Wicked Peace

Gay Longworth is twenty-nine and lives in Old Street, London with her husband. *Wicked Peace* is her second novel. Her first, *Bimba*, was published by Pan Books in 1997 and is being developed by BskyB in association with Marc Samuelson Productions. She is currently working on the third.

Also by Gay Longworth

Bimba

Wicked Peace

Gay Longworth

PAN BOOKS

First published 2000 by Pan Books
an imprint of Macmillan Publishers Ltd
25 Eccleston Place, London SW1W 9NF
Basingstoke and Oxford
Associated companies throughout the world
www.macmillan.co.uk

ISBN 0 330 39149 6

A CIP catalogue record for this book is available from
the British Library.

Typeset by SetSystems Ltd, Saffron Walden, Essex
Printed and bound in Great Britain by
Mackays of Chatham plc, Chatham, Kent

To Adam Spiegel

Falling?

Acknowledgements

My paternal grandmother, Lydia, regretfully died when I was three; I fought with my cousins over ownership of her surviving sister. My great-aunt Vava Van Stolk Basilewitch is an inspiration to anyone who meets her. Fiercely intelligent, beautiful and funny, she's still going strong.

My maternal grandmother, Judith Randal Roberts, 'Rannie', died in the Fall of 1998. She was a wonderful grandmother to all seventeen of her grandchildren, adding our names and birth dates to a charm bracelet as each one came along. She died soon after the christening of her first great-grandson – I don't think she had any room left on her bracelet for more.

They say the second book is the hardest. I hope so. It couldn't possibly get any worse. I'd like to thank all the people who've been more patient, more understanding and more encouraging than a wet-nurse. Stephanie Cabot and Eugenie Furniss at William Morris Agency: no one should read a book as many times as you've had to. I apologize to Philip Adler if Stephanie's expenses were unusually high – it was always an emergency. Arabella Stein, Mari Evans, Clare Harington, Lucy Henson – thanks for putting up with me. A deep and special thank-you goes to Felicity Gillespie: despite being overworked and ill, she took time to read *Wicked Peace* and then went through it page by page giving me the hardest advice there is to give. Constructive criticism. Another goes to Dee Poku, where would I be without you? For all things medical I'd like to thank Dr Caroline Foster, a very cool paediatrician who makes motherhood look easy.

For all things pharmaceutical, and a million and one other favours, I'd like to thank Dan Patel, the untitled king of Pimlico. For information regarding the police force, many thanks to Chief Superintendent Paul Scotney. I'd like to thank Milly Pack for steering me through the justice system. Thank you to Madame Maurin for all things relating to Paris, except the S&M scene which is entirely thanks to Conti and Doon. Still waters . . .

A special thank-you goes to my mother. The best sounding board a confused writer can have.

Lastly I'd like to thank the editing skills of the Topless Trio of Playa – Stephanie Longworth, Princess Poku and Thalia Murray – I will never forget the cries of 'Pass me the sunscreen', 'Where are the fags?', 'Who's got chapter five?'

Wicked Peace

Prologue

Jane Wellby stood in front of the mirror and studied her naked form. Her parents knew nothing about the still-life sculpture that stared back at her. And they never would. It was probably better that way. Illusions should remain illusions. And parents should remain parents. She stroked herself, letting her hands run over her chest, breasts and stomach, stopping just above her pubic hair. They'd never asked her about sex. Or drugs. Or anything. But she knew why. It was so obvious. Jane looked around her bedroom, overly decorated, pink and floral, she hated flowers and she hated pink. Her stepmother's taste. Not hers. Not her father's, certainly not her mother's, just Sandie. Everywhere she looked. There was Sandie. The woman had broken up their family, split it open, leaving the three constituent parts reeling from separation. And her, the pappy unprepared child, exposed to too much, too young. Her stepmother had been poisoning them ever since. And now there was nothing left but her reflection. And an overriding feeling of fear. Uncertainty. Until now. It was time to tell everyone what Sandie Wellby was really like. Jane found a blue dress with a daisy print and put it on. Her father had bought it for her. It was knee-length and had short sleeves. She put a pale pink cardigan over the top, white plimsolls then stood back. Perfect. Jane ran down the stairs two at a time, the dress billowing around her knees. She sprang like a cat down the last three and landed on the highly polished wooden floor. The rubber soles squeaked as she skipped over the hall. She looked behind her and smiled at the marks she was leaving behind. She knocked on a door, without waiting for an answer she opened it. The man at the desk turned, smiled and put his pen down. Jane ran to her father and kissed him on the cheek.

'Good morning!'

'You're up early.'

'I wanted to see you off.'

'Your mother called. I thought you were asleep,' he said.

'You spoke to her?' she asked excitedly.

'Of course.'

'What about?'

'You. How long you're staying.'

'Till Sunday,' said Jane, patting her father's cheeks.

'You won't be bored?'

'No. You said you'd be home early for tennis and the Whittons are coming tomorrow,' she said smiling.

'It'll be a good weekend then.'

The study door opened. A well-dressed woman stood in the doorway, she held on to the handle tightly as she took in the scene. Jane leant closer to her father's ear. 'She didn't knock.' The man nudged her playfully.

'Jane, your mother called.'

'I know. She and Daddy had a nice long chat.'

The woman's eyes narrowed. Imperceptible except to Jane. She'd learnt to read the signs.

'Jane, would you excuse us, I'd like to talk to your father before he goes to work.'

'Daddy?'

'Off you go, sweetheart. Don't forget, tennis.'

Jane kissed her father. 'I'll be ready.' Jane closed the door behind her and ran back across the hallway. Then she stopped.

Sandie listened to her stepdaughter's receding foot-falls. 'I wish you wouldn't do that,' she said in a hushed tone.

'Do what?'

'You know what I'm talking about.'

Jane crept silently back to the door.

'It just makes it easier.'

'For you maybe.'

'Sandie, I've got to go.'

'We need to talk.'

'Can't, I'll be late.' He gave her a quick kiss on the lips and left the room.

A few minutes later, when her temper had subsided, Sandie followed her husband. Jane stepped in front of her. Sandie's hand went to her heart. 'Jane!'

Jane winked at her, ran over to the staircase and, taking them two steps at a time, quickly disappeared round the bend. Sandie couldn't see the smile on her stepdaughter's face. But she could feel it. Sandie looked at the recently polished floor and saw the marks.

'Shit,' she said in a hoarse whisper.

Chapter One

Chapter One

Cat held her microphone low and waited for the reply.

'Absolutely not. Just because we're old doesn't mean we don't have sex,' said the elderly lady. 'And don't be put off by the wheelchair either.'

Cat smiled nervously.

'What? Can't I say sex on the radio?'

'You can, it's just' – Cat pressed pause on her minidisc – 'maybe this isn't good subject matter after all.'

'Darling, it's brilliant, these old biddies are at it day and night. I haven't heard so much headboard banging since Oxford.'

'That didn't go on when you were at university,' said Cat.

Amelia shook her head. 'You're right, we were all virgins until your generation came along and invented it.'

'Such wit.'

'The walls are so thin I could stick my nail scissors through and watch. No one builds anything properly these days. How about getting a spy camera and branching out into television.'

'This is definitely a bad idea.'

'Even better, live show on the Internet.'

'What!'

'We have classes.'

'That's enough. You're becoming a danger to society.'

'Come on, Cat, it's a great idea. Sex over seventy. These old boys have been surviving without Viagra for years. It's very topical, darling. The gentleman across the corridor was offered it by a well-dressed man at the bus stop the other day. Drug dealing in the geriatric ward, definitely newsworthy.'

'Imagine what would happen if they did get their hands on it,' said Cat laughing. 'None of you would get any sleep.'

'One doesn't sleep at this age anyway,' said Amelia. 'Which goes back to my first point. What would you prefer — a good rollick between the sheets or another game of solitaire.'

'I hope you're all practising safe sex.'

'Lord, no, it's only done to induce a heart attack.'

'A quick exit.'

'Exactly, think about it, we could put this place on the tourist map, swap male octogenarians with other retirement homes. Most of them aren't aware of their surroundings but they can still get an—'

'Gran.'

'Everyone will be so disappointed, I've already got lots of volunteers longing to show off to you.'

'What about Nurse Cleveland?' asked Cat.

'Clearly she's never had sex, so there would be no point interviewing her.'

'That's not what I meant.'

Amelia winked.

'Don't go spreading rumours to those horny old devils that swinging is to be added to the list of Sunday activities,' insisted Cat. 'You'll have a riot on your hands.'

'My lips are sealed.'

Cat looked at her watch. 'Shit.' She kissed Amelia. 'I'm late.'

CAT'S MIND WAS ALREADY in the editing room by the time she pulled out of the home. The culminatin of a week's unpaid work experience at BBC Chelmsford. It would be her longest solo report. If she got to the editing room on time. Cat instinctively put her foot down. If she couldn't secure a job after the radio journalism course ended she'd know the gamble with her career had failed. Then what would she do? Twenty-eight, unemployed. She glanced at the clock. One fifteen. If she listened to the recording now, she could plan the edit. Cat put her left hand behind her and searched for the mini-disc on the back seat. She couldn't feel it. She glanced quickly around, located it and grabbed the strap. Turning back she caught a glimpse of something on the road, close to her front wheel, alive. Panicked, she hit the brakes and swerved. She wasn't quick enough. Cat didn't feel a thud but she heard a fearful noise. The car skidded across the road, bumped up against the steep grass verge and stalled. Her heart punched her ribs in protest as she held her breath, too terrified to turn around and see what she'd hit. A child? A fox? A pheasant? A child? A child? 'Please God, don't let me have killed a child.' She opened the door and put one foot out. Still staring ahead, she swivelled to the right. Delaying the inevitable. 'You've got to look.' Cat turned and frowned, she had skidded a fair way, there was something on the road. Blonde. Cat felt sick. A head? She looked around quickly. No body. Not a head. An animal? She walked closer. Some improvement to a child killer at least. A fox? Whatever it was, it wasn't moving. Cat stood over the corpse.

'Shit,' said Cat as she saw the unmistakable flash of colour. Collar. She'd run over someone's pet.

'Come on, pick it up, it can't hurt you.' *Not now anyway.* As she carried the small dog to the grass she heard a metallic tinkling. Two silver discs hung off the leather strap. Shit, she didn't want the dog to have an identity, a home, people who loved it. Pretend it's a rabbit, she thought, just think rabbit. People hit rabbits all the time and leave them to get ingrained in the road's surface. The White Rabbit immediately hopped into her mind and barked 'too late' at her. She lowered the dog on to the grass. It was no good, her head was now filling up with disturbing images of pigtailed girls in gingham dresses crying out in heartbroken voices, 'Toto! Toto! Where are you, Toto?' The size of the dog had also begun to gnaw at her conscience. She had killed someone's puppy. Perhaps the pigtailed girl had been given the puppy to compensate for the death of her own parents. Now Cat had killed that too, the girl would grow up, never able to get close to anyone and live a lonely and troubled life collecting stuffed animals that couldn't die on her . . .

ENOUGH WITH THE MORBID imagination shit. As the gingham dress faded, Cat knew hit-and-run was off the day's specials. She crouched down beside the animal to feel along the leather collar until she found what she was looking for.

'Lucy,' read Cat. 'Shit.' Definitely a little girl's dog. The guilt tightened. Lucy resided, until Cat had brained her with the bumper, at Cedar Hall, Old Harlow, Essex. The telephone number was not supplied, which wiped out the anonymous phone call possibility. She had no choice, despite the risk of being branded a pet killer; Cat would have to return the puppy to its rightful owner. Chelmsford would just have to wait for its fascinating bus story. Cat walked back to the car in a remorseful daze and dialled the newsroom at the station. She got the fat controller. The woman hadn't warmed to her. Cat explained her predicament.

'So you've hit a dog,' said the woman. Clearly not believing her.

'Once I've told the owners I'll come to the station, you can put the package on the later—'

'We won't have time later.'

'But—'

'Look, according to you, you're halfway home, though it's a funny route back from the Colchester bus station. However, we'll send your assessment to the college.'

'But—'

'But what. We can't hold up news pieces because you go rambling. I'll explain to the bus company. We'll get one of the full-time staff to do the report again. That's my other line.'

The phone went dead.

'Bitch,' said Cat, staring at the phone. She'd been working like a slave for five days, she'd barely eaten, and she'd slept badly in BBC accommodation just to be dismissed like an irresponsible schoolgirl. If they'd liked her, they'd have given her some leeway. Depressed, Cat made an eight-point turn and drove back towards the Essex heartland. She found the one-road village, but no signs of a house large enough to label itself a hall. She asked at the pub expecting incomprehensible directions, putting an end to this sorry trail, but he was ever so helpful. Cat resigned herself to an unwelcome reception.

'Follow the lane behind the pub, can't miss it.'

Cat returned to the car and drove up the single-lane

track. The publican was wrong, there were no signs of a grand house as far as she could see. Then she rounded a corner and saw what could not be missed. Stone pillars. With lions on. She instinctively shifted the gearstick into reverse. The gearbox let out a gnarling cry. Cat whipped her foot on to the clutch just as the car stalled. The lions glared at her. So much for doing the good Samaritan thing, she should just leave the dog at the lion's feet and go. People who needed to be protected by fifteen-foot-high gates and imperial cats were not likely to send her off with an understanding wave. She really was sorry about the accident, but she wasn't going to throw herself to the lions over the death of a privileged dog. She opened the car door, stepped out and immediately saw the publican. He was watching her.

'Damn.' She got back in.

THE GRAVEL CRUNCHED UNDER her tyres as she drove through the gates. Cedar trees flanked the long driveway. Not a blade of grass was out of place.

'Shit,' said Cat loudly. She watched the publican shrink in her rear-view mirror as she drove towards certain persecution. Cat rounded another corner and saw the house. It was a beautiful, pale limestone, three-storey house. Wide sash windows framed by blooming wisteria spread out either side of a pillared front door. Cat reluctantly turned the engine off and peered through her windscreen. Maybe it was a health club for wealthy self-obsessed women, and the dog belonged to some ageing romantic novelist who was in there for her fourth thigh tuck of the year. But no women in white towelling robes appeared and there were no other cars parked in front of the house. Cat dismissed the theory. Maybe it was the estate of a rich old widower who could build ramps in the west wing and rescue her grandmother from a perennial diet of semolina pudding. Cat got out of the car and waited for a while, just in case a butler appeared, but nothing happened. Carrying the animal like a gift, she approached the large double front door. Two stone dogs sat obediently to attention at the base of the pillars. Maybe she could lie Lucy down next to them, to petrify with the others. Eternally stoned. Maybe she should lie down? Improve on an otherwise bad day. Cat saw the ceramic button inscribed with the word 'Push'. She fingered the smooth, cool surface and felt like someone had just handed her a bottle labelled with the words 'Drink Me'. Finally, she took a deep breath and pushed. Still nothing happened. She rang again, and when that too went unanswered she decided that she had fulfilled her moral obligation to the family and she could do no more. She placed the dog on the step. A note would have to suffice. She set off back to the car to find a pen. Cat stood breathing in the country air, chewing the end of a biro, and mentally constructed some soothing words of remorse. She had one blank piece of paper. 'Dear' she wrote, then stopped. Dear who? Cat tore off the first strip of paper. 'To Whom It May Concern', she ripped that off too, too formal. 'To Lucy's owner. It is with a grave heart I write this note . . .' Cat tore the page again. Bad turn of phrase. Two more errors and she was left with no choice but to write a few simple words, there was no room for more. She searched the front door for a letter box, but there wasn't one. She couldn't stick the note under the dog's collar. She was walking back to the car to find an envelope when she saw a hand-painted sign-post. Tradesmen's Entrance. She wasn't plying her wares, but it was worth a look. Cat folded the note, put it in her pocket and followed the gravel driveway around to the back of the house. The crunching of small, sharp-edged flint accompanied her every step to a courtyard, there the gravel ended and with it the reassuring noise of her own footfalls. She stood on the clean grey slate tiles and looked at the redundant stables in front of her. Everything was still, a perfect composition of rural life with no signs of life. Cat expected to find muddy boots, beaten up bicycles, gardening tools, toys. Something. Anyone. But there was nothing. Not a breath of air. No wind in the trees. No guttural calls from the wood pigeons that perched on the roof. Cat's heart skipped a beat when her ear became accustomed to the silence and picked up a vague sound. It wasn't a sound as such, more of a vibration. Cat leant her ear towards the courtyard, listening, then straightened up.

'Hello!'

The thick walls soaked up her voice.

'Is anyone there?'

Still nothing. Cat walked up to a window and saw an

immaculate kitchen inside. There wasn't a dirty vessel in sight, nothing on the draining board. Along the wall was a vast kitchen dresser displaying a matching dinner set. Cat counted twenty of everything. That scared her more than the lions. Either it was a film set or the resident had an obsessive cleanliness disorder and what she could hear was the carpets being vacuumed for the fifth time that day. Cat crossed the courtyard and put her head through an open stable door. The room was full of drying flowers, Cat inhaled the stale, musky aroma, this woman clearly had too much time on her hands. Cat began to imagine her. Neurotic definitely. The long-suffering wife of a city bore who makes excuses about coming home. Essential to have a hobby when your husband is screwing around. They never had children, he blames her. All she has is her house. Her fortress. Alternatively, she could be a wide-hipped mother of three who goes pink in the cheeks after one G&T. Mungo, Flora and Cosmo have flown the nest of course, taking their muddy boots and old bikes with them, leaving her redundant. A no-sex, good-cause woman. Cat leant against a garage door. Whatever the version, Cat did not envy her and her big, all-matching house and manicured garden. Poor woman, she'd probably given her life to her family and been entombed in the process ... Cat snapped out of her hallucination. The garage door was vibrating. She moved away and stared at it perplexed. Surely the woman wasn't vacuuming the garage? Cat placed her hand gently on it and spread her fingers. They quivered involuntarily.

Whether it was proverbial curiosity or a feeling that all was not well, Cat reached for the T-shaped handle. It turned easily and with one strong pull the bottom of the garage door swung out.

Cat was on the ground, coughing, disorientated as a cloud of exhaust fumes enveloped her. With her hand over her mouth, she scrambled away from the smoke now billowing out of the half-open garage door. She couldn't see the offending exhaust pipe, but she could hear the engine still churning out its deadly fumes. Cat's skin prickled. Deadly fumes? Why had she thought that? Surely the car had been left running as an accident? Images flashed through Cat's mind. No mess. No loose ends. No one around. No life.

'Oh God.' Without further thought, Cat pushed the garage door all the way up, took a deep breath and with her face stuffed down the front of her T-shirt she disappeared into the smoky interior. She didn't make it the first time. But she did the second.

Cat instinctively pulled the hose out of the car's exhaust pipe, sooty paper fell out with it. She stared at it until her eyes stung. The hose was bright green, easily lost on a lawn, but a convenient guide in a fume-filled garage. With her eyes half closed through fear and tears, she felt along the hose until she reached the driver's door. The inside of the car was thick with smoke but she didn't need to see to know what was inside it. The odds for there not being a sad soul sucking the end of the pipe were a million to one. For a few seconds Cat couldn't move. Then she quickly pulled the hose and felt it fall about her feet. She tried to go for the handle, but her hand kept retracting. Fear and guilt. Should she get some help? There was no help. She was the help and she was wasting precious seconds. Holding her breath, Cat forced her hand to lift the handle, she opened the car door, felt for the key and killed the engine. The killing engine. Already a shadowy outline had begun to form, Cat leant into the car and screamed as a face loomed at her.

'You're alive, you're alive, keep breathing. I'll get you out of here.' Cat was shouting out of nerves, she reached for the seat belt and unclipped it. 'Keep breathing.' But the person didn't move again. 'Wake up! You're . . .' Cat's voice trailed off as she watched the ever-thinning smoke create the illusion of movement. In the confined space of the car's interior Cat watched a figure take its full, fearful form. It was a girl. A young girl. Pretty. Pretty fucking dead. Horribly dead. Blue and dead. And she was staring straight at Cat with fixed, rigid eyes. You're too fucking late. Cat had no idea whether it was a fraction of a second or a full scarring hour before she started running. All she knew was that she was running.

Chapter Two

'Police, no, ambulance. Both, shit, I don't know. Police.'

'What is your situation?' It was a man's voice.

'What do you mean?' Cat was nearly in tears.

'Are you hurt, madam?'

'No, I'm . . .'

'Where are you?'

'There's a girl, in the garage. I think she's, well she is d—' There was a noise. Above her.

'Madam, what is your situation?' Cat, for the first time since escaping the garage, became aware of her surroundings. She was in a spacious hallway, bending over a round mahogany table, her face two inches from a bowl of dried flowers. The noise came again. A door closing. She looked up. A majestic staircase ascended and circled away from where she stood. She was clutching a telephone she couldn't remember finding in a house she had thought was empty.

'What is your location?'

'Shh,' she said to the voice then placed her hand over the receiver. Someone was in the house who hadn't been before and they were coming down the stairs.

'Is she locked in the garage? Is the girl hurt? You must tell me, otherwise I cannot help. Hello? Hello?'

A high-heeled shoe. Then another. Two calves. Two knees, one bending, one straight, one bending, one straight. Good legs. A hand. Red nails. Big ring. It clicked against the banister.

'What has happened to the girl?'

The two women stared at each other. The stairmaster spoke first.

'What are you doing in my house?' *Dried Flowers*.

'What has happened to the girl?' *Killed herself*.

'Are you a friend of Jane's?' *No*.

'Who is the girl?'

'Jane,' said Cat.

'Who are you talking to?' asked the man and the woman simultaneously.

Jane's mother. The Police. Jane's ignorant mother. 'The police,' answered Cat quietly. This was no way for a mother to find out.

'Is she in trouble?' *Was*.

Cat spoke slowly and clearly to both. 'I'm at Cedar Hall, Old Harlow, Essex. I need an ambulance and a police car as soon as possible.' The woman on the stairs paled significantly, but did not move a muscle.

'What has happened?' said the voice down the phone.

Cat and the woman stared at each other. 'I'm sorry,' she said to Jane's mother.

'What are you sorry for?' said the voice.

'All of this,' replied Cat. She closed her eyes, not able to look as she delivered the news. 'There is a girl in the garage. She has killed herself.'

There was a sharp intake of breath from Jane's mother.

CAT CLIMBED THE STAIRS to where Jane's mother sat, staring into a void, and lowered herself down next to her. No one spoke for a long time. Cat didn't know what she should do, so she just waited.

When the woman spoke, it was in a slow whisper. 'Are you sure it's Jane?'

'No.'

Another long pause. 'I should make sure then?' she said, looking at Cat questioningly.

Cat didn't think the woman was seeing her properly. 'Maybe you should wait, it might be easier to do it with someone else here.'

'You're here,' said the woman, stilted, but unequivocally.

'Yes, but . . .' *This has got nothing to do with me.* The woman stood up abruptly and waited. Cat reluctantly followed. She was right, Cat *was* there, involved, but until that point she hadn't been aware of it. As Cat followed the woman back down the stairs and across the hall, she was conscious of the polished floor beneath her feet. Of the weight of the door as she held it open. Of the immaculate kitchen she had no recollection of being in. The back door was open too, but she couldn't remember opening it. Cat followed the woman out into the fresh air. It *was* fresh. The wind had whipped up the noxious gases and hidden them in the clouds. But the sight of the green hose lying along the cement floor of the garage made Cat's chest tighten. The car's interior had cleared and she could already see the brown curly hair spilling over the side of the leather seat. As she looked at it, she imagined it growing, oozing out of the skull like a Girl's World doll. Dead head, dead hair, still growing. Sour bile rose briefly into the back of Cat's throat. Unable to look again she cast her eyes down and concentrated on the first object that caught her eye. She didn't take her eyes off it until the identification had been made and they were back out in the courtyard. Yes. It was Jane.

As they returned to the kitchen the phone began to ring. The dead girl's mother walked back into the hall and stared at the object next to the dried flowers. She turned back to Cat. Cat frowned, but the woman just continued to stare at her. Her inaction was further unnerving Cat as the phone continued to ring.

'Would you like me to answer it?' asked Cat in a cautious voice. The woman nodded. Cat felt herself being reluctantly drawn deeper into the surreal situation, but her pity for the disorientated woman forced her to pick up the phone.

'Cedar Hall?'

'Jane?'

Cat swallowed.

'Who is calling please?'

'Oh, sorry, is Sandie, um, Mrs Wellby, is she there?' *There's a woman here . . .*

'Who's calling please?' repeated Cat.

'It's Simon, Simon Proudlove. Who is this?' Cat covered the phone with her hand.

'It's Simon Proudlove,' said Cat to the woman. Cat watched her outstretch a hand and walk towards the phone. She took it. Cat noticed her hand was steady. For a moment the woman didn't say anything. Cat waited.

'Simon, Jane is dead.' Cat couldn't hear the reply, but it was a while before the woman talked again. 'Just get Robert, I can't tell him over the phone. Please go and get him, bring him here.' She paused again then shouted, 'Of course I'm sure it's her, she's gassed herself in the fucking car.'

Cat took a few steps back and retreated into the kitchen. She was American. The woman was American. Cat kept walking, she didn't want to know who Jane Wellby was, or Sandie, or Robert, she didn't know these people. But outside in the courtyard an ambulance had pulled up, followed by a number of police cars. Too late, thought Cat. Too fucking late. A dominating, round-shouldered man approached Cat and told her to wait. His

imperious manner didn't require an answer. She was
stuck with nothing to do but witness the methodical
removal of a corpse and contemplate her disappointing
finale at the station. She should have left the bloody dog,
it wasn't as if Jane would miss her now. A doctor came,
declared Jane dead and left. Dogs and their owners,
thought Cat. The police flocked around Mrs Wellby who
seemed to float among them. At one point she began to
offer them drinks, apologizing to them, as though she had
forgotten her manners. Everyone declined, but she
returned to the house nonetheless. The short, stocky
policewoman who had been shadowing her followed her
inside. They were waiting for the moment it hit her,
thought Cat. But suicide wasn't like that. It wasn't like
ordinary death. It came with strings attached. She should
know. When her father committed suicide, it didn't come
as a shock, there were no histrionics, no tears. That's how
she feels, thought Cat, it was in her every move. The
policewoman and Mrs Wellby returned carrying a picnic
table and tray of coffee respectively. Despite their previous refusals, everyone received the drinks gratefully.
Clearing corpses was thirsty work. Cat looked at the
mugs. A matching set. She remembered the kitchen.
Twenty of everything. On display. Cat suddenly gasped
aloud, a policeman looked at her suspiciously, Cat put
her hand over her mouth and pretended to cough. All
that time she'd been snooping, all that procrastination, all
that dallying. Meanwhile a girl quietly asphyxiated herself
to death and she could have stopped it. Panic rose like a

geyser in her chest. She coughed again and blinked back the tears that sprang up and burnt her eyes. But the garage was full of smoke, the engine must have been running for hours. Hours. The image flashed before Cat's eyes. She certainly looked long dead. The yellowing grey leather that clung to her skull wasn't flesh. It was just something that kept the bones together. What Cat had seen wasn't a person, it was a carcass. She couldn't have saved that. Cat watched as the police emerged from the garage carrying plastic bags containing the hose and the scrunched-up pieces of paper. She didn't want to be around when they put the body into a plastic bag and brought that out.

TYRES CRUNCHED ON THE gravel. A man got out before the car had fully stopped. Sandie was already running towards him. He saw her, called her name in a voice that was painful to listen to. They embraced. This was not a spectator sport, she should excuse herself and go. She had no place being there. Long minutes passed while everyone stood quietly, listening to the man's sobs. Cat sat hugging her knees on a mounting block, trying to make herself as inconspicuous as possible. She'd been there three hours. Jane's father eased himself off his wife's shoulder when he heard the sound of his daughter being brought out on a trolley. Bad timing. Mr Wellby pointed at the body bag. He kept pointing as he walked slowly towards it, tears spilling down his cheeks, mouthing unheard words. He only stopped walking when his index finger touched the thick layer of plastic that provided his daughter with her first crude coffin.

'Open it.' Cat heard him say. The wind had begun to pick up, the day was turning colder and the blue sky was now coated in a thin blanket of grey. He repeated the words and then, when no one volunteered, he looked up. 'Please?' It sounded like the voice of a seven-year-old. Cat looked away again. The noise of the plastic zip echoed around the three walls of the courtyard then followed the wind and the smoke upwards. Mr Wellby lifted his daughter's body and rocked her awkwardly.

'No, Janey, no.' Cat involuntarily glanced back. The same curly hair escaped over his arm. Cat felt sick. Jane's father looked up at the waiting ambulance man who could only shake his head sympathetically. Mr Wellby searched the rest of the faces. Most of them looked down, a few shrugged, finally his gaze rested on his wife. 'Tell them,' he begged. 'Tell them, Sandie. Tell them little Janey would never kill herself. She had no reason. No reason in the world. She was happy, a perfectly normal happy little girl. *Tell them.*'

All eyes were on Sandie, she was clenching her lips together so hard it looked like she was wearing white lip liner. Finally she said, 'I don't know, darling, I don't know what happened.' She took his arm and led him away from the trolley. The ambulance man quickly zipped up the bag, the sound hit hard, Mr Wellby's legs buckled. It took two policemen to get him inside.

Cat watched as Robert Wellby grabbed their arms, pulling them towards him. 'There was nothing wrong with my daughter.' He shouted in their faces. 'Nothing!'

Cat looked at Sandie Wellby. The expression on her face was unfathomable. Simon Proudlove, the man she had spoken to on the phone, the man who'd delivered the shattering news, walked up behind Mrs Wellby and squeezed her shoulder. They watched Mr Wellby as he was carried into the house. 'She's being so strong,' mumbled Cat to herself.

'Who?' said an approaching police officer.

Cat looked up. No one had spoken to her for hours. 'Jane's mother.'

'Her,' he said raising his arm. Cat couldn't believe he was pointing at Mrs Wellby, in front of everyone. 'That's not Jane's mother. That's the second Mrs Wellby. Jane's *step*mother.'

'Oh,' said Cat. That changed things.

THE POLICE DISAPPEARED INTO the house, leaving Cat alone to watch the unceremonious deposit of Jane Wellby's corpse into the waiting ambulance. She'd seen a body before, lain out alongside a funeral pyre in India. It had seemed rather beautiful at the time, but then she'd been safely seated in the front row of a tourist boat, bobbing up and down on the Ganges. Near enough to get the photo, but far enough away for the scene to seem surreal. A Kodak Believer. This was different. The image of Jane's face was printed into her brain. Cat could see through the layer of plastic as clearly as if it wasn't there. The bag could not disguise the body of Jane Wellby. Everyone knew what was inside. Cat looked back to the house, the cellophane-wrapped house, and shook her head softly to herself. Cat watched the paramedics close the ambulance doors. It was time she left too. The Wellbys had caused her enough trouble. Cat was walking across the courtyard when she heard angry voices from the kitchen.

'Of course I'm fit to drive,' said the voice. Cat turned around. Mr Wellby, closely followed by his wife, came storming out of the kitchen. 'It can't be anyone, goddammit, some stranger. She was our only daughter, of course I have to tell her myself.' The accent was English. Very English. Very angry.

'I understand that, Robert. I just don't want you to drive. Please, honey, let me drive, or Simon if you'd prefer.' She looked questioningly at the man who had delivered Robert home. 'I'll take you,' said Simon, nodding vigorously.

'What's the point, you'll get stranded in London.'

'Actually my other car is in London, it would be easy.' Sandie and Simon looked hopefully at Robert.

'Mr Wellby,' said the policeman in charge, 'I need to ask you some questions.' Robert turned on him.

'What!'

'I know this is a difficult time, sir, but—'

'How dare you. My daughter is dead. There are no questions.'

'Unfortunately we have to, sir. It's routine.' The policeman replied impassively.

'Fuck routine. Who the hell are you anyway?'

Sandie held her hand out to the policeman. Show . . . 'This is Detective Chief Inspector Bramley, darling.' And Tell . . . 'You met just a few min—'

'You are not going to stop me telling my first wife that our daughter is dead.' Cat wasn't sure whether Robert Wellby was talking to his wife or the policeman, but the policeman answered.

'Certainly not,' he said, stepping back from him.

'Good.' Robert turned but instead of going to the car he marched back indoors.

'Darling? Where are you going?'

'I can't remember the bloody address.'

'What?' said Sandie, to his receding figure.

'Did Mr Wellby have custody?' Bramley asked Sandie.

'No, Jane lived with her mother,' said Sandie. 'Well, most of the time.'

'Yet Mr Wellby doesn't know the address?'

'The shock,' said Sandie. 'He's in shock.'

Bramley and Sandie walked slowly back towards the hastily constructed picnic table and poured coffee for two. Sandie held the cup with both hands and stared at the garage.

'What was she like, your stepdaughter?'

Sandie's eyebrows arched. 'I'm probably not the best person to ask.'

'Stepchildren can be a handful.'

'You have no idea,' she sighed.

ROBERT RE-EMERGED HOLDING AN *A-Z*. Sandie immediately put the coffee cup down and went over to him, flicking easily through it and showing him the quickest route. Robert snatched it back. 'I know,' he said impatiently, before walking briskly to the waiting car.

Bramley intercepted. 'I really must insist you allow someone to drive you.'

'I'm perfectly capable.'

'Sir, I wouldn't be doing my job if—'

'I'll take you,' said Simon, putting his hand on Robert's shoulder.

'No,' he said, shaking it off.

'Honestly, Robert, it is the least I can do.'

'Why?'

'What?'

'Why is it the least you can do, Simon? You're not part of this. This isn't your family.'

'Robert!'

'Never mind, Sandie.'

'I want everyone out of here,' said Robert angrily.

'Please, let's try to be calm, Robert,' he said nervously.

'Be calm! Be fucking calm! Christ!' shouted Robert Wellby looking up at the sky. He turned on Simon. 'My daughter is dead. Dead! What do you suggest I do? Throw a fucking barbecue.' Cat winced. Robert swivelled round and pointed at Bramley. 'I'm not answering your questions.' He looked around at the four remaining police officers. 'Get out of my house, all of you – now.' He exhaled loudly and looked straight at Cat. She tried a sympathetic smile.

'Who the fuck are you?' Everyone turned.

Cat's eye's widened. 'Catherine Amelia Torrant,' she said, suddenly back at school.

'Who?' he barked, taking a menacing step towards her.

Cat coughed nervously, she looked around for assistance, then at Sandie, who seemed to re-register her.

'Catherine Amel—'

'I got that, thank you,' he shouted. 'But who are you and what the fuck are you doing here?'

Bramley looked at her warily. He knew the girl had found Jane, but it never occurred to him that she was a stranger to the Wellbys. Everyone, including him, had assumed she was a friend of the family, or of the daughter's, staff, daughter of staff. All of the above. None of the above. Tick (B).

'She was in the house,' said the second Mrs Wellby. 'On the telephone.' Cat nodded encouragement. 'You were on the phone to the police. You told them about Jane. I mean me, told me.' Robert looked at his wife questioningly. Cat relaxed. It was premature. He suddenly turned on her again. 'You live around here?' Cat shook her head. 'Where do you live?'

'Fifteen Aubrey Street. Angel.'

'Angel?'

'In London,' said Cat.

'I know where bloody Angel is, how did you get into my house?'

'I, I can't remember.'

'What!?' bellowed Robert Wellby.

'The door, I suppose. Look, I can't remember. I found Jane and ran. The next thing I knew I was on the phone to the police.'

'So, you are a friend of Janey's from London. Of course Angel is very close to her mother's house,' said Mr Wellby, less aggressively. 'She didn't tell me you were coming to visit. Did she tell you?' Robert turned to Sandie. Sandie didn't respond. She didn't even move. She just stared at Cat.

'I wasn't visiting,' said Cat quietly. 'Actually, I– I don't know your, um, daughter.' Cat wished she were on Mars. 'I . . .'

'Why *are* you here then?'

Cat swallowed nervously.

'What were you doing here, Miss Torrant?' asked Bramley.

Cat looked straight at Robert. 'I'm afraid I've got some more bad news for you.'

Robert Wellby laughed at this. 'You think there could be any *worse* news?'

She'd said more bad news, not worse, but didn't think this was time to argue semantics. Everyone was watching her. She continued. Slowly. 'I had a road accident. I was coming here to report it to you.'

'Why on earth should we want to know?'

Cat looked him in the eye and devoid of expression informed them of the second death in the family.

IT WAS THE FIRST time she saw Sandie Wellby cry.

ROBERT GOT INTO SIMON'S car. Bramley leant into the open passenger window.

'Now what?'

'Thank you for agreeing to be driven. Please send my condolences to Jane's mother.'

Robert relented slightly. The man was only doing his job. 'Thank you,' he said.

'It must have been difficult for you. Your wife and daughter at odds with each other.'

'What are you talking about? Simon! Let's go!'

'No problems at home then?' Bramley persisted.

Robert pointed at him. 'I know what you are trying to insinuate. Jane and Sandie were very good friends. Very good. Simon!'

Bramley stepped away from the car and watched as Simon relinquished Sandie from an embrace.

'Who is Mr Proudlove?'

'My wife's partner. Business partner.'

As Bramley watched the younger man climb grace-fully into the car, a bad taste rose in his mouth. He summoned his sidekick, Detective Sergeant Mike Chambers, and whispered something into his ear. Together they watched the Mercedes estate pull away then returned to the picnic table.

As CEDAR HALL RETREATED in the side-view mirror, Robert eyed the bright yellow Ford Fiesta with suspicion. His daughter was dead and some *stranger* had found her? No, thought Robert, Catherine Amelia Torrant was in some way connected. But how? And why? His mind raced as the powerful engine distanced himself from the scene of his daughter's death. But the guilt, that would never disappear. He slammed his hands on the dashboard.

'Stop the car, Simon.'

'What?'

'Stop the fucking car. *Now!*' Simon skidded to a halt just before the crossroads. Robert's face had drained of all colour. 'I can't let you drive me to Fiona's. Please—'

'We have to talk about what happened earlier—'

'No, we don't.'

'Robert, what is going on?'

Robert looked at him as if he were an imbecile. 'Jane is dead. Nothing else matters.' He got out of the car, walked around to the driver's side and opened the door. Simon did not move. 'You wouldn't understand anyway. You don't have family. You don't have children.'

'Robert, I . . .' he paused. 'Your family is my family.'

'Simon, you are in business with my wife, her friend – not family. Neither you nor she has lost a daughter.

She was my daughter. I have lost her. *I* have. So when I ask to be alone, I expect you to leave me the fuck alone.'

'Of course,' said Simon quietly. 'I'm sorry.' He put one leg out of the car. 'Please drive carefully though, if anything happened to you, Sandie would kill me.'

'Don't tell Sandie anything. Not with all this going on.'

Simon got out of the car. 'You know you can trust me, but she should know. How long has this been—'

'Just tell her to cancel the Whittons.' Simon nodded and watched the car leave. He listened to the engine until it was lost among the sound of rustling trees. He turned around and started the mile-long walk to Cedar Hall. His surrogate family home. His surrogate family. They meant more to him than they would ever know. And now this had happened. Robert trusted him – what was he going to tell Sandie? What could he tell Sandie?

THE NEEDLE SHOWED 140 miles per hour. Robert passed every car at speed, some hooted, others flashed their lights. He didn't care, he just wanted to go faster, drive off the end of the world. Anything rather than tell Fiona that her only daughter was dead. Dead. Twenty-three little years. Suicide? Who would believe that? He shook his head, no one. Why? Because she wasn't sup-posed to die. Not his daughter. Not his baby. The sun was descending over London. The mirrored buildings of the City glinted orange. Serene, mocking, glaring down at the mortals. Canary Wharf, erect and ridiculous. Still mostly empty. A waste of space. A waste of time. Of life. He'd spent more hours in that square mile than the sum total of his daughter's waking hours. And for what? To have his family disintegrate. To be disgraced. But suicide? If *anyone* was going to do that in his family . . . Robert steered the car to the side of the road and got out. He was on a flyover and alone. The East End spread out below him, shimmering in the red light, waterways and cranes, empty buildings, businesses long gone bust. Pointless, utterly pointless. He stood, battling with the confusion then leant forward, spread his arms wide and screamed for all of London to hear:

'It's my fault! Goddammit. It's my fault!'

DETECTIVE CHIEF INSPECTOR BRAMLEY from the Harlow CID made her go over her story three times. Cat was exhausted, pissed off and deliberately unhelpful, but he wouldn't take the hint.

'So you're a journalist who happens to kill the Wellbys' dog on the day that their daughter decides to kill herself?'

'Why would I lie?'

'No one said anything about lying. We are just trying to establish the facts.'

'With all due respect, officer—'

'Detective Chief Inspector.'

'With all due respect, Detective Chief Inspector, I've told you the facts.'

Bramley turned away.

'I should have left the bloody dog to rot.' She mumbled.

'What was that?'

'Nothing. Can I go?'

'As long as we can get hold of you.'

'I've given you my address already.' Another policeman appeared from inside the house.

'Beats me, y'know. A young girl kills herself, in her own home, to the utter amazement of her father, and she leaves no note.'

'Careful,' said another. 'That's how rumours start.'

'No note? Are you sure? Why didn't anyone tell me?' Cat watched them curiously. 'Christ Almighty, what else do you fools think we're missing?'

'A dead dog,' said the WPC rounding the corner.

Chapter Three

One look at her ex-husband was enough. Something had happened to her daughter. There was no other reason he'd darken her doorstep. When he failed to speak, she knew it was bad. Very bad. Fiona slammed the door in his face. It was a reflex action. She waited for the mottled form of Robert to disappear, for time to rewind, for the impossible to happen. He remained on her doorstep. It could only mean one thing. Jane was dead.

'How?' asked Fiona through the door.

'Let me in, Fiona.'

'How?' she screamed.

Robert paused before answering. Fiona watched his shape sharpen as he leant on to the glass. 'She was in the car—'

'I told you that car was too fast for her,' said Fiona pulling the door open angrily.

Robert righted himself. 'You don't understand, she was in my car.'

'How dare you let her drive—'

'She wasn't driving it,' he said, silencing her.

Robert watched as Fiona digested the information. Waiting to see if she knew, but she didn't. 'Oh, my God, Sandie! Tell me they're not dead. Please?'

'Sandie wasn't in the car,' he said, hovering on the threshold of truth.

'What?' said Fiona. 'Who was driving the car?'

'I don't know how to tell you this . . .' Death was unimaginable, but suicide – that was unacceptable.

'Tell me what?' said Fiona grabbing his upper arms. 'Where's Jane? What's happened?'

'It seems,' said Robert slowly, 'it seems that Jane . . .'

'What?!'

'She killed herself, Fi.'

'Don't be so ridiculous. What the fucking hell are you saying?'

Robert took her hands in his. He'd forgotten how small they were. 'I wish it wasn't true, Fi, but it is . . .'

'Shut up. Where is she, where's Jane?' Tears betrayed her and began to fill her disbelieving eyes.

'She took her own life, in my car, I wish it weren't true but it—'

'Shut up.'

Robert didn't respond.

'Stop saying that,' Fiona reiterated furiously, turning away.

Robert quietly closed the door behind him and followed Fiona down the hallway into a kitchen.

'I don't know why you are doing this, but I want you to stop.'

Robert stared at her.

'What have you done, Robert, what have you done to her?'

Robert shook her. 'I don't know what happened. I wasn't there. Simon appeared from nowhere, told me that there'd been an accident. A fucking accident. I suppose he thinks Jane attached herself to an exhaust pipe *by mistake.*'

'What?'

'She gassed herself out in the car, my car.'

'Jane?'

'Yes, Jane!' shouted Robert. 'Why didn't you tell me something was wrong?'

'What?'

'Stop saying what? Aren't you listening? Jane killed herself, you're her mother—'

'There was nothing wrong with my daughter. You don't know what you're saying. She would never do something like that.'

The silence was louder than the shouting.

'I saw her, Fiona,' he whispered.

Fiona crumpled into a chair. 'Who found her?'

'Some girl, I don't know.'

'Why?'

'She says she—'

'No. Why Jane? Why Jane?'

'I don't know. We're her parents, what did we miss? What did we do wrong?'

Fiona frowned at him. 'Wrong?'

'We are her parents.'

Fiona looked at the calendar on the kitchen wall. 'Oh, no,' she said slumping over the table.

Robert's gaze followed Fiona's. 'What?'

'The date, Robert.'

'What about it?'

Fiona stared at him in disbelief. 'It's ten years.'

'No,' said Robert sharply.

'To the day, Robert,' she said bitterly, pointing to the calendar.

'Fiona, it has nothing to do with that.'

'What else could it be?'

'Fiona, girls do not kill themselves because their parents got divorced years ago.'

Fiona looked up at him. 'To the fucking day.'

Robert looked at his ex-wife with fury in his eyes. 'It has got *nothing* to do with that!'

'Look, I don't know where the bloody dog's gone. It was dead. God, maybe it was just stunned. It happens. I know someone who hit a kangaroo on the road in Australia, they dressed it up in a jeans jacket and sunglasses and took photos of themselves with it, then the bloody thing came round and jumped off with their traveller's cheques
and passport in the pocket.' No one was smiling. 'Police didn't believe *them* either,' she added as an afterthought.

'Okay,' said Bramley, 'from the top.'

Cat imagined herself doing a tap-dance routine, *five, six, seven, eight* . . . 'I was doing a report in Colchester. You can listen to it if you like. I hit the animal driving back to the station.'

'How did you get into the house?'

'Don't know.'

'Did you break in?'

'No.'

'How do you know if you can't remember?'

'I'd remember that.' He scribbled on his pad. 'Then I phoned the police.'

'Oh, yes. We've got that on tape.'

'Why?'

'Normal procedure.'

'This is ridiculous, you are asking me questions as if you think I had something to do with all this. It's tragic that a young girl should take her own life, but I can't see that it's got anything to do with me.'

'And you are quite sure that you have never met the deceased?'

'Quite sure.'

'And the family?'

'Yes.'

'Yes, you're sure or, yes, you have met them?'

'The former.'

'You've met the former?'

Cat pulled a face at the policeman. 'Does this feel absurd to you, or is it just me?'

'I wouldn't be so cocky if I were in your shoes.'

He was not a slight man, it was unlikely her suede mules would suit him. 'No, probably not.'

He was about to start on at her again, when the WPC called him. 'We've got everything we need, I think we are ready to move out now.'

He nodded and turned back to Cat. 'Right, we've got your car registration, your address, telephone number, and we know where your grandmother resides.'

'I know.' She sighed. 'I gave them to you. Remember?'

He narrowed his eyes. 'You're not thinking of leaving the country any time soon?'

There was an endless stream of cheeky answers to that one, but she decided that none of them were suitable. A tiny anxiety monster was tugging at her trouser leg. The police were not joking. They really did believe she could be involved. A set-up. Locked up for a crime she didn't commit. After twenty years of rotting in gaol, some hot-shot young lawyer from the States would prove her innocence, get her acquitted, fall madly in love with her and then she'd get offered one million dollars for the movie.

Not Cat's idea of a fast buck.

'MY SKID MARKS!' SHE exclaimed loudly. Everyone stared. 'On the road. My tyres.' Still no one was with her. 'I skidded, when I hit the dog.' A collective 'ahh' from the audience, they'd finally caught up. 'That should prove my side of the story.'

'So would dog hairs on the bumper, but we didn't find any of those,' said the woman in uniform.

'WPC Clement,' said Bramley looking at Cat, 'call the coroner.'

Cat's head ached. She couldn't take any more insinuations. 'Can I please go?' Bramley nodded. She made her way to the front door, unaccompanied, and jumped when the doorbell rang loudly just as she opened it. If Mrs Wellby had answered the door in the first place her only problem would be a dead dog. Now wouldn't that be nice.

'Hello,' said the redhead smiling at her, 'you must be Jane.' Cat opened her mouth. The redhead tilted her head to one side. 'Hmm, Sandie has mentioned you.' Cat closed it again. 'Could you tell your stepmother that if she wants to rearrange today's cancelled hair appointment, I can pop in any time over the weekend.' Cat found herself nodding. 'Thanks. See ya.' The redhead turned on her heel and began to climb back into her red Mazda MX5. With one, bare, fake-tanned leg still on the gravel, she called out to Cat, still standing stupefied in the doorway, 'It's Suzie, by the way.' She waved, swung her leg into the car, closed the door and revved off along the gravel driveway. Cat looked back at the house as she got into her car. Sandie Wellby was standing at a first-floor sash window. The vacant expression from earlier had vanished along with her dog, what glared down at Cat now was as hard as granite and as angry as hell.

WPC CLEMENT KNOCKED LIGHTLY on Mrs Wellby's door and entered. She was standing at the window, clutching the thick chintz curtains.

'Mrs Wellby?' asked the policewoman when she didn't turn around. 'Are you all right?'

Sandie Wellby shook her head.

'Why don't you lie down.'

She shook her head again. 'I just can't believe it . . .'

'It isn't uncommon, Mrs Wellby, for parents to find their child's suicide completely incomprehensible.'

'She wasn't my child,' said Sandie turning around.

'I'm just saying this might be very difficult on your husband.'

'You think so?'

Clement ignored the sarcasm. 'Suicide often reveals some painful truths. There are some numbers you might want me to leave you.'

'I'll be fine, thank you.'

'I was thinking more about Mr Wellby.'

Sandie stared at her. 'Oh. Yes, of course.' Sandie took the leaflets and returned to her place at the window.

'There was one more thing?'

Sandie turned her head slowly.

'Is there a place that Jane may have left a note to her father?'

'A note?'

'It is usual in suicide cases, especially among younger people.'

Sandie didn't reply for a while. 'Perhaps she posted it.'

The policewoman smiled politely. 'We'll be leaving in just a moment, is there anything I can do before we go, or someone I can fetch?'

'No, thank you.'

'Will you be all right, Mrs Wellby?'

She nodded and watched the policewoman leave. She steadied herself against the windowpane. 'I don't know,' she whispered after the door had closed.

Chapter Four

Sandie saw Simon at the curve in the drive five minutes after the last police car left her property. Her eyes kept slipping out of focus, she wondered whether it was a side effect of the fumes. She blinked and looked again. It was definitely him. She ran down the stairs, pulled open the heavy wooden door and went to meet him.

'What happened?'

'I'm sorry, Sandie. He had to go alone. It was important to him.'

'You let him drive?' Sandie sounded at breaking point.

'I'm sorry,' repeated Simon.

'He'll probably kill himself too.'

'So they're sure it was suicide?'

'Of course they are,' said Sandie. 'What else would it be?'

Simon paused. 'I don't know, sorry, you just never know with the police.'

'For God's sake, Simon, the last thing we need is vicious talk about suspicious circumstances. We've all just got to keep our heads.'

'Yes, quite. Sorry.'

'Stop saying sorry, Simon. It's not your bloody fault Jane killed herself.'

'Well, quite. Is there anything I can do?'

'No. The only thing I asked you to do, you couldn't.' She couldn't keep the anger out of her voice. Simon stared at the ground. 'You'll have to take care of business,' she said trying to handle the situation better.

'Of course,' said Simon. He did anyway.

'I'll need to be here for Robert. Oh God, what are people going to say? What will his office do?'

'No one is going to say anything. Jane obviously had problems we knew nothing about.'

'Simon, we live in a big house in a small village. I'm an American. Robert is a well-respected banker. People will say a great deal.'

'You should go away,' said Simon quickly.

'What and leave Robert and Fiona?'

'I meant you and Robert. Death is an enormous emotional strain, Robert will need time.'

'*Life* is an enormous emotional strain. Death is easy, and anyway that office won't give him time off.' She rubbed the palms of her hands into her eye sockets. Simon was relieved she couldn't see the expression on his face.

THEY REACHED THE HOUSE. 'He said something about cancelling the Whittons,' said Simon.

'Hm?'

'The Whittons?'

Sandie stared at him blankly.

'Are they coming for dinner?'

'Who?'

'The Whittons.' Simon frowned. 'Sandie, are you all right?'

'Oh, damn! The fucking barbecue.' Simon looked confused. 'A treat for Jane.'

'Can I help?'

'No. I've got to make some phone calls anyway. After the crematorium, the Whittons will be a cinch.'

'No burial?'

'No. Jane didn't want to be buried.'

'Really?'

Sandie nodded. 'She told me so herself. A couple of weeks ago actually,' Sandie paused. 'Christ, Simon, do you think she was trying to tell me something? Something I missed?'

'No, come on, old girl, maybe she just wanted someone to know. Had it planned? I don't know.' There was no response from Sandie, so Simon continued, with difficulty. 'Look, best you call Robert. He's at Fiona's. Probably be nice if he brought her back with him. She probably shouldn't be alone.'

'Yes,' said Sandie smiling. 'Yes, that's a great idea. I'll

call now. Thanks, Simon.' That way she could keep an eye on them both.

'I am sorry, Sandie.'

'For what?'

'That this had to happen to you. You don't deserve this.'

'No one deserves shit like this, it just happens.'

'Not true, shit like this just happens to the wrong people.'

Sandie smiled sadly and shook her head.

'You are too good,' he said, 'too good.'

HALFWAY HOME EXHAUSTION SWAMPED her. Cat pulled into a garage and repeatedly scalded her tongue on thick black coffee. It didn't help, by the time she parked outside her flat in Angel, she was a wreck. Cat pulled herself up the stairs to her flat, struggled with the lock and crawled along the corridor to her small sitting room. The television was on, which meant Dan had arrived. Cat collapsed on to the sofa and closed her eyes. She didn't even have the energy to call his name. A sickly sleep smothered her and she rolled into a ball to protect herself from it.

'Hello, sleepy head,' said a distant voice. Cat smiled, opened her eyes slowly, and turned on to her back. Dan leant over the back of the sofa and planted a sloppy kiss on her lips. 'Where have you been all my life?'

Cat blinked at him. 'I'm so glad you're here.'

'Are you okay?' Dan put his hand, his insured hand, to her forehead. 'You look terrible.'

Cat put her arms around his neck and pulled herself up. 'I found a dead girl.'

'Well finders keepers,' said Dan smiling nervously. 'But I don't think you and Anna have the room.'

'No, I mean I *found* a dead girl.' Cat's lower lip began to quiver before the words were fully out. 'She'd gassed herself to death in her father's car.'

'Oh God, Cat,' Dan slid down next to her and wrapped himself around her, 'you poor thing.'

Cat started crying properly as Dan started to stroke her long, dark hair. 'And I fucked up at the station. Just because I didn't get one story in, bastards. The police wouldn't let me go, it wasn't as if I wanted to be there. I'm so pissed off.' Dan let Cat cry, if she wanted to blame the tears on the radio station, she could. He wasn't going to press her on a subject as perilous as suicide.

A TAXI CAME TO pick him up to take him home. Sandie was relieved to see him go. She needed time to think. She started tidying up the kitchen, bland, mundane motions keeping out the blackness. She turned the television on, then off again. It was hard to know what to do, now that no one was watching. She wondered whether she would ever cry for her stepdaughter. She doubted it. Eventually, when she thought she had given them enough time, she rang Fiona's number and got the answering machine.

'Fiona, it's Sandie, hello? Are you there? I want to know if you're both—'

'Hello, Sandie,' said Fiona, picking up the phone.

'Fiona, I am so sorry, I don't know what to say . . .'

'I know. It's a terrible shock. I had no idea she was unhappy.'

'You didn't?'

'Was she?' Fiona looked at Robert who was turning a tumbler of whisky round and round in his hands. He looked up. 'Sandie is saying she *was* unhappy.' Robert frowned. 'What was she unhappy about?' Fiona said into the phone.

Now was not the time. 'Fiona, it's been a dreadful day. We're all at our wits' end.'

'But there must be something, some clue. Did she leave a note?'

Sandie listened to Fiona's breathing down the phone. 'The police think she may have posted it to you, or she left you something, a message,' she continued tentatively, 'one that only you'd recognize?'

'The date,' replied Fiona immediately.

'What about the date, Fiona?'

'Ten years ago we told her,' she said beginning to cry again.

'Told her what, Fiona?'

'That we were getting divorced.'

'Really?' said Sandie slowly.

'To the day,' repeated Fiona.

Suddenly Robert downed the drink and slammed the glass on the table. He glared at the telephone.

'We'll get to the bottom of this,' said Sandie, unaware, 'but not now. It's late.' She glanced at her watch. It was eleven twenty. The day stretched behind her like a year. 'Will you both come here. There's plenty of room; I can look after you both. Please?'

'That's kind, but I think I'd rather be at home. All her things are here, you know.'

'I'd hate for you to be alone, Fiona, please think about it.'

'Okay.'

There was a pause. 'Can I have a word with Robert?' Fiona held the phone out towards her ex-husband. He stood up from the sofa then walked out of the room. Fiona closed her eyes. She couldn't cope with this.

'Sandie, I don't think he's up to talking at the moment. Let me try and settle him down a bit and I'll get him to call you. Will you be awake?'

Sandie was completely thrown. 'Awake? What am I . . . Of course, yes. Take your time. I'm glad you have each other.' Now was not the time to consider her feelings, there would be time enough for that.

FIONA SAT ON THE sofa. It was warm. She moved to the adjacent cushion. Why would a healthy, happy 23-year-old gas herself in a car? Surely there should have been signs. As hard as she tried, she could remember nothing that indicated to her that her daughter, her only child, had found herself in a hole so deep, so suffocating, that death was the only exit. She'd have known, surely? Depression was disguised in many forms, yes, but not in happy, sociable, chatty, confident girls. Jane always went out, she seemed to have lots of friends, she spent hours making plans, always had a scheme on the go – to travel, to make money, to live. To live dammit. Fiona had dined out on the success she and Robert were as divorced parents. It seemed like the split had hardly affected their thirteen-year-old daughter. She was certainly never neglected. Robert had even come over in the weekdays to do homework with her. That was more than most fathers could boast. True, Sandie was around before the ink had dried on the petition, but she had never been the cause of the divorce. Fiona and Robert knew that. Fiona climbed the stairs to her daughter's bedroom. She stared at the wooden door for some time, remembering.

'Mum, I've put my sheets in the laundry basket for you, but I can't find a clean duvet cover.'
Fiona stood at the bottom of the stairs and looked at her daughter. 'Didn't you take your old one to your father's?'
'Oh yeah, damn.'
'Doesn't matter, I'll have those ones cleaned and back on your bed by the time you get back.'
'You don't mind then?'
'No. Of course not.'
'You'll put them on while I'm away?'

'Yes. I should probably buy you a new one anyway.'
'And get rid of Pooh? No way,' said Jane laughing.
'Daft thing, it's virtually see-through, it's so old.'
'It would be a waste of money buying a new one, I'd
never use it. So, promise me you won't throw it away
while I'm at Dad's.'
'I wouldn't dare. Now come downstairs, I've got some
disgustingly good doughnuts that I can only justify having
in the house while you are here.'
'Coming.'

Fiona pushed the door open. The Pooh Bear duvet cover lay flat and clean on the bed, just as she had promised it would. But her daughter had reneged on the deal. She hadn't come back. She'd known she wasn't coming back, too, that was why she had insisted her mother not throw away the duvet. It was for her sake Jane wanted it kept. A reminder of the little girl that had grown beneath it while she slept. Fiona stared at the faded bear with his hand stuck in the honey pot. Not much of a trade-off, was it. The rest of the room was very tidy. Well it would be. Jane would not have left a messy room behind. It was a strange way of communicating, but worked for them. Jane had been allowed a lot of freedom since she was quite young. It was necessary if she were to spend equal time with mother and father. She had passed her driving test first time and had worn a route between the two houses ever since. The system worked well. If Jane was going away for one night, her room was left messy, bed unmade, wet towels on the floor, clothes everywhere. Two nights, the same. Except for the wet towels. Three nights to a week, the bed was made, the clothes were piled up on the armchair in the corner and half of her bottles had been cleared off her dressing table. Any longer than that and the room was cleared of all debris and all the clothes were put or taken away. The room Fiona stood in now was immaculate to the point of being sterile. If only she had been in it herself at any point in the last few days she might have realized something was wrong. Jane was supposed to be home the day after. Sunday lunch. It was planned, some of Fiona's friends were coming over, Jane knew about it. Fiona calculated quietly to herself. Five nights. Five nights away did not mean immaculate. It meant almost tidy. Some-times tidier than others, but definitely not immaculate. Why hadn't she been in the bloody room? Fiona sat in the small blue armchair below the window. The room screamed at her.

'Was it a sign, Jane? Did you think I'd come into this room, and know you were planning on being away for a long, long time? Did you think I'd come after you?' The tears sprang up again. 'I would have, darling, I would have. If only I'd come into your bloody room.' Fiona didn't have the energy to cry again, but the tears continued to slide listlessly down her face. She stared at the neat room accusingly, as though every polished surface, every neatly lined bottle and pot, each cushion piled symmetrically on her bed, every CD squarely in place, was responsible for killing her daughter. Fiona wiped her face on the curtain, a material that had been chosen so carefully and was now so insulting. Insulting because it had been given so much importance. She straightened in the chair, she must try and hold on to some semblance of rational thought, Jane would not have left her life to dangle on something as precarious as a tidy room.

'. . . Mum, I've put the sheets in the laundry basket for you, but I can't find a clean duvet cover.' Fiona stood at the bottom of the stairs and looked at her daughter.

'Didn't you take your old one to Dad's?'

'Oh yeah, damn.'

'Doesn't matter, I'll have those ones cleaned and back on your bed by the time you are back.'

'You don't mind then?'

'No. Of course not.'

'You'll put them on while I'm away?'

'Yes . . .'

'You'll put them on while I'm away?'

'Yes . . .'

'You'll put them on while I'm away?'

'No . . .' Fiona sunk to the floor. 'I was tired, Jane, it had been a long day. I knew it would be a long day that Tuesday, I was running the shop, you know, my friend's antique shop as a favour. I'd had two frames to finish and the shopping to do. You see, I didn't have time to do it myself, Jane. I asked Rosa to do it. You know, lovely

Rosa who helps me clean every other week. She did it. She ironed Pooh and put it back on your bed. I didn't do it. I never went into your room. There was no need you see, Jane, I had no reason to go in there. I'm sorry, I'm so sorry . . .' Fiona crawled across the carpet, knelt alongside the freshly made bed and laid her head upon it. It didn't even smell of her little girl, it smelt of a bloody Spring Meadow.

CAT SAT BOLT UPRIGHT, her eyes searching for something to focus on in the darkness as the image of Jane Wellby faded from her mind. She looked at her watch. It was three in the morning. Dan must have carried her to bed because she was still in her clothes. She watched the rise and fall of the duvet next to her and envied him his sleep. Cat peeled off the covers and sat on the edge of the bed. Her jeans were clamped to her clammy thighs and her hair stuck to the back of her neck. She undressed in the darkness, put on a towelling dressing gown and went downstairs to the sitting room. The green light from her computer winked at her. She automatically walked over to it and switched it on. The screen glowed reassuringly at her, coating her in a thick electronic light, coaxing her to exorcize the ghosts. Cat began to write down the events that had led her to Cedar Hall, but it didn't help. Jane Wellby's death had hit her hard in a place that wasn't open to assault and she didn't know what to do about it. Cat walked through to her small kitchen, put on the kettle and dialled the number of the one person she knew who never slept before dawn.

'Cat?'

Cat was relieved. 'How did you know it was me?'

'Contrary to what I said, darling, since the fractured hip there haven't been many lovers to have late-night chats with and anyway, you're the only one with my direct number.'

'I didn't wake you?'

'Hardly, the best hours are just in sight. Anyway, I've been doing a bit of corridor wheeling.'

'I thought you said—'

'Hush now, not that sort. Just changing the names around on the door tags and doing a bit of research for your radio programme. I bet Radio Four pick it up.'

'I doubt it,' said Cat. 'You be careful you don't get caught.'

'And get a hundred lines to write. Have my Batten-burg cake allowance cut, my pocket money stopped.' Amelia paused, Cat wasn't laughing. 'You're sober. What's wrong?'

Cat laughed. 'I love you.'

'You're not sober.'

'I am, I am.'

'So,' said Amelia, 'if you haven't called to gush drunkenly down the telephone, what's the matter?'

Cat told Amelia about her journey home. When she finished Amelia was quiet. The kettle had boiled. Cat stared at the puffs of steam as they swirled under the electric light. Smoke. Fumes. Asphyxiation. Death.

'Are you still awake?' said Cat eventually.

'I was thinking about Angelo Romano.'

'Gran, don't. This has got nothing to do with him.'

Amelia sighed. 'It's a trigger mechanism.'

'What are you talking about?'

'To make you think about Angelo, Clara, Dan.'

'Dan? What's he got to do with the people who we mistakenly refer to as my parents.'

'You see.'

'I'm being flippant. I didn't call to talk about them.'

'You never talk about them.'

'There's nothing to talk about.' Cat heard Amelia sigh heavily. 'Don't do this. I'm freaked because I found a body in a garage, maybe if I'd got there sooner I could've stopped her.'

'Who are you to say she wanted saving?'

'She was so young. How bad can things have been? She had a lovely home, a dog, family, most people would give anything to have that.'

'Anything, Cat?' said Amelia deliberately.

'I'm not talking about me. I have the perfect family. You. It happens to be all I need—'

'Cat?'

Cat looked up startled. Dan stood in front of her. His eyes squinting against the harsh kitchen light.

'Who are you talking to?' he asked.

'Gran.' *Dan. The police. Dead Girl's Mother. Dead Girl.*

'Yes, darling?'

'What's wrong?' asked Dan.

'I couldn't sleep.'

'I know,' said Amelia. Cat sighed. She couldn't cope with another three-way conversation.

'I was talking to Dan,' said Cat into the phone.

'Tell him to make you some hot chocolate and read you a story.'

Cat smiled. 'That'll work will it?'

'It did when you were a little girl.'

'All right. I'm sorry I rang in the middle of the night.'

'Listen to me, my precious thing, you ring me whenever you need me, day or night.'

'Okay, Gran. I love you.'

Cat replaced the phone slowly and looked at Dan. He pointed to himself.

'What?' asked Cat.

'I'm here, Cat. Me.'

'You were asleep,' she offered.

'You could've woken me up.' Dan busied himself with a pack of herbal tea. He spoke with his back to her. 'You cried in my arms until you passed out from emotional exhaustion, then, when you feel like talking about it, you go to Amelia.'

Cat squirmed, remembering the uncontrollable tears. 'I'm sorry about earlier.'

'Cat, that isn't what I'm saying.' She looked at him uncertainly when he faced her. 'Oh, it doesn't matter,' he said, passing her the tea.

'Thanks.' Cat took it and blew the surface gently. Dan watched her, shaking his head, as she swung through the jungle of her own thoughts.

'This is exactly what I'm talking about,' he said quietly. 'You completely exclude me without even realizing it.'

'Hm?' she said, looking up at him.

'Never mind.'

'What did you say, Dan?'

'Never mind. I just worry about you.'

'I was just pissed off about the stupid bus story. I'm fine now.'

Dan took her hand, pulled her to him and kissed her forehead. She relaxed as he held his lips against her skin. Then she closed her eyes. Jane Wellby stared back. Cat jolted.

'What is it?'

'Nothing, let's go to bed.'

'Cat, please, talk to me . . .'

'Really,' said Cat, forcing a smile, 'I'm fine.'

Chapter Five

There was a note on the fridge door, stuck there with Cat's Elvis Presley magnet.

GONE TO GET BREAKFAST — BACK IN 5.

She groped at the fridge door and stared blindly in. She closed it again and sat at the table waiting. She didn't have the energy to put the kettle on. She wanted fuss. She wanted to be taken care of. She didn't know what she wanted.

'How are you feeling, sleepy head?' asked Dan climbing the stairs two at a time. He had a pink and white striped plastic bag in his hand, which meant he'd only been as far as the corner shop. Cat watched him pile the white bread, butter and marmalade on to the kitchen table. Two blocks on, he could have got them cappuccinos and fresh croissants, but she didn't say anything. Dan poured the instant coffee into mugs and filled them with boiling water. Cat watched him. He was tall, much taller than Cat, with thick, slightly wavy brown hair. The bridge of his nose was flat and narrow and he had an enviable jaw line. His eyes were the colour of conkers.

'Sorry about last night,' she said, 'not much of a romantic reunion was it?'

'You know a simple headache would do if you're not in the mood.'

'And be threatened with two Nurofen?'

Dan rolled his eyes.

'You know what,' said Cat, pulling the middle of a slice of bread out and rolling it between her palms, 'I think we should go and spend some of that money your hands earn and have a laugh.'

Dan watched her eat the dough ball.

'What?' said Cat.

He shook his head. 'I'd love to but I'm afraid I've got a bit of a confession to make.'

'Don't make it,' said Cat putting her hand over his mouth. 'Ignorance is bliss, Gran told me that.'

'Ignorance is bliss, life is unfair and a truth is stronger than a lie . . .'

'All right, Dan, you've made your point. Confess all.'

'I've got to go into college.'

'But it's Saturday.'

'I didn't get a chance to tell you last night.'

Cat felt a strange heat behind her eyes.

'It's a weekend seminar given by my tutor for all the Ph.D. students. I have to go.'

'Right. Well, if you have to,' she said biting her lip.

'I'm really sorry. I don't want to leave you on your own.'

'I'll be fine, I'm feeling fine already. Really. I was just tired.'

'If it was a modelling job I'd cancel it, but I can't get out of this.'

'My fault for wanting brawn and brains.'

Dan put coffee and marmalade-covered toast on the table and pushed her gently on to the chair.

'Eat,' he said. 'I'm going to run you a bath and ease a little of my guilt if that's okay.'

Cat nodded.

LEAVING CAT IN A lavender-scented bath, a small fortress of toast soldiers in arm's reach and with fresh coffee, Dan crossed the demarcation zone and entered Anna's part of the house. Only colour and accoutrements marked the division of territory. Anna's place was a mixture of pink and purple; Cat's was green and blue. In Anna's bathroom the quantity of beauty products was alarming, in Cat's they were minimal. In Anna's the sofas and chairs were covered in fake fur and PVC, in Cat's, well, she went to Anna's most of the time anyway. Dan and Anna had been at Cambridge together, in fact, Anna was the most famous fringe act to come out of Cambridge University, having been spotted by a casino king, taken to Las Vegas and launched into the big time. The legal change of name to Anna Prokton did concern his parents temporarily, but other than that he'd experienced a mess-free, meteoric rise to Divaship. Dan and Cat loved him only a little less than he loved them. Anna was reclining on the sofa with a cold press over his eyes.

'Hangover?' said Dan sitting next to him.

'Oh, Danny boy,' Anna peeled the jelly mould off his face, 'what treats me to a visit on this fine morning?'

'I have a favour to ask.'

Anna sat up. 'This better be good, I've got hyenas in my head.'

'Would you mind looking after Cat today?'

'My throat, darling, I can't afford to catch a bug.'

'She hasn't got a bug, she had a scare, accidentally stumbled across a suicide victim yesterday.'

Anna raised one eyebrow, challengingly.

'It's true. Then the police gave her a hard time about it.'

'I would've thought that was the sort of radio news your Lois Lane would love,' said Anna, slumping back against the sofa, feigning exhaustion.

'Anna, you probably don't know this, but Cat's father committed suicide.'

'Cat doesn't have a father. Try another.'

Dan stood up and walked to the bay window that looked over the narrow street.

'Sorry,' said Anna sitting up straight. 'That was stupid. I know her mum pissed off to Australia, I just presumed it was a one-night stand situation. I thought she'd never met her father.'

Dan continued to stare out of the window. 'She

didn't. He was some playboy Italian, I don't know the details, just that something happened and he gassed himself in his sports car. Never even wrote her a letter, nothing. Anyway, this girl yesterday, she was in a car too and I just think that—' Dan cleared his throat. 'I can't be here.' He turned back to Anna. 'Please, it's important.'

Anna approached his old room-mate and put an arm around his shoulder. He often marvelled at the curse of being male, having watched Dan struggle with it for years. So much bubbled beneath the surface but so little burst through.

'Why didn't you tell me before, about Cat?'

'She doesn't like anyone knowing, she thinks they'll feel sorry for her or something. Don't say anything, Anna, just pop in to say hi and stay. Okay?'

'Sweetheart, I've got just the thing.'

'It's too early for tequila,' said Dan, backing out of the room.

'Yuck, don't speak of such things. I'll be up in a minute.'

Dan smiled to himself. Anna had never got ready in anything less than an hour. But this time he surpassed himself. Twenty minutes later, just as Cat appeared in a bundle of towels, Anna knocked on the door. Under his arm he carried a basket of videos, face packs, hair removing devices that looked medieval and his own specially prepared herbal tea.

'Tisane, darlings?' Anna called from the kitchen doorway. Dan watched Cat smile, then look knowingly back at him. He kissed her before she could argue that she really, *really* was fine, picked up his jacket, winked at Anna and left.

'What's he told you,' said Cat, kissing Anna hello and staring into the basket.

'Nothing, darling, I thought we could have a beauty day, I've got something here you won't be able to resist.'

Cat ignored the video cassette Anna was waving around. 'Bullshit, Anna, you've been talking. I knew that bath thing was a trick'

'Dollybird, boys don't have conniving conversations like that.'

'But you're not a boy, so spill.' Cat clicked her fingers.

'Bitch. I most certainly am a boy, which is why I know they don't tell each other anything.' Anna smiled. 'Your pores are blocking, it is time for a girly day.'

'You are a gender whore, Anna Prokton.'

'Tell me about it, I'm a 32-year-old man with a 32-year-old woman's anxieties. Now spread *that* on your couch and eat it.'

'I don't need babysitting, whatever Dan told you.'

'I've got the first Remington Steel series on tape,' he said tauntingly.

Cat relented. 'Okay, sit.'

Anna blew her a kiss. 'Baby.'

IT WAS ON LEVEL nine, the interval programme, set for thirty minutes. She had seven minutes left to go and despite the burning in her legs and lungs, she would not stop. She would not be defeated by a fucking step machine. She would do fifty lengths in the pool next, maybe sixty, anything to bring on the endorphin rush and rid her of the weighty grogginess that had descended upon her like the LA smog. Sandie stepped on, climbing the insurmountable. She knew there were more important things to do, but she couldn't cope with the mental stress of doing them. Robert couldn't take responsibility for his daughter even when she was dead. During their seven years of marriage, Jane had been their only problem. In regard to his daughter he could be blind, ignorant and stupid. None of which he was. Which made it harder to circumnavigate. She was his Achilles heel. His weakness. Sandie could never criticize him, she wasn't a parent, what did she know? Well, she knew this – a parent who could see no wrong in their child was a dangerous parent. And produced dangerous children. She loved Robert, but Jane . . . The image of Jane's lifeless body filled her head. She had been poisoning their family for years. Death by noxious fumes was about as ironic an ending as could be. It was *almost* funny. From her unique perspective. Of course no one else could know that. She'd have to get everything just right, say the right thing to the right person, get the level of mourning right for her position. Mourn too little and she'd be open to criticism, mourn too much and she'd get even more. After all, she was only the *stepmother*. Sandie marched on. She must handle this well. Two minutes to go. The pain was almost enjoyable.

'Come on!' she urged herself on. It was the first voice she'd heard all day. It sounded good, even if it was only her own. The house had been so fucking quiet. 'Come on, Mrs Wellby,' she said again, almost smiling, 'you've done things like this before, you can get through this.' Thirty seconds. She closed her eyes, head down, the sweat dripped on to the digital screen, not long now, just a few seconds more . . . Three, two, one. The last step lowered slowly to its resting place. She breathed heavily as the machine congratulated her. She left her exercise room and jogged down the staircase, out of the French windows, across the lawn, into the walled rose garden to the swimming pool.

ROBERT WATCHED HER.

SHE KICKED OFF HER Nike trainers haphazardly, peeled off each sock, threw them aside and then pulled her cycling shorts and G-string off in one. She pulled the sports top over her head, chucked that down too, took three long steps and did a racing dive into the shallow end. She wasn't allowed to do that, it set a bad example for Jane, friends of theirs had a child in a wheelchair from diving into the shallow end. It was a house rule at Cedars. Robert didn't want anything happening to his precious daughter. God forbid there should be an accident. Then again, maybe an accident would have been better. Incomprehensible, but unaccountable. There would be no one to blame but fate. Sandie completed the length underwater, bursting through the surface when she reached the deep end.

'What the hell are you doing?'

'Robert!' It was a shock seeing him, suddenly, as if he had appeared from nowhere. 'When did you get back?'

'What the hell are you doing?' he repeated slowly.

'I, I'm . . .' She felt embarrassed. Exposed. 'I'm sorry, I needed to clear my head. I felt terrible all morning. You should've phoned, I was worried.'

'You have no clothes on.' Robert sounded disgusted.

'I'm sorry,' she repeated, holding herself close to the side of the pool, trying to obscure her nakedness. 'I thought no one was here.'

'Very good, darling, no one is here, that's right, no one is here at all and why? Because Jane is dead. Jane is dead, Sandie, and you go skinny dipping. Very good indeed.'

'Robert?' she said, hurt, 'please, I'm sorry. You're right. It was insensitive.'

'Insensitive.' He laughed. 'It's fucking inexcusable.' He stalked off down the path through the rose bushes to the narrow-arched wrought-iron gate. At the gate he turned and shouted. 'Why did she do it?' He wasn't shouting at her really, she knew that, he was shouting at himself, at God, that omnipresent being who was supposed to have the answers, at anyone who would listen, at Jane. Sandie watched him leave, then swam to the bottom of the pool and looked up at the blurry, chlorine-

soaked sunrays dancing above her. She'd have to tell
them some things about Jane. Hint at her unhappiness.
That way they might accept her death and leave it at that.
It was called damage limitation in her country.

AMELIA WATCHED ANNA, IN a black pencil skirt, high
heels and a pink shirt tied around his midriff, flounce
down the path towards her swinging his handbag and
calling her name. Cat, in jeans and a T-shirt, strolled
calmly a few paces behind.

'Amelia!' called Anna more loudly than necessary.
'Darling!' Amelia glanced at the inmates around her, she
could always rely on Anna to upset a few of the stuffier
old ladies and give a little life to the old gents.

'What a lovely surprise,' said Amelia, kissing Anna.

'You are never going to believe what's happened,
your granddaughter has a knack, a knack, I tell you. She's
a genius, brilliant. Jon Snow move on out, Cat Torrant is
taking over.'

Amelia looked behind the gesticulating Anna Prokton
to Cat who stood with her hands on her hips waiting for
the sideshow to finish.

'Hi, Gran.'

'Drugs?' said Amelia, bypassing Anna.

'They might help.'

Amelia mouthed, 'Are you all right,' to Cat, who
nodded. Anna was still squealing. 'Tell her, tell her. Oh,
I'll tell her. There we were happily ensconced in front of

the darling Pierce Brosnan and who should pop into the storyline but our own wicked American stepmother.'

Amelia leant round Anna again. 'Translation please?'

'It seems that the dead girl's stepmother is an actress.'

'And?'

'And? And? Amelia, she kissed Pierce. What more proof do you need? She must hang.'

'Cat, call a nurse, Anna is checking in.'

Anna looked at them both like they were imbeciles. 'There wasn't a note.'

'They didn't find a note,' said Cat, correcting him.

'The girl was very ugly,' said Anna, as though that might be reason enough for the beautiful American actress to do away with her stepdaughter.

'I didn't say that,' said Cat.

'You said she looked repulsive.'

'Anna, carbon monoxide does strange things to a girl's complexion, and if you wouldn't mind, I'd prefer it if you changed the subject.'

'Look, Chelmsford sent her packing because of one missed deadline. Well she'll show them what she's made of when she hits them with the Wellby scandal.'

'American Actress Takes Role Of Wicked Stepmother Too Far, this is Cat Torrant for Channel Four News, Death Row.'

'Perfect.'

'Tabloid junky,' said Cat sitting down next to her grandmother.

'I don't think Cat should get involved in this,' said Amelia quietly.

'Why not?' asked Anna.

Amelia looked sideways to Cat.

'It's okay, the shameful secret is out.'

'It isn't shameful.'

'Gran, I was joking.'

'I don't think suicide is a very humorous matter.'

'Gran, I can handle this.'

'Anna,' said Amelia, 'would you mind getting us some tea?'

'Gran, stop it.'

'No problem,' said Anna.

'Stay where you are,' said Cat. 'This isn't about him. It's got nothing to do with him.'

'He was your father, Cat.'

Cat winced. 'He wasn't my father. I don't have a father. I barely have a mother. Anna's right, I need something that'll make BBC Chelmsford regret their hasty decision. What's a bus story compared to murder most foul.'

'I thought it was suicide,' said Amelia, still resisting.

'They called the coroner,' said Cat.

Amelia didn't say anything for a while. She remembered the funeral like it was yesterday. Decade hopping was something that came with age. She had gone to Italy alone and alone she had watched as the donator of half Cat's genes was lowered into the ground. A giver and waster of life. She thought she'd better understand the man who had never shown any interest in his daughter, but she should've followed her own advice. Ignorance *is* bliss. He turned out to be nothing more than a selfish gigolo who killed himself after being diagnosed with prostate cancer. Cat was better off without him, not that she'd had that choice. It was Amelia who'd taken that away from her when she sent her own daughter, Clara, to Florence with nothing more than a few words of advice. *Italians make excellent lovers, but whatever you do don't marry one.* She never thought her daughter would take her quite so literally. Clara didn't believe in abortion. Nor in motherhood. The baby was going to be put up for adoption until Amelia took one look at her, Catherine Amelia, and stopped the process. Clara stayed with them until her figure returned and then she left. Amelia became mother, father, sister, brother, aunt and uncle. She was Cat's whole family. Cat put her hand on Amelia's arm. 'Come on, Gran, you've never protected me in my whole life. It's a little late to start now.'

You're wrong, thought Amelia, all I've ever done is protect you.

Cat turned to Anna. 'When I was bullied at school, she sent me right back with the words, hit them if you have to. She made me do three jobs to pay off my college debts, my pleas of exhaustion falling on deaf ears.'

'Quite right too,' said Anna.

'I'll be fine, Gran, honest. All I'm interested in is doing a good investigative piece and salvaging my reputation.'

Amelia was about to say something when a young nurse arrived at their table on the stone terrace. 'Excuse me?' Cat didn't recognize her. 'Mrs Torrant, I was wond— Oh, I apologize, I didn't realize you had guests today.' She consulted her list, then frowned. 'I'm sorry, but you haven't signed in, I haven't got either of you on the list, I must insist—'

'Oh bugger off, we're talking here.'

'Mrs Torrant, you must try and curb—'

'I said,' continued Amelia, not in the mood, 'bugger off.'

'I've been warned about you,' she said. 'Please don't swear.'

'I can't help it. I've got Tourette's syndrome.'

'Bollocks,' said the young nurse.

Anna laughed. Amelia threw him a withering look. Anna stopped laughing. 'Didn't anyone teach you to respect your elders. Now, get out of my sight before I start using swear words that your wee mind doesn't understand.'

The young girl walked backwards a few paces before turning and walking back to the main house.

'Cheeky devil,' said Amelia.

'You've got to give her points for effort.'

'She didn't seem too bad,' said Cat.

'You don't understand, if you don't scare the new ones off the first time round, they pester you all the time.' She put on a squeaky voice. 'Come on, Mrs Torrant, a general-knowledge quiz game will keep your mind ticking over. We need a last team member for the relay race on wheels. Croquet? Booooole? Mrs Ticklebottom needs a partner for the square dance . . .' She threw up her hands. 'You will not catch me dancing with other incontinent women. The next thing you'll know I'll have my nightie stuck in my pants, a tea cosy on my head and chocolate biscuit smeared all over my face. Forget it.' Cat went over and gave her a kiss, Amelia held her hand and squeezed it.

'Do the men dance together too?'

'Anna, most of the men round here smoked their legs off years ago. And those who didn't can't dance. It's God having the last laugh. The painters go blind, the musicians go deaf and . . .' Amelia checked herself. 'Anyway, at least that nagging little strumpet won't be' – a large shadow loomed over their table – 'back.'

But she was. And she'd brought reinforcements of the worst kind. Nurse Cleveland.

'Okay, Mrs Torrant, let's get your guests registered and while we're at it put you down for a Sunday activity,' said the new nurse, empowered by the stalwart presence of Nurse Cleveland.

'Don't be ridiculous, girl.'

'Everyone has to do something, keeps the brain ticking over.' Amelia looked at Anna who nodded sympathetically, then pouted at the nurses.

'We know you, Cat, but you, madam, are . . .?' Anna winked at Amelia. Cat made a silent prayer and wondered whether the moment of expulsion had finally arrived.

'That,' said her grandmother, lording it up, 'is Miss Anna Prokton. A force to be reckoned with on the stages of London's West End.'

'Oh, an actress,' said the younger nurse with awe.

'No,' contradicted Amelia, 'a drag queen.'

Anna removed his blonde wig and bowed. 'Charmed I'm sure. Fantastic uniform,' he said admiringly. 'What size are you? No. Wouldn't work. Your breasts are smaller than mine.'

'Please, sir,' admonished Nurse Cleveland.

'What, honey? We're all girls here.' He eyed the large nurse up and down. 'Well nearly.' Anna pouted. 'Now let me autograph that little ledger of yours.' Anna signed his name in a flurry of ink over the page then held it away from himself in order to admire it. 'Probably worth a bit of money.' He handed it back to Nurse Cleveland. 'Haven't I seen you somewhere before, nurse?' She shook her head. 'You look awfully familiar.' She shook it more vigorously. 'Ever been to Madame JoJo's?'

'No.'

'Climax?'

'Certainly not.'

'Captain Pugwash?'

'What?'

'Tool Shed?'

'Out!'

Anna scratched his chin. 'No, I don't think I've ever done a gig there.'

'Leave!' Nurse Cleveland pointed towards the car park.

'Up yer bum!' yelled Amelia gleefully.

'Right that's it. I want your notice of departure immediately.'

'Why?'

'For being rude and disruptive, Mrs Torrant.'

'Nurse Cleveland, you misunderstood me. That's Anna's name. Well, that's what it means. *Anaprokton*, it's Greek.'

Nurse Cleveland looked desperately at Cat. 'Ancient Greek, to be precise,' said Cat, knowing the routine.

'I studied it at Cambridge,' said Anna.

Defeated, Nurse Cleveland turned on her heel and began to walk back up to the main part of the building. Two hundred yards up the path she turned back and said in a loud voice, 'Deuteronomy, chapter twenty-two, verse five!' The mismatched gathering stared nonplussed after her.

'Christ,' said the young nurse crossly, 'reminds me of the claptrap the nuns used to quote at me at the convent.'

'What does it mean?' asked Anna.

'Never paid that much attention to the Old Testament,' said the girl.

'The only part I could relate to was when two angels visited old Mr Lot and the men of Sodom, without exception, shouted, "Bring them out so we can have intercourse with them." After that it gets a bit gloomy,' said Anna winking. 'Too much fire and brimstone for my liking.'

The young nurse giggled.

'Moving neatly on to the subject of Sunday Activities, which I believe are forbidden in the eyes of the Lord,' said Amelia hopefully. 'What are you going to do about them?'

The nurse scrunched up her little face, then smiled broadly. 'Nothing.' Everyone smiled.

'What's your name, honey?' asked Anna.

'Katie O'Leary.'

'Well thank you, Katie.'

'Well that's okay, Anna.' She smiled sweetly and left.

'Well I never,' said Amelia, wheeling herself back to face the table. 'We might have found us an ally in this godforsaken place after all.'

SANDIE FOUND ROBERT IN the meadow. He was on his knees. In tears. Sandie's heart cracked at the sight of him. But it quickly filled with the sediment of anger. This was all Jane's fault.

'Darling,' she said tentatively, kneeling in front of him.

Robert took her face in his hands. 'I'm so sorry.'

'It's okay, I'm sorry too, I don't know what I was thinking. Shock.'

'I know,' said Robert, 'I should've been here. Sandie, I've made so many mistakes, I don't know how to tell you.'

'Ssh,' she said, stroking his head. 'You were a wonderful father to Jane, this isn't your fault.'

Robert looked up. He stared at his beautiful wife for a full minute. 'I don't deserve you.'

'Robert, darling, you make me happier than I ever thought possible. Recently things have been—' She sighed. 'Maybe we should go away, together. This is going to be very hard, but we'll survive. I love you. We'll be okay.'

'But Sandie, you don't understand. It's my fault she's dead . . .' The tears began again.

'It's not your fault, you gave that girl everything.'

'You don't understand, I—'

'Listen to me, you're in shock. That's all. It's natural for parents to blame themselves. You didn't do this to her. You couldn't hurt anyone. Robert, you are a good man, we need time to get back to how it was.' Sandie pulled his face towards her, kissing the oversized tears off his face. His sobbing increased as he kissed her back. Sandie shifted her weight and lowered them both on to the uncut grass.

NURSE CLEVELAND REAPPEARED.

'Oh, no, the blot on the landscape is back.' They all turned. This time she had the police.

'They're going to have me physically removed,' said Amelia. 'Get ready for a real news story, child. Has anyone got a camera?'

'Gran, stop being so melodramatic. It's not you

they're after. The dead girl, remember, that's why they're here.' They looked at each other then turned to face the policemen. Bramley looked at the three of them from behind one of his officers. An old woman, a transvestite and a possible murderer. Give him a murderer any time.

'Catherine Amelia Torrant?' asked the young officer.

'Yes?' said Cat and Amelia.

'Well, which one is it?'

'Well, officer, I'm Amelia Torrant and this charming girl is my granddaughter, Catherine.'

Cat turned to Bramley. 'Do you always work on Saturday?' she asked, trying to hide her nerves.

'That depends on whether members of the criminal element are giving me the run around, Miss Torrant.'

'Ooh, don't talk to me about criminal members,' giggled Anna. 'Take, take, take and no give makes any member criminal in my opinion.' Cat elbowed him.

Bramley gave him a look of disgust. Anna thought about squaring up to the stocky policeman, but the last time he had done that he'd been threatened with a truncheon. Though not in the way one would expect to be threatened with a truncheon. He turned away. Bramley considered it a victory. He looked at Amelia.

'We'd like your granddaughter to escort us to Harlow Police Station, there are a few matters concerning the death of Jane Wellby that we would like to clear up.'

Cat's eye's widened. Black saucers.

'Why do you need me?'

'Best we discuss that at the station.'

'But I already told you everything.'

'It seems some inconsistencies have arisen regarding the suicide, we need your fingerprints, Catherine.'

'Please call me Cat,' she said. 'I automatically feel as if I'm in trouble when anyone calls me Catherine.'

'Well, there's a coincidence,' said Bramley, 'you may well be.'

Chapter Six

Cat looked at the black ink on her fingertips and listened to the tape rewind. It clicked off loudly. The door to the interview room opened and a man in jeans and a yellow Ralph Lauren shirt walked in.

'Cat, this is DS Mike Chambers, I'd like him to listen to the tape as well. Sit down, Mike.' Bramley pressed play. Once again her disembodied voice filled the small stark room in the modern police station, like so much else, purpose-built. Its purpose to isolate and intimidate the captive, the architect had done a fine job. She looked at the machine on the table and listened to her own, but unfamiliar, voice:

'Who is the girl?'

'Jane.'

'Is she in trouble?'

'I'm at Cedar Hall, Old Harlow, Essex. I need an ambulance and a police car as soon as possible.'

'What has happened?' There was a dramatic pause.

'I'm sorry,' said Cat's voice pathetically. Cat cringed.

'What are you sorry for?'

'All of this.'

The policeman pressed stop then looked at Cat. She spoke first. 'Well, if you stop the tape there of course it sounds odd, but I wasn't talking to the person on the phone. I was talking to the woman who I thought was Jane's mother, and I was about to tell her that her daughter was dead. You'd be sorry.' She looked desperately at the other policeman opposite her. 'Wouldn't you?' They stared back at her. 'Why would I want to hurt someone I've never met before?'

'We've only your word that you had never met her before, Miss Torrant. Miss Wellby not being here to corroborate.'

'That,' Cat replied, horrified at what Bramley was insinuating, 'is uncalled for.'

'Well, you did name her on the phone.'

'I've explained that.' *Or are you deaf?* There was a knock on the door.

'WPC Clement entering the room at' – the officer glanced at his watch – 'fifteen oh three and handing DCI Bramley a note.'

Bramley read it, looked warily at Cat, then handed it to the policeman next to him. Cat continued to sit in disbelief, reality suspended. She could've been watching one of the many police series on the TV, except that she was not in the comfort of her own home.

'They are your fingerprints on the hose, Miss Torrant. All over the thing actually.'

'Well they would be, I pulled it out.'

'Pulled it out or put it in?'

Cat shook her head. 'Pulled it out.'

'And the body itself, did you put that in, or pull it out?'

'Neither.'

'Funny, your fingerprints are all over Jane's body too.'

'I . . .'

'And the seat belt.'

'Because I undid it.'

'Suicide victims don't usually strap themselves in, is that why you took it off?'

'I didn't take it off—'

'You just said you undid it.'

'But only because I thought she was alive, I was trying to get her out, that's why I undid the seat belt.'

'That would be easier to believe if there were other fingerprints on it apart from yours. But there aren't.'

Cat didn't know how to respond.

'You could have put it on and taken it off again.'

'Why would I have done that?'

'That is what we are trying to do, cooped up on this fine Saturday afternoon, to answer that question. A lot of things don't add up about your version, including the timing. The bloke who runs the pub at the end of the drive tells me that you asked directions to Cedar Hall at two o'clock. But your call to the police was not until three minutes to three. What were you doing for that hour?'

Cat remembered the lions. Wanting to turn back. Ringing the bell. Waiting. Constructing the note. Snooping.

'Let's go one step further,' he said, leaning towards Cat.

WPC Clement looked at Bramley nervously.

'You killed Jane Wellby. Later you go back to "discover" the death, but she still has a pulse. You have to wait before raising alarm.'

Bramley leant in towards her, breathing heavily. Cat stared at him but all she could see were the events at Cedar Hall, the kitchen, the dried flowers.

'What time did she die?'

'That's a strange question for you to ask,' replied Bramley.

'*What time did she die?*'

'Between one and two thirty.'

Cat pushed herself away from the table, a wave of nausea threatening to overwhelm her. 'It was my fault.'

'In what way, Catherine?'

'Because,' *you idiot*, 'I was there. I was there, trying to do the right thing by a dead dog while a girl was choking to death a clean air's breath away. I could have saved her.'

'Settle down,' said Bramley, 'there's no need to get hysterical.'

'Isn't there? You keep telling me I killed her, well I didn't.'

'You didn't save her either.'

Cat was rendered speechless by the scathing words. There was a knock on the door. A policeman put his head in the room and held up a manila folder. Bramley signalled for him to bring it over. He looked back at Cat.

'Tell me, what was your impression of Mrs Wellby?'

Cat couldn't take much more. 'Well she was doing a fine act of the bereaved stepmother when you lot turned up, but she was totally calm when I told her.'

'Why would she act up to us?'

'Because she's an actress of course.' The police officers looked at each other. 'You didn't know?' Cat felt relief flood through her. 'American TV actress. She's called Sandie-Ann Surly. I looked her up on the Internet, she was very well known in TV dramas during the seventies and early eighties. Guess she gave it up to move into her new role as lady of the manor. I don't blame her, it's a nice house, right up there with Beachy Head in the most likely places to commit suicide. She was there you know. I rang the bell but got no answer, that's why I went round the back. Turns out she'd been there all along.'

'Maybe she turned up while you were looking for a way in,' Bramley said in his self-satisfied manner.

'I wasn't looking for a way in. I was looking for someone to give Lucy to.'

'Who's Lucy?'

'The dog I ran over.'

'What if I told you that Mrs Wellby claims to have been out walking the dog.'

'Impossible. I killed the dog.'

'That's the same dead dog that has mysteriously disappeared.'

No one said anything for a while. Bramley opened the file and leafed through the pages. His eyes rested on one.

'Shit,' he said, under his breath.

'I swear I had nothing to do with this girl's suicide,' pleaded Cat.

Bramley looked up. 'Nor did she.'

CAT'S GRANDMOTHER AND ANNA were waiting for her. They both started talking at once, but Cat silenced them. They were escorted down a corridor, Anna's heels clicking on the linoleum floor as he pushed Amelia along. Amelia took her granddaughter's hand in hers and stroked it. Cat looked down. Amelia's ring picked up the light from the electric strip above and threw it back in Cat's face. Cat blinked but the image of the ring stayed imprinted in her vision. A diamond ring. Cat let go of Amelia's hand and stopped walking. She turned slowly back to the police officers walking behind her.

'Mrs Wellby wears a diamond ring.'

'Possibly. She's a very wealthy lady.'

'It's what I saw first, on the banisters.' She closed her eyes again, recalling everything in minute detail. 'A hand on the banisters and red high-heeled shoes.' She opened her eyes. 'Hardly the kind of footwear you walk a dog in.'

'Cat,' said Amelia warningly.

'What happened after you told her?'

'We both went back into the garage to make sure it was Jane.'

'Did you touch the hose again?'

'No,' said Cat, 'I couldn't bare to look. In fact, I concentrated on Mrs Wellby's ring. She had her hands clamped behind her back.'

'So Mrs Wellby *didn't* touch the hose when you both re-entered the garage?'

'Cat!' said Amelia again.

'Let your granddaughter answer the question.'

Cat studied the policeman's face. 'You told me you'd only found *my* prints on the hose?'

'I said nothing of the sort. I said your prints were the only ones on the seat belt. I never mentioned anything about the hose.'

'Look, maybe she did and I didn't see.'

'But you've already told me you didn't look at anything else apart from her diamond ring, on her hand, clamped behind her back. She didn't touch the hose did she, not while you were both in there?'

Cat couldn't answer.

'Jane Wellby had a bruise on her head, she was probably unconscious when she was put in the car. Murder is a very serious matter.'

Cat looked down at Amelia who'd watched the policeman run circles around her granddaughter. 'Answer the question, Cat,' said Amelia.

'It's okay,' said Bramley, 'she already has.'

SANDIE LINKED HER ARM through Robert's as they watched his first wife's car approach. He continued to stare straight ahead but after a moment he began to speak.

'I'm sorry about earlier. I just kept thinking . . .'

She squeezed his arm as he continued to watch the car pull up in front of the house. 'It was too soon, I shouldn't have pushed you.'

'You didn't, I just . . .'

'It doesn't matter. As long as we are together and we love each other, everything will be fine.'

'I can't pretend nothing's happened. Frolicking in fields, what if someone had seen?'

Robert took a step away from her and waved at Fiona as she pulled up.

'I didn't want you to feel like that. Robert?'

He half-turned. 'Never mind, darling. Not now . . . Fiona.' He pulled her car door open and she stepped out. They hugged. Sandie stood back and watched, a sad smile on her face as she waited her turn to console Fiona. 'What about me?' she wanted to scream as the embrace stretched on. 'What the fuck about me?' But she couldn't, she knew that. This was not her time; she looked up at the sky and wondered if it ever would be again.

'Come on, you two, come inside. You probably both need a drink.'

Fiona looked at her over her ex-husband's shoulder and nodded. 'It's been a long time since I had a drink in the afternoon.'

'I'll make tea if you'd prefer,' replied Sandie. Ever ready and willing to help.

'Actually, I'm desperate for a drink. I just didn't want to start alone. I was worried that I might not stop.'

'You had Robert with you,' said Sandie.

Fiona opened her mouth to say something, caught the look on Robert's face and changed her mind.

'Let's get you inside, Fi,' he said, smiling tensely at the two women. As Sandie followed the two of them into the house she gently poked Robert in the back. He half-turned. 'Not now, darling.'

THEY STOOD AROUND THE island in the kitchen with mugs of coffee laced with whisky. Fiona stared out of the window towards the garage door. 'I had to come,' said Fiona.

'We're glad you did,' said Sandie.

'I wasn't going to, but the police came this morning,' she said after a while, then looked back at Sandie and Robert. 'They scared me.'

'How dare they? I refused to answer their questions, interfering—'

'Why shouldn't they ask questions?' asked Fiona. 'Or is it only me that thinks Jane committing suicide is the most ludicrous notion I've ever been expected to believe.'

'What did they ask you?' said Sandie, noticing her husband stiffen with tension.

Fiona turned back to the garage. 'Actually it was more

what I asked her, I wanted to understand the signs that I must have missed. The only thing out of the ordinary was that Jane had completely tidied her room. The policewoman told me that suicide victims often do that, it leaves less mess for me. She says Jane was saving me from having to go through her things.'

Sandie took Fiona's hand. 'I know this is hard. Maybe it would be easier if you saw her, you know, went to say goodbye. They say it is very important, Fiona. It might assist the grieving process and help you come to terms with this.'

'I don't want to come to terms with it, Sandie. I was her mother.'

'Not now but—'

'That's enough, darling,' said Robert putting his hand on Sandie's arm. She glared at him. 'Shouldn't we concentrate on the funeral, get things arranged. Do it properly. Start a family plot in the churchyard.'

'We can't do that, Robert,' said Fiona. 'We aren't one family, we're two. We can't play happy families with corpses.'

Why not, you did it when she was alive, thought Sandie angrily.

'No,' continued Fiona unaware, 'we have to choose. Naturally, I'd like her grave near me, there are some lovely churches in Islington.'

Robert opened then closed his mouth. He turned away; Fiona went back to staring out of the window.

'I believe,' said Sandie, slowly, 'that she wanted to be

cremated.' Jane's parents snapped back to face her, quizzical, uncertain. 'There are different ways, I spoke to the people at the crematorium. I thought you and Robert could go over the options, well, maybe later.'

'Cremation?' Robert looked at his wife.

'How do you know, Sandie? How do you know that?'

'Well,' said Sandie, aware of the delicacy of the situation, 'it's just she has mentioned it a few times to me.'

'When?' said Fiona, sounding close to tears.

'I don't know, you know, when you have those conversations. Life, death, belief-type conversations. You know,' she said, mostly to Robert. Hoping he'd back her up. He didn't.

'What were you having conversations like that for? She was a child for God's sake.'

'Robert, she is . . . sorry,' Sandie took a deep breath in, 'was twenty-three years old. She was an adult with plenty of opinions about things, strong opinions at that.'

'You should not have been talking about death to her,' he repeated.

'I wasn't talking to her. I was talking with her. She told me that she would prefer to be cremated than buried and I agreed with her. I remember it, because it wasn't that long—' She stopped talking.

'. . . All those maggots.' Jane feigned a grimace. 'No thanks. Fry me any day, but don't stick me in the ground.'

'I agree. After all, they only have to dig you up again later to make room for the new multi-storey car park.' Jane laughed, it made a pleasant change. 'If anything ever happened to me, you'd remember what I said, wouldn't you? About being cremated. You know what Mum and Dad are like, they'd want a mound of ground and a large headstone to go and mooch over. I'd prefer my ashes to go up in fireworks, it'd be fun.'

'Well, I wouldn't be around to witness it. I'd be long gone.' Sandie tried to change the subject.

'I'm talking about if something should ever happen to me now. An accident. Would you do it, Sandie? Would you put my ashes in a rocket, throw a party for Mum and Dad and send them up into the sky for all to see? Would you do that for me?'

'Nothing is going to happen, so this is a senseless conversation.'

'Yeah, but if it did.'

'It isn't going to.'

'But if it did, Sandie?'

'It's not going to.'

'I'm not saying it is going to, I'm saying *if* it did, then promise me you'll do that. Help cheer everyone up. Promise me?'

'They say "if" is the longest word in the English language.'

'Promise me.'

'Okay. I promise.'

Sandie looked up at Fiona. 'Maybe she was trying to tell me something.' The idea of a rocket was totally inappropriate now, but the cremation was a must. 'She made me promise that if anything should happen to her, she would like to be cremated.'

'Well then,' said Fiona, 'cremation it is.' Sandie was pleased. 'I suppose,' Fiona said with no humour, 'we could always split the ashes.'

BRAMLEY, WITH DS MIKE Chambers standing at his side, spoke to the team.

'Right lads,' said Bramley, Clement felt her blood pressure rise, 'the coroner concurs with the initial pathol-ogy findings. Neither set of prints are Jane's and she had a partially developed bruise on her head. We're dealing with suspicious circumstances.'

'So what now?'

'The inquest will be adjourned pending a criminal investigation, which starts now with the immediate fam-ily. Mrs Wellby was the last person to see her alive, so we start there. Personally I don't think we'll be looking much further.'

'Not very intelligent,' said Mike, 'leaving prints all over the hose.'

'Murderers are stupid, that's why they get caught.'

'But sir, you don't know that they're hers,' said Clement.

'Actually—'

Bramley interrupted Mike. 'No, Clement, I don't. But I'll bet my handicap that they are.'

'Why?'

'I had a stepmother, leaves a certain imprint on you.'

'Oh.'

'Clement, don't look at me like that. I want you to call the paper. Let them know we've got an OJ case of our own.'

'What about the press office?' she said, hiding her irritation.

'Unofficial tip-off, Clement, just follow my orders. Keep your mouth shut and you might actually learn something. Right, let's make this slick, boys.'

WPC Clement held her tongue, retrieved her hat and followed her boss and three others out to the car park. For the hundredth time she wondered what she had done to deserve a boss like Bramley. As the door closed behind her the phone started ringing. After fourteen rings it stopped. Unanswered.

SANDIE REPLACED THE PHONE. How could she organize a cremation without a body? Fiona appeared at the top of the stairs. Sandie looked up. 'I thought you were supposed to be getting some sleep. Do you want some Valium?'

'No thanks. I was just going over in my head something you said on the phone last night.'

Sandie knew and dreaded what was coming next. 'What was that?'

'About Jane being unhappy, as if *you* knew she was unhappy.'

'Come on, let's go and sit in the rose garden. I'll tell you what I know, but no doubt you'll know most of it yourself. After all, you are her mother.'

'Was.'

'No, you are still her mother. You'll always be her mother.'

They left the house by the French windows.

'Summer. What a terrible time of year to choose to die.'

'I doubt there is a good time,' said Sandie.

'Maybe, but at least in winter you could blame it on the weather.'

'Fiona, people don't kill themselves because of the weather.'

Fiona stopped walking. 'Why not? She didn't have any other reason.'

Sandie walked on to the gate of the walled garden and opened it. She turned back to Fiona.

'Jane loved life,' she said. Not sounding quite as determined as her words.

They walked down the gravel path in silence. Where it met the other path, they sat. The stone bench was warm. Fiona picked up a pile of gravel and let it fall through her fingers bit by bit. Sandie closed her eyes and listened to the sound. She was not going to start this conversation. It had to be Fiona.

'The policewoman who came to my house said she'd spoken to you.'

'No one has spoken to me,' said Sandie. 'I mean, not officially.'

'She was trying to tell me that we, Robert and I, well, she said suicide mostly shocks the hell out of . . .' Fiona dropped the remaining gravel and shook her head as if to change the scene in front of her. 'The garden looks stunning, Sandie, you've done so much to it.'

'Thank you.'

'When did you plant the roses?'

'Fiona . . .'

'No seriously, it's new isn't it?'

'We've had it for three years, Fiona.'

'For that long, really?' She turned suddenly to Sandie who was staring straight ahead. 'Why don't I believe this is happening? Is this happening? Really? Jane, this whole thing?'

Very slowly Sandie turned and looked at her husband's first wife, mother of her stepchild.

'I can't bear this,' said Fiona.

'Obviously this has come as an enormous shock to you, I can't even begin to imagine how you are feeling, I don't even know what to say.'

Fiona searched Sandie's face. 'Part of me wants you to say nothing.'

'I understand that.'

'No you don't. The reason why I don't want to talk about why Jane did this is because –' Fiona stood up and

walked a few paces away from the bench '— I don't want
to know why Jane did this. Just like Robert, I don't want
to have to deal with why Jane did this. The more I talk
about it, the less able I am to convince myself that Jane
hasn't done this, that it's all a joke, a misunderstanding. It
can't be real, this can't be real.' Fiona walked around in a
small circle, her voice rising to a painful crescendo. 'I sat
in her room at home last night, and actually convinced
myself that this hasn't happened. Why? Because I don't
want to have to tell people my daughter committed
suicide. The thought of them flocking over with tins of
soup and tea, like it's going to make a difference, like that
is going to assuage my guilt because I, her mother, didn't
know she was unhappy.'

Fiona stopped circling and let her disorientated vision
anchor itself on Sandie. 'But you knew, didn't you?'

'Sit down,' said Sandie extending her hand to the
woman.

'Why didn't you tell me?'

'Fiona, sit down.'

'Why?'

Sandie pulled Fiona down sharply. 'Nothing your
daughter has ever done led me to believe she would take
her own life. Nothing, and believe me, there have been
plenty of issues I've had to take up with Robert about
Jane. If I had ever thought that she'd do this, ever, she's
part of Robert . . .'

'You're right, I'm sorry. I'm sorry.' Fiona fought to
regain control.

'So am I.' The two women sat side by side on the bench staring out at the array of rose bushes.

'That isn't to say, however,' said Sandie, holding on to Fiona's hand tightly, 'that Jane didn't have her problems. She did. She had problems.'

'What sort of problems? Why didn't I know about them?'

'You heard the policewoman, children keep things from their parents as well, if not better, than parents keep things from their children.'

'We never fought in front of her, ever,' said Fiona defensively. 'We made sure the split didn't affect her, I doubt she even knew it was happening. We were very good about it.'

Sandie sighed, how could you make a blind man see?

Fiona understood the essence of Sandie's long breath. Once again she tried to reign in her fear of the truth. 'What sort of problems did she have?'

'I don't think this is the time, Fiona. You need to take this one slowly.'

Fiona braced herself as she ran through a shopping list of the worst it could be. *Drugs? Bullying? An abortion? Rape? The divorce? The divorce? The divorce?* 'Tell me,' she said, 'I have to know.'

Sandie paused. The quiet before the storm. 'Jane had a big problem with her looks,' said Sandie.

'What? I don't believe it.' Fiona searched Sandie's face. 'Her looks, she killed herself because of her looks?'

'I'm just telling you what I know. Her weight distressed her.'

'Don't be so ridiculous, she isn't overweight.' Sandie didn't correct her use of the present tense.

'I told her that. Heavens above, I come from the most weight-obsessed place on earth, it infuriates me.'

'Jane wasn't like that.'

'I'm not saying she was, but she did suffer sometimes about her looks. Maybe something happened that pushed that suffering into despair.'

'No, we'd know about it.'

'Why would you? You heard what the policewoman said, parents often have no idea.'

Fiona thought about this for a moment. She'd always bought Jane's favourite food when she was staying with her, it was her way of saying 'hi, darling, nice to have you home', maybe she did put pressure on her to eat it . . .

'. . . darling, dinner is ready.'

'Coming . . . Oh, Mum, you haven't been slaving away over a hot stove again.'

'Hardly. It's only lamb stew and mashed potato. But there is bread and butter pudding for afterwards.'

'I'm sorry you have to cook for only me.'

'I like cooking for you, you silly thing. When I'm on my own I never cook. It makes a pleasant change. So stop blithering, wash your hands and come and eat.'

'There should be more than two of us, that's loads.'
'Rubbish, you can eat all that, easy. Now sit down and
start refuelling . . .'

'. . . now, come downstairs, I've got some disgustingly
good doughnuts that I can only justify having in the house
while you are here . . .'

Well, she supposed, it could be construed as force-
feeding, but Jane never complained, then again, there was
that one time . . .

'Diet pills,' she said horrified.

'You let her take diet pills?'

Fiona stood angrily. 'You gave them to her,' she said
accusingly.

'What?'

'About a year ago, I remember, I found them in her
trouser pocket.'

'Diet pills?'

'Little yellow ones, of course I confronted her, and
she told me what they were, she told me you gave them
to her.'

'Why on earth didn't you say something?'

Fiona looked around embarrassed. 'She said they were
herbal, and I thought, well if you take them then . . .'

'For God's sakes, Fiona, do you think I'd work my
ass off on a step machine if I thought there was a wonder-
drug to take?'

Fiona looked like Sandie had slapped her in the face.

'I don't take pills, Fiona.'

'Come on, you've already offered me Valium and I've only been here a few hours.'

'For extreme circumstances. I was only trying to help.'

'What about Melatonin?' Fiona continued in an accusing manner.

'I don't take Melatonin. I don't take diet pills.'

Fiona bit her lip. 'Shit,' she whispered.

'What?'

'Jane had some other pills, white ones, she told me they were Melatonin, something about cell regrowth during sleep.' The words dripped in implausibility as they fell from Fiona's mouth.

'Your daughter had a collection of pills and you didn't do anything about it?' said Sandie amazed.

'It didn't happen at the same time, and anyway she told me you gave them to her.'

'Fiona, I'm allergic to Melatonin. You should've taken those pills off Jane the moment you found them and had them tested. I'd bet you they weren't diet pills or Melatonin.'

'What are you saying, that Jane was taking drugs?'

Sandie frowned, then put her hand on Fiona's thigh. '*I* didn't give her those pills, Fiona. I swear to you.'

'Not even the diet pills.'

'Fiona, if she was taking diet pills why did she enrol at the local Calorie Carers Club in town?'

'What?' Fiona couldn't believe she was hearing this.

'She didn't tell you?'

'Tell me what?'

Sandie started shaking her head, she was a fool to ever have trusted that girl. 'Jane desperately wanted to go,' said Sandie angrily. 'I said it was ridiculous, she burst into tears and said how would I know what it felt like to be a little elephant when I was so tall and thin. Finally I agreed,' Fiona opened her mouth to say something, 'not with her being overweight, Fiona. I agreed to take her, I thought she'd take one look at the people who really do suffer from weight problems and decide she was fine after all. I even spoke to a woman there about it. She said I should bring Jane in and they would have a consultation. In retrospect I suppose that was foolish, of course they were going to suggest a "trim-up" programme, how else do they make money. Jane said it sounded like a great idea and that it was nice to have someone to talk to. So I paid.'

'You paid for Jane to go to Calorie Carers?'

Sandie nodded. 'She told me you wouldn't mind as long as I went with her. So I did. It really did seem to help her. I don't know, maybe it was too indulgent and made things worse.'

'When was this?'

'The course ended about three months ago, she didn't mention things for a while, just said thank you and it had worked. Of course, I couldn't tell the difference, but it is all a question of how you see yourself. I tried to say something to Robert but he wouldn't hear of it. He thinks counselling is for the insane, not for his daughter who, basically, in his eyes, was perfect.'

'You sound angry.' Fiona picked up more gravel, this time throwing each little stone as far as she could.

'I'm not, I'm sad. I knew when I met Robert that Jane was the most important girl in his life, I only asked to be the most important woman in his life. The difference is enormous – there should have been plenty enough room for both.' She needed Fiona on her side. Now, more than ever. 'I just wanted everyone to be happy.'

'I do know that, Sandie, sorry. It's just inconceivable she'd want to go to a place like that—'

'Like what?' It was Robert. He stood before them, one hand clamped around a large tumbler of whisky, the other adjusting his sunglasses. The sun had slipped below the tree line. Fiona responded by taking a slug of whisky.

'I've sent that bloody woman home,' said Robert to Sandie. 'Dusting at a time like this.'

'Oh shit,' said Sandie. 'I'm sorry. She probably doesn't even know.'

'I don't want anyone here, Sandie, do you understand, poking their noses in, spying, tattling to the villagers.'

'Mrs Daniels wouldn't do—'

'I mean it, Sandie, keep her away from the house. And that fucking gardener of yours.'

'He is—'

'Christ, Sandie, can't you just do—'

'Robert,' interrupted Fiona, attempting to rescue Sandie, 'we've been talking about Jane going to Calorie Carers.' Fiona missed the look of despair that flickered over Sandie's face before she lowered her head.

Robert lit a cigarette, and threw the match on the ground, before retrieving his drink from Fiona. 'It was nonsense,' he said. 'Sandie said she had a problem, but heavens above, I'd have seen it.' Sandie continued to stare down at her painted toenails.

'She did say she mentioned it to you and you didn't seem very interested.'

'What's that supposed to mean, Fi, that I turned my back on my own daughter?'

'No, just that, I don't know, maybe as parents we were too close to see.'

Only if you are not looking, thought Sandie.

'Nonsense. If you ask me the person most likely to put ideas about weight in Jane's head was you,' he said stabbing his cigarette at Sandie. 'Always on that bloody step machine!' Sandie opened her mouth to retaliate but she wasn't quick enough. 'You should never have taken her to Calorie Carers, she was a child. They aren't just little adults, Fi knows that. I know you haven't had any children, but you must have some maternal instinct in there somewhere.' The cigarette came perilously close to Sandie's breast. 'To protect, that is what parenting is all about. Preserve your child from the harshness of reality. What do you do? Take her to a place full of fat desperate women paying for anything that will give them a straw to clutch on to.'

'How dare you?' said Sandie quietly. 'Jane was a very opinionated 23-year-old. Not the squeaky seven-year-old you wanted her to be. The trouble with you English is that you won't talk about anything until it is too god-damm late. If I didn't talk to her who the hell did she have? Certainly not you. Or do you think that would have been better? To be more like you and not talk to her at all. Great fucking parenting.'

'That's ridiculous, I spent enormous amounts of time with her—'

'Oh, yes, with her, absolutely. No one can accuse you of not spending time *with* her but talking to her? Actually talking to her?' She turned frantically to Fiona and started counting off her fingers. 'The theatre, the cinema, the swimming pool.' She turned back to her husband. 'Anywhere where you didn't have to actually talk to her!'

'That is bloody ridiculous,' Robert shouted back.

'She should have seen a professional therapist.'

'Oh God,' said Robert. 'How predictable can you Americans get.' He turned to Fiona. 'She is obsessed with that psychobabble.' The patronizing tone hung heavily in the air.

Fiona watched Sandie's chest fill out. She knew Sandie well, she knew that Robert had opened himself up for dissection. But she hadn't thought it would be quite so harsh.

'You think so, do you? All that psychobabble may be a waste of time to you, you are perfectly in control, aren't you, Robert? Safe job, good-looking wife who bought a fabulous house. You have no idea. You can't imagine what it would be like when the world outside panics you so much you cannot leave your house, when misery sucks at your soul, when no one will listen and no one understands. People go to psychiatrists because they haven't got anyone else to talk to. When they need their wounds attending. When they need attention. They say suicide is the ultimate attention-seeking ruse. Well she's got your attention now.'

Fiona inhaled sharply, her hands shot up to her mouth.

'Not interrupting anything, am I?' Everyone turned. Chief Inspector Bramley stood at the gate of the rose garden.

'Not at all,' said Sandie, standing up, 'we were just coming back indoors.' She walked past her husband without looking at him.

'Well, there's a coincidence. I need you indoors myself.' Bramley was smiling.

'Fine. Let's go. I'm glad you are here actually,' said Sandie, 'I've been trying to ring you. I had no luck so I gave the crematorium your number.'

'How convenient.' He was still smiling.

For a fraction of a second Sandie frowned. She must have misheard. 'It helps the healing process.'

Bramley made a little noise. It sounded like a laugh. Even Robert had noticed. 'Sandie is organizing everything, I'm afraid Fiona and I have been knocked out of orbit. I can't seem to . . .' his voice faltered. Sandie walked back to him and took his arm.

'Perhaps that explains why you failed to show up at the police station, Mr Wellby. It really would help our inquiries.'

'Inquiries?' Fiona looked at the police officer.

'Yes, madam. May I ask who you are?'

'This is Mrs Wellby. Jane's mother,' said WPC Clement stepping forward. The two women acknowledged each other. Bramley looked from Robert to Sandie to Fiona. A very cosy threesome.

'I am very sorry about your daughter, *Mrs* Wellby.' He threw a mocking glance in Sandie's direction. 'I'm afraid I have some further, quite disturbing news. Shall we go inside?'

'Why?' said Robert.

'What is it?' asked Fiona in a panicked voice, clutching the bevelled edge of the bench.

WPC Clement looked sympathetically at her. 'This would probably be easier inside.'

'Tell me now. I know she had problems, Sandie's told me, it's okay, I know.'

WPC Clement glanced back towards her boss. 'It's not quite as easy as that I'm afraid. I'm sorry—'

'Mrs Wellby,' said Bramley pushing Clement to one side, he abhorred sympathy, it was a weakness, 'your daughter didn't commit suicide.'

Fiona felt the stone beneath her go cold.

'I knew it,' said Robert, 'it was an accident.'

'Possibly,' said Bramley, 'we'll know more after we have searched the premises. I have a warrant here.'

'What for?' asked Robert.

'For the weapon that may have killed your daughter, Mr Wellby.'

Stunned silence. Robert and Sandie stared at each other, then he pushed her away and marched furiously towards Bramley, his arms outstretched, as though he were aiming for his neck. Two policemen stepped in front of Bramley, but Bramley told them to step aside. 'Let him come,' he whispered. But Robert didn't go for Bramley; he went for the paper. Standing inches from Bramley's face he read the warrant.

'Jesus God, why?'

'There are a number of reasons.'

'A number of reasons? What are you talking about? Who would want to kill my little girl? A number of reasons? A number?' Robert turned back to his wife and ex-wife. 'Fi? Sandie?' Fiona was slumped forward on the bench, she'd been sick all over her feet. Sandie had disappeared. WPC Clement saw the wooden door in the side wall bounce on its hinges and pointed to it.

'Go and get her!' shouted Bramley. One of the officers ran towards the door and the second back through the wrought-iron gate from which they had entered. WPC Clement approached Fiona Wellby, removing a handkerchief from her skirt pocket. Robert Wellby stood motionless, staring aimlessly at the vomit.

'Come on,' she said softly, easing Robert out of the way, 'let's get you cleared up.' Fiona did not respond. WPC Clement lifted her legs out of the dark pink suede loafers and put them down on a clean area of gravel. She leant forward to wipe Fiona's mouth. The woman appeared to have gone into a trance. As the cotton touched her cheek, Fiona's arm moved sharply and she gripped WPC Clement's wrist with force. She still looked down, but she spoke firmly to the policewoman.

'Sandie's gone to tidy up.' Then she closed her eyes and started sobbing. WPC Clement left Fiona Wellby on the bench and ran down the gravel path, wishing, not for the first time, that she was wearing trousers.

Chapter Seven

Cat emerged from the car and saw Dan at the end of the street. Perfect timing. She jogged down the road towards him, he opened his arms and she careered into them.

'Where've you been? I've been calling.'

'I was taken in for questioning about that girl's death, they think she was murdered.'

Anna approached the couple and Dan looked at him over his girlfriend's shoulder.

'Great nanny you turned out to be,' he said, winking to Anna.

'Doll, if your girlfriend has a penchant for leaving her fingerprints all over murder scenes, it isn't my fault. Hacks, they'll do anything for a story.'

'Bitch,' mumbled Cat into Dan's shoulder.

'I take it they let you go?' said Dan lifting Cat's chin.

'Only because I implicated that American woman.'

'What?'

'She's being overdramatic,' said Anna.

'Coming from you,' said Cat, then turning back to Dan. 'She isn't going to kill her own stepdaughter, leave her fingerprints everywhere and not have an alibi, it's stupid.'

'Well, I guess she didn't think you'd turn up and run her alibi over.'

'Okay, you two, enough. Inside,' said Dan. 'It's Saturday night, I've had one of the most boring days of my life and I need a drink.'

'She was probably high as a kite on vodka and Valium like all good failed actresses are.'

'That's what I need,' said Dan, holding the front door open.

'Actually she did seem spaced out.'

'There you go, she was boozing, had a fight with Jane, hit her over the head and then panicked. Simple.' Anna smiled triumphantly.

Dan pushed Anna in the back. 'Write the script, it would make a great TV movie.'

'Maybe that's her angle?'

'Inside!'

'You know what we all need,' said Anna, going straight through to his living room and turning on the assortment of heart-shaped fairy lights. Cat collapsed on to the leopard-fur-covered sofa and Dan went up the small flight of stairs to the bathroom.

'Put the lid back down,' called Anna after him.

'What do we all need?' asked Cat.

'A night out on the town.' Cat groaned. 'Cat Torrant —' he clicked his fingers '— it is time.'

Cat looked around nervously. 'Time for what?'

'For you to get out of those jeans.' Anna stood up. 'Time for fun, frolics and good ol' femininity.'

'No way,' said Cat belligerently.

'Come on, a night at Madame JoJo's, get those morbid thoughts out of her head.'

'I wasn't having morbid thoughts.'

'It's written all over your face. Glitter is the only answer.'

'All right,' said Cat standing up, 'but you're not dressing me up like a Barbie doll. I'm quite happy in my—'

'Jeans and T-shirts, yeah, yeah,' Anna yawned, 'I know.'

'Tell Dan I've gone upstairs, it won't take me long.'

'Don't rush, it'll take me ages.'

Anna opened the bathroom door as Dan flushed the loo.

'Do you mind,' he said primly.

'Sweetheart, you haven't got that much to hide. Cat's gone to get changed, we took a vote, you're both coming to the show tonight.'

'Is she up to it?'

'She's fine, I think you were being a little over-protective actually, she really does seem cool about it all.'

'I don't know what worries me more.'

Anna began to remove the day's warpaint. 'Though she is interested in the family unit, she talked non-stop about the Wellbys on the way home.'

'What did she say?'

'That the rule safety in numbers doesn't apply to family. Her and Amelia are a safe, manageable unit, dead 23-year-olds and lethal blonde stepmothers only go to prove that extended families are not happy families.'

'I don't think she needs to prove that to herself. Cat is not the nesting type.' He looked at himself in the mirror when he spoke. 'She makes that very clear.'

Anna pushed a line of toothpaste on a brush and passed it to Dan. 'You've got lecture breath,' he said, waving a hand under his nose.

'Cheers.'

Anna waited until Dan had a mouth full of brush and foam before he continued with his thesis. 'Unless of course she's freaking out because her body clock is betraying her, or her heart, in which case she'll be looking for an antidote?'

Dan turned open-mouthed to face Anna, toothpaste froth pooling in his cheeks.

'Spit,' said Anna. 'Do you know what she thinks about kids?'

'Split perineum, that's what I think about kids,' said Cat, leaning in the doorway. Dan spat his toothpaste on Anna's hand.

THERE WAS A LIGHT on under Robert's study door. Fiona looked at her watch. It was now past one in the morning. The police had spent hours searching the house.

They had taken prints off everyone including Sam Clough the gardener and they'd called the daily back. Robert was furious, convinced their privacy was in jeopardy. When the police finally finished they left behind a heavy air of suspicion. No one talked about what questions they'd been asked. Sandie immediately disappeared into her gym to 'work off the tension', and Robert had disappeared into his study to work. They couldn't hide forever. Answers had to be found. Fiona tapped lightly on the door then opened it a few inches. Robert was slumped over his desk. Fiona panicked at the motionless shape. 'Robert?' He stirred.

'Stupid woman,' whispered Fiona to herself, as she went in.

'Must've fallen asleep,' said Robert, rubbing his face. Fiona saw an empty bottle of whisky in the wastepaper basket.

'Do you want one?' said Robert holding up another. Fiona shook her head. 'Do you mind if I do?' She shook her head again and closed the door behind her.

'I was wondering,' she said, 'whether you could decipher anything, when they questioned you?'

'Why? What did they ask you?'

'They were pretty soft on me, kid gloves I guess.' She fell silent. Kid gloves. Put on for bereaved mothers. 'They wanted to know where I'd been on Friday afternoon, of course.'

'Really?' Robert had avoided that question.

'Hm.'

'And?'

'And what?'

'And where were you?'

Fiona looked at her feet awkwardly for a moment. 'With Jo,' she said.

'Your friend?' he said in a tone she couldn't fathom.

'Yes, Robert, my friend.' They fell into another uncomfortable silence. She didn't want to talk about what she and Jo had been doing all Friday afternoon. It made her feel sick. 'What did they ask you, Robert? The police?'

She watched as he leant against the desk, holding the tumbler in one hand. 'Basically, whether Jane was happy.'

'What did you say?'

'That she was, I mean, Fiona, she was happy, wasn't she?'

'Well I always thought so,' she said, sounding less convinced than her ex-husband. 'They kept wanting to know if the relationship between Jane and Sandie was strained, but all I could say was that she was always very happy when she was at home with me in London. I mean, sure she had bad moods, the odd sulk. And she left the language school in Paris, but it wasn't serious, she was just homesick, wasn't she?' Fiona paused. 'She was happy, basically, she was happy. I think.'

'You're right to think so, I don't know why the hell Sandie is talking about Jane like she suffered some kind of depression. That she tried to cause problems between us. She told all that to the police for God's sake. Why would she do a thing like that, why would she lie?'

'How do you know what she said? Have you talked to her?'

He shook his head. 'The policeman made it very clear to me what line my wife was taking. I just don't understand it.'

'Come on, Robert, if there was a problem between Sandie and our daughter we would have known about it. Jane would have told me.'

'And not me, is that what you're saying?'

Fiona sighed. 'You work very hard, Robert—'

'I work very hard,' he said, beginning to raise his voice, 'to give my family everything I can, to keep everybody happy, to . . .' He slammed the drink down on the desk.

'To provide, Robert?' She'd heard that bullshit line enough to last several lifetimes. 'You don't need to provide any more.'

'What the hell is that supposed to mean. You think I married her for the money?'

Fiona was shocked. 'God, no, I—' She caught her breath. 'I'm sorry.'

'I am not the one to blame here, I haven't done anything wrong. All I've ever done was try and keep everyone happy. And Jane was happy. Fiona, I may not have done many great things in my life, but,' his voice was beginning to crack, 'my daughter was happy. I did that, goddammit, I did that.'

Fiona approached him. 'Ssh,' she said, putting her arm around him. They should at least be able to find strength in each other over their daughter's death. 'We'll get to the bottom of this,' she said as he leant his head against her shoulder.

'That's what I'm afraid of,' he said in a whisper.

THE LIGHT FROM THE study spilled over the lawn as far as her feet. Leaning against the trunk of the cedar tree, Sandie watched her husband and the first Mrs Wellby embrace. Robert was going to regret this. They all were.

ANNA BURST INTO MIME. The crowd roared. Made up to the nine hundreds, he pranced on the stage of the illustrious Madame JoJo's. His fans watched intently.

'You look gorgeous,' said Dan.

'What?' shouted Cat, her hand cupped round her ear.

'Never mind,' he said, shaking his head, it was no good trying to talk over Anna, he was just too bloody loud. He was doing a particularly kinky version of 'Lola'.

Cat took another sip of her flamboyant pink drink, nearly gouging out her eye with the umbrella but at least she she felt better than when she had left the police station. Dan laughed at her and took another swig of his beer. Very manly. He didn't like the umbrellas, thought people might misinterpret his sexuality.

They watched his old room-mate stalk up and down the stage, a little harem of transvestites behind him, joining in with the L-O-L-A- Lolas. The crowd loved him. 'Another one?' shouted Dan. Cat nodded enthusiastically. She leant up on to the balls of her feet and kissed Dan on the mouth. He smiled. Cat smiled back. He picked her up and hugged her.

'You are a strange girl, Cat Torrant,' said Dan loudly in her ear.

'Not as strange as some,' she replied looking around. The music died down, Anna took his bow, the crowd continued to roar their approval.

'I'm sorry I wasn't with you today.'

'Amelia and Anna were, it's fine, promise.'

'Cat?'

'Yes, Dan,' she said, laughing at him.

'Will you promise something?'

Cat pursed her lips. 'Is this a trick question?'

'Of course.'

'Go on then,' she said, putting her hands in her jeans pockets.

'Don't go after this Wellby story, Cat. Leave them.'

'I wasn't going to go after them, you make me sound like a mercenary.'

'I don't mean it like that,' he said.

'How did you mean it?'

Dan rubbed his eyes with his finger and thumb. Bad timing.

'What do you mean?' she asked again, impatient.

'A girl died, Cat. I'm worried. I don't want to see you affected by it.'

'But I am affected by it. I can see her now, you know, right in front of your face.'

'I don't really mean it like that either.'

'Anna is right, there was no way I could get back to the radio station, I was told to wait by the police. The woman at the station just told me to piss off, like it was my fault. If I do the story at least they'll know it wasn't through incompetence that I didn't go back.'

'Cat, I think it goes a bit deeper than that.'

'It's my career, Dan, that is all I'm worried about. I'm twenty-eight, most of the people on my course are much younger than I am, I've been a student for nearly a year and I need a bloody job. I'm hardly going to get a glowing report from Chelmsford am I?'

'You know what I'm trying to say, you're just refusing to acknowledge it.'

Cat frowned. 'Can we change the subject, please?'

'Fine. I'm going to the bar.'

DAN WAS RETURNING WITH the drinks when Anna appeared, hyped up from his act and glistening with sweat.

'That was fucking fantastic,' he called out to them.

'What charming modesty,' said Dan, handing him a cocktail of dubious colour.

Anna grinned broadly and fluttered his fake eyelashes. 'It is hard to be modest looking like this.'

'I'd kiss you,' said Cat, 'but I'm scared you'd crack.'

Anna shooed them both away. 'I shall take your drinks, but not your insults, tonight is a night to worship me, and if you won't I know just the little darling who will.'

'Where?' said Cat and Dan in unison. They knew Anna too well.

'That boy over there,' he whispered. They both turned. 'Don't both of you look. God you are useless.' He hit Dan with his fan. 'The one next to the speaker, on his own. Now, quick, he's not looking. I'll need more than this pansy drink before I do anything.' He clicked his fingers at the barman. 'Tequila. Shots. Three.' Anna turned back to Cat, who was shaking her head at his arrogance. 'Darling,' he said, 'they expect it. So, do you think he's sexy?'

'Anna, he's wearing leather chaps and a furry pink codpiece. You're asking the wrong person.'

'Dan?' said Anna, turning away from Cat in despair.

Dan gave the boy a furtive once-over. 'Bit skinny for my liking.'

'That's my man,' said Cat smiling.

'Yuck,' exclaimed Anna, 'I can't breathe for all this heterosexuality. Move aside, I'm off to pinker pastures.'

Cat grabbed his arm. 'We'll stop. Promise.'

'Doll, I don't want you to. And I don't want you to stop me either. Comprendez?'

Dan had been studying the prey. 'He looks like he's off to a Village People party. Nobody dresses like that.'

'Darling,' purred Anna, 'I'm not interested in what he looks like in clothes. So don't be such spoilty-pusses. It's all right for you two, I'm single. He is young, male and eager to please.' Anna could be very matter of fact about his sex life. Beggars, and all that. 'And this isn't the first show he's been to, either.'

'That's even more suspicious,' said Cat.

'Hey, Cat, stop pissing on my fire. He's gorgeous, or he will be after this.' The drinks arrived. They downed the tequila like professionals. Anna spat out his lemon and exhaled loudly. 'Now I'm ready!' he exclaimed.

'Go for it,' said Dan, grimacing as he sucked the lemon slice. Anna smiled broadly at him and flounced off.

'You know you shouldn't encourage him. That boy looks like a freak.'

'Anna can look after himself.'

'I know, it's just—'

Dan grabbed her round the waist. 'Aren't you forgetting how we met, you wicked woman?'

'That was quite different,' Cat said tartly. 'I wasn't wearing a furry pink G-string, nor did I throw myself at you.'

'That's what you think—'

They were interrupted by Anna who arrived with his little admirer in tow. Within three seconds Cat knew she definitely didn't like him. And it wasn't just his pink pants. He was just too in your face, too up Anna's bum.

She loved Anna when he was being a girl, and when he was being a boy. It was when he was being both that she couldn't quite handle it. She worried about him. The boy caught her staring. Her tentative smile was not returned. Cat tugged on Dan's shoulder, he looked down at her and knew instantly that she wanted to go. He put his beer bottle to his lips, drank the last quarter of it, placed it on the table in front of them and took Cat's hand.

'Hey, Anna,' he said, 'I think we are going to call it a night. You coming with us?' Bad choice of words, thought Cat as she watched the smile on Anna's face grow.

'Oh, yes,' he said, 'but not with you, darlings. You two trot along now, I'll see you tomorrow,' he gave pink pants a sideways look, 'maybe.' The boy moved a step behind Anna and turned away from them. Anna sighed. 'How coy.' Cat didn't think so. Cat didn't think he looked the coy type. Men in leather chaps and furry pink codpieces didn't get sudden attacks of shyness. He wasn't being coy, he was skulking in the shadows. She went to kiss Anna goodbye and whispered in his ear. 'You sure you won't come back with us?'

'Absolutely not.'

'Please?'

Anna poured another large tequila. 'No. Catareena, this is my night. Go home with Dan and do filthy things to him, I'll see you tomorrow.' Dan was nodding. Pink pants was staring at her and Anna was shooing her out of the club. She was outnumbered three to one.

A GREEN GLOW EMANATED from the radio-alarm clock as it effortlessly closed down the minutes till dawn. No ticks to metronome her to sleep. Fiona didn't like clocks that didn't tick. She liked to hear the passing of time. Digital clocks meant you looked up occasionally to see a few more minutes had passed, uncelebrated. So much of life was like that. She was fifty years old. Countless minutes had passed and she hadn't even noticed. She stared at the luminous numbers. Another irreplaceable minute gone. Fiona sat up in bed. She'd left the curtains open to get more breeze, the night was stifling, but it wasn't helping. The shadows were disturbing her. She pushed back the sheet and swivelled off the bed. Her bare feet sunk into the deep, woollen carpet. It was cream, but the lights from Harlow had turned the sky a strange colour and the carpet looked a sickly orangey purple. The whole room was tinged in it. The chintz couldn't compete. Everything in Cedar Hall was overly decorated. The matching palettes made Fiona want to get hold of a bright red glossy paint and do a Jackson Pollock on the wallpaper. Nothing was out of place. Nothing was ugly. *Except my daughter.* Her cotton nightie slipped down her legs as she walked around the guest bedroom. Cedar Hall was Sandie's house all right, Jane hadn't left much of a mark. At least at her home in Islington there were childhood toys, adolescent mess, individuality. Crumbs, coffee cups, photos, old coats. She wished she could get in her car and go home to feel closer to Jane. But the police had made it clear she wasn't to go anywhere. Fiona opened the door of the guest room and padded softly down the corridor. The police tape was still across the doorway of Jane's bedroom, she ducked under it and closed the door behind her. It was messy. Not that messy, but messy enough. Still, it didn't look like a room her daughter would have spent time in. It was so . . . twee. Must have been Sandie's choice. Fiona frowned. She'd never even been into this room. Wasn't that strange? A child's bedroom was very important. It was their territory. Their zone. Fiona shivered. It felt so empty.

'Ridiculous,' she said to herself, crossing the room and opening up a cupboard. A brand new pair of Adidas trainers lay on the floor in their box. Robert probably bought them. He spoilt her. But his parenting wasn't in her jurisdiction any more, so she couldn't do anything about that. Then again, Adidas trainers weren't the most obvious thing Robert would buy Jane. He didn't encourage tomboyishness. Maybe Jane had bought them for herself. Fiona picked them up. They'd definitely never been worn. Fiona flicked through the rest of the wardrobe. One Rip Curl T-shirt, a pair of combat trousers, both with the labels in, unworn. She rubbed the material between her fingers, frowning at the crispness of the cotton. Not unworn; never to be worn. Fear trickled into her. Never to be worn. Suddenly the bedroom door opened. Fiona let out a startled cry.

'You are not allowed to be in here, Fiona,' said Sandie.

'Bloody hell, you scared the living daylights out of me!'

'You aren't supposed to be in here. The police said.'

'She'd been on a shopping spree,' said Fiona holding out the clothes lamely. 'Why would a suicidal girl go shopping?'

'You should be in bed.'

'I can't sleep,' Fiona replied angrily. 'Look at these clothes. She had a bump on her head, Sandie, she had a wardrobe full of new clothes, what the hell does it mean?'

'I bought her the clothes,' said Sandie, less aggressively.

Fiona frowned. 'You did?'

'You need your sleep,' said Sandie, adopting an authoritative tone again.

'You bought her all these?'

'What about it, Fiona? Robert tended to go the Laura Ashley way, if you know what I mean. I thought she'd like something a bit more . . .' Sandie looked at the clothes and shrugged, 'trendy.'

'Obviously not, none of them have been worn.'

Sandie took the clothes from her. 'Obviously,' she said.

Fiona felt another sort of edginess creep over her. 'When did you buy them?'

'Fiona, it's been a long few days for all of us. You're tired, I'm tired. Take these and go to bed.' Sandie pulled a bottle of pills from her dressing-gown pocket. Fiona shook her head. 'If you can't sleep you won't be able to cope with any of this.'

'I don't want them.'

'Fiona you need to be strong. You need to sleep in order to be strong. Take them and go to bed. Everything will seem less sinister in the morning.'

Fiona felt her resistance ebb. Sandie was right, she was tired. Exhausted. Drained. One good night's sleep and she'd be able to cope. She let Sandie usher her back to her room. She left the bottle by the bed. 'Take more if you wake up,' she said pulling the thick curtains closed. The only light came from the corridor, illuminating Sandie as she sat in the corner of the room, and began to tell Fiona about the time the two of them and Jane had gone dry-slope skiing. It had been a truly hilarious afternoon. A rare memory. Fiona felt the weight of the Valium in her limbs as she listened. Her body pressed heavily into the mattress. She was sinking into sleep. As her eyes finally closed she saw Jane standing behind Sandie with her hands around Sandie's neck. Sandie was laughing or choking, Fiona couldn't tell which. She slept for fourteen hours.

'WHAT'S BEHIND THE MYSTERIOUS beaded curtain,' said Anna as they entered the boy's studio flat.

'The Promised Land,' said the boy with a wicked smile.

'Take me to it, Moses!' Anna knew he was slurring

his words. He turned his back to the curtain and stumbled over to the sofa bed. His legs were beginning to wobble.

'First another drink.' The boy passed him a glass of clear liquid. Anna found it difficult to hold, let alone drink, but his admirer was there, offering a helping hand. Anna saw the track marks on his arm as he poured the thick, clear liquid into his mouth. Anna swallowed hard to keep the liquid down.

'Shit,' he said holding the scarred arm. 'Fucking idiot.'

'Me? You're the one who's here.'

'What? I don't take drugs.'

'Maybe not knowingly,' he said laughing.

The boy's face oscillated in front of Anna.

'I don't feel very well.'

'Who's the fucking idiot now, faggot?'

Anna held the smile, a stage smile. Scored into his face.

'Did you hear me! You're fucked, so what the fuck are you smiling about?' The boy took a swipe at Anna, knocking him on to the floor. He gagged. Nothing came up.

'Please,' mumbled Anna, 'please don't hurt me.'

'You've done that yourself.'

'Money, take it, anything.'

'Oh, I will, don't you worry about that.'

Anna used his arms to push himself up. He hoped he could get down the stairs before he passed out. There had been an awful lot of stairs and he was only too aware that his minutes of consciousness were numbered. Anna knew what it was like to be drunk and this wasn't it. The heavy burning in his belly, the tingling in his fingers, the inability to throw up, waves of 'other worldliness' that periodically engulfed him, the loss of feeling in some places and the hypersensitivity in others. He tried to speak, to beg for help, but he couldn't do that either. The boy was watching him.

'Show time,' he said, then stepped over the small coffee table, heaved Anna up off the floor, dragged him across the wooden floor and pushed him through the beaded curtain. Anna fell forward on to his knees. He put his hands down to stop himself from falling on his face and felt the plastic sheet beneath him. Anna started praying. Three men emerged from the shadows. He immediately stopped praying. He was a dead girl.

'Strip him,' said one of the men.

In his imagination Anna stood up, tall and strong, he started running, dressed in an emerald gown encrusted with rhinestones. He had lovely long white Grace Kelly gloves on. He ran over green fields, jumped over trees, leapt over lakes and hopped over hills. His heels gave him no trouble and not a hair fell out of place. Though he slipped in and out of consciousness and felt very little, everything that happened next was recorded for posterity both on celluloid and cerebrally. At least a film could be erased.

IF SHE HADN'T HAD the nightmare, she wouldn't have seen the car. Unfortunately, all she saw was the back of a smartly dressed man get into the driver's seat of a black saloon car and unhurriedly pull away. She looked at her watch. Bad girl, thought Cat, staying out this late. At least Anna had the good sense to use a reputable cab company to get him home. No doubt he'd be sending her out for vegetable and vitamin juice from the local health food shop as a peace offering to his liver. Cat stood, clutching her pillow against potential peeping Toms, looking out of the window. It was early summer, light by six o'clock, and a grey hazy mist hung over Angel, cool, but with a promise of improvement. There was no way she was going to be able to sleep again, not only were her curtains too thin to keep any proper light out, but Dan, in his own inimitable way, was snoring like a hippo. She decided to do something she had never done before. Never even contemplated doing before. She was going to go for a jog. She gathered the necessities out of her bedroom, Dan turned in his sleep when the cupboard door creaked, pushing most of the duvet off him. He lay on his side, his legs splayed, revealing a round white bottom on one side and hand-held balls on the other. A string of dribble stretched from the corner of his mouth to the pillow. Cat tilted her head, it was without doubt the most unattractive sight imaginable, though more frightening even than that was the fact that she found it endearing. Cat was always more emotional after good sex. And they'd had that. Dressed in the cycling shorts she'd never cycled in and Dan's T-shirt, she let herself out of her flat.

AT FIRST SHE THOUGHT it was a tramp wrapped in a plastic sheet. There was a homeless man who lived around the area, but he chose to sleep in bigger doorways. It wasn't until she saw the pink fluffy material poking out from between his fingers that Cat knew it was Anna.

'Shit,' she exclaimed kneeling down beside him. 'Anna,' she whispered into his ear. 'Wake up, Anna, it's me.' The ball tightened. Cat walked round him, unsure of what to do. She tried again. 'Anna, love, try and stand up, I'll get you indoors.' Anna opened his eyes, looked at Cat, then closed them again. He was naked under that plastic sheet. But that didn't scare her half as much as the look he'd just given her. She stood up and pressed the buzzer marked Torrant, one long hard push, followed by lots and lots of little ones. On the third long push, Dan's groggy voice crackled at her.

'Who the—'

'Dan. It's me, I'm downstairs, I need your help.'

'Cat, what the hell are you doing?'

'Just come down now, and bring Anna's key.' Dan didn't reply but the door opened twelve seconds later. He hadn't wasted any time putting clothes on. Dan lifted Anna, who refused to uncurl, and carried him indoors. He had opened his eyes a few times, but had said nothing.

The plastic sheet slipped off him as Dan lowered him on to the sofa.

'What the hell do you think happened to him?' Dan asked Cat as she handed him one of Anna's kimonos and draped a blanket over him. Cat pointed at the pink fur still caught in Anna's grip.

'Pink pants,' whispered Cat. 'That bloke was wearing some. I knew it. He looked like a rat. Anna's watch has gone, his wallet, his earrings for God's sake,' she couldn't help the tears. 'They've taken everything.'

'Come on, Cat, calm down. We better get him into a bath,' said Dan. 'He smells like he's been in the sewers.'

Cat watched as Anna winced like an oyster in lemon. 'I don't think that's a good idea, Dan,' she whispered.

'Why not, he's obviously been sick on himself.'

She took his arm. 'It's not just sick he smells of.'

'Oh, please—'

'Look at him for God's sake. He's been raped, the worst thing we could do is put him in the bath. We should phone the police.'

'No. Wait. Let's just try and get him to talk first.' Dan sat next to him on the sofa. Anna instinctively curled back into the foetal position. His head on his knees, his arms tight around his legs, the blanket pulled over his shoulders. But when Cat sat on the other side he sat bolt upright and stared at her.

'Look what the Cat's dragged in,' he laughed maniacally. 'Look what the Cat's dragged in, Cat's dragged in,

Cat's dragged in, dragged in, dragged in the drag queen, the drag queen—'

'Stop it.' It was Dan. Anna stared at him next.

'I've been bad. Punish me, punish me, push me, push me, push, push, push, harder, harder, harder. *Stop it!*' Anna suddenly looked up at the ceiling and moaned. The moan lasted two minutes. Anna had sung in the choir at Cambridge, the moan was a lament. It was too much for either of them to bear.

'Get an ambulance, Dan,' said Cat. He nodded, not trusting himself to speak. It was when he reached the telephone that Anna seemed to return to them.

'Please don't phone them,' he whispered. He grabbed Cat's wrist with the hand that didn't hold the G-string. 'Please.'

Cat looked back at Dan, he nodded at her. 'Okay, Anna, no ambulance, but you must tell us what happened.'

'I want a bath.'

'Told you,' said Dan.

'No bath, Anna, until you tell us what happened.'

Anna started crying. 'Don't come near me, Cat, I might kill you.'

'Who raped you?'

'Cat!' It was Dan.

'It was that boy wasn't it. I bloody told you.'

'Stop it.'

Cat grabbed Anna's arm. 'We've got to go to the police.'

'Leave him alone, Cat.' Dan forcefully removed Cat's arm and stepped between them.

'He'll regret it.'

'I know better than you what to do in this situation,' Dan said inexplicably.

'What is that supposed to mean?'

'Can't you see he isn't up to this.'

'He isn't up to this because someone has attacked him and unless we find out what has happened, the fucker will do it again. It was him, wasn't it, Anna? Jesus Christ, they even took his clothes.' Cat was too angry to cry now.

'Cat, that's enough. Let's get you into the bath.' Anna smiled at Dan gratefully.

'He'll get away with it.' Cat tried to block their way, but Dan pushed her aside. He held her away at arm's length.

'Some things are more important, Cat.'

Chapter Eight

Sandie Wellby stared at the plastic-wrapped hammer. They had found it in her gardening apron in her workshop during their search of Cedar Hall. Now the police were back with two excellent pieces of news. She sighed. Firstly, the circumference of the hammer matched the bruise on her stepdaughter's head and secondly, her fingerprints were all over it. She would have told them the fingerprints were hers, but they had been too busy, crawling over her house like bugs, soiling it with their ill-educated bigotry and prejudice, to ask. She watched them now as they picked up precious vases, peered unknowingly at the craftsmen's stamps on the bases and replaced them heavily with a look of contempt. No one liked the American. It didn't take a genius to calculate her popularity, the fact that they stared at her as if *she* was the scum of the earth was proof enough. She knew what they were doing, they were waiting for her to break down and confess. Confess to the murder of her stepdaughter. It was ludicrous. She would never say anything self-incriminating, she had done enough cheap court dramas to know all the pitfalls. They would have to come up with more than a lousy hammer to get her arrested, which explained why the informal scaremongering was taking place in her house and not the police station. Bramley couldn't arrest her, she knew that, but boy did he want to.

BRAMLEY WAS IN A quandary. His problem was that the hammer belonged to Mrs Wellby, and it had been found in her apron. Her fingerprints would not prove beyond reasonable doubt that she had used it to smash her stepdaughter over the head, before placing her in the car, strapping her in and turning on the ignition to leave her to die. The girl would never have come round, slipping peacefully into death. No struggle, no attempts to escape. A simple murderous suicide. There was a bruise, yes, and it was made by a blunt instrument like a hammer, but it was not *definitely* that hammer, nor did it kill her – the autopsy clearly stated death by carbon-monoxide poisoning. But Sandie Wellby couldn't have been sure of that or why did she flee the garden? She was guilty. He was sure of that. WPC Clement, fit for a girl, had cut her off at the kitchen door. She had a cloth in her hand claiming she was about to return to the rose garden. Via the courtyard? How stupid did she think he was?

FIONA WAS STILL IN a state of severe shock. Her daughter – murdered? The police hadn't actually come out and said it, but it was perfectly clear that they thought Sandie was involved. It was preposterous. Sandie couldn't harm Jane. To even entertain the idea was obscene. Sure she had a different perspective on the child, what step parent didn't, but it was ridiculous to think she could've had a hand in her daughter's death. Fiona had prayed so hard that Jane hadn't killed herself, now she wished she hadn't. The very fact that other parents of other children were as stunned as she had been had lent Jane's suicide an explanation of sorts. There was a lot she probably didn't know about Jane. Like most parents. She could almost, in time, have got a handle on that. But now? Now she couldn't mourn her daughter's confusing, premature departure, because Jane hadn't chosen to die. Her life had been stolen from her. Now it was a murder case and the police talked pointedly about Jane as if all she had ever been was a corpse. And all Sandie had ever been was the cause. They hadn't even bothered to confirm her where-abouts on the Friday afternoon. Why should they? She was Jane's mother. Statistically, she probably didn't even need an alibi. If she was lucky no one would ever know that while Jane was being murdered, she was thrashing about . . . Fiona ran from herself, up the stairs, away from the accusations and insinuations. Away from her indefensible but unbreakable silence. No one stopped her. Fiona reached Jane's bedroom, pulled the police tape until it snapped in her hand and slammed the door behind her. It was only then she noticed the key. Like Jane countless times before her, she turned it and locked herself away from the rest of Cedar Hall.

SANDIE WATCHED FIONA RUN from her. She too noticed how no one tried to stop her, block her, follow her, watch her. No, it was quite understandable why she should be put to bed, left alone to grieve. The only time anyone had offered Sandie help was when a few misguided policemen had thought Jane was her own flesh and blood. That all changed when they learnt the truth, why should they console her, she was just the *stepmother*. Sandie looked around the kitchen, all these people, she thought to herself, all these people staring at her for no other reason than that she was the stepmother. She had come to expect it from people. Ignorant people with preconceived ideas. But she never thought Robert, her own husband, the man she loved, would be the worst culprit of all. He had disappeared into his study, claiming pressing business. What could be more pressing than defending your own wife, thought Sandie bitterly. Had she misjudged him? It would cost her dearly if she had.

'Okay, Mrs Wellby, seeing as we are all here, let's go through where you were on Friday.'

'Again?'

'Yes, again.'

'Robert went to work, Jane was at home. Her course was one of the first to have exams, she had no reason to go to college so she was staying here while the weather was good. I had done a workout and then spent about an hour in my study organizing some sample books to be delivered to the shop in Colchester. I waited for my hairdresser to turn up, which she didn't. In fact,' said Sandie, remembering seeing Suzie's red Mazda from her window, 'she turned up later that afternoon. Talked to that girl, she must have got the time wrong.'

'Where does she work?' Sandie pulled a card out of her wallet and handed it to the policeman.

'And then?'

'Jane and I had coffee.' That much at least was true, thought Bramley to himself, they'd found it in her stomach. 'It was nearly one o'clock. I must have worked longer than I intended because I was late taking Lucy out for her midday walk. Which I did. I returned early because I had a terrible headache, I thought I was getting a cold so I went for a nap. I woke up and came downstairs, which was when I saw the girl on the phone.'

'When you got back from your walk, did you see Jane?'

'No. There was a note in the hall saying she had gone to the video store and would be back. I went straight to my room.'

'And what time was that?'

'Two o'clock. Exactly.'

'You are very precise for a woman who doesn't wear a watch.' Sandie beckoned Bramley to follow her. In the hall stood a finely carved mahogany grandfather clock.

'In just a few moments,' said Sandie, 'you will realize why I keep such good time.' At quarter past the hour the clock chimed melodically, filling the hall with the sound. She smiled patronizingly at him. 'So much for your detective work, Detective Chief Inspector Bramley.' She turned and walked back into the kitchen.

'I don't suppose you have Jane's note?' Bramley wasn't going to let the woman get away with her haughty behaviour. She had planned it well, but murderers always slipped up. Eventually.

Sandie looked at him with contempt. 'You know perfectly well that I haven't got it. It must have been thrown away in all the commotion that followed.'

'One of my officers has paid a visit to the video shop. No sightings of Jane.'

'Gee, really?'

'Mrs Wellby, this is a serious matter.'

'Then take it seriously!'

Bramley waited for his temper to subside. 'Catherine Torrant rang the doorbell just after two with your dog in her arms. Can you hear the bell from your room?'

'Yes.'

'But not on Friday.'

'I told you, I had a headache, I needed a rest. I took two headache tablets that must have made me fall asleep very quickly. Where is Lucy, if that girl killed her?'

'We are still looking into that, Mrs Wellby.'

'No, you are not, you are interrogating me. I think I should get my lawyer if this is going to continue.'

'Do you feel like you need a lawyer, Mrs Wellby?' asked Bramley smugly.

'With you around, yes.'

There was a screech of tyres outside, a car door opened and slammed. Sandie didn't look up: one more 'gift' from a concerned neighbour and she might just hit *them* over the head with her hammer. Or perhaps it was an overzealous policeman, ready with the handcuffs and a dead dog, desperate to whisk her off and make an example out of her. If you're rich and American in this country – you *will* be caught. She should send e-mails to her few American friends over here and warn them not to entertain the idea of murder. They may look fat and stupid, but the British copper is more tenacious than you'd think. The kitchen door opened. Sandie didn't even bother looking up, the only person she wanted it to be was Robert. And he hadn't come out of his study.

'Sandie, what's going on?' Simon ran up to where she sat and crouched at her feet.

'Simon, oh God, where've you been?' For the first time since the beginning of this, Bramley heard a trace of vulnerability in her voice.

'I'm so sorry.'

'Why didn't you come?'

'I didn't know, I was in the bloody Lake District. I thought you'd want time alone.'

'The where? Why?'

Simon didn't answer; instead he began to turn away from her, taking in the hovering presence of the police.

'Simon?'

He let go of Sandie's hand and marched up to Bramley. 'You must be mad, Sandie couldn't hurt a fly, this is preposterous.'

'What is preposterous?' asked Bramley, condescendingly.

'That Sandie could have anything to do with Jane's death.'

The corner of Bramley's mouth flickered up for split second. 'Why do think that?'

'The local paper's been calling the office incessantly. Whatever Jane has done, Sandie has got nothing to do with it.'

'Is that so, Mr . . .?'

'Proudlove. She'd never assist a suicide. I know her.' He looked intently at Sandie. 'I know her.'

Sandie smiled at him. 'Thank you, Simon.' It was more than her beloved husband had done.

'Well that is all very nice, Mr Proudlove,' said Bramley. 'But I'm afraid we aren't dealing with a suicide any more.'

Simon glanced back at Sandie, then to the police officer. Bramley watched as the information began to sink in. 'An accident?' he asked, not quickly enough.

'I don't think so, Mr Proudlove. Which only leaves death by unlawful killing, and I'm afraid that is what we're dealing with here.'

'Where's Robert?' said Simon.

'Don't you want to know who or why?' said the policeman walking up to him.

Simon looked around the room. 'Where's Robert?'

'He's in his study, working,' said Sandie.

'Jesus Christ, can't he put an end to this nonsense. Go and get him, now.' Sandie went to the kitchen door.

'Who are you exactly, Mr Proudlove, that you feel it is your duty to involve yourself in the Wellby family. Are you family?'

'You leaked the information to the press, didn't you? Whipping up a witch-hunt based on nothing.'

'Where were you between one and three on Friday afternoon?'

'I'm not answering your questions. Jane killed herself.'

'No, Mr Proudlove, there were two sets of prints on that hosepipe, Mrs Wellby's and Cat Torrant's. We were *never* dealing with a suicide.'

'That girl?' said Sandie, still at the doorway.

Bramley swung round, furious with himself. 'I think we should continue this at the station,' he said.

'When did you get her prints?' asked Sandie.

'Criminal record I bet?' said Simon.

'I think we ought to talk to Mr Proudlove alone, DS Chambers,' said Bramley, trying to deflect the attention away from the hosepipe.

'I knew it,' said Sandie, 'she was lying about Lucy too. She's responsible for this.'

'Mrs Wellby, we took her prints and matched them,

she doesn't have a record,' said DS Chambers, trying to be helpful.

'When?'

'Where were you on Friday, Mr Proudlove?' said Bramley, raising his voice.

'When?' shouted Sandie.

'Saturday morning,' said DS Chambers.

Sandie walked slowly back into the kitchen and right up to WPC Clement. 'Why did you chase me?'

'Excuse me?'

'You tore after me like I was an escaped convict. Why?'

'Because she suspected your prints were on that hose,' said Bramley. 'And she was right.'

Slowly, Sandie turned. 'You hadn't taken my prints, Detective Chief Inspector. You had no reason to suspect me, yet batgirl here held me in an arm lock until the cavalry showed up and I want to know why.'

'Mrs Wellby, I'm sure she didn't mean to panic you, she was just taking precautions.'

'Bullshit! I want to talk to your superiors. I want to know on what grounds you obtained the search warrant.'

'Your stepdaughter had a bruise on her head and left no note. That's why we applied and obtained a search warrant. So please, don't threaten me, Mrs Wellby. I know you didn't touch the hosepipe when you went into the garage with Miss Torrant, so you must have touched it earlier.'

'And how do you know that? I can't remember you being there.'

'Because Cat Torrant has informed me that you had your hands clasped behind your back the whole time.'

'And you believe her, a young girl, in a beaten-up old car, who broke into my house for no reason.'

'She ran over your dog, Mrs Wellby, and was decent enough to do the right thing by letting you know.'

'Where is she then, Detective Chief Inspector Bramley? Tell me that.'

'We'll find it.'

'Her. Lucy is a bitch.'

'Well you know what they say about dogs and their owners.'

'Get out of my house. If you think that I am going to make this easy for you, think again.'

'Cat Torrant is prepared to swear on the fact that you kept your hands clasped behind your back all the time you were in the garage. Swear on oath. Thou shalt not give false evidence, remember that commandment?'

'If I were a religious person, which I am not, and I lied on oath about touching the hose it would be because I was guilty. In which case I think I'd have more to worry about breaking that particular commandment. I touched the pipe as I went into the garage just as she says she did. It is her word against mine. You came here on Saturday with the sole purpose of finding evidence against me and I want to know why. What have I done?'

'Everyone is a suspect.'

'Bullshit! No one chased anyone else.'

'No one else ran,' said Bramley smugly.

'I did not run. You just presumed I did because you had me down as guilty before you even got here, you narrow-minded piece of . . .' Sandie paused. 'Unless, unless you already knew they were my fingerprints.' She eyed Bramley. 'What did you do? Remove something from my house *without* my permission. Remind me what is the ninth commandment?' Bramley did not answer. 'Something about stealing I believe. Are you a religious man?' asked Sandie. 'You ought to watch out for that hand of God if you are.'

'What is going on here?' Robert rocked unsteadily in the doorway.

Simon marched up to him and whispered tensely into his ear. Robert pushed him away.

'The police are leaving, darling,' said Sandie, rushing to his side. 'You can go back to your study, I'm sorting it.' She knew she was talking to him like a three-year-old, but she didn't want a scene. Robert was difficult to predict when drunk. Not because he could react in a million different ways, but because he'd never been a drinker. She took his arm then looked challengingly at Bramley. 'They're leaving before I change my mind about being co-operative and file a complaint of harassment. They will not be taking anything away with them. Least of all me.' She looked seriously at her husband. 'Jane killed herself.' The pain in her voice filled the words. 'She killed herself.' Once more with conviction.

THE POLICEMEN BEGAN TO filter out of the house. Robert escorted Bramley to the front door. Sandie and Simon were alone in the kitchen.

'Thank God you turned up,' she said. 'That damned girl, who is she, can you find out?'

Simon put his finger to his lips. 'I'm sorry I didn't come sooner. I thought you and Robert would need time alone.'

'Simon, what were you doing in the Lake District?'

He walked towards the kitchen door. He could see Robert talking to Bramley.

'Walking,' he said absently.

'You hate walking. What were you walking for?'

'Hmm?'

'Were you there alone?'

He turned back to her briefly. 'Um, yes.' He turned back and continued to look out into the hall.

'Simon, what are you looking at?'

'Oh, nothing, I need to speak to Robert, sit down, you need a rest.'

ROBERT AND BRAMLEY STOOD on the stone steps of the front door.

'I know this is hard for you, sir, but your daughter wasn't suicidal, was she? Never in my experience as a police officer have children killed themselves without leaving an explanation for their parents. Never. Think about it, if there is anything you want to tell me, it will be in complete confidence.'

'You are talking about my wife,' Robert spoke through gritted teeth.

'No, I am talking about your 23-year-old daughter. Jane.'

Robert shuddered at the sound of her name. 'She was a lovely girl. A wonderful daughter.'

'And Mrs Wellby, is she a wonderful wife?'

Robert stared at him. 'Absolutely,' he said.

'Difficult isn't it, knowing where your loyalty lies?' said Bramley, turning away from the doorway. 'You probably felt split down the middle.'

'Sandie wouldn't have hurt Jane.'

'No note. No fingerprints,' said Bramley matter-of-factly.

'An accident then.'

'Mr Wellby, how do you think you accidentally wedge a hose into an exhaust pipe then jam it into a car window, climb in, belt up and turn on the ignition?'

Bramley watched Robert Wellby pale. 'I don't know,' he said quietly.

'Are you sure about that, Mr Wellby?' Bramley dipped his hat and turned away from him. Robert watched the last of the police cars disappear around the corner in the drive. When the dust settled, he turned to go back in. Simon was standing directly behind him.

'Jesus!' exclaimed Robert. 'What the fuck are you doing?'

'Robert, you haven't told Sandie. What's going on? Are you okay?'

'What kind of fucking stupid thing to say is that? No, Simon, I'm not okay.' Robert put his hand over his chest and breathed slowly.

'I didn't mean to frighten you.'

'You didn't.'

'Listen, Robert, the police are going to try and mess with your head, don't let them.'

Robert looked incredulously at Simon. 'What are you doing here?'

'Trying to help. This is getting completely out of hand. You and Sandie need each other right now.'

Robert softened slightly, his shoulders dropping by inches.

'Robert?' Sandie was standing in the kitchen doorway.

'What's happening?' he asked looking at her.

Sandie rushed over to him. 'I don't know, my love, I don't know. But we'll find the answers. Together.'

'I'm sorry, I . . .'

'It's okay, I'm here for you.'

'I'm sorry,' he said again. Sandie pulled him to her.

'You do know that I wouldn't do anything to Jane, don't you?'

Robert nodded. Sandie exhaled loudly. 'Okay,' she said, holding him tightly. 'Okay then.'

Simon retreated from the reunited couple to the staircase and saw Fiona, standing at the top of the stairs watching them. When she saw him, she sprang backwards as if she'd been burnt and retreated out of sight. Simon heard her rapid footfalls disappear down a corridor. He looked back at Robert and Sandie who remained oblivious. Simon began to climb the stairs. Halfway down the corridor was Robert and Sandie's bedroom. The door was ajar. Simon pushed it open and saw Fiona standing at the bay window, staring wide-eyed at the driveway below. She was clutching a thick blue notebook.

'Fiona?'

She swung round, holding the book out in front of her like a crucifix. 'Go away,' she shouted.

'What is it? What's that?'

Fiona's face turned purple as she stared at him. She didn't answer.

'Breathe,' he said softly. Fiona started to shake. Moving slowly, Simon walked to the bedside table, picked up the phone and dialled 999. Quietly he asked for the ambulance service but before he could be put through he heard the dim sound of sirens. Four police cars were racing back up the drive. Fiona dropped the notebook. It lay open by her feet. Simon immediately recognized the writing. He read the first few lines, picked it up and started turning the pages frantically.

'Oh, shit!' The police cars were at the door. As he ran from the room he heard the doorbell.

'Don't open it!' he screamed, reaching the top of the

stairs. He was too late. Sandie was in handcuffs. Someone was reading her rights.

'Get off her!' Robert was shouting.

'Where is she?' said Bramley to Simon as he ran down the stairs.

'Get a lawyer, Robert,' said Simon, ignoring the policeman. 'Now!'

'What the hell is going on?' Sandie pulled against WPC Clement's firm grip. All those exercises and she still was no match for this dumpling of a policewoman. 'For Christ's sake,' she shouted into Bramley's face, 'I'll have your fucking badge for this.'

Bramley smirked at Sandie then turned to his officers. 'Go and find Fiona Wellby. And bring the book.'

'You better have a very good explanation for this, this disgusting behaviour.' Robert turned back to his wife. 'It's all right, darling. We'll sort this out.'

But Sandie wasn't listening to him. She was watching Fiona being helped by two policemen down the stairs.

'Jesus,' said Robert, following his wife's gaze. 'What's happened to her?'

'She's all right, Mr Wellby, she's just had a bit of a shock.'

Robert stared back at Bramley. 'What are you talking about?'

Another policeman ran ahead of Fiona and handed Bramley the thick blue book. Bramley tapped it against his hand. 'It seems,' said Bramley, 'that your daughter left a suicide note after all.' He glanced back at Sandie.

Robert tried to grab it from him, Simon held him back. 'What is it?'

Bramley looked beyond them both to Fiona, who was backing away from the gathering, a look of terror in her eyes. 'It's okay, Mrs Wellby, no one is going to hurt you. You did the right thing by ringing us.'

'Ringing you?' said Sandie.

'Fiona?' said Robert.

'This is ridiculous, get these things off me.'

Fiona shrank at the sound of Sandie's voice.

'What's happened to her,' said Robert.

'Shit, Sandie,' muttered Simon.

'What?'

Bramley pointed at an officer. 'You, take Mrs Wellby home. Make sure she isn't alone.'

'What the fuck is going on?' Sandie's voice filled the hall like a clap of thunder. Silencing the air around her. Then lightning struck.

Fiona lifted her right arm and pointed at Sandie. 'You killed my daughter.'

Robert looked like he'd received an invisible blow to the side of his head. He righted himself, dazed. 'What are you talking about?'

'She killed Jane and *you* let her.'

'Shut up, shut up, Fiona!' shouted Simon.

'You killed my daughter, you killed my daughter, you killed my daughter, you killed my daughter, you killed my daughter . . .'

Sandie stared back at Fiona. The eye of the storm.

Chapter Nine

Dan and Cat kept a vigil over Anna for three days. He drifted in and out of sleep, was sick regularly and bloodied his sheets often. Still he refused medical help and still he refused to talk. In fury and frustration, Cat had taken the sheet and the pink furry G-string and hidden them in her car. She wanted someone to pay, but she was alone. Cat stood at the small oven in her kitchen and stirred the new batch of home-made chicken soup. Cat didn't think Anna would be venturing out for a while, but she couldn't stay with him indefinitely. She was behind on her final radio package, then they were given a week off before the three-week TV course started. It was only now that she'd been forced to stop for five minutes that she realized how madly busy college had kept her. Perfectionism was a plague, when she thought about Chelmsford undoing all her hard work, she felt sick. And then she felt guilty about self-obsessing when Anna was downstairs struggling to get out of bed in the mornings. She wanted to lean on Dan, but he had enough on his plate without having to worry about her. Cat was staring dolefully into the saucepan when the phone rang.

'It's me.'

'Hi, Gran.'

'How is he?'

Cat turned the heat down low and sat at the kitchen table.

'A bit better than this morning. I seem to be finding it harder. I cried like a baby after I spoke to you,' said Cat. 'I see this expression come over his face, it's so sad.'

'You must be careful that he doesn't slip into a depression that he can't get out of. You've got to nip this in the bud, Cat.'

'It isn't like he's been chucked, Gran,' she said, trying to keep the frustration out of her voice. Amelia's stuff and nonsense approach to life was difficult to handle, even after twenty-eight years of it.

'I realize that, darling, but once you're down there, it is very difficult to get out. Bolting himself indoors isn't going to help.' Cat pinched the bridge of her nose. How did life change so quickly? One minute you're all swilling tequila, the next you're clinging on to your sanity by a thread. One minute you've got a daughter, the next she's gassed herself out in your car. One minute you've got a mother the next she's pissed off to Australia. The difference between blissful ignorance and unshakeable truth is one split second.

'So what do you think?'

'What?' said Cat.

'My proposition. Weren't you paying attention?'

'Sorry.'

'Darling, get yourself and Anna down here, I'll explain then. I've got to go, I have a date.' The line went dead. Getting Anna out of bed had taken forty-eight hours, getting him dressed another twenty-four, getting him out . . .

DAN AND ANNA WERE watching television when she went back down. 'Hey,' she said chiding Dan, 'I thought you were supposed to be going to a lecture.'

His eyes flickered over Anna. 'It wasn't important,' he said. Amelia was right. This couldn't go on indefinitely.

'Anna,' she said, plonking down on the sofa between them, 'how do you feel about getting out of the flat?' Anna shrugged. 'It might help,' she continued.

Anna looked at Dan. 'It isn't a bad idea,' said Dan. 'We are running out of supplies anyway.'

'Okay,' said Anna listlessly. 'If you think so.'

'Good girl,' said Dan.

'Hardly,' he said as he got up and went to the small flight of stairs that led to his bedroom and bathroom. Dan and Cat watched him take cautious steps before he turned around to face them when he reached the top. 'This isn't going to be easy is it?'

Cat shook her head. 'But you've got us, and we'll do everything in our power to help.' Dan nodded and Anna went into his room to dress.

'Poor bastard,' said Dan. 'It makes me sick, how could anyone do that, raping a bloke for pity's sake.'

'Dan, a woman is raped every five minutes in this country. Every day in the paper there is a story about it, don't tell me you haven't noticed them. Of course it happens to men.'

'Sure, but somehow it seems worse, guys raping guys.'

Cat frowned. 'I don't think I understand what you mean by that.'

'Well, you know, imagine if it had been me . . .'

'That would be terrible too.'

'Yes but, if you're not used to . . .' Dan shrugged. 'Never mind.'

Cat stood up. 'Are you telling me that rape is worse for a straight man than a gay man or a straight woman because he isn't used to having something up there?' she said in a tense whisper.

Dan winced. 'You know what I mean, that sort of thing fucks with a guy's head.'

'That's the most stupid thing I've ever heard come out of your mouth, Dan. You should consider what you're saying before you bring up this theory in public.'

'Why are you so cross?' he said, mystified.

'That fact that you have to ask me makes it worse.' She shook her head.

'I'm just making an intellectual point—'

'About penetration?' Cat was losing her temper. 'Real sensitive, Dan.'

'*Sensitive?* That's rich coming from you.'

'What's that supposed to mean?'

'You know.'

'No,' said Cat crossing her arms defensively, 'I don't.'

'Doesn't matter. We've all been cooped up in here too long. I need to get out.'

Cat grabbed his arm as he walked past her. 'This has hurt me too, you know. I've been sneaking off to have baths so I can have a good cry without anyone hearing me.'

'Why didn't you come to me?'

'You? You were busy holding Anna's head above water.'

'So you call Amelia.'

'Not this again, Dan.'

'You'd prefer to sit in a cold bath than admit you need someone to talk to.'

'I have someone to talk to.'

'Well she won't be around for ever, then what are you going to do? Perhaps you could think about getting some training in before . . .'

'Don't stop now, Dan, carry on. Before what?'

Dan didn't say anything.

'Bastard,' whispered Cat.

'Cat I'm—'

'Don't speak to me.' She walked out to her car in a

daze. When Anna walked out of the front door he was wearing jeans, a T-shirt and a bewildered expression. Snap.

'. . . SEPT 4TH 1992. I AM *fighting for survival. I know that now. It is obvious she hates me. More than hates me, despises me, detests me, that is the only excuse for her behaviour. Yet no one knows, no one can see it. She is a better actress than we credit her for. I see her with her friends, hear her on the phone to Mummy. You would have thought she treasured me if you heard those phone calls. But she doesn't. I love Daddy but he is blind and I am too afraid to tell him because he loves her and what would I do if he didn't believe me. I can't tell Mummy either, I do not want to put more stress on her, she worries so, tries so hard to make it up to me, if I told her my stepmother was the devil – she would blame herself. What am I going to do? God give me strength to cope with the foul things she does and says. She is clever, she bruises me only on the inside, I sometimes wish she would go ahead and do the vile things she threatens me with. Then I'd have proof. But what would life be like then. Deformed. Disfigured. Unlovable. I was only fourteen when my life became a living hell. Oh, she was fine when she first arrived. Presents from America, the latest toy, I was stupid then, I was taken in. I thought she was a friend, come to stay. For ever. Spending Dad's money. Living in our house. I know she'd prefer it if I didn't visit, but then she'd win. And I'll never let her do that. I want my life back. Help me, God.'*

Bramley replaced the diary on his desk and looked at his surrounding officers. 'That is one of the few excerpts

I can stomach to read aloud. Jane Wellby was tormented by that woman for years. The last entry sums it up.' He handed out photocopies to the room.

'. . . *May 28th. I'm scared, really scared. If anything happens to me I want to be buried in the churchyard that my parents were married in. Happier times. But who can I tell? No one would believe me. I think my stepmother wants to kill me, I can just imagine how they would laugh at me . . .*'

'So much for wanting to be cremated,' said DS Mike Chambers, 'looks like Mrs Wellby wanted to get rid of the evidence.'

'Very good. Now it seems the worst abuse came in fits and spurts, it wasn't continuous. There is a pattern there that we should look into. Now Mr Wellby says he had absolutely no idea that this was going on, he's a businessman, let's find out if he travelled. If he did, when, we can match the dates. That would explain his ignorance.'

He continued to read. '. . . *February 12th. Today was one of the worst days of my life. The humiliation can get no worse. I want to die. She dragged me into that dreadful place, Calorie Carers, told the woman I had a problem and compared me to all those disgusting fat women in there. "My daughter has a small problem," how dare she pretend to be my mother. The only problem I have is her. She's the one who tells me I'm fat, ugly, worthless, she does. Standing there in her revolting G-string and cycling shorts, bending forwards, sticking that tight American arse in my face and asking me if I think she looks good. Of course she looks good, she's plastic. She left me there, with all those fat people, they told me to take my clothes off, they measured me and weighed me, and ummed and ahhed and embarrassed me, they pinched my waist with pincers. How could she do this to me? I thought we were going shopping. She is trying to destroy me, I must be strong . . .'*

Bramley looked around the room. 'Clement, you're a woman, you go to Calorie Carers first thing in the morning – might even think of signing up with them yourself.' He laughed.

'What about the hairdresser, sir, shall I check up on her at the same time?' She would never rise to his bait but her stomach tightened that little bit more.

'What for? If you want to get your hair done, don't do it on taxpayers' time.'

'To find out why she didn't make Mrs Wellby's appointment.'

'Haven't you read this,' he said, waving the A4 sheets.

Clement nodded.

'Then you know this girl was threatened with unspeakable sexual violence by Mrs Wellby, so who gives a shit that she didn't get her hair done. Now, I want to make this quick and concise. We know who's guilty of Jane's murder, we just need enough evidence to put her away. Got it?'

Everyone got it. Even Clement. She knew what it was like to be bullied, put down, tormented. She knew what it was like having no one on your side. Well she wasn't going to end up like Jane Wellby, trapped, powerless to defend herself. She was going to fight, men like

Bramley had to be stopped. Jane's death was the sad end to years of victimization, Clement was going to do everything she could to make sure Sandie Wellby was punished for what she had put her stepdaughter through. And when that was over, she'd get Bramley.

'DARLINGS, ISN'T IT EXCITING — Anna, you look simply wonderful as a man, but please do not pull the waistband up around your nipples.' Anna yanked his jeans down. 'Much better. The thing is, I do think that there is more to all of this than meets the eye.'

'Like you don't already know,' said Anna, throwing a look at Cat who mouthed 'sorry'.

'Well, I certainly don't know everything, but being an expert at eavesdropping helps.'

This was not the answer Anna or Cat were expecting. 'What are you talking about, Amelia?'

'The dead girl of course.' More looks of confusion. 'Oh, for heaven's sake, don't you read the local rag?'

'How many times have I told you, Gran, that's not a newspaper—'

'Well, darling, it is all Fuhrer Cleveland orders. It's on account of the size of the print and the calming stories,' she said imitating the nurse. 'I have to smuggle in anything more highbrow than that. Anyway, none of that is important, because for once her inability to understand the subtleties of life has resulted in something tremendously exciting.'

Cat stared at her grandmother, had she finally lost it?

'Oh, please stop looking at me like that, young lady, I'm not going mad. But I have found you a real story, one that'll silence your opposition for ever and give you that last radio project that's bound to put you back at the top of your class. You might even discover a little about yourself in the process.'

'Get the nurse,' said Cat.

'Okay, okay, I'll start from the beginning.'

Anna sat down on a chair, crossed and then uncrossed his legs. Why Cat wore jeans was beyond him. They were exceedingly uncomfortable, lifting and separating in all the wrong places.

'When you've quite stopped fidgeting.'

'Sorry.'

'I was having a quiet cigarette by the lake when I happened to overhear—'

'Gran?' Disbelieving her grandmother already.

'Okay, when I happened to wheel accidentally too close to Mr Blaine and his visiting daughter, Camilla Simpson,' she conceded, then went on, sidetracked, 'Mr Blaine, absolutely charming man, widower, seems very fond of his daughter, she's a teacher you know.' Cat frowned at Amelia. 'Anyway, Jane's death was reported in the local paper, just a small piece, but they were discussing it, our case.' Cat and Anna looked at each other, *our* case? 'Well it was only polite of me to tell them of my own involvement in it, and Camilla and I talked about it at length. She taught Jane you see—'

'Ah,' said Cat, finally seeing where this was leading.

'Twice. At school when she was a child and then again when she went into higher education. Camilla is now principal of the college Jane was taking a course at. The first and most interesting point is Camilla didn't know that Jane's parents were divorced until Sandie Wellby called her up about the course. Camilla had been very confused until she realized that Sandie was Jane's stepmother. Well, of course, she was too discreet to ask when the divorce had taken place, assuming it had been a recent thing because Jane always made quite a song and dance about her mummy and daddy at school, about what a perfect little family they were.'

'Didn't she ever meet Sandie Wellby?'

'Well, that's what's so strange,' said Amelia, talking enthusiastically, 'she met Jane's mother and father often, they would always come to the school plays, parent nights, whatever, together, Fiona and Robert. Apparently it is "modern thinking" to call everyone on first name terms. Disrespectful if you ask me, but there you go. Camilla Simpson believed Fiona and Robert were happily married and Jane never corrected her. But Robert and Sandie Wellby have been married for seven years, which means Jane lied to everyone and what does a lie do?' said Amelia opening up her arms dramatically. Cat knew the answer to this one, she'd been brought up on it, she smiled back at her grandmother.

'It covers a truth,' they said together.

Anna looked perplexed. Cat explained. 'When I was younger Gran always told me the reason not to lie was because a lie had a life of its own. Its job was to cover the truth, but the truth is stronger than the lie, and the lie could not cover it completely because it was weak, and it would flap about and eventually it would expose the truth beneath it. So, rather than fib in the first place, deal with the truth, before it deals with you.' She paused. 'Well, something like that anyway.'

Anna knew exactly what she was talking about and it was nothing to do with Jane Wellby.

'So you think that Jane was hiding something?'

'And it's up to you two to find out,' said Amelia nodding.

'I don't think this is really my thing, Amelia. Thanks.'

Amelia put her skinny hand on Anna's knee. 'Take some advice from an old lady. Focus on this. It will help.'

Anna's bottom lip started to tremble. 'What have you told her,' said Anna, turning on Cat. Cat opened her mouth.

'Anna,' Amelia's voice was as soft as duck down, 'I lived through a war, I got to see men broken in many forms. Cat didn't tell me anything I wouldn't have seen with my own eyes. You need time off to heal.' Tears pricked his eyelids as Amelia stroked his head. 'Wouldn't it be nice to have something else to think about. A reason to get up in the morning?'

Anna sniffed. 'How did you get to be such a wise woman?'

Amelia took his hand. 'We've Cat to thank for that.'

'I've got nothing to do with it.'

'Yes, you have, as you grew older, I grew younger. If I hadn't had you to teach me, this crazy modern world would have got the better of me.'

'It certainly got the better of me,' said Anna.

'And me,' said Cat.

'But we're going to change all that,' said Amelia brightly. 'Find some answers, get Cat a grand finale for her course, it'll be a damned sight better than sex over seventy.'

'What?' said Anna.

'Never mind,' said Cat.

'And we may even solve a murder, who knows – it might be fun.'

'Strange sort of fun,' said Cat.

'Darling, I am thinking about you too.'

'What do you mean?' said Cat.

'Just ride with me on this one. Please?'

'You did find the body—' said Anna.

'And it can't be coincidence that I met the teacher—' agreed Amelia, nodding encouragement.

'Or that we saw Sandie-Ann Surly on that video—' confirmed Anna.

'And that I hit a dog that has seemingly disappeared—' said Cat.

'And that you both know Paris so well.' Anna and

Cat turned back to Amelia. 'I told you not to look at me like that . . .'

'PLEASE, ROBERT,' SIMON WAS begging now, 'go to the police station and give her your support.'

Robert shook his head. 'I was doing that when Fiona found the diary.'

'She is your wife!'

Robert looked up, slowly. 'And Jane was my daughter, Simon, can't you understand that?'

'Your marriage has been the envy of everyone. How can you turn your back on that? Defend the living, Robert.'

'Even if they are responsible for the dead?'

Simon cursed under his breath. He walked up behind Robert and put his hands on his shoulders. They stood there for a while, looking out of the study window over the neatly manicured garden. Robert's shoulders felt like breeze-block under his shirt. Rock solid. Solid rock.

'You don't really believe that Sandie could hurt Jane?'

'You haven't read the diary, Simon.'

'Jane is like any child, perfectly capable of making things up.'

'Not like this.'

'Like what?'

'Leave me alone, Simon.'

'For pity's sake,' said Simon, quietly, 'the woman picks ladybirds off the driveway so that they don't get squashed. She has looked after you and Jane for years.

She deserves a medal for putting up with you and Fiona, always playing the proud parents.' Robert's shoulders tightened under Simon's fingers, one more knot. 'She is a saint and you cannot even see it. She wouldn't harm your daughter. Think about it, Robert. Think about the Sandie you know and love.'

He didn't answer immediately. 'Do I know her, do you? She's an actress, Simon, that's what she does.'

'I can't believe I'm hearing this. How long have you been married?' Simon walked round to the side of his desk. 'Seven years, Robert, seven fucking years. Doesn't that count for anything?'

Robert didn't answer.

'Well, I'll tell you something, if she was my wife, I'd do more than send my lawyer.'

'Thomas Hallifax is the best.'

'Big fucking deal. She needs support, she needs to know you care. Remember her, now, in your head,' Simon closed his eyes. 'This beautiful, intelligent, funny woman, your wife, always ready to help, to support. She carries you, Robert, like she carried your daughter, but she does it with such grace and good nature, you don't even notice.' He opened his eyes slowly. 'She deserves your support.'

Robert had turned around and was watching him. 'She's got yours hasn't she, eh, Simon? Your support. That's not all is it? She's got you, your love.' He laughed, spitefully. 'Of course, and all this time I thought you were just a content bachelor. You are in love with my wife. God, you've been so obvious, I can't believe I didn't see it.' He was still laughing.

'What the hell have you got to laugh about?'

Robert stopped laughing and turned abruptly away. 'Oh, my God.'

'What?'

'Get out of my house.'

'What on earth for?'

Robert was pacing the floor in front of the window. 'Jane tried to tell me.' He looked up, his lips parted, a thousand thoughts racing through his head.

'Tried to tell you what?' asked Simon, his voice quavering slightly.

'You're nervous.'

'Only about you going insane.'

'I'm not going insane, for the first time in a long while I have great clarity of thought.'

Simon started walking to the door. 'Look, you're obviously very shaken up, I'll speak to you tomorrow. Just go to the police station.'

'Jane knew, didn't she?' Simon stopped walking. 'Now I have your attention, don't I?' said Robert.

'I don't know what you are talking about. I think you should lie down.'

'Which room do you suggest I lie down in. You probably know the colour schemes better than I do.'

Simon didn't move.

'How could I have been so stupid. Jane told me, every time you came by, she told me. Jane knew, she was trying to warn me what you two were up to.' A tense laughter rippled through his throat. 'Why is Simon here all the time, Daddy?'

'This is bullshit, Robert. I never came here.'

'You even talk like her. All those times I've come home and you were here. Carrying your little sample books. Very ingenious. Bet you giggled about that.'

'What do you think your wife does, Robert? *I* work all hours God sends, she swings by a couple of the big houses from time to time, and that's really where her interest in the company ends. I may well be her plaything, but not in the way you think. I never came here unless I was invited by the both of you.'

'Jane called you her toyboy, I thought it was a joke—'

'Forget it. I'm sorry I even came here. I'm sorry I was sent to get you from work, *work*, Robert. Remember that day, when I found you in your *office*? You expect me to be loyal to you, to carry your little secret, and then you do the gentlemanly thing of accusing me of fucking your wife.'

'Get out of my house!'

'Your house. Don't make me laugh.'

'How dare you . . .'

'Cut the sanctimonious bullshit, Robert. You should take a closer look at your own life before you start condemning others. Sandie didn't have a hand in your daughter's death, nor did I, but you, Robert old chap, you may not be so guilt free. She wasn't a child you know, by any stretch of the imagination.'

Robert picked up a whisky tumbler from his desk. Simon managed to close the door behind him as the glass shattered against it. Robert sank into his chair.

'Dad. Dad.' His daughter's voice, calling him. 'Are you home?' The door opened, his daughter stood in the frame, smiling. 'You *are* here. I think you are going deaf in your old age.'

'Well thanks a lot. Come in, I've been meaning to have a word with you.'

'Yeah?'

'Plans. What do you want to do this weekend—?'

'I won't be here Sunday. I'm going back to Mum's.'

'Oh yes, Saturday then. Would you like to have some friends around.'

'Not really, we could just spend it here. Together.'

'What about going to the go-cart track?'

'Well, if you want to, but I'd rather just be at home.'

'I'll get the Whittons over for tennis then. You like their boys, don't you?'

'Yes, but—'

'In fact, why don't we have a barbecue, get a few others over, make a day of it.' Jane shrugged at him. 'Sandie does such a great barbecue, I'm sure she won't mind.'

'Okay, Dad, if that's what you want.' Jane's voice was flat.

Robert turned back to his desk. 'Good, good, that's settled. I'll phone some people up now.' Jane hadn't even made it fully into the room. She hesitated. 'Anything else,

poppet,' he called over his shoulder. He already had the
phone in his hand.

'You don't have to do this for me, Dad, I'd be quite
happy to just—'

'Anything to make my little girl happy.' He smiled and
started punching in numbers he'd found in his address
book. 'Hello, Veronica. Hi, it's Robert Wellby. Fine, yes,
Sandie is as wonderful as ever, how are you?'

'She's not.'

Robert turned slightly. 'Hang on, Veronica.' He put his
hand over the receiver. 'What did you say?'

Jane looked at her father. 'Nothing.'

'Oh.' He removed his hand. 'No, just Jane,' said her father
down the phone. 'She fancies a barbecue on Saturday,
what are your lot up to? Great . . .'

Jane closed the door behind her.

Robert Wellby walked out to the courtyard and sat on
the mounting block. He stared at the garage door as tears
rolled down his face, until all the light of day had gone.

Chapter Ten

'It is very good of you to see us, Mrs Simpson.'

'My pleasure, please, come in. And call me Camilla.'

'I'm Cat and this is An—'

'Drew. Andrew. I'm Cat's researcher. Leg man. Um . . .'

'Pleased to meet you, Andrew, Cat.' Everyone shook hands. 'Come in.'

'So,' said Camilla Simpson as she showed them a seat in her sitting room, 'your granny tells me you are a radio journalist.'

'Not quite. I'm at the London College of Printing, still learning.'

'Well it's a good place to learn. Difficult to get into isn't it?'

'It took me three goes.'

'There's dedication. Very impressive. Doesn't surprise me, your grandmother is an extraordinary lady. Growing up with her must have been quite a minefield.'

'She told you.' Cat was very proud of the way Amelia had brought her up, but she was also very private about it. She'd learnt the hard way that not having a mummy and a daddy and a goldfish was seen as freakish by some people who should have known better.

'Actually, Cat, she told my father. I think he has rather a crush on her.'

'Old devil,' said Anna.

'She told me she had a date. I wasn't really paying attention.' Cat saw the photo of a smiling couple in their sixties on the mantelpiece. 'I don't think it was like a proper date.'

Camilla's eyes followed Cat's. 'It's okay, Mum died a few years ago now, I'm delighted he has found an equally high-spirited friend. He only moved to the home because he was lonely. At first we thought it was a mistake, and then he noticed Amelia.'

Cat didn't say anything.

'Mrs Simpson . . .?' said Anna, changing the subject. 'Would you mind if Cat recorded the interview?'

The woman hesitated.

'It would never be aired, would it, Cat?'

Cat looked away from the photo. 'Oh, no. Well, unlikely.'

'What's the subject matter?'

'Jane Wellby. I'd like to find out what happened to her.'

Camilla twisted her wedding band around her finger.

'I'm not looking to point the finger of blame at anyone,' said Cat, wanting to reassure the woman.

'Why are you doing it then? Whether she was murdered or committed suicide, someone is to blame.'

'Mrs Simpson, no one is to blame for a person's suicide, except for that person—'

'Cat,' said Anna gently.

'Anyway,' continued Cat, without looking at Anna, 'the police are convinced she didn't take her own life.'

Camilla Simpson sighed. 'I'm afraid I agree with them. Jane Wellby wasn't the type of girl to kill herself.'

'So it's okay,' said Cat, inserting a mini-disc into the machine. Camilla nodded.

Holding the microphone equidistantly between them, she pressed record.

'Mrs Simpson, you are the head teacher at the newly integrated Harlow college of further education. Before that you taught at a grammar school in Stoke Newington, both of which were attended by Jane Wellby?'

'Yes,' said Camilla.

'What was Jane like to teach?'

'Well I only actually *taught* her when she was ten, so . . .' Cat waited for her to finish her sentence. She didn't.

Cat pressed on. 'Was she a happy child?'

'Yes. Quite strong-willed. Liked to boss the smaller kids a bit, but nothing serious. A pretty common characteristic in an only child. There was talk about bullying but it turned out not to be Jane.'

'Was she clever?'

'Very. Though you wouldn't know it now. I mean . . .' Camilla bit her lip. 'Sorry . . .'

'It's okay, go on.'

'She was a bright child but not a good pupil. She ended up at Harlow college because she'd failed her A levels. Twice. But she shouldn't have.'

'Did the standard of her work slip dramatically?'

'Her records show a steady decline. But as I said, I wasn't involved in her education between the ages of ten and twenty-three.'

'But she was a troublemaker?'

'An attention-seeker would be more accurate. She'd tell elaborate stories about her parents and their incredible holidays, it didn't make her very popular, I'm afraid.'

'But her parents were divorced,' said Cat surprised.

Camilla shrugged. 'I don't know when. Jane obviously didn't like to see it that way.'

'What did the school in Stoke Newington do about her grades?'

'I believe Fiona Wellby was asked whether there was something wrong at home, she was totally taken aback by the school's concern and categorically stated that Jane was a joy at home, ergo any problem she had at school was the school's fault. I left the school around that time.'

'Isn't that what all parents say?' asked Anna.

'No, most parents will do anything they can to halt a decline in performance.'

'Could she have been hiding something?' asked Cat. 'Abuse of any kind?'

'No. I don't think Jane was abused, abused children aren't as demonstrative as Jane was. Even at ten, she was a very strong-willed, opinionated little girl. She'd grown into quite a manipulative young lady. I don't want to talk badly about the dead, but she wasn't the –' Camilla paused '– well the nicest pupil I'd come across.'

'What do you mean?'

'She was disruptive. And she was still at it. I received some complaints from her teachers. She was moody, short-tempered, tired all the time. Someone did mention drugs, but it's difficult to know what kind or how much. A lot of kids experiment with drugs in this area. This time I tried to talk to Fiona, I got a similar response.'

'Even though you knew there'd been problems before.'

'It sounds strange but I don't think Jane, or Fiona Wellby for that matter, knew we'd crossed paths before. I'd got married, had children, my husband died.' She paused. 'I barely recognize myself sometimes. I never mentioned having been at the Stoke Newington school. I didn't want to put them on the defensive.'

'I'm sorry to hear about your husband.'

'He was ill,' she said. 'Would either of you like some tea?'

Cat turned the tape off. 'Yes please.' They watched Camilla go.

'Poor Mrs Simpson.'

'Poor Jane Wellby,' said Anna. 'She obviously had severe problems, I can't believe no one did anything about it. The moodiness, the tiredness, classic symptoms of depression.'

'And why weren't her parents interested in what the school was saying? Talk about denial. If I so much as grazed a knee Gran would come racing over to check the school weren't underplaying it.'

'Sounds to me like something was seriously wrong at home and everyone was denying it. Even Jane. Hence the stories. She was a mess.'

Camilla returned with a tray. 'I know what you're thinking' – Cat surreptitiously pressed the record button – 'that Jane was a victim, that the school and college failed her. She wasn't a victim. By any stretch of the imagination. She embellished everything, she liked the attention she got showing off all the new toys her *parents* bought for her. The teachers used to talk about it in the staffroom.'

'Well her parents are rich.'

'I don't want to talk out of turn, but the money in that family is Sandie's. Fiona and Robert weren't rich in their Stoke Newington days.' Camilla poured out tea.

'What sort of toys?'

Camilla shrugged. 'She was the first to have a compact-disc player, playstations, that sort of thing. Divorced parents often overcompensate their children by giving them presents. I probably should have guessed that was what was going on, but she was no longer in my class.'

'Mrs Simpson, you've been very helpful,' said Cat. 'No one could've known what would happen.'

'I presume the police suspect Sandie Wellby, Jane's stepmother.'

Cat didn't want to admit her part in that presumption. She shrugged inconclusively.

'Well, if they ask me, I'll tell them that Sandie Wellby was the only one of them who ever seemed concerned about Jane's education. Robert and Fiona told the college she'd failed her A Levels because she'd fallen in with a bad lot. When she failed again, they rewarded her by sending her to La Croix language school in Paris. Not cheap. That didn't work either. She was back early. Finally I get a call from Mrs Wellby. Help, what do we do about Jane? I thought it was strange that Fiona was talking in an American accent. That's how I discovered the existence of Sandie Wellby, when she called to ask my help because she was worried about Jane. Not her mother or her father, but her stepmother. She's probably the only sane one among them. There's no way she killed Jane. No way.'

'I WONDERED WHEN YOU'D get to us.'

WPC Clement looked at the women uneasily. If Bramley had rung Calorie Carers and booked her an appointment for a practical joke, she would not rest until she had his badge. 'Excuse me?'

'You're here because of the Wellby girl. I read it in the local paper. Absolute tragedy. I suppose you have arrested her.'

'Who, madam?'

'The stepmother of course. That poor girl, we did everything we could for her, she was a wreck. A terrified wreck.' Lynne Reed was delighted to be involved in something for once that did not involve calorie counting.

'I think we had better sit down and start from the beginning. You are?'

'Ms Reed, I am the manager of Calorie Carers, we pride ourselves in—'

'Thank you, is there somewhere we can talk?'

'Certainly,' said Lynne Reed, slightly put out by the young policewoman. 'Come through to my office.' WPC Clement sat down amongst a terrifying array of low-cal produce and instantly felt hungry. Extraordinary *Before* and *After* photographs sat triumphantly on Ms Reed's desk. Her 'favourite pupils', she announced in an evangelical manner. Clement stared at the pictures, not entirely convinced that the *Afters* had any biological relationship to the *Befores*.

'Have you ever used our services?'

Clement glanced down herself, she'd never thought she had needed to, but now, just looking at her thighs, they seemed to spread before her very eyes. She looked up quickly. 'Wasn't she a bit young to be coming here?'

'We have clients as young as sixteen.'

'Sixteen,' repeated Clement, horrified.

'It is never too young to start adopting a well-balanced diet.' Clement glanced again around the room, on the way out, a pile of chocolate-flavoured soya bars, totally fat free, perched at grab level on a trolley. And only £2.98 for the culinary delight. Clement looked back at the woman in front of her and though she tried to stop herself, she couldn't help herself from disliking Ms Reed. She bet herself a Deep Pan Pizza that there was a packet of milk chocolate HobNobs tucked away in Ms Reed's bottom drawer. After all, she wasn't so very thin herself.

'They came in together in February, got the "trim-up" deal, post-Christmas piggery.' Lynne Reed snorted at her joke. 'Quite a bargain actually. At first I thought they were an ordinary mother and daughter, then I realized that she was totally dominating the conversations, telling my associate that Jane was very nervous and just wanted advice.' Clement jotted everything down in Pitman's shorthand. The most valuable tool of her trade.

'Were you present then, at the time of the conversation?'

'I was in the room.' Clement looked at the woman. 'Very close.' Clement said nothing. 'Standing next to them actually. Overseeing. I'm the manager you see.' Clement nodded and smiled and drew a thick line through all her previous notes. The woman was not to be trusted.

'Do you remember how Mrs Wellby introduced Jane?'

'How do you mean, exactly?'

'What did she call her?' Lynne frowned. 'Daughter, stepdaughter, friend.'

'Oh.' Lynne was thinking hard, the policewoman wouldn't be asking the question if there was not something strange about it. She took pot luck. What damage could it do? She had much more juicy information than that to impart. 'Daughter.'

'You sure about that?'

'Oh yes,' said Lynne, certain she had answered correctly. 'Quite. Of course, I found out soon enough that that was not the case. Jane Wellby had more to watch out for than her weight.' Lynne had been cracking that little joke since the news had broken.

'Would you mind expanding on that.'

'Expanding,' Lynne laughed through her nose, 'good pun.'

Clement clenched her lips into a smile. 'You were saying?'

Well, thought Lynne, if the woman wasn't going to appreciate her humour, was she really the one to divulge her secrets of the Wellbys to? It was such sensitive information. 'What I have to tell you may shock you a great deal, WPC Clement. It is *very* crucial to your case. Shouldn't we go to the station and talk to your boss, Detective Chief Inspector Bramley isn't it? He helped me with a very troublesome neighbour problem.'

'Really.' Clement sighed inwardly, the last thing she could bear was being forced to listen to eulogies of that pig. She took that back, pigs were always getting such a hard time.

'Indian family, always cooking, a constant smell of curry. Turned out the old woman didn't have her correct papers. She got sent home. Thankful for the flight, I should imagine. The others soon followed suit. Marvellous man.'

'Yes, isn't he. What is your address, Ms Reed?'

'Twenty-six Chalk Row. Is that important?'

'Just for the file.' Clement scribbled down the number and made a note to look into Bramley's little eviction order.

Lynne Reed stood up. 'Shall we go then?'

'There's no need, I should be able to get everything I need now.' Lynne sat down reluctantly. 'How did she seem to you – Jane Wellby?'

'Very distressed. The moment her mother, oops, sorry, stepmother,' Clement looked at her pitifully, 'had left and we got Jane talking—'

'Who is we?'

'My associate who signed her up.'

'Can I talk to her?'

'No need, we were both there.'

Clement smiled. 'I'll need to, none the less. Procedure. You see Jane wrote in her diary that she found the whole process of being measured and weighed very humiliating. Is that a fair recollection do you think, Ms Reed?'

Lynne paused for a while.

'. . . If you wouldn't mind just popping in here, we'll take all your measurements in just a jiffy and jot you out a wee chart. That way we can see our goal, Jane, start moving you in the direction of where you want to be. The perfect you.'

'In here?'

'That's right. Just pop your clothes on the chair. I'll be back in just a mo.' Lynne went to fetch her measuring kit. She re-entered the room seconds later to turn up the heating. Lynne took one look at Jane and quickly left the room to fetch her associate. 'Don't know why you took this one on, her figure is fine, nothing more than a little excess flesh. Who does she want to be, Twiggy?' Lynne Reed was a trifle behind the times.

'What do you mean?'

'Come with me. I'll show you.' Lynne and Carla re-entered the room. Jane stood in the middle of the room on a podium they used to do the measuring, her hand on one hip, surrounded by mirrors.

'Jane, dear.' Lynne paused. Embarrassed. She wasn't often confronted with absolute nudity. Jane turned and looked at the two women. Something in the look made Lynne incapable of continuing.

Carla, who boasted a more robust personality, finished for her. 'There is no need to remove all your clothes, Jane. You can put your underwear back on.'

'Oh,' said Jane. Then added in a less patronizing tone, 'I've never done this before.'

'That's okay, dear,' said Lynne, 'everyone is always a bit unsure the first time.'

'Well, Jane,' said Carla, 'doesn't seem like we have much work to do on you, we'll take the measurements, but I can tell from just looking at you that you are carrying very little excess weight. If any.' Jane stared at her blankly as she put one leg through each hole of her knickers, it wasn't until she had fixed her bra strap that her demeanour changed. Suddenly she crumbled before their eyes.

'I told her,' whispered Jane.

'Pardon?' said Lynne.

'She said I had to come here and stand next to the fat people, because that is what I am, fat and ugly.' She started crying immediately. Lynne rushed over to her and let her talk and sob into her shoulder.

'. . . My associate left at some point, I don't think she heard much of Jane's terrible tale. Her stepmother had all but convinced her that she was an ugly, worthless rump. Good for nothing. I suppose she thought we would pander to her and take her on regardless—'

'Which you did.'

'No, well, yes and no, depending on how you look at it. She needed help, that much was obvious, which I think we provided in a friendly ear.'

'I see,' said WPC Clement.

'She made me swear I wouldn't tell anyone.'

'Did you ever think she was in danger?'

'Well, yes and no. Looking back I see she was in mortal danger, tried to tell me on several occasions, but couldn't bring herself to, and no, because I suppose, being in this business you do meet girls who are crying out for attention. Overeating is just one way of showing it. I will never forgive myself,' she whimpered, 'for not heeding that poor child's cry for help.' Clement could almost see the pulpit.

'Try not to upset yourself, Ms Reed. If I could ask you to do something for us,' she paused, dramatically, 'for Jane.' Ms Reed nodded her head vigorously. 'Could you write down everything you remember about what Jane said to you and "pop" it over to the station as soon as you are able.'

'I will not sleep, I will not—'

'Any time in the next day or so will do.'

'Certainly.'

Clement rose to leave. 'Where can I find your associate?'

'Holiday. Two weeks,' she answered quickly.

'I see, and her name?'

Lynne paused. She really did not want anyone butting in on her scene. 'Carla Hammond,' she offered, finally. Carla had an awful grasp of people, she was a terrible judge of character, unlike herself. Lynne watched the policewoman leave, she really should find a way to tell DCI Bramley what happened, he seemed like such a kind, decent man with traditional values and honour, he would certainly take her story seriously. He wouldn't let a woman like Sandie Wellby get away with it. Serve her right for being too bloody perfect. Lynne pulled open her bottom drawer and pulled out a half-eaten packet of biscuits. She broke one in half and popped it in her mouth. 'Mrs Lynne Bramley,' she said, her mouth full of milk-chocolate HobNob.

Chapter Eleven

Cat drove Anna slowly away from Camilla Simpson's house and headed back towards Harlow.

'Well I'm completely confused now,' said Cat.

'Hm,' said Anna absently.

'Are you all right?'

'Yeah, just tired. You know what I think – that they're all in on it. Too busy projecting the image of happy family to even look into trouble at school. That's bollocks. This has got child pornography written all over it. She was probably on drugs too.'

'Surely not, they looked so . . .'

'Reputable? One of their games could've gone wrong, they all panic and shove her in the car, that's why there wasn't a note.'

'That's sick. You've got a sick mind.'

'People *are* sick, Cat. Just because it's a nice middle-class family, doesn't mean it doesn't go on.'

'But Camilla said she wasn't a victim . . .'

Anna wasn't listening. He was back in that room. '. . . *Life is brutal. In here you are at my mercy. You are nothing. No one loves you. No one is coming to help you. You have to be punished. We are going to reduce you to nothing. And when we are finished with you, you'll have a scar so deep you'll never recover. We'll have made you what you are. Your soul belongs to us, your loyalty lies with us, you will never betray us . . .*'

'Anna, are you all right?'

He shook his head. 'Stop the car, I need air.' He opened the passenger door before Cat had even tried to slow down.

'Close the door!' she shouted. 'I'll pull over.' Cat turned into a residential street and braked hard.

'I need air!' Anna could taste the pink fur in his mouth. He jumped out of the car, grabbed a lamppost and clung on to it, sobbing and breathing hard. Cat walked tentatively towards him. She put her hand on his shoulder.

'It's too soon, I feel so sick,' he whispered. 'So sick.'

'Come here,' Cat tried to turn him round.

'Don't touch me. I'm polluted.'

'No you're not.'

'I did this, Cat. I did this to myself.'

'What?'

'I looked up that verse, you know, the one that fat nurse shouted at us, me, rather.'

'And?'

'*No woman shall wear an article of man's clothing, nor shall a man put on woman's dress; for those who do these things are abominable to the Lord your God.'*

Cat looked at her denim-clad legs. 'Looks like we are both heading for a fiery ride,' she said as she put her arms around Anna.

He pushed her away again. 'Leave me alone.'

Cat took his shoulders and shook them gently. 'We'll sort this out, there are people who can help.'

'No.' Anna looked away. He'd fight it, just as soon as he had the strength to do so. 'I can't do this Wellby thing, they are bad people, I can't cope. Sorry.'

'No, I'm sorry, I didn't think it would go into such murky territory.'

'The girl is dead. It was hardly likely to be all roses and light. It's just shit, Cat. The world is a shitty place and shitty things happen. God knows what happened to that girl, she is probably better off dead.'

Cat didn't think he was talking about Jane Wellby any more. 'Anna, don't say that. It isn't true.'

'It'll go on happening, Cat, you're not going to stop it.'

'You could try, Anna.'

'What is that supposed to mean.'

'Nothing.' Cat turned away.

'You think I can go to the police. Cat, you saw me. I went with that kid knowingly. Everyone saw it, I was all over him.'

'That doesn't give him the excuse to—,' Cat couldn't say it, not to his face. 'Never mind.'

'Cat, he didn't rape me.'

'What do you mean?'

'It wasn't him.'

Cat took hold of his shoulders. 'What do you mean?'

He was about to continue when a voice called out in the distance. Neither of them would have taken any notice of it, were it not for the name.

'Jane! Jane Wellby! Cooeee!' Cat looked over to the houses. A woman was approaching them, Cat looked back, there was no one behind them. She turned again, the woman continued to walk towards her smiling and waving. Cat stared at the redhead, then remembered.

'Oh, shit!' she said, turning back to Anna. 'Hide me.'

'Too late,' said Anna.

'It's the hairdresser from the Wellby's house. She thinks I'm Jane.' Anna frowned. 'It's a long story.' Cat looked nervously behind her. 'Shit, I'll have to tell her.'

'She must know that Jane is dead?'

'Jane!?' shouted Suzie, getting closer.

'Then again, maybe not,' he said. 'Cat, if you want to find out more about Sandie Wellby and Jane, you'll be much more productive if she still thinks you are Jane.'

Cat opened her mouth, aghast. 'I can't do that.'

Anna turned her around by the shoulders. 'Do you want to find out the truth or not?'

'But . . .'

'Do you?' She nodded. 'Well then.' Anna gave her a gentle shove.

'Suzie, hi, how are you?' she said in a slightly strangled voice.

'Oh, I'm sorry, not interrupting a lovers' tiff am I?'

'Hayfever,' offered Anna, wiping his eyes from earlier.

'Oh, I've got a lovely aromatherapy oil that can help you with that, why don't you come to the salon, it's just around the corner.' Cat looked at Anna, he gave her a barely perceptible nod.

'Thanks.' They began walking. 'Um, do you work mostly from the salon?'

'Half and half. I like the visits, there is big money in this area, oops, sorry, probably shouldn't say that to you.'

Cat smiled at her. 'I don't mind.'

'And three days in the salon. Couldn't live in London, too big. And all the decent-looking blokes are gay,' she said smiling at Anna. 'That doesn't help a single girl like me much. It suits me here. Now let me see if we have that oil, you put it in the bath, helps you breathe.' She let them into the hair and nails salon. 'It's small, but it's mine.'

'How did you recognize me?' asked Cat.

'The car first. Don't see many bright yellow fiestas, actually I thought you'd be a Clio type,' she giggled. 'Then I saw you hugging this fine-looking man.' Suzie smiled at Anna. 'And I thought, hello, Mrs Wellby never told me about a boyfriend.'

'You obviously talked a lot about me then.'

'Not like *that*, it was all good. You don't mind, do

you? She asked me if I would come and do your hair, she said you didn't seem to like it, can't imagine why,' she said looking at Cat. 'It's beautiful. So dark.'

'Actually I'm going grey.'

'You're not are you?' exclaimed Anna, horrified.

'I've got all sorts of magic potions that can cure a little bit of greyness, let's have a look.' Cat bent her head forward and her dark hair slipped either side of her face. 'It's in clumps, behind the ears.' Anna and Suzie examined her head. It looked like the monkey cage at the zoo.

'Lordy, girl,' said Anna, in a very Anna Prokton way, 'they're everywhere.'

'Hmm,' said Suzie, sounding infinitely more professional. 'I see what Sandie meant about a problem. It's not right at your age.'

'So, what else did my stepmother say?'

'Sweetie, if you are having troubles with your stepmother, I suggest you go talk to her yourself.'

'What makes you think we are having problems?'

Suzie looked confused. 'I don't. She's very fond of you, Jane, you must know that. I know step parents aren't that much fun, but she is a lovely lady, if she wasn't married to your dad, I bet you'd get on like a house on fire.' Cat looked down, thinking about what she should say next. 'Look, love, if Sandie does anything wrong it's because she worries about you. That's all.' Suzie went to a cabinet and chose a selection of hair tonics.

'How do you know all this stuff?'

'I do Sandie's hair once a week, she's stuck in that big house, your father working ridiculous hours, she's probably lonely. A hairdresser's job is only partly about cutting hair. I don't pry, but I'll listen.'

'You're right, sorry, didn't mean to be impertinent.'

'That's all right, love, my skin is thicker than that.' Anna grinned at Cat. Anna Prokton would have had something to say to that, but without the togs he didn't feel up to it. He was beginning to quite like Andrew, soft and sensitive type . . . 'Now you say this gorgeous-looking bloke isn't a boyfriend,' she said, looking straight at Anna.

'Um.' Anna shot Cat a look. 'No. He's not.'

'You wouldn't mind if I asked him out for a drink myself then would you?' she said, still looking at Anna.

'Be my guest, Suzie, be my guest.' If Suzie had taken her predatory eyes off Anna for one second, he would have given Cat the finger. Instead he smiled and watched Cat nearly wet herself behind Suzie.

'So how about it, big boy?'

Anna nearly choked. 'I, well, I'm not really up to a relationship at the moment.'

'Sweetie, who said anything about a relationship?'

'Suzie?' It was Cat, realizing she should rescue Anna from the rampant redhead.

'Hmmm,' said Suzie, still not turning round.

'Why did Sandie cancel her hair appointment on Friday?'

'You should know, darling,' said Suzie turning finally. 'You're the one who phoned and cancelled it.'

FIONA DROPPED HER BAG and linen jacket on the floor, kicked the front door behind her, and walked slowly along the narrow hallway. It had taken her days to get home. Robert was a mess, the police wanted to know everything they had ever done, anything that Sandie and Jane had done together, they wanted evidence that would back up the words of the diary. *Surely you must have noticed something*, that is what DCI Bramley had said to her. *Something? Anything?* At the bottom of the stairs, she looked up, waited for a moment and then entered the kitchen. She was still expecting Jane to appear. Explain the diary. Tell everyone it was a joke, a project. Something. Anything. How could she not have seen it? There were twenty-one messages on the answering machine, she'd been away four days, word was out, the jungle drums had been beating. Fiona couldn't be bothered to listen to any of them; she went straight to the coffee percolator. She spooned the last of the coffee into the filter, filled the machine with water and waited for the comforting gurgles to fill the room. She couldn't remember when she had last done something normal, like shop. Valium clouds were still drifting around her head, she had lost her grasp of time. Before the arrest Sandie had given her a vast quantity of pills, she could barely remember what had happened on what day. Had that too been part of Sandie's plan, to keep her asleep and unobservant, so soporific that she wouldn't ask too many questions regarding the death of her child. Like, how did she get that bruise? Or, where the fuck were you while she was choking to death? She watched the coffee pot fill impatiently, needing the caffeine like an addict. She took a cup from the cupboard and pulled the jug out to pour what was in there into her mug. Percolating coffee dripped on to the hot metal plate below. It hissed. Fiona got an irresistible urge to put her hand on it and push down so hard that her hand melted away. She couldn't imagine what it would feel like, but she wanted to know, her hand edged towards the heat, it hovered there, the temptation growing. What was she doing? She replaced the jug quickly. Her mind was playing tricks on her. It had happened as she drove back from Cedar Hall, the central reservation had looked so inviting. To turn the wheel, to feel the impact . . . She'd pulled away from it instead and had driven home in the slow lane trying to ignore the irresistible urge to inflict upon herself a more tangible pain than the one that was consuming her soul. The coffee was thick and strong, she sat at her table, wrapped her hands around the china and sipped incessantly. She thought about Jane, about Sandie and Robert, trying to remember something, anything that would give her a clue as to what was going on.

'I thought I'd ring this morning and wish you happy Easter, we'll be on the mountain most of the day.'
'Mum! Great to hear your voice, how's the snow?'

'Perfect, the sun is out, and I already look like a strange inverted panda. How is everyone at Cedars?'

'Dad is really well. Looking very handsome, he's lost some weight.'

'Sandie is doing a good job then.' Fiona was laughing.

'He's done it by himself actually. Everything all right with the skiing party?'

'Oh, yes, but our girly holiday seems to have been thwarted by the appearance of Jo Attlewood and his brother's family. Remember him? We were good friends a long time ago, he's been living in Argentina.'

'No.'

'Yes you do, tall, rather handsome actually, took us sailing on the Solent one summer.'

'Oh yes. I remember. Drip. Never liked him. Sailing's boring.'

Fiona paused. 'Oh, well, he's going tomorrow.'

'I'd like to go skiing with you. Maybe Dad could come along.'

'Sandie is the one you want, her skiing is the best.'

'No I don't.'

'Are you all right, darling?'

'Yes, fine, I just don't see why everyone thinks Sandie is so good at everything.'

'You and I can organize a trip for next year then, darling, how about that? You can bring a friend.'

'Great. Dad has just come in, he is waving at you, sends his love. We miss you. Easter isn't the same without you.'

'Can I have a word with your father?'

'He's rushing out, sorry, he's just gone. Golf.'

'Now that *is* boring.'

'He only plays when he wants to get out. Know what I mean?'

'Sure. I've got to go, the girls are waiting.'

'Bye, take care.'

'You too, send my love to Robert and—'

'Sure will. Bye, Mum.'

Fiona snapped out of the daydream at the sound of her front door closing. She stared wide-eyed for a moment, listening to the footfalls on the floorboards. Her stomach tightened with nerves.

'Jane?' She called out tentatively.

'Ola, Meeses Wellby.'

Fiona bit her bottom lip hard and swallowed the disappointment. Would this ever pass? 'Rosa,' she said, and waited for the short, portly woman to enter the room.

'Meeses Wellby, you not well?'

'Sit down, Rosa, I have some terrible news to tell you.' The Spanish lady crossed herself and sat down. She took Fiona's hand instinctively. Fiona couldn't speak, the words stuck painfully in her throat.

'Jane—' Fiona swallowed, trying to keep a lid on her emotions. She couldn't even tell her cleaning lady, how the hell she was going to cope with the rest of the world.

'Jane?' repeated Rosa. Fiona nodded. 'She is ill?' Fiona bit down on her lip hard and shook her head slowly from side to side. Rosa crossed herself again. 'Sweet Jesus. She is going to be all right?' Fiona shook her head faster, large tears dropping on to her lap.

'Oh no,' Rosa's fat hands went to her mouth, she prayed silently for a couple of seconds then leant forward, gathered Fiona into her arms and let her cry into her shoulder.

'She is at peace, Meeses Wellby. The Lord will protect her now.'

Fiona pulled away and looked straight at the woman. 'But he didn't, did he, and nor did I.'

Rosa frowned. 'Meeses Wellby, you are excellent mother. She was not easy, you couldn't watch her all the time.'

'You don't understand, she was killed, murdered.'

Rosa crossed herself. 'Go upstairs, you need rest. I will bring fresh coffee. You lie down.'

Exhaustion enveloped her like a lead suit, Rosa was right, she needed rest. Get control. At the kitchen door she turned. 'But the police are coming, they need to see Jane's room . . .'

Rosa crossed herself again.

'What is it, Rosa?'

'I . . . I . . .'

'What?'

'I tidied it. I'm sorry . . .'

Fiona held on to the wooden door frame. '*You* tidied it?'

'I'm so sorry, Meeses Wellby, I was only trying—'

'Was it a mess?'

Rosa hesitated, she didn't want to get Jane into trouble, but she wouldn't lie. 'Was why I tidied. It was a very big mess.'

'Oh God.' Fiona's knees began to buckle. Rosa ran to her as she slipped on to the floor.

'I'm sorry . . .'

Fiona clutched her stomach and wailed. Rosa pulled a rosary from around her neck and started repeating the Hail Mary.

AMELIA PLACED THE DAFFODILS into a vase and smiled. The phone rang.

'I've only just got back,' she said immediately.

'From where?'

'Oh sorry, darling, I thought you were someone else.'

'Really, something you want to tell me?'

'No. How did it go with Camilla Simpson?'

'You know her father fancies you.'

Amelia looked at the rich yellow flowers. 'Tell me something I don't know.'

'Gran, a little modesty please.'

'He drools every time I go near him.'

'If you are using dribbling as a benchmark, the entire population at Heaven's Gate has hot pants for you.'

'I said drool not dribble.'

'Same difference.'

'Entirely different consistency.' Amelia was chuckling.

'I think you are getting worse.'

'I like to think of it as improving with age. Like a fine wine. Talking of which, how are the plans for Paris coming along?'

'I'd like to go and check out this language school. I mean if Jane was being abused at home, why go back early, it doesn't make sense. The trouble is, I don't think Anna is up to going and Dan and I have had a fight. We don't seem to be talking at the moment.'

'Well for heaven's sake, sort it out, I'm seventy-seven next year. I'll be talking the same language as my great-grandchildren by the time they're born.'

'I thought I'd break the Torrant family tradition and have a child *in* wedlock.'

'Did I bring you up to be this cheeky?'

'Actually—'

'That was a rhetorical question, young lady. Anyway, I didn't think you were the marrying sort.'

'I'm not.'

Amelia whistled. 'Which puts you in a slight muddle, doesn't it?'

'Gran, shut up.'

'Charming, and there was I about to offer you a Parisian weekend break.'

'We can't afford it.'

Amelia's wicked laugh tinkled down the phone. Cat feared that laughter. 'What have you done?'

'A terrible thing.'

'Not your diamond brooch, I told you—'

'Worse.'

'You haven't started selling off parts of your anatomy?'

'I couldn't give them away. No, I've transferred all the money from your mother's deposit account into mine.'

'You haven't.'

'She hasn't used it for years, it is just sitting there. The next time she comes over to England it will probably be for my funeral, if she bothers, and it'll be too late by then.'

'How on earth did you do it?' Cat didn't know whether to be angry or impressed.

'I was the one who set it up, I've got all the numbers and they ask such silly questions. Date of birth, not something I am likely to forget, mother's maiden name, I mean please, and when did I last use the account. Easy, she was last here four years ago.'

'You are wicked.'

'I like to think of it as—'

'Gran, how much?'

'Tuppence.'

'Gran?'

'Enough for four Eurostar tickets and a bowl of moules marinière.'

'Gran?'

'Seven hundred and forty-three pounds and eighty-one pence. We lost three months' interest because I didn't give them notice.'

'Well,' said Cat after a moment's thought, 'it's probably high time my mother took us on holiday.'

'I don't have to put it back?'

'Nope. You are absolutely right, it will do us all the world of good.'

'Olé!'

'That's Spanish.'

'Same difference.'

'I hardly think the French would agree.'

Chapter Twelve

WPC Clement walked up the street looking for the salon. She looked at her watch nervously, if she hurried, there would be time. Bramley had sent her off to do a routine check into a garage suspected of handling stolen cars. One not very tall policewoman and seven lads stripped naked to the waist, coated in engine grease and impertinence. Life was too short, she decided, as she headed off in the opposite direction. She'd tell Bramley the garage was shut. Clement reached the salon. It was 'closed' according to the black and gold sign on the door, but she could see someone moving about inside. This was obviously not a beauty salon for working women, it opened at ten and closed at five-thirty. WPC Clement sighed, chance would be a fine thing. She tapped lightly on the door. The redhead turned, pointed to her watch and shrugged. She tapped again, this time holding her badge up to the glass door. Suzie frowned and stepped tentatively towards her.

'Yes?'

'I'd like to come in and ask you some questions, just routine.'

'*I* haven't done nothing.'

'I know that, it is regarding a client of yours.' Suzie nodded and opened the door wider. Clement entered and was immediately struck by the pungent smell of chemicals and hairspray. She sneezed.

'Bless you. I've just put the kettle on, do you want a cup?'

'Thanks.'

Suzie busied herself making tea. 'It's that Mrs Baker. I told her not to have the Auburn Rose, wouldn't suit a woman of her years, but oh no, she insisted, and then screams blue murder when she ends up looking like a summer pudding—'

'It's not Mrs Baker.'

'Oh,' Suzie frowned again. 'Well then,' she said, passing Clement the tea and sitting down, 'who?'

The policewoman paused for effect. Suzie thought she might have forgotten.

'Mrs Wellby.'

'Sandie,' exclaimed Suzie affectionately, 'never given her the blue rinse, if you know what I mean.' Clement did not.

'Did you know she has been taken in for questioning?'

'Who by?' Suzie was obviously two curls short of a perm.

'The police. In connection with the death of her stepdaughter.'

Suzie sprung out of her chair, knocking it over and dropping her tea. 'You having me on?' Oblivious to the scalding wet patch on her skirt. 'Jane? Jane Wellby? Oh my God.' Long red fingernails clawed at her face. 'That's terrible.'

'You didn't know?' said Clement, crouched on all fours trying to contain the puddle of tea.

'How could *I* have known? Jane, dead, Lord have mercy.'

'Why don't you sit down.' Clement picked up the chair with one hand, carried it over her head in an arc and placed it safely down on dry ground.

Suzie stared blankly at the wall, then shook her head. 'Strange. I mean it feels like I was talking to her five minutes ago.'

'Death in these circumstances is always a shock.'

'What circumstances?'

'Did you not read about it in the paper?'

'What paper?'

WPC Clement shook her head. 'Doesn't matter.'

'Dead, and to think, all this and I never managed to do her hair.'

'Jane's?' Asked WPC Clement frowning.

'Hers as well, yeah, oh, she won't like all that attention with her hair not being right. You know I thought Jane was acting a bit strange like, how did you say she died?'

'I didn't.' Clement didn't know who was more confused.

'Oh. Sandie always wanted me to do Jane's hair, said it was pretty dry and horrible. Must say, I was a bit surprised when I saw her, I mean her hair was beautiful, wasn't it? All that long dark hair.'

WPC Clement had been to the morgue. She frowned. 'Are you sure you are talking about Jane Wellby?'

'Course I'm sure, she was in here asking me questions about Sandie. I said to her, if you are having problems with your stepmother, then you should talk to Sandie yourself.'

'What sort of problems?' asked WPC Clement, quickly opening her notebook.

'She didn't say.' Suzie sighed. 'I can't believe it, it was only yesterday.'

'It seems like that sometimes,' said WPC Clement kindly. Her words did not seem to have the desired effect, Suzie looked increasingly baffled. The police-woman was beginning to feel foolish for coming to the salon. The hairdresser could obviously tell her nothing about the accused except her favourite shampoo.

'Was she a good customer?' she asked, wanting to end the chat politely, give in and go to the garage.

'Sandie? Oh yes, the very best. Always polite and charming – tipped the girls who washed. She'll tell the police everything she can to help find out what happened to Jane. You can be sure of that. What did happen to her by the way?'

'She was found, asphyxiated in her father's car.'

'No! Lock herself in did she, by accident?'

WPC Clement was amazed by how little the woman knew. 'Actually, it *looked* like she did it on purpose.' Suzie frowned. 'She killed herself, or so it seemed.'

'You having me on? Topped herself?' Clement nodded. 'Jane Wellby?' Clement nodded again. 'No way. Excuse me, but I don't for one minute believe you.'

'Why not?'

'Because there was nothing wrong with her. Perfectly happy when I saw her, had a bloke and everything, whizzing about in her car.'

'A man? What did he look like?'

'Tall, good-looking, she said there was nothing going on, but I saw them clinging on to each other like their life depended on it. Maybe he chucked her?'

'Let's not jump to conclusions,' said Clement. 'How old was this man?'

'Difficult to tell, he had good skin, lovely blue eyes. Somewhere between thirty and forty.' Suzie frowned again. 'Surely she wouldn't have killed herself over him. It must have been an accident.'

'Actually, what is more likely is that someone else killed her and made it look like suicide.'

Suzie stared at the policewoman. 'Murder?' she said, after several seconds.

'I'm afraid so.'

'My God, you ain't safe these days, could've been a burglar or a random madman. I tell you, it's not safe these days—'

'Suzie, I'm sorry to have to tell you this, but it is Sandie Wellby who is being questioned in connection with Jane's death.'

'Well she would, like a mother to that girl she was.'

'I mean in connection to how she died.' Suzie stared at her. WPC Clement tried to read her expression. There was none. Suzie left her with no alternative than to be blunt. 'Sandie Wellby has been arrested for the murder of her stepdaughter Jane.' Surely there was no room for incomprehension this time, but still Suzie's response surprised the policewoman.

'You must be mad,' exclaimed Suzie, 'that woman wouldn't even use hair dye.'

WPC CLEMENT WAS IN a quandary. Suzie had seen Jane with a man. That threw open the field of the investigation but Bramley only wanted to narrow it. There was no mention of a boyfriend in the diary, in fact she'd stated she had no friends because her confidence was so low. Bramley would rip Suzie to pieces. With little up top but follicles, Suzie wouldn't last a minute. Then Bramley would punish her for not going to the garage. She could predict his well-aimed jocular digs. A hairdresser isn't going to improve *your* looks. Ha bloody ha. She'd be back to square one. It probably wasn't worth it. Clement marched towards her car. If she had long, tanned legs and the brain the size of a pea Bramley would probably like her more. If she had Sandie Wellby's enviable cleavage, breasts fifteen years older than her own but more gravity defying than Clement's had ever been, would men have fallen at her feet instead of falling over themselves to get away from her? She was tired of dragging her confidence up from around her ankles and forcing it to stay up. She envied the Cat Torrants of this world, bright, beautiful, intelligent, long dark— WPC Clement stopped walking. She turned slowly and looked back to where she had walked from. Hair like that was memorable, it made an impression, it stole the show. Almost. Clement began walking back to the salon. She bet the usual. The hair so described by Suzie belonged not to the poor bullied and beleaguered brunette, now lying on a slab, a line of aluminium staples down her chest holding together the seam left by the pathologist's knife, but to Cat Torrant. The girl with no dead dog, no alibi and an unfortunate habit of turning up in places she didn't belong.

WHEN WPC CLEMENT RE-ENTERED the door to the salon, Suzie was painting her nails black. A sign of respect, she said.

'I've cancelled all my appointments for today,' she said to the policewoman.

'I'm sorry to hassle you like this, but I need to ask you a few more questions.'

'Yeah?'

'You said that Jane had long black hair.'

'That's right, to about here.' Suzie pointed to halfway down her upper arm. 'Beautiful. Can't understand why she hated it so.'

'She told you that.'

'Nah, Sandie did. She certainly thought Jane hated her hair.'

'What else do you remember about her, Jane?'

'My height.'

'Five foot nine, ten?' said Clement, looking Suzie up and down.

'Sadly not in real life, it's the shoes. That's what the beauty trade is all about, creating illusions.' Suzie smiled at her own wisdom. 'I'm pretty small in real life.'

Clement looked down. The shoes that donned the redhead's feet were more scaffolding than footwear, WPC Clement's heart sank, four-inch heels. And some. Jane was five foot five. Suzie's height, minus the heels. Cat was the tall one. Another pizza melted away.

'Course I'm talking about in me heels. Jane was the same height as me in me heels. No one ever sees me without them.' She smiled, suggestively. 'Ever.'

'Was Jane wearing them, high heels?'

'Nah. More of a jeans and T-shirt girl, well that's what she was wearing yesterday.'

'Yesterday?'

'Yeah, like I said, it was only yesterday.'

WPC Clement smiled. Deep Pan. Cat Torrant had

been impersonating a dead girl. Hardly the impartial act of an accidental pet killer. One large pizza coming up. 'Suzie, will you come to the police station with me. I need to show you some photographs.'

'Styling like?'

'No. Not really. I'll explain on the way.' WPC Clement put her arm around Suzie's shoulder and led her towards the door, picking up the hairdresser's keys for her and passing them over.

'Oi. Mind me nails.'

THE GARDENER READ THE note. That girl had been a bitch to him. He had watched her cause trouble for all the years he'd worked for the Wellbys and managed to stay out of it. Now this. Mr Wellby didn't want staff in the house, not even the daily was allowed in, Mrs Wellby had made that very clear before she got carted off. Mr Wellby was mourning, she said, and he had a lot of work to do. Well Sam Clough could see right into his study from the garden, and Mr Wellby had very clearly been doing neither. He stared at the wishy-washy writing on the crumpled piece of paper and cursed himself silently for choosing that day of all days to clear out the guttering around the courtyard. If only he had stuck to mowing the lawn, he would not be faced with the prospect of having to go in and talk to the man. He reread the few, deliberate words and realized he had no choice. Sam entered Cedar Hall through the kitchen door. He scraped his boots on the metal rack obsessively, then stepped cautiously into the sunlit room. He shivered. He would hand the note over and go straight back to the garden. That way he would bring as little attention to himself as possible. Mr Wellby would do the right thing with it. He hoped. Sam Clough's knowledge of the interior of the house had been amassed from looking in. Mr Wellby's study was the first bay window above the herbaceous border on the left of the French windows, overlooking the largest of the three cedar trees. He stood outside the door and knocked.

'Come in.' Robert replaced the phone and turned around. For a moment he thought it was Simon. He had hoped his old friend would return, look him in the eye, and deny the accusations.

'Sorry to bother you, Mr Wellby.'

'What is it?'

'I found this in the drains in the courtyard.' Robert Wellby frowned. Was his wife's absence going to mean dealing with household queries as well as an empty bed, dinner for one, silence and solitude? He'd have to sack him. And the woman. They'd freeze Sandie's assets soon enough. Then he'd have to follow suit. No one would believe that he didn't know what was going on, he'd be as condemned as his wife. Everything he'd been trying to hold together was falling apart.

'Mr Wellby?'

'What?'

'It was next to your garage, sir.' He continued to hold the piece of paper out to Robert.

Robert looked at it for the first time. 'What did you say?'

'It's a note. I think you should read it.' Robert was out of his chair and grabbing at Sam's hand before the words were out of his mouth.

'Jesus, man, why didn't you say!' He cupped his hand around the paper as though it might disintegrate before his very eyes and stared at the rain-washed writing. Sam Clough watched him take three steps towards his desk, place the paper down, splay his large hands either side of it and lean right over. The gardener lowered his gaze and waited to be dismissed. He didn't see Robert charge at him. Suddenly Sam Clough found himself with two feet clear off the ground, encircled by his employer's arms.

'Oh God!' cried Robert, tears still on his face. 'Thank you.'

One of Sam's wellies was slipping off his foot. He hadn't wanted thanks, attention. He had just wanted Robert Wellby to do what was right for once.

'How can I ever thank you?' he was shouting in Sam Clough's ear. Sam moved his head away, fearful that the noise would set off his tinnitus again. Robert lowered the gardener back to the ground. 'I'll get her back, Mr Clough. With this.'

DARREN WHITE DEPOSITED THE pay packet in his bank account. Who'd have thought he would ever have a bank account. He walked away from the Barclays Bank in Soho Square with a swagger. He was going places. Hardly the average corporate ladder route, but at least he was moving in a direction that was different to the one he'd been going in all his shitty little life. Hell bound. Now he had a job, not one he'd be informing the social securities about of course, but it was a job. He passed a scabby girl sitting under a cash-point machine. *Spare any change?* To pay the fucker who controls this patch, you've got to be kidding. He walked past her. She wouldn't last long on the streets if she'd got herself into that mess. A junkie *and* beholden to a turf deal, she'd never get to keep enough of the money she begged to buy herself decent dope, she'd be on the meths and glue before the summer was out. And she'd be dead before winter. Or worse. He'd watched them come and go for years. He had a habit, yes, but it was a good one. His boss got him quality gear. Christ, he deserved the odd perk, it wasn't like his life had been a long line of merry moments. Darren kicked an empty beer can. He didn't want to think about that. His family had cursed him. He could never be good, but he could be better and he didn't have to be like them. He'd keep doing what he was doing until he had enough money in that sweet little bank account of his and then he'd buy himself a ticket and get the fuck out of this sordid city. Did he have a guilty conscience about what he did? Answer the question with a question Darren. Did they have a guilty conscience about what they did? Did his sweet, caring mother have a guilty conscience about what she did? Did her clients have a guilty conscience about what they did? Did the authorities have a guilty conscience about what they'd done? *No.* They didn't. So why the fuck should he?

Chapter Thirteen

Simon sat in his car in the police station's car park. He'd been there twenty minutes now and had not moved a muscle. How could he go and see her and bring no news of her husband? But how could he tell her the truth? They'd been friends back in LA when he had unsuccessfully tried to act. Sandie had always helped him out and this was how he was repaying her. Deserting her. Simon put his hand on the key and turned it, the well-tuned engine sprung obediently to life. He slid the gearstick left and down. To R. He would reverse out of there and pretend he'd never been. Simon stared at the gearstick. R for run rabbit, run rabbit, run, run, run. He was a coward. R for renounce. He'd never get away with it. R for retribution. Sandie would have been expecting at least one of them to come, and neither himself nor Robert could face it. R for rebuff. Whoever said men were cowards was correct. Uncomfortably correct. R for fucking pathetic. Simon squeezed the steering wheel until his nails dug painfully into his palms. Eight half moons etched into his flesh. The pain did little to relieve his self-loathing. He could no more face Sandie than himself. All he had to do was bring his foot off the clutch, roll backwards from the building and away from responsibility. Simon clutched the wheel and closed his eyes. His left leg had turned to cement, his knee locked in position. A brittle noise clipped above his head, he looked up startled and saw black talons tapping out his treacherous act on the windscreen, followed by red flaming tendrils swooping down on him ready to take him to the fires of hell. To punish him for his sins.

'Wotcha, Si.' Suzie smiled at him through the glass.

Simon was so stunned by the image his foot jerked off the clutch; the car lunged backwards, shuddered and stalled. The red lights on the dashboard glared angrily at him, but he didn't need modern technology to alert him; the thud had been enough. Simon staggered out of the car and clambered around to the boot where WPC Clement lay on the ground, her face sheet-white, clutching her knee. He remembered her from the day of Jane's death, not a very tall girl. Knee-high to a bumper. The sudden impact from the lurch of the stalling Mercedes Estate had forced WPC Clement's left kneecap back into itself. He could actually see the knee swell before his very eyes. The poor girl looked in agony, but the only clamour of anguish came from Suzie. Simon took off his jacket and placed it under Clement's foot. He had read somewhere that elevation was good, but it could have been architectural advice in a building manual. The poor girl hadn't said anything.

'Suzie, for God's sake, call for an ambulance, get help.'

He crouched down next to WPC Clement and took her hand. 'I am so sorry, I don't know what I was thinking. I can't believe I was so stupid.'

He looked around the empty car park. 'Someone help here!'

Suzie returned with Bramley.

'What have you done, Clement?'

Clement's fingers tightened around Simon's hand. He looked down at her. She smiled at him. It was a covert smile. Simon squeezed back.

'Where the bloody hell have you been all morning? I asked you to go and have a look at the garage, not have a service.'

'This poor thing is lying on the ground because I nearly ran her over.'

'Oh, it's you, Mr Proudlove,' said Bramley, peering down his nose. 'You know I can see the car park from my office.'

'Really,' replied Simon. 'Where's the ambulance?'

'Yes really. You drove in here, sat in your car for a good fifteen minutes and then you reverse out again. You weren't looking very happy, Mr Proudlove, and happy is the man who does *not* take the wicked for his guide – got something on your mind you'd like to tell me about?'

Simon stood up slowly. He was closer to forty than he ever imagined being, but he was a fit man, and he was tall. He looked like an athlete compared to Bramley. Simon did not try and hide his loathing of the policeman.

'I could have killed this young woman and all you are interested in is asking questions about my sex life. Not quite the decency one would hope to expect from a police officer, is it?'

Bramley smiled triumphantly. 'I hardly think decency is a subject you would be happy to delve too deeply into at present.'

'And what,' said Simon, beginning to lose his temper, 'is that supposed to mean?'

Bramley almost winked at him. 'I think you probably know exactly what I mean.' The two men stared at each other.

'Excuse me?'

Simon turned and looked down at Clement. He knelt back down.

'I think I'm going to pass out,' whispered Clement through gritted teeth.

'Christ,' shouted Bramley, 'and all over a bit of a bruise and, don't tell me, that time of the month which she has at least twice a month.'

'I'll go and get some ice and find out where that ambulance is,' said Suzie, not enjoying the floorshow. Bramley watched her as she walked away from them. 'Quite a girl.' He turned back to Clement. 'For heaven's sake, get up.'

'Surely she shouldn't stand.'

'Mr Proudlove, I think we have more important things to discuss. Follow me please, and Clement, though I'm sure it is a favoured position of yours, lying on your back with your legs spread is not the sort of image I like my officers to portray to the world. You *will* get up. And that is an order.'

'Jesus Christ, man—'

Bramley pointed his finger at Simon. 'You are in no position, none at all, to judge. If I were you I'd keep my eyes down, my mouth shut and hope that the DCI is in a forgiving mood. Right, let's get moving.' Bramley started walking off in the direction of the station house. Clement stretched out an arm to Simon.

'I really don't think you should move.'

'I'm going to get up on to my feet if it kills me.'

Simon laughed. 'You remind me of someone.'

'Don't tell me, your mother.'

'Oh no, she was a timid little thing. Gentle.'

'I'm not sure I like where this is going.' She was smiling, but Simon could see the pain through it.

'Why don't you wait until the ambulance gets here.'

'And risk Bramley standing over me again? No way.'

'Come on then,' he put his hands under her arms and eased her up off the ground. She paled further.

'It's dislocated, I can feel it.' Clement swallowed the desire to cry.

'I'm so sorry.'

'It was an accident.' She was upright now, balancing on one leg. 'Christ Almighty!'

'What?' exclaimed Simon.

'What the hell is *she* doing here?'

Simon looked in the direction of the car park entrance. A yellow Ford Fiesta pulled in off the road. 'What about her?'

'Where the hell has Suzie gone?'

'Are you all right? I think you might be suffering from delayed shock.'

'Suzie!' cried Clement, not listening to Simon.

'I need help here!' shouted Simon to the array of cars. 'Hello!?' Clement seemed to be getting heavier in his arms. He looked down at her. Her eyelids were flickering up and down, every time they opened more of her brown iris disappeared back into her skull. Simon shook her.

'Stay with me, come on.'

She opened her eyes one more time. 'You see, long black hair.' Then she passed out completely. Cat climbed out of her car to see WPC Clement collapse on to Simon Proudlove. She almost brought him down with her. Cat ran over. Simon stared at her suspiciously, as far as he could work out everything would have been fine if it wasn't for her.

'What's happened?' asked Cat as she ran towards them.

'Why do you care?'

'Excuse me?' said Cat, then realized he had been at Cedar Hall the day she had found Jane. 'Oh,' she said.

'Oh indeed. What are you up to, why are you always here?'

'What?'

'Go and get some help, or go away, I don't want to speak to you.' Cat didn't move. 'Go!'

'What?'

'Just go.'

Cat moved backwards. 'I'll get some help.' Simon didn't answer her. Cat saw the side door and ran straight to it, went down a long dark corridor and finally found the reception. The only people in it were two old men.

'Excuse me?' said one of them.

Cat looked over. He was pushing an old Victorian-style pram. She frowned.

'Can you help me?'

'With the baby?'

'Oh no, it isn't a baby.'

'Look I can't, I'm—'

'The other man just left us, went off with some pretty girl. It's disgraceful.'

'I'm not actually the police. I think you'd better wait.'

'Who are you then?'

'Catherine Amelia Torrant.' Cat turned round at the sound of her name. Bramley stood in the doorway she'd come through.

'Detective Chief Inspector, how nice to see you

again.' He beckoned her over. Cat sighed, all she had wanted was a quiet word with the policewoman. 'This saves me a journey to London. Would you mind waiting in interview room one, you should remember the way,' he said condescendingly. 'There are some questions I would like to ask you, it's regarding the—'

'Thanks, I think I can guess.'

He held the door open. 'This way.' Cat re-entered the hallway and let herself into the interview room.

'Where the bloody hell is the duty officer?' asked Bramley.

'He went outside.'

Bramley looked at the old men with recognizable disrespect. 'What?' he said rudely.

'And the other one went off with some lady. I suppose you can help us?' He began to lift something out of the pram.

'Who left you in charge of a baby?'

'Oh no,' said the old man playfully, 'it's not a baby.'

'Thank God,' said Bramley. Dead babies were not good for PR. He disappeared after Cat.

The two old men looked at each other and shrugged.

SIMON WAS GETTING CRAMP in his leg. WPC Clement was still away with the fairies, and that bloody girl had not come back. When he heard a vehicle turn violently into the police station, he thought that the ambulance had come at last. He couldn't turn round for fear of dropping Clement. But he waited for a reassuring hand on his shoulder, and the reassuring thud of the paramedics bag landing at his feet. He got neither.

'Simon! Simon! Everything is going to be all right. I've got the answer. I can prove Sandie had nothing to do with it. Nothing. Look.' Robert Wellby ran towards his friend holding up a scrappy piece of paper. Simon could not turn round to look at it and had absolutely no idea what Robert was babbling about. 'Please don't be cross with me,' Robert continued, 'I'm sorry, about what I said. I didn't mean it, I was just angry.' He walked round to face Simon. As yet, he had made no reference to the girl slumped in his arms. 'She left a note. I'm going to get her now.' Then Robert ran off. First Bramley, then Cat Torrant and now Robert. So much for third time lucky. The pins and needles were spreading.

'I WANT TO SEE my wife. I insist on seeing my wife. Where is Bramley?'

One of the two old gents said quietly. 'There is a queue.' Wellby stared at the men for a few moments, then looked back at the empty desk.

'Hello? Hello?' Robert leant over the counter. 'Sandie!' he called. 'Sandie!'

Bramley re-entered the waiting room. 'What the hell— Oh, Mr Wellby, I suggest you come with me. I've discovered some things I think you should know.'

'No, I've got something you need to know. We were wrong, about the diary.'

'Really?' he said, not attempting to hide the sarcasm. 'Let's go through, shall we?'

'Excuse me?'

'What!' Bramley turned towards the old man.

'I was wondering whether we could see the man in charge?' Bramley looked at them as though for the first time. They looked the grumbling types.

'No.' He marched out after Robert Wellby.

SIMON WATCHED THE AMBULANCE take WPC Clement away. She hadn't regained consciousness and Simon was gripped with the fear that the external injury was there just to hide the potentially fatal injury that continued to bleed unchecked inside. Skin, disguising the damage within. The devil within. Recently Simon had been plagued with a need to believe. To believe that all this added up to something bigger than the separate components. He had turned to God and God had pointed to the Bible, and the Bible had condemned him before he had reached the end of Genesis. He walked slowly to the building. He could hear the shouting before he had climbed the outside stairs. He walked into the reception area and straight to the side door.

'You can't go in there,' said one of the elderly gentlemen.

'Watch me.'

At the end of the long corridor was Sandie, led by the Custody Officer. His stomach tightened. She looked amazing. There was not a scrap of make-up on her face, her hair was pulled back and the expensive baubles that usually adorned her throat and fingers were gone. Nothing sparkled, yet she seemed more precious at that moment than she had ever been. He did not notice Robert watching him. Nor Bramley watching Robert watching Simon as he stared at Sandie. Bramley was the only one with a smile on his face.

CAT WATCHED FROM A crack in the door of interview room one. Sandie Wellby had been arrested and it was purely her fault.

ROBERT TURNED TO HIS wife. 'My love,' he said, 'everything is going to be fine. I'm taking you home.' Sandie looked confused. That was not what she had been told. 'Take those things off her,' said Robert pointing at the handcuffs.

'I'm afraid I cannot do that, Mr Wellby.'

'She wrote a note, what more do you want?'

'A note?' It was Simon.

Sandie hadn't been able to see him, standing at the dark end of the corridor. 'Simon, is that you?'

'I'm here.'

'You were supposed to come earlier, what kept you?'

Simon remembered sitting in the car. 'Um, things got suddenly busy in the office, that's all.' Bramley raised an eyebrow.

'You mean we still have customers?' asked Sandie. 'I thought ostracism would be official by now.'

'Oh no, nearly all the clients have rung to give their support.' This was an even greater lie than the one before. Sandie smiled. *Thank you.*

'Anyway,' said Robert, 'none of that matters, you'll be talking to them yourself soon enough.'

'As I said, Mr Wellby, I don't think that will be possible.'

'Why not, you took her away and I let you and now I'm telling you to let her go.' He turned back to Sandie, still standing at the top of the corridor. 'Please forgive me, I can't stand it without you. Say you'll forgive me.'

Pain and betrayal pinched Sandie's vocal cords. She had imagined this scene over and over during the last forty-eight hours, her plea of innocence, the words that would strike his heart and unite them again. He was the only one who could release her. Without him she didn't stand a chance.

'Please, Sandie, please. I was paralysed by Jane's death, incapable of thought, I was prepared to believe anything that anyone told me. God, Sandie, I'm so sorry. Jesus, my daughter kills herself and I refused to see that anything was wrong, you tried to tell me, that whole business with Calorie Carers, I see that now, I see that. But she wrote a note, my love, she wrote a note.'

'Mr Wellby,' said Bramley, 'I think we better take a look at that note.'

'Do you forgive me?' Robert Wellby's voice was near

breaking point. 'Please, Sandie.' He broke past Bramley, and ran up the corridor to his wife. For a moment the Custody Officer thought about performing a neat kick-boxing movement, to stop him getting to his goal, but as he approached she softened – this was better than any bodice ripper.

THROUGH THE CRACK IN the door Cat could see the back of Simon's head, Bramley's profile and Sandie and Robert at the opposite end of the corridor, embracing. It was the sort of hug people gave each other at the airport. The heart is full of love, the head is full of images of twisted burning metal as the plane plummets 30,000 feet to the ground. Hold tight it might be the last.

'ABOUT THAT NOTE?' SAID Bramley as he approached the clutching couple. Robert reached into his jacket pocket and stretched his hand behind him. Sandie did not look up and Robert did not turn around. Bramley brought the piece of paper up to his face and squinted at it. 'Can we get some light in here?' The Custody Officer left her ward and pulled up the plastic slatted blinds behind her. Sunshine poured over the length of the corridor, illuminating Bramley, then Simon and stretching as far as Cat's feet.

'Where did you say you found it?' Bramley asked Robert.

'The gardener found it, in the guttering outside my' – he paused, remembering – 'garage. Jane must have attached it to the door, maybe she thought my wife would come downstairs and see it and stop her. Maybe the wind blew it off. They say most people who try and commit suicide are only crying out for help, I don't think she really meant to die.'

Bramley shook his head. 'How very sad,' said Bramley not meaning it. Cat nearly said something from her hiding place. 'You're sure it's your daughter's handwriting then?'

'Yes,' said Robert. 'Absolutely.'

'Same handwriting in the diary is it, sir?' Robert blinked several times. 'The same writing that lists times and events over the preceding seven years when your wife bullied and belittled her.' He paused for effect. 'Do you think that might be the reason why she killed herself?' The soft tone in his voice did nothing to hide the harshness of the words. Cat saw Robert's fist clench. His right arm jerked outwards. Sandie grabbed it and held it against his side.

'I don't believe my wife capable of doing those things,' he said, through clenched teeth.

'You understand we will have to look into that, Mr Wellby?'

'You can do whatever you goddamm like, just give me back my wife. My daughter wrote a suicide note, Detective Chief Inspector.'

'What about the diary?' He would not let this one go. Cat was shaking her head. This was surely not the way to conduct a murder inquiry.

'She was confused,' said Robert. Sandie finally lifted

her head off her husband's shoulder. She sighed and smiled at him.

'You really believe that do you, Mr Wellby?' Robert stared at Sandie. He nodded. 'I see. Well, let's see what her parting words were shall we?' Cat could have killed him for his insensitivity. He continued, '"To everyone to whom this life meant something, I am sorry. Please forgive my weakness and leaving in this cowardly way."' Bramley looked up. 'Very moving.'

Simon walked towards the policeman. 'You have disrupted this family enough, Bramley. Let Robert take Sandie home.'

'You'd like that wouldn't you, Mr Proudlove. But I know all about you, and if anyone is guilty of disruption, it isn't me.'

'How dare you.' Finally Sandie found her voice. 'You come into my home, you falsify evidence against me, haul me off, keep my family and friends away from me and each other at the one time we should have been there to support each other in grieving the tragic death of my stepdaughter. When evidence is presented to you, logical evidence that explains the truth, you start firing off at those who have done nothing but protest my innocence. Jane killed herself, Detective Chief Inspector, and *that* is her suicide note.'

A door squeaked. A new streak of light crossed the one from the window. Cat walked into the corridor.

'What the hell are you doing here?' It was Robert, but Cat wasn't listening. She was staring at Sandie. Simon tried to stop her walking past him, but she yanked her arm away and clutched her hands over her heart. She couldn't believe she was doing this for a second time.

'What is it?' said Sandie. 'What's happened?'

'I'm so sorry,' Cat said, also not for the first time.

'What are you sorry for this time?' asked Sandie, reasonably calmly, given the circumstances.

'The note,' she said slowly. Sandie, Robert and Simon all nodded warily. Cat bit her lip, looked down at her feet, exhaled, brought her head up again and looked at Sandie Wellby. 'I wrote it.'

'You did what!?' exclaimed Sandie.

'I'm sorry, I must have dropped it when I discovered Jane. I was supposed to leave it with the dog.'

Sandie actually laughed. 'The dog, of course. The dog I was taking for a walk while you were killing it. What is *wrong* with you – have you not got a life of your own, or do you just want to fuck up mine? Jesus Christ, I've been asking myself over and over again while lying in my disgusting little cell what the hell you are up to. Why the hell you were in my husband's garage in the first place? What you were doing there? And don't start giving me any shit about Lucy. You say I never touched the hose, and now you say Jane didn't write that suicide note, in fact, the only person who has put me in this hell is you, and I want to know why, goddammit—'

'Hey, I've got nothing to do with this.'

'Except for finding my husband's little girl dead and

now claiming you wrote her suicide note.' Sandie turned to Bramley. 'You aren't going to believe her are you?'

'Why? You worried, Mrs Wellby?' His tone was not pleasant. 'About your status, hmm? After all, if Jane didn't write that, we have nothing that can place her at the scene of the crime voluntarily. If you see what I mean.'

'There is just as much evidence against her,' said Sandie pointing at Cat, 'as there is against me. Jesus Christ *she* could have killed Jane. This could all be part of some mad plan to frame me.'

'This girl is lying,' said Simon. 'It's obvious.'

'Mr Proudlove, with all due respect, shut up.'

Simon frowned at the policeman. 'Don't you want to find the truth?'

'Oh, I do, trouble is, people like you make that a little difficult.'

'It's her you should be talking to in that manner, not me.' Simon pointed at Cat.

'Is that so. Mr Proudlove, where were you between twelve thirty and one thirty last Friday?'

'I told you.'

'Amuse me.'

'Visiting a client.'

'One Mrs Dewhurst. You told me that you saw Sandie and the dog in the meadow as you drove past.' Simon nodded. Robert was now watching him intently. 'But that cannot be, can it, sir?' Simon's eye's narrowed. 'Mrs Wellby was allegedly in the meadow between one fifteen and one thirty. But you arrived at Mrs Dewhurst's at one thirty. You can't make that journey in less than forty minutes, even if you are driving at dangerous speeds. I don't think Cat Torrant is the liar here. No, Mr Proudlove, that sin lies at your doorstep.'

Robert took a step away from his wife. She grabbed him.

'I forgive you, Robert,' said Sandie, 'I forgive you for how you acted before, but I need you now, you have to believe me. I did take Lucy out for a walk and I did return home and go to bed. I did not kill Jane, Robert; I could not kill something that is part of you. I love you, now support me, support me now, Robert, or it's over for all of us. That girl no more killed Lucy than I killed Jane, for God's sake, you must believe me, I love you—'

'Excuse me?' Everyone turned. The old man with the pram entered the hallway.

'No unauthorized personnel are allowed in here.'

'Is that so,' said the old fellow, looking the crowd over. 'Well, I'm not staying. I just thought I would let you know that I have never been so despairing of figures of so-called authority, or so horrified by the lack of intelligence, collective or otherwise, in this building. You make me sorry I fought so long and so hard for Britain's future generations if this is all we can come up with. I nearly died for you, now I pay for you, I expect to be, at least, acknowledged by you.' No one said a word. The man turned the pram around, as if to leave.

'What's in the pram, sir?' asked Bramley nervously.

'None of your business. I would no sooner leave a living animal in your care than a fallen man in battle. Good day.'

'An injured animal?' said Cat. Sandie started shaking her head.

'Yes.' The man looked at Cat with tired eyes.

'A dog?'

'A bitch, actually.'

'Oh perfect,' said Sandie sardonically, 'you've got grandpa in on it.'

Cat nodded. 'A Norwich terrier?'

'What did you do, kidnap my dog?' said Sandie, still eyeing Cat angrily.

'Is she yours?' asked the elderly gentleman. Cat shook her head, unable to look at Sandie. 'She's a beautiful little thing, sweetest nature. She's been well loved, that is why I wanted to find her owner, put them out of their misery.' He lifted the animal out of the pram and lowered it to the floor, one of her legs was in plaster.

'Lucy!' It was Sandie. 'Come here, my little one.' The dog scampered, as best it could, along the corridor. 'I told you that girl couldn't have killed her, I told you. I was taking her for a walk, she must have run off when all the ambulances turned up. See.' She held up the dog. Only then did she seem to notice the plaster for the first time. 'You didn't have to injure her. What kind of people are you?'

The old man stared at the woman. Bafflement seeped into his eyes. 'Excuse me?'

'What the hell have you done to my dog?' Sandie's

resolve to be strong was slipping away from her. 'What could I possibly have done to offend you?'

'Madam, I have no idea what you are talking about. All I know is that when we found your dog she was nearly dead. In fact she had crawled under a fallen tree and was waiting to die, would have, too, if we hadn't found her. She had some bad bruising, a broken leg, and serious dehydration. Looked like a car had hit her, she slipped in and out of consciousness for the first few days. It's been touch and go, madam, touch and go. The only thing I have done to your dog is nurse her back to health. If you want someone to blame, find the evil creature that hit her in the first place.' Suddenly Cat knew how Sandie felt. All eyes on the pet killer.

'I'm sorry,' muttered Cat.

The old man cottoned on. 'You?' he said. Cat nodded, biting her lip.

'How disappointing,' he said.

She had never felt so ashamed of herself. 'I'm sorry,' she said again.

'I wouldn't be sorry if I were you,' said Bramley in a tone that did not sound in the slightest bit consolatory. 'A damaged dog is a small price to pay for justice.' Cat was confused. Sandie wasn't. 'Oops, there goes your alibi, Mrs Wellby, and just in time too.' He looked at his watch. 'Our additional twenty-four hours was up. Five more minutes and I would have had to release you. Now isn't that a shame, eh?' Robert Wellby steadied himself against the wall. 'Thanks to you, Cat, looks like Colchester Prison will be opening its doors for its first septic celeb. Any last words . . .?' No one spoke.

'No press,' said Robert finally.

ROBERT AND SIMON WALKED out of the building in silence, a gleeful Bramley escorting them to the car park. Cat walked behind them, the leper. Sandie Wellby had been remanded in custody. She would be formally charged with the murder of Jane Wellby the following morning and taken to Colchester to await trial. No one had mentioned bail. Lucy had been given back to the two old men. That was Sandie's decision. Robert looked like he had the day Jane had died – broken. Simon tried to comfort him, but Robert physically pushed him away. Simon pointed a finger at Cat and looked at her with loathing. 'This is your fault.'

'I know it looks that way, but I promise you my involvement is purely accidental.'

'And you expect anyone to believe that?'

'It's the truth, I swear.'

Simon turned away from her and walked briskly down the front steps. At the bottom a giggling couple emerged from behind the building.

'DS Chambers! What is going on?'

The couple looked up nervously.

'Sir?' he said, rearranging his uniform. 'I was looking after Miss Moore, she had a shock.'

'Shit,' whispered Cat, trying to turn away. Once again. She was too late.

'Jane!' Everyone stopped moving. 'Jane, thank God,' cried Suzie breathlessly, mounting the steps two at a time. 'They told me you were dead.' Suzie put an arm around Cat's shoulders. 'Oh, Mr Wellby, you must be over the moon to have your daughter back. Does Sandie know?' Suzie stared at him. 'Oh, don't cry, please.'

Cat couldn't bare to look.

'Accidental?' sneered Simon. 'Come on, Bramley. Do something.'

'Go home, Mr Proudlove.'

'But—'

'Go home.'

'This is a fucking farce!'

'I said go home.'

Simon looked at Cat for a full minute before turning away.

Chapter Fourteen

Darren watched the fat man die. It wasn't easy but he had no choice. He couldn't call an ambulance and he couldn't get him to a hospital. He wouldn't have survived anyway. It was all over in a matter of seconds. Darren knelt by him and rested the dead man's head on his knees. He brought the rug on the floor around his near naked body. He had hoped he'd at least succeed in surviving life without succumbing to killing another person. He'd had the opportunity. He'd had the cause. But he'd never had the will. Darren stared at the bulbous body, the rolls of flesh that hung in concentric rings around the man's torso. He'd eaten himself into an early grave. His heart was probably thankful for the excuse to pack in, tired of pumping fat-laden blood through cholesterol-lined arteries.

'Your greed just saved your life. Some people have all the fucking luck.'

Darren had spent most of his life not knowing when

he'd be fed. Breakfast at his house was a fag and a slap when he was a kid. He still couldn't stomach a big meal. Darren pushed the man's head off his lap and stood up. He couldn't go back to blowing German businessmen on the top level of multi-storey car parks for a fiver. He had a front-door key. Very few people could know what a precious thing that is. Now he was going to lose that because some fat fuck couldn't stay alive. He kicked the body.

'There goes my fucking savings account, you big ape.' All Darren's shitty little life, somebody had come along and ruined things. If everyone had just left him the pissing alone, he would have been fine. Not now. Now it was too late. Darren felt his surface body temperature drop as the heat of his anger sucked itself into the very core of his soul. Backdraft of fury. For a split second he hovered on the boundaries of sanity, then the heat roared out of him. He kicked the dead defenceless man again. And again. Darren buried his foot into his father's head. The man who had beat up on him. Then his stepfather's chest. Another man who had beat up on him. His 'uncles' appeared one after another. One by one he beat them back. The spongy form below him reformed as his mother. His loving mother who had used him on her punters. He kicked her in the head too. And his 'guardian' who had locked him in cupboards, the staff at the home, his ex-drug-dealer girlfriend who had got him hooked on heroin and taken all his money. He kicked his life to shreds. His Shitty Little Life.

FIONA SAT IN HER kitchen. The letters of condolence were piling up on the table, but she couldn't bring herself to read them. Let alone respond. Dear Cousin Sue, isn't it tragic that the woman I saw as my saviour, who took my family off my hands, should end up destroying it . . . Dear Gillian, the woman who I haven't spoken to in years who wrote a gloating letter about the perils of divorce, fuck you, I had a life, I was proud of that. Dear Man Next Door, no I don't believe Sandie really did all those things. Dear Fiona Wellby, thank you for your letter, I too hope this is all one horrible mistake and that Sandie will forgive you for making that call. Dear Dad, I'm sorry I can't give you a funeral date yet, you see they won't release the body . . . Not that they knew where to bury her. Jane had requested, according to her diary, to be buried in the church where she and Robert had married, which was a little odd, because they had been married in a registry office in Reading where Fiona's parents had lived. Hardly the fairy-tale wedding. It was the early seventies; Fiona hadn't even worn white. She'd worn beige. How telling. Fiona shuddered at the thought of it, and continued to shudder when she thought of her daughter alone, frozen, in a metal cubicle with a plastic tag on her toe. Naked, most likely. Naked for all the young med. students to have a good gawk at. They had never even talked about sex. She didn't even know for sure that Jane had had sex. She was twenty-three so it was more than likely, but she didn't know for sure. She always thought they would get around to having that conversation when the time was right. Well the time was wrong – always would be now. Who had Jane had sex with? Who would she have told? Fiona tried to remember intimate details of her daughter's life. They weren't coming back to her. Worse, she couldn't remember if there was anything worth remembering. Were most mothers like that with their children, were there always great voids between parent and child, why didn't she know her daughter? Why? What were her religious beliefs? Did she believe in reincarnation? Life after death? Had she experimented with drugs? Had she ever been brought breakfast in bed? What did she want to be when she grew up? Fiona's hair was falling out in greater quantities as each day went by, she stared at the clump in her hand. Her daughter was dead and she was the one who was decomposing. The phone rang. Fiona listened as the answering machine picked up the call.

'Listen, I'm beginning to really worry. Please, please call me at the hotel. You're never there, there are a thousand messages on this machine, and there's no answer at the studio. Where are you? Are you ill, my darling, I'm going insane with worry . . .' Fiona covered her ears at the sound of Jo's voice and ran out of the room, slammed the door and leant against it. The doorbell made her jump. For a moment she thought about hiding upstairs, playing dead, but that was an insult to those who'd had their life taken away from them. She still had her life, she should live it. Or was it an insult to go on, as if nothing had happened? Should she just leave it up to time? The Healer. Would it eventually make life bearable, let her forget? But to forget would be an insult . . . What the hell was one supposed to do when one's daughter died, who was there to tell her? The doorbell rang again just as the phone did. She answered the door.

'Mrs Wellby?'

'Yes.'

'Delivery from Sun Travel, would you mind signing here?'

Fiona frowned. 'You must be mistaken, I'm not expecting anything from the travel agents.'

'Well here are two tickets, in your name, all paid for by the look of it. I'd take them if I were you, what have you got to lose?'

'You sure you've got—'

'Mrs Wellby, maybe it's a surprise, anniversary of something, I don't know, I'm just the delivery man, if there's a problem, I suggest you ring Sun Travel.'

She took the thick envelope, printed and signed her name, then walked back to the kitchen. When she finally opened it, the printed itinerary informed her that one F. Wellby, Mrs, and one J. S. Wellby, Miss, were expected at Stansted Airport at 14.35 on the following day, eleven days after Jane's death, to catch a plane to Lisbon, Portugal. The two printed words at the bottom of the page startled her. Happy Fiftieth. Two tickets. One to her, as a gift for making it to fifty, and one to her daughter, for not.

FIONA PICKED UP THE phone and dialled Sun Travel. She had used the local travel agency for longer than she dared to remember. One of the many joys of being an independent middle-aged woman was the enormous amount of travelling she could do. Most of her married girlfriends had to fit their holidays around their husbands or children. She didn't have a man she had to organize her life around. And Jane she packed off to Cedar Hall. It was easy. For her. Jane hadn't even complained. Or had Fiona just not heard?

'Sun Travel, good morning, Vanessa speaking, how can I help?'

'Vanessa, it's Fiona Wellby here.'

'Hi, what can I do for you?'

It was weird talking to a normal person. A person who didn't know. 'I've just been given a holiday, to Portugal. I think there must be a mistake.'

'No mistake. I believe it is a birthday present.'

Fiona was taken aback. 'From you, but that's ridiculously generous—'

'Fiona, you are a good client, but not that good.'

'Must be from Robert then, he's probably forgotten to tell me, given everything that has happened recently.'

'What's happened recently?'

'Oh dear, I don't do this bit very well . . .' She paused.

'Are you all right, Fiona?'

'The thing is . . .'

'Listen,' said Vanessa not wanting to press a delicate

subject out of the woman, 'it wasn't Robert who booked the holiday, it was Jane. About a month ago.'

'Jane?'

'Paid for it with money she had saved. So that solves that mystery.'

'Jane?'

'Yup. It is a surprise, she wanted to give you a really special birthday. It's the big 5—0 after all. She told me, hope you don't mind—'

'But Jane's dead.'

'You look bloody well on—' Vanessa stopped. 'Excuse me?'

'Dead. She was found in my ex-husband's car last Friday.'

'Found?'

'In the garage,' said Fiona staring at the tickets. 'Are you absolutely sure it was Jane?'

'Fiona,' said Vanessa, 'I issued the tickets to her myself.'

She put the phone down and walked in a daze to a photo of Robert and Sandie on the mantelpiece. Jane had been in it. She'd cut herself off the end, saying her hair looked frizzy. Fiona could still see Jane's arm tucked into her father's. If she imagined very hard she could bring Jane back to that photo, like her dreams could bring her back to life. Sandie looked as beautiful as ever, smiling radiantly at her. The more Fiona looked the more the nature of the smile changed. From genuine to guilty, from welcoming to wicked, from maternal to murderous.

The frame had smashed into the corner of the kitchen, glass splintering across the tiles, before Fiona was aware it had even left her hand. The doorbell rang again, followed by insistent knocking and when that went unanswered, shouting. It was Robert.

'Fiona! I know you are in there. Fiona! It's me, let me in.'

'Fuck off!'

That shut him up for a few seconds. But he persevered. 'Fiona, open this door or I will break it down.'

Fiona slid down the wall and put her hands over her ears. 'Leave me alone.'

'Please.' The voice was quieter now. 'Please, for Jane, come with me to the magistrates' court. I cannot do this without you.'

ANNA WAS LAUGHING. It was the first time Cat had seen him laugh since the attack. 'God,' said Cat shaking her head, 'to think I only went there on my way back from Gran's to see the policewoman. I didn't even know they had arrested Sandie, I couldn't believe it when they led her out.'

'Well, at least something good has come out of it, think of all the information we've got, Calorie Carers, the dog . . .' The door to his flat opened, he hadn't bolted it, it was another good sign. 'Dan,' said Anna, surprised. 'Hi?'

Cat tensed. She hadn't spoken to him since their argument.

'Come on in, your terrible girlfriend has just been

telling me about the trouble she has been getting into. Sleuthing suits her.'

'Really, what kind of trouble?' he said going over to Anna and squeezing his shoulder. Manly affection. He didn't squeeze hers.

'She went to the police station in Harlow to get some information when the whole Wellby circus turned up and she was right in the middle of it. Robert Wellby, Jane's dad – shall we open a bottle of wine? Cat, do the honours—'

She walked through to the kitchen area avoiding eye contact with Dan. She retrieved a bottle of chilled red wine and the corkscrew from the second drawer on the right from the hob. It was always there. Anna was meticulous like that. She opened the bottle, carried it and three wine glasses upside down in her right hand, and returned to the sofa. Suzie the hairdresser had just turned up. Anna was in peals of laughter again.

'I can't believe you would do such a thing,' he said looking at Cat.

'I'm fine thanks, how are you?'

'She's only been dead for a few days and you are walking around impersonating her. I think it is disgusting. Imagine if someone did it to you. Pretended they were Amelia after she died.'

'Don't you fu—'

'Oh,' he said standing up, 'so it's all right you walking around pretending to be someone's dead daughter, but God forbid they should do it to you.'

'It was an accident,' said Cat.

'Isn't it always.'

'What is wrong with you?'

'And dragging Anna into it. Don't you think he's been through enough!'

Anna stopped pouring the wine. 'Hang on a moment, Dan, you're being a bit of a prick if you don't mind my saying. There, I've said my piece, don't bring me into this any further.'

'Well it doesn't seem a great way to recuperate.'

'Which is why I wasn't with her, but I wish I had been. I spent the day here alone. It wasn't very nice. Next time I'll go.' Anna pushed himself off the sofa. Dan and Anna looked at each other. 'If I'd had company, maybe that wouldn't be necessary.' In his heels he had always towered over Dan, but without them they stood eye to eye.

'Nice. Do love a bit of emotional blackmail,' said Dan defensively.

'Well, where have you been?'

'I didn't leave this flat for three days, remember?'

'Sorry to inconvenience you, but I think it will take longer than three days to get over this little hitch, so please don't belittle what happened to me by dragging it into a domestic.'

Cat chewed her lip. Dan looked like he'd been slapped. 'So you told him, did you?' said Dan, to Cat.

'Of course I didn't.'

'What didn't you tell me?' said Anna, also looking at her.

'It doesn't matter,' said Cat, who hated confrontations.

'Well that sums it up nicely.'

'Dan,' said Cat, 'you started this. Not me.'

'Hounding the Wellbys started this.'

Cat frowned. 'That is not true and you know it,' said Cat, amazed at his ability to twist things.

'What did start it then?' asked Anna, taking a long drink.

'You don't want to know,' said Cat looking pointedly at Dan.

'All I'm saying is that this Wellby thing is none of your business.'

'Dan, did you grace us with your presence today with the sole purpose of being a wanker?'

Dan and Cat turned and looked at him.

'I think you'd better go,' said Anna. 'You're a negative influence and a pain in the arse.'

'Fine,' said Dan.

'Good.'

Dan turned to the door. Cat threw a frantic look at Anna, who signalled she shouldn't protest. She watched in stunned silence as the door clicked shut behind him.

'I don't believe he just did that,' said Cat going to the window.

'I do,' said Anna. Cat waited for him to explain. But he didn't.

THEY SAT LIKE HUSBAND and wife, side by side, waiting for the proceedings to start. The room was beige. Like her wedding dress. It no longer agreed with Fiona's taste, these days she preferred ruby red, royal purple and bottle green. Beige was like flesh. A flaccid colour.

'Don't you think you should talk to her?' said Fiona. 'Get her side of the story.'

'I can't.'

'You've got to.'

'I just can't. I can't bring myself to look at her.'

Fiona could. Sandie was staring at Robert. What a mess. If she were asked to give evidence, what would she say? That she'd always admired Sandie. That she liked her sense of humour? That she trusted her with her daughter's life. Had, sorry, that was *had* trusted her. Robert was still squeezing her hand. She pulled it away and wished, once again, that this whole thing was not happening and that Jane was pulling a fast one and would at any moment appear laughing. A door opened behind them. An immaculately dressed young man walked into the court-room. His chin was square and his eyes were piercing blue, his shirt was starched and his jacket was lined in turquoise satin. LA meets Essex. Fiona looked back at Sandie. This time they spoke. Don't make a show out of this, said Fiona with her eyes. Don't make me have to, said Sandie in return. Two old gents sat in the back row. Fiona only noticed them because of the dog. It was under the old boy's coat. Quiet little thing, would hardly have known it was there. And what if Lucy hadn't been in the road? Cat Torrant wouldn't have come to Cedar Hall. Maybe none of this would be happening. Sandie's story of her daughter's misery would have gone on unchecked. The police would not have set up camp at Cedar Hall and Fiona might not have sought sanctuary in Jane's bedroom. She might not have been the one to find the diary. What would she have done when the tickets arrived then? Fiona imagined herself in Portugal alone. The second ticket in ashes. She shuddered. Robert put a reassuring arm on her shoulder. It felt like the pressing hand of God. Fiona sat frozen under its weight. Ashamed by her own thoughts. She was not fit to be a mother.

THE BARRISTER FOR THE Crown Prosecution Service stood up. 'We ask the court to acknowledge the arrest of Mrs Sandie Anne Wellby for the murder of her step-daughter, Jane Sara Wellby, aged twenty-three. The murder was unprovoked, in fact, when the facts are more closely examined, it marks the sad end of a long and drawn-out torture that the defendant subjected the deceased to for a number of years. We request she be held at HMP Colchester until a trial date is set.' The magistrate nodded, the lawyer sat down. The man in the tailored suit and blue eyes stood up. He introduced himself as Marcus England, QC for the defence, Sandie's lawyer. Robert's head snapped up at the sound of the American accent.

'I don't believe it.'

The alarm in his voice worried Fiona. 'What's wrong?'

'She called him of all people. Where's Hallifax, I sent her Hallifax.'

'Who is he?'

'A smooth-talking yank, look at him, what the bloody hell does Sandie think she's doing?'

Fiona looked back at Marcus England. He was making his statement to the judge.

'Why don't you like him?' said Fiona.

'Shh, let me listen.'

Why did she let him talk her into coming, thought Fiona, as Robert pitched himself forward in his chair. He did not take his eyes off Marcus England throughout the proceedings.

'I request all charges be dropped against my client on the basis that the only evidence against her is circumstantial or has been falsified. In fact Detective Chief Inspector Bramley here had his men harass Mrs Wellby at her home before they had any evidence to even put her at the crime scene. They still do not have such evidence.'

'I have read the file, Mr England, we go to trial.'

'In which case I request bail immediately.'

The prosecutor stood up. 'Your Honour, the CPS would be exceedingly grieved if Mrs Wellby were allowed bail. She is a rich woman, she has two passports, if she wanted to do a vanishing act, she could.'

'Your honour, Mrs Wellby has a large amount of money invested in this country, not least in Cedar Hall, and her interior design business in Colchester. She has no intention of abandoning either. On the contrary, she is worried about her assets, which amount to a large amount of money, being dismantled by her husband.' Robert searched the courtroom, saw Simon, then looked away, a look of hatred on his face. 'She is innocent, but she is rich, your Honour, she also believes she has been framed. If that is the case, your Honour, we must ask by whom. Generally we should look to the person who stands to benefit from Mrs Wellby's incarceration.' It was a fraction of a movement, but everyone watching noticed, as Marcus England flicked his eyes over Robert Wellby. 'We will prove her innocence. Grant her bail, your Honour, so that she still has something to go back to when this horrible ordeal is over.' Robert looked ill, but no one looked more distraught than Sandie. The magistrate was silent, the room that had seemed so bland seemed suddenly alive with colour, awash with pigments of expectation. The magistrate turned to Sandie.

'Mrs Wellby, you have no criminal past, and the physical evidence against you is not strong, however, I have read the words of a young girl whose life, it seems, has been made a misery. She names you as the culprit. No one else has seen these tendencies in you and for that reason I will grant you bail, but the conditions are these.

You must report to the police station once a day and you are requested to leave your passports with the court.'

'Thank you, your Honour,' said Marcus England.

'My pleasure, Mr England, but I haven't quite finished. Bail is set at two hundred and fifty thousand pounds. Court is adjourned.'

Sandie stared at Marcus, he nodded, things had gone well for today. He hadn't expected to get out of there for less than five hundred thousand. For two fifty he needn't have got a banker's draft. People began to filter out of the courtroom, its dreariness returning with every departure. Bramley came over to Fiona and Robert. 'I guess it's time to get yourself a lawyer.'

'Excuse me?'

'A lawyer. Your missus is going to get dirty. Best you're prepared.'

'Excuse me?' Robert said again. Bramley looked at Fiona. She didn't like the policeman, but she knew where he was going with this.

'He is trying to tell you that Sandie's defence may well point the finger at someone else.' Robert's eyes darted between the policeman and his ex-wife. Funny, thought Fiona, he wasn't usually this dim. 'You, Robert,' she said, 'Sandie is going to blame you.'

Chapter Fifteen

The doctor looked at the photo on Amelia's bedside table. It was one of Cat and Amelia in mid–unrestrained laughter. He admired her and the way she had brought up Cat. He saw her not as an old woman in a wheelchair but a young and accomplished mother. Which explained why he approached her check-ups with more trepidation than most. The door opened.

'Oh, sorry, doctor, didn't mean to disturb you.'

'Nurse O'Leary, come in. We're finished.'

'Everything okay?'

'Strong as an ox.'

The door to Amelia's bathroom burst open. 'Katie, thank God you're here, I'm falling apart, I can't even put my stockings on by myself.'

'Amelia,' said the doctor, 'you should have asked me.'

'Dear, oh dear, a man can take them off, but he should never see them being put back on. Completely ruins the mystique. Remember that,' she said pointing at Katie.

Katie nodded seriously. 'What on earth are you doing with your stockings off at this time of day anyway?'

'The good doctor here always asks me to remove some article of clothing or other.'

Katie looked at the doctor. He winked at her. 'Office perk. Amelia has the best legs at Heaven's Gate.'

Amelia shrugged. 'And to think, he believes he is flattering me? The mind boggles.'

'I don't know,' said Katie, 'Mrs McCron's pins aren't bad.'

'Mrs McCron,' Amelia protested, 'have you not seen the colour of her varicose veins?'

'Now, now, Amelia,' said Katie. 'Put those claws away. Anyway, I've got the finest legs in Heaven's Gate,' she lifted her skirt, 'by some margin.'

'Hussy,' said the elderly lady, 'but just you wait. Nurses evolve in a peculiar form. They all start lean and pretty in their little white uniforms and black stockings, then the next thing you know, they look like colossal Cleveland with mountainous breasts that cover the midriff range and beyond.'

'And to think,' said Katie, 'I only stopped by to tell you a certain gentleman is waiting for you by the fountain.'

Amelia glanced at her watch. 'Damn, I'm late. Katie, please, my stockings?'

'Young love?' said the doctor.

'Christ no, wouldn't want to go through that again. This is old lust, much less painful.'

Katie helped Amelia dress then wheeled her out to the fountain. Mr Blaine was waiting, dressed in pink, holding a rose. Amelia smiled. Her granddaughter was not the only one getting a story out of the Jane Wellby case. She smiled gratefully as she took the rose.

'Where to today?' said Mr Blaine.

'I spotted a new Italian on the way back from my hydrowhatsit class. Are you feeling strong enough for a two mile push?'

'It just so happens, Mrs Torrant, that today I am feeling Herculean.'

'You know what, Mr Blaine, so am I, so am I,' she said as he turned her chair towards the car park. 'And, by the way, call me Amelia. I think the coast is clear, let's get out of here.'

'I've been wondering how a mischievous thing like you wound up in this place.'

'I don't think you really want to know, Mr Blaine.'

'Call me Bertie, and you're wrong, I do. In fact, I'd like to know everything about you.' Amelia smiled. His timing was perfect.

'Well, the thing is,' she said as he wheeled her down the lane, 'I seemed to adopt a problem with ovens . . .'

'Ovens?'

She smiled to herself. 'Dreadful modern things. All those knobs these days, they really aren't necessary.'

'So what happened?'

'I burnt my house down while preparing hot hors-d'oeuvres for my bridge four. Luckily, I always kept my most precious belongings in a vanity case which I kept packed at all times just in case of an emergency. This was one of those emergencies. The kitchen was well on its way when we noticed. My bridge partners helped remove the few bulky essentials. By the time the fire brigade arrived we'd set up the game in the garden. I wasn't concerned for my furniture.' She turned and winked at Mr Blaine. 'Drunk all the good stuff years ago.'

'That is terrible. You must have lost everything.'

'Oh no, I called a grand slam in diamonds, and having been doubled then re-doubled by my partner, I made the call triumphantly. In fact, I made a profit.'

'So you came here?' said Mr Blaine, pausing to wipe his forehead with a handkerchief. A pink one.

'Not exactly . . .' There was another house and another fire, finally she was forced to admit that ovens no longer suited her. She did horrible things to the microwave that was provided for her by Cat, complaining afterwards that she always baked her potatoes in silver foil for an hour and a half. Needless to say, neither the potato nor the 'nuclear box' survived. The final straw was delivered when she fell down two flights of steps, but unlike Mrs Hope in the Sunday supplements, she knew help was not on its way. It was Cat who eventually found her. During her stay in hospital for the fractured pelvis, they discovered a suspicious-looking growth in her colon and, to add insult to injury, whipped great sections of it out and replaced it with a port-a-loo.

'A wheelchair and a colostomy bag put me here, I

didn't want to be a burden on my granddaughter and anyway, I realized my courting days were probably over. Walking with a limp is one thing,' she said smiling, 'walking with a slosh and a limp is quite another.'

'Oh, I don't know,' said Mr Blaine, 'I think you wheel wonderfully.'

'You know what, Mr Blaine, I may be pleased to have ended up in this decaying death hole after all.'

'I'll drink to that. As soon as I have a full-bodied Chianti in my hand.'

'What about you, Bertie, how did you end up here?'

'Families,' he said. 'But let's not go into that.'

MARCUS ENGLAND HELD THE door open for Sandie. She stood for a moment, afraid to go in, but this was her home. Her bastion. It was from here she would launch her attack. She had not done all this to be beaten. No way. She was not going to lose everything she had worked so hard for. Sandie's stiletto heels clicked satisfyingly across the wooden hall. She noticed the flowers immediately and made a mental note to go and thank Sam Clough. At least someone had expected her to return. Even if it wasn't her own husband. Damn him. Damn him and his bloody daughter. Any remorse, any guilt she had felt she'd left behind in her cell; let the police have it. They needed a dose of the stuff. Marcus walked up behind her, just as the image of Fiona being helped down the stairs by two policemen remoulded itself from her memory. He put his arm on her shoulder. It should have been Robert's. Why hadn't she thought of checking Jane's room? She knew Jane was keeping something from her, but a diary – Jesus Christ – it never even crossed her mind she would do something like that. Now it was Sandie's turn. Revenge of the Killer Stepmother. The perfect B-movie. Her old agent would have loved it. Through Marcus she would tell her accusers what Jane Wellby was really like. Robert would end up wishing he had stood by her from the beginning. The phone started ringing. Marcus tried to stop her going to it. He knew who it would be.

'Robert?'

'Mrs Wellby, this is *Essex Daily Press*—'

Sandie slammed the phone down. Marcus walked up behind her and began to massage her shoulders.

'Press?'

Sandie nodded, leaning back against his strong hands. It felt good.

'They've been calling. I think we better change the number.'

'What about my friends? I'm going to need them more than ever.'

'Sandie, the only time the phone rings it's the press. Or some mad woman screaming blue murder about child abuse or quoting sections of the Bible.'

Sandie turned around and faced him. 'My friends haven't called?' He shook his head. 'Letters?'

Marcus had thrown the worst ones away.

'I'm getting hate mail? I don't fucking believe this. They can all go to fucking hell.' The phone rang again. Sandie picked it up before Marcus could. 'Yes!' she barked angrily into the phone. 'Sure. I'll be here.' The phone rattled on the crook.

'Do you think that is a good idea?' said Marcus. Sandie pulled him closer to her and put his hands on her shoulders. He began to rub. 'You worry about the legal side and leave the rest to me. And get me a copy of that diary, I'm going to punch holes in it so large there'll be nothing left.'

SIMON STARED AT THE two of them through the window. He had parked at the pub and walked the half mile drive to the house in order to give himself time to think. Time to rehearse what it was he wanted to say. What he had to tell Sandie before the situation got worse. And it could. As he watched her rock gently in the man's arms he wished he had screeched up the driveway, horn blaring, done a handbrake turn and skidded loudly to the front door. He didn't want to see this. Secrets should stay secret. It was the only way anyone survived.

MARCUS HEARD THE CRUNCH of gravel as Simon turned to leave. Their eyes locked for a second, before Sandie became aware that the mood had changed and straightened up. As soon as she saw Simon she rushed over to the front door.

'Simon! For Christ's sake, why the hell did you lie to the police? God, if you know anything about me, you should know that I can look after myself.'

'I wanted to help,' he said, not quite looking at her.

'Well next time you want to help, keep your fucking mouth shut. Do you know what it looked like, you lying for me like that?' Simon nodded. 'You may as well have locked the fucking door yourself.'

'I was trying to—'

'Oh, stop bleating, Simon. It's pathetic. Some help. First you lie, poorly, if you don't mind me saying, and then you don't even bother to come visit.'

'I was trying to work things out, what should I do?'

'Don't *do* anything, Simon. Have you learnt nothing from our partnership? You don't do anything unless I tell you to. That is how it works, how it has always worked. For fuck's sake, the most crucial time of my life and you decide to ad lib.'

'How dare you. I keep that business going. You don't do a bloody thing.'

'You wouldn't have a business if it wasn't for my money.'

Simon looked at her stunned, then lowered his voice. 'Now I know how Robert feels.'

'What's that supposed to mean? Have you spoken to him? Does he think I killed his daughter? Why didn't he visit me? Why didn't you visit me? You don't think I'd—'

'Of course not.' Simon ran his hands through his hair.

'I didn't come to fight with you. Please, we are friends. Don't do this.'

'No, Simon. Friends do not desert one another.'

'I gave you an alibi.'

'I had an alibi,' Sandie shouted angrily back.

'Oh yes. Lucy. Great fucking alibi, how does a dog get taken out for a walk and run over at the same time?'

Sandie glared at him. Her expression changed. As soon as the aggression left her face, the tiredness began to show. 'I don't know,' she said, quietly, to herself.

The vulnerability softened him. He stepped towards her with an outstretched hand. 'Truly, I only wanted to help you.'

'Thank you, but I have Marcus to do that,' she said, still looking at her feet.

'I can see,' Simon replied sarcastically, withdrawing his hand.

'Now what are you implying?' Simon raised an eyebrow. 'Get away from me, Simon. Get away from my house. If you are not going to support me, you are against me. There is no room for half measures. For once in your yellow-bellied life you are going to have to choose, make a stand, for pity's sake.'

'Sandie,' said Simon, pleading.

'Just leave.'

Simon began to back away from the front door. Robert had thrown him out, Sandie hadn't even asked him in. Well, she knew nothing about him. Nothing. He'd show her. Shouting and screaming was not his way.

Loud words last as long as their sound, it is the quiet ones that linger. A few whispered well-delivered words are so powerful that they are ingested by the soul and repeated for ever. Simon turned towards the drive. She had her way. He had his.

MARCUS GUIDED HER BACK into the house and closed the heavy wooden door. Sandie shuddered when she heard it close. Everyone she needed was deserting her. They all had someone else to turn to. Fiona had the role of grieving mother. She could not be short of support. Robert had Fiona. Simon had Robert. Who the hell did she have? Marcus put his other arm around her shoulders and nodded slightly towards the staircase, it was the same gesture he had made to Robert in the courtroom. It was a very commanding gesture.

'Bed,' he said. Sandie nodded and allowed herself to be led upstairs.

FIONA AND ROBERT SAT in the offices of Tatham, Henry, Hallifax & Co. She had agreed to let him stay in her house, since he couldn't return to Cedar Hall now Sandie was out on bail. She'd given him Jane's keys then immediately regretted it. He sat with a large notebook open on his lap in which he'd listed the evidence of their daughter's abuse that both of them had failed to see when she was still alive. Not for the first time, Fiona contemplated life without Jane. Not without Jane now, without Jane ever. What if she had never given birth to the child?

People would think her as evil as Sandie if they knew how she really felt about motherhood. Every woman was supposed to be thick with maternal love. As soon as that ring was on her finger, it was the first question that came out of everyone's mouth. When? Not if. So she'd done it. Thought it would help a lagging relationship – how stupid could you be? It had felt wrong from the very beginning. Wasn't she supposed to be in love with her child? But Jane had been such a strange child. Wasn't she supposed to lay her life down for her child? She'd help her certainly, but die for her? The trouble was Fiona loved her own life. She wasn't going to live vicariously through her husband and child. It would have killed her. So she had saved herself and killed Jane instead. She had tried to teach her daughter to be strong, independent, brave, to go and explore in the garden, to be adventurous, but Jane had never really wanted to play. Instead she would sit quietly at her mother's feet. All the other mothers would say how well-behaved she was but Fiona remembered wishing Jane would cling less. She remembered, with discomfort, being embarrassed watching other children idle away the hours playing contentedly with other children. Not Jane, she always came back to Mummy. Maybe if they had had another child then Fiona would have learnt to be more forceful. But the mistake had been having the first, having a second wasn't going to make amends. Make it up to Jane, that was the best she could do. Make it up to Jane and never let her think she was the reason for the divorce. So she let her child cling and spent her life as a parent compensating for the rest. They had all been playing 'let's pretend' for years. She looked over to her ex-husband. She even did it with him.

'. . . So we've got the holiday tickets to Portugal, the diary, the absence of a suicide note . . .' continued Robert as though he were reading out a travel checklist. Passport, money, ticket – check. 'Of course, I have no real alibi, I was in the car between meetings. Popped into a pub for a sandwich and read the paper before going back to the office. Someone will remember.'

'How is work, are they being understanding?' asked Fiona.

Her ex-husband looked at her. She thought he paled slightly but then he said. 'Fine. Fine. Everything is fine. They are being very thoughtful.'

Fiona nodded and returned to her thoughts. The waiting room reminded Fiona of Jane's old teacher's office and the times they had been summoned in the light of some disturbance or other. Of course, it was never Jane's fault, she just seemed to be in the wrong place quite often. After one particularly nasty incident involving scissors and a thigh, not Jane's, they had been called in during the middle of the day. It turned out that Jane had been the victim of some rather nasty bullying and, at her wits' end, had lashed out in self-defence. Jane broke down in tears and recounted a list of incidents where the girl had got her by the throat, a half nelson, stolen her gym kit, etc., etc. Fiona frowned, now what had that girl's name been? She had left the school shortly afterwards. In fact, Fiona had found it hard to believe the girl could inflict such pain, she was really quite little. Damn what was it? When her parents took her away, everyone agreed, it was as good as admitting her culpability. They even got a written apology from the teachers. Lottie something . . .

'Robert, what was the name—' A door opened. An immaculately dressed girl walked in. Should be Jane, thought Fiona painfully, as she had done every time she had seen a living breathing girl around the same age as her daughter.

'Mr and Mrs Wellby?' Fiona frowned. Why did that sound so damaging? Robert stood up. 'Mr Hallifax will see you now.' They were shown across the wood-panelled corridor. Mr Hallifax stood to greet them.

'Robert,' he said, extending his hand, 'so sorry to hear the news.'

'Thank you, Thomas, it has indeed been a shock for all of us. This is Jane's mother.' Fiona tried to smile. At least he hadn't said, this is my first wife, like he usually did. Why hadn't these things annoyed her before? First wife. Like it was something to be proud of. Robert nudged her.

'What?' she said, confused.

'Thomas was asking you whether you would be interested in any counselling.' Her frown deepened. 'For grief,' continued her ex-husband. Fiona looked from one to the other of the two men. Both suited and smiling. Snap.

'I know it sounds a bit strange, but it is company policy. We see many victims of crime. If you bottle your feelings up for years and years they can cause long-term damage and explode suddenly without warning,' said Mr Hallifax. 'We have some numbers, that's all.'

'Excuse me?' said Fiona looking strangely at him.

'People who can help sort out the subconscious, you never know what goes on in there.'

Fiona raised a finger and opened her mouth, as if she were going to make an important point. But nothing came out. The two men continued to smile vacantly at her. The silence became more pronounced with every passing second.

'Fi,' said Robert, putting his hand on her arm. She turned to face her ex-husband. Then closed her eyes. She had been so stupid.

'Fi?' repeated Robert.

'What the hell am I doing here?' she said, suddenly opening her eyes.

'Mrs Wellby?'

'Lottie Hawk,' said Fiona. 'Remember her?' Robert shook his head. She mimicked him. 'No,' she said, 'of course you don't. Excuse me I have to go, I just can't be here, sorry.'

'Fiona, please, I need you.'

She turned back at the door. 'What *you* need? I can't do this Robert. We are divorced. Don't you see? I need to deal with the death of my daughter. You can deal with the death of yours. We can't do this together, we're divorced. Separated. Annulled. Split,' she said breaking her hands apart. 'At least we can be that now. At long last, we can at least be that.' She opened the door and ran out of the neat, patronizing office.

'Fi?' cried Robert after her. 'Fiona?'

THOMAS HALLIFAX HAD SEEN plenty of grief, family disturbances, men and women break down, it was only to be expected. He was paid more than a therapist so didn't mind doing a little of their work. Now was time for him to take charge.

'Leave her, Robert. She has been under a lot of strain. I'll get my secretary to send her a list of top therapists. Anyway if I am to understand what you said on the phone, this meeting really isn't about her.'

Robert turned slowly towards the man. 'Except that she gave birth to Jane. Minor as that may be in your eyes.'

'Quite. And subsequently no one is going to accuse her of any malpractice. Mrs Wellby isn't going after her. She is going after you.' He raised his eyebrow dramatically. 'In fact, I think it is best if Fiona is not seen as too supportive. You are not fighting this together.' Robert frowned. 'Sandie is going to say that you framed her in order to have her incarcerated and thereby gain monopoly of her funds. Money is indeed a strong motive, but love, that always gets the jury going. Perhaps you were doing this for Fiona, so that you could once again be joined. Only wealthier this time round.'

'Are you mad?'

'I can quote many a case of that ilk. Very *Death on the Nile* I grant you, but you'd be surprised what people do for money.'

'Do they kill their own child, Thomas? Is that terribly common?' Robert's voice was rising. 'Why not just kill Sandie for fuck's sake.'

'Too obvious,' said Thomas, ever the lawyer.

'What!'

'Sit down, Robert.'

Robert took a step towards the lawyer. 'You think I could kill my own daughter? That I could hit her over the head with a hammer? That I . . .? Do you?'

'Robert, I wasn't suggesting anything like that, I was merely—'

'Fiona is right, I'm leaving.'

'*I* don't think you did anything,' said Thomas, obsequiously, trying to placate his client, 'but I'm a lawyer, I am trained to think a certain way. And if that thought came to my mind, then you can bet your life that it also came to Mr England's. So let's start from the beginning and prepare ourselves for all the possibilities they may throw at us and get you ready. Okay?'

Robert nodded but couldn't speak. He was waiting for the surge of fury to ebb away, then he sat. From heaven to hell. How had he fallen so far, so quickly?

'Right,' said Mr Hallifax, taking a seat behind his broad desk, 'the first thing we do is get all the post forwarded to you. If we don't get our hands on it, they will. Shall I have it forwarded here or to your work address?' Robert shook his head. 'A friend's perhaps. One you can trust.' Robert shook his head again. 'Fiona's then?' Robert didn't move for a few moments, then nodded slowly. 'Right,' said Thomas Hallifax matter-of-factly, 'Fiona's it is. Secondly, we will need to get your personal belongings from Cedar Hall. It is her house, she'll be back there, that gives her lots of time to find incriminating evidence.'

'There isn't any,' he said defensively.

'Are you sure about that? You do know everything you tell me is in confidence. I do need to know everything so that we are prepared for all eventualities.' Thomas smiled thinly.

Robert looked up slowly. 'My daughter is dead, don't you think you should be concentrating on her life, rather than looking for inconsequential inconsistencies in mine?'

'Well I . . .'

'I didn't kill my daughter, Thomas.'

Chapter Sixteen

The journalist and the photographer were prompt. Too prompt. They sat in her drawing room, drinking coffee from an incomplete set, pretending to like her. She shouldn't have done this. She was so angry with Robert, her husband, who had turned against her again at the first sniff of trouble. If that girl hadn't been there ... It was no good, if, if, if, didn't change the fact that she was being charged for the murder of her stepdaughter and her husband had her down as guilty. For better for worse? For richer for poorer? Fat chance. But she couldn't say any of that. The only option she had was to lie. Something she was getting increasingly good at.

'Did you love Jane like she was your own daughter?'

What kinda question is that, dip shit? 'Of course, she was the only child I knew.'

'Fiona and Robert remained very good friends, did that cause problems asserting your ability to discipline Jane?'

Discipline Jane? What a joke. 'I believe that Fiona and Robert were entitled to bring up their child as they saw fit.'

'Must have annoyed the hell out of you?'

Like you would never believe. 'No.' Sandie was forced to smile through the minefield of questions, knowing that none of her answers sounded convincing.

'Mrs Wellby, you are absolutely resolute that you are not guilty.'

'Absolutely.'

'So who do you think killed your stepdaughter?'

Now there is a tricky question. Sandie paused. 'I really don't know.'

'A lover?'

I doubt it. 'She was very secretive in that department.'

'You say Robert adored his daughter, loved her to the end of this earth?'

They say that love is blind. 'Yes . . .'

'Nothing ever strike you as peculiar about their relationship?'

Yes, but not in the way you are thinking. 'Absolutely not. Don't tell me fathers aren't allowed to love their daughters any more.' Her coffee mug landed heavily on the marble-topped table. The questions were futile and annoying. 'Just because I didn't kill Jane, doesn't mean that Robert did. There are a million possibilities, but no one is going to find them if they concentrate on me. Now if we could wrap this up—'

'Mrs Wellby, just one more question. Did Jane love you?'

Sandie frowned. 'Of course she didn't. I was her stepmother. That's like having an adversary passed to you on a plate.'

'Must have caused problems for you, between you and Robert.'

'Robert and I are just fine, thank you.'

'Really? I was told he had moved back in with Fiona.'

'What?' She stood up, her guard slipping from her like warm butter. She stood exposed, vulnerable, easy prey. 'Well, yes, it is normal, of course they would seek solace in each other . . .' This was getting too much, the façade was cracking, she had to stop the interview before she said something stupid. She had not taken into account the stress of the last few weeks, she was not handling this well. 'Will you excuse me, I have a lunch meeting with my lawyer, can't keep him waiting, costs too much.'

'Of course, Mrs Wellby, thank you for agreeing to see us. We can show ourselves out.'

Sandie nodded and left the room, crossed the hallway and into the kitchen. She pressed the internal phone line and buzzed through to Marcus who was working in Robert's study. 'Marcus, I've got to get out of here before I go mad. How about lunch at The Fox, I'll book us a table, and call Bramley, I think I know how he got my prints . . .'

The reporter replaced the phone and joined the photographer on the front step. 'I didn't get a picture.'

'Never mind, we'll go and get one at The Fox, take a look at the actress when she isn't acting.'

CAT WAS LEAVING THE computer teacher's office when she saw Bramley. She ducked behind some students as he got out of his car. She watched him eye the crowd of students as they spilled out of the college entrance. He passed close by her, but did not see her. Following the problems her hair had caused, she had remembered to tuck it up under one of Dan's woolly Tibetan hats. Instant student – just add ethnic weave wear. She blended in nicely. He wasn't going into the computer block, so Cat decided to follow him. She kept her distance but never lost sight of him as he walked through the corridors. Finally he reached a fire exit door which led out to a grassy courtyard. Boys were lying topless on the grass. Cat was momentarily distracted. It was a while before she realized she had actually stopped walking and had started staring. Things must be bad if she was beginning to ogle young men. She was beginning to show her age. She tore herself away from the undulating mass of half-naked bodies and followed Bramley to a building on the northern side of the courtyard. After a few moments she followed him in. She walked down the corridor. It was designed like most of the colleges she had ever been in. Each classroom had a double door, painted a hideous colour, with a window. Cat saw Bramley approach three solemn-looking girls in sensible clothes. They didn't seem to fit in with the rabble she had seen out on the lawn. They were wearing knee-length skirts and cotton shirts. So much for the power of femininity, thought Cat. They were sitting straight-backed, feet firmly on the floor, on wooden chairs next to an open window. Luck was on her side. She jogged softly back down the courtyard and moved into position under the open window. She couldn't catch every word because of the noise going on around her but what she did, she scribbled in her note pad. Amy? Emily Hasson. Rachel? Good Friends. Someone in tears. Feeling responsible. Why – Br. (short for Bramley). Problems at home. With stepmother. Didn't come forward. Jane didn't want us to. Why – Br. Scared. Of stepmother – Br. Yes. No. Girls arguing about something. What about Dad? – Br. Cat couldn't get the answer. The girls were sobbing. Cat was trying to get nearer to the window when a sweet smell wafted past her. Marijuana. She looked up nervously. It was going straight into the open window. She ducked lower and looked around her. She didn't want Bramley to have a reason to put his head through the open window and seek out the smell. Cat edged along the front of the building and turned the corner. Sure enough, in the shade of the building sat a young lad, cross-legged, halfway through a tightly rolled joint.

'Are you mad?' said Cat.

He looked up and smiled. 'Hi.'

'There is a policeman in that classroom,' she said

pointing frantically at the brick wall. He looked confused. 'Your smoke is going straight through the window.' He still looked confused. 'Round the front.'

'Shit.' He looked at his joint sadly, then broke the lit end off. 'Thanks,' he said to Cat. She shrugged and crouched back down to return to her place under the window. Moments later the lad appeared next to her. 'Why are the police here?' Cat put her finger to her mouth. She was busy writing notes. Church?? Regularly?? Did she believe – Br. Absolutely. Jane Wellby found God, she wrote and underlined. There were more tears from the girls above her. Guilt, wrote Cat.

'No way,' said the lad, looking over her shoulder. Cat pulled the notebook to her chest.

'Do you mind.'

'No,' he said, smiling still. 'Do you want a fag?' Cat looked at him, he was holding out a packet of Benson and Hedges. 'Fag?' he said again.

Cat shook her head. He frowned. 'Don't smoke,' she added by way of explanation.

'Really?' he said, not sarcastically. 'Weird.' He broke off the filter of the cigarette, tucked it into his top pocket and put the rest of it in his mouth. Cat watched him. 'Takes a thousand years to decompose, very unhealthy,' he said tapping his breast pocket. Cat wondered whether he was talking about a nipple ring. She smiled and marked him down as a nutter. 'My name is Julian,' he said smiling at her. 'But everyone calls me J.J.'

'My name is Catherine,' she replied in a whisper. 'But everyone calls me Cat.'

'I take photos. I'm going to be a photographer,' he said, also lowering his voice.

She studied him for a moment. 'I'm trying to be a journalist, so do you mind?'

'Mind what?'

'Shutting up,' she said trying not to lose her patience.

J.J. didn't seem to hear her. 'It's that Jane Wellby isn't it? Those girls didn't have a chance against a girl like that.'

BRAMLEY WHISTLED TO HIMSELF as he walked back past the heathens on the grass and pitied the poor taxpayer. Bloody good-for-nothing students, not a solid employee among them. Let alone a copper. But he would not let the sight of them lessen his good mood. Those girls had confirmed everything he had read in the diary and more. Sandie Wellby was not getting out of this one. He couldn't have wished for better witnesses if he had ordered them hot off the press. Three girls, timid and shy, as girls should be, in his opinion, all feeling personally responsible for not having gone to the authorities sooner with the information they had on Jane Wellby's personal life. The jury wouldn't blame them though, oh no, not good little girls like that. No they would blame the person responsible for all this grief and for the death of a young girl. Sandie-Ann Surly, two-bit American actress turned killer. Jane Wellby, the girls would weep, our dear friend, confided in us the mental anguish and torture she went through at home at the hands of her stepmother. They would verify to the jury how Jane, quite rightly it seemed, was convinced no one would believe her. The only people she could confide in were her three college friends and the pages of her diary. The girls would reaffirm the power the actress had over friends and family, and warn them not to be taken in by it themselves. They would cry on the stand, Bramley would make sure of that, just as they had in front of him. Did they believe Jane, oh yes, they would say, but who could they tell? Jane was adamant they kept it secret. Why? Because she was terrified of losing the love of her father and mother. Everyone adored Sandie. Why would anyone believe her? To avoid that, she told her friends, she would endure anything except death. Did Jane Wellby want to die? No, your Honour, she wanted to live, maybe study therapy and counsel others that had been in her position. Bramley smiled, as he thought of the three perfect witnesses for the prosecution. He called into the police station.

'Mike, is that you?' he said, getting into his car.

'Yes, Gov.'

'Let everyone know the kids at the school knew all along about what was happening to Jane. It came out almost at the beginning of their course. Jane had been really quiet and these three girls who knew each other from their previous schools felt sorry for her. Then they found her in tears one lunchtime and they tried to comfort her. She started by saying she was having trouble at home, never specified. Then it would be fine for a few weeks, then she would be in tears again. The girls can just about remember vague times, I bet, if we push them, we can match it up to the diary dates. They'll be coming in to make an official statement at the weekend, so I want a list of the dates by then.'

'I think it's nearly finished anyway.'

'Good. They are prepared to go to court but are scared about coming face to face with the family, especially the second Mrs Wellby. Maybe we can get counsel to go over things with them, practise. Get on to it. Has she checked in yet?'

'Who, Gov?'

'Who do you think, you blithering idiot, the Queen Mum?'

'Sorry, Gov, not with you.'

'Sandie Wellby,' said Bramley with despair. He stared out of the window and resigned himself to the fact that he was surrounded by idiots.

'Oh, Mrs Wellby, yeah, she's checked in. Had a smooth-looking bloke with her too. Said he wanted a copy of all our interview records and a copy of the first search warrant and the fingerprints from the hose, which he says are not admissible because of how you obtained her fingerprints and—'

'I don't want to know, Mike.'

'But, Gov, she wanted me to ask you if she could have her mug back.' Mike sounded perplexed. 'She says the set doesn't match up without it. God knows what that was about.'

'She's barking mad, don't worry about it. Ignore her. Instead I want you to call Calorie Carers and tell Ms Reed I will be with her shortly.'

Bramley hung up. Fucking lawyers. Stirring things up. The world would be a better place if there were no lawyers and the guilty went to prison, and not, as was more often the case, on holiday with money won in damages by lawyers who were too fucking clever for the likes of the average juror. What was the world coming to? Fucking mug. Bramley started his car, as he pulled out of his parking place with one hand, he pushed his electric window down with the other. 'Mug? What fucking mug?' he said, smiling. From his glove compartment he pulled an unmarked jiffy bag. He took the mug out of it, hooked it loosely under his right index finger and as he drove away from the college he dangled it out of the window. At the corner he dropped it. It smashed just as Bramley put his foot on the accelerator and turned into the traffic.

'Oops.'

CAT'S SCALP WAS BEGINNING to itch. She couldn't wait any longer and anyway, Bramley was already pulling out of his parking place, he wouldn't see her. She turned her back to the car, tugged the hat off and bent forwards to let her hair escape.

'God, that's so much better.' Cat flicked her hair

back, then ran her fingers through it a dozen times. By the time she turned around, Bramley's car had disappeared into the traffic. She was hungry. Her new-found friend had disappeared.

'J.J.,' she called out.

'Yeah,' replied a voice, not too far away.

'Where are you?'

J.J. stepped out from behind a tree. 'Here,' he said emphatically.

'Fancy something to eat?' She wanted to know anything he could tell her about Jane Wellby.

'At college?'

'We could go somewhere else if you'd prefer.' J.J. eyed her suspiciously. 'I'll pay,' she said helpfully. He narrowed his eyes in concentration, thinking hard, his head swaying from side to side. Cat reckoned he was weighing up the pros and cons of going off with some stranger he had never met before who followed policemen around and was engrossed with the life of a dead girl. She didn't begrudge him the deliberation. Finally he straightened up. 'Come to think of it, I am hungry.'

'Great. Let's go.' Cat and J.J. set off down the road to find a cheap café. She had offered to pay but she only had fifteen pounds to her name, so cheap was essential. She wondered if she was doing the right thing, if he took five minutes to decide whether he was hungry or not, questioning him on Jane Wellby might be more arduous than she could cope with. Then he answered the question for her.

'If you really want the low-down on that girl you should talk to my half-brother. He's the one who knew her. Actually they had a thing for a bit.' J.J. pulled a face. 'Not my cup of tea at all, but there you go, just because we are blood related doesn't mean we have to share the same desires and dreams, eh?' Cat nodded. She was beginning to like J.J.

'Where would I find your half-brother then?'

'He manages a posh bar in Chelmsford – Madison's, do you know it?' Cat shook her head. 'No, can't say you look the type. Dreadful place, but they flock there in their thousands.'

'Jane went there?'

'Oh, yes. Quite the little groupy. Flashing her Amex,' he said, 'and the rest.'

'Really?' She thought about Amy, Emily and Rachel. It didn't seem likely.

'Look, if you don't believe me, talk to my half-brother, he'll tell you what Jane is really like.'

'Is?'

'Yeah? I'd love you to write an exposé on her.'

'J.J., haven't you heard the news?'

He frowned. 'What news?'

'Jane was found dead in her father's car last Friday.'

'No?'

Cat nodded.

'Come on,' he said, 'we've got to go and see my half-brother now.' Cat looked nervous. Chelmsford wasn't on her way home. 'Please, I haven't got a car, he needs to know this.'

Cat was suddenly nervous. How did he know she had a car? Maybe she was being set up. If Jane really was murdered, getting into a car with a stranger was not such an intelligent thing to do.

J.J. shook his finger at her. 'None of that bad karma stuff, Cat, thoughts like that give you bad energy, and there isn't any need for concern.' He had an angelic face under all the hair. 'I'm perfectly safe,' he said. 'Trust me, you want an honest opinion of Jane Wellby, you've got to talk to him.'

'Okay,' she said eventually. 'Let's go and meet J.J. senior.'

They crossed the road and started walking to her car. 'Actually,' said J.J., 'his name is Paul.'

'So, Ms Reed—'

'Please, call me Lynne.' Bramley smiled at the woman. 'Would you like a drink? Coffee? Tea?' Lynne paused, a knowing look on her face.

'No, thank you,' he replied.

Lynne's smile lessened. 'I'm so glad you managed to find time in your busy day to come and see us. I knew Jane terribly well, you know,' Lynne Reed said dramatically. 'Dreadful business.'

'Indeed,' sighed the policeman. Women were all right, he supposed, but they always made so much noise.

Waiting to see whether he now had her attention, he started again. He opened his notebook. 'So, Ms Re—'

'Oh now,' Lynne cackled, 'aren't you the funny man. It's Lynne to you.' Lynne had been reading an article earlier about the attractiveness of being coy. Men, according to the magazine, liked women who were girly, it was less threatening, left the man thinking he was in control. Lynne liked the idea of Detective Chief Inspector Bramley being in control of her.

Bramley inhaled deeply. 'Lynne,' he said. She smiled. 'I was hoping you could make an official statement for the case against Mrs Wellby.'

A look of uncertainty passed over her face.

'It's routine. It means we can use your statement in court.'

'Well I—' She paused. 'What's going to happen to her, Mrs Wellby?'

'That's up to the court to decide. Look, nothing you said contradicted anyone else, in fact it was very helpful.'

'It was?'

'Yes.' Bramley forced a reassuring smile.

'So Jane really was bullied by Mrs Wellby?'

Bramley nodded. 'It looks that way.'

'Well, I'd love to help you, but it's my lunch break and I'm absolutely starving.'

'Oh, later then.'

'Sorry, I'm off to a three-day dieting seminar at the NEC.'

'This is important,' said Bramley.

'Well,' Lynne sighed dramatically, 'there is only one thing for it. Join me for lunch.'

'That wouldn't be appropriate, you being a witness.'

'Oh poppycock, it's only a sandwich.' She stood up. 'I'll get my coat.'

Bramley nodded. He needed an adult witness like Lynne Reed.

'I'll just tell the girls.'

She was back in five minutes with fresh lipstick, newly brushed hair, and pinker cheeks than when she had left. 'Let's go then,' she said. 'The café looks full, we'll go to the pub.'

'Fine.' He could do with a pint.

'I'll drive.'

'Drive?'

'Trust me, Detective Chief Inspector,' said Lynne steering him towards the door.

'Um, call me Douglas.'

Lynne nearly sang. Mrs Douglas Bramley. That would do nicely.

'TURN RIGHT HERE, CAT.'

'Okay.' They had been driving for fifteen minutes along the A414 and were now on the outskirts of Chelmsford. Cat had pointed out Cedar Hall as they drove past it. J.J. whistled. No wonder Jane could afford to buy Paul all those things. Apparently, over their four-month affair, she had bought him a leather jacket, an expensive watch, designer clothes. As J.J. explained, Paul had only been a barman back then and he couldn't always rely on the tips.

'So when did their affair end?' asked Cat.

'About two years ago. She was doing retakes, I think. Or not doing them as the case may be.'

'How did it end?'

'Very abruptly. Paul was a mess.'

'I'm sorry.'

'She fucked him, Cat. Real bad. He's back on his feet now, but it took a while. Didn't go near the girls for ages, and he has always been one for the girls.'

Cat looked over to J.J. 'What about you?'

He smiled innocently. 'I prefer to look at them through a lens. It's here on the left,' he said pointing out the window. Madison's was a low-level cream building with a long window designed to look like the New York skyline. There was parking enough for sixty cars and a no trainers or soiled clothes policy. Before she entered she knew it wasn't her *kinda place*. Inside a list of expensive cocktails adorned the walls, written in cartoon chalk: HIGHBALL, 5th AVE., BLOOMINGDALES. Cat and J.J. exchanged glances as they crossed the highly polished wooden floor. The bar was not full, a table of female office workers celebrating a departure drank cocktails out of jugs, a few men propped up the bar, other than that it was empty. The waiter practised his 'flair' behind the bar. J.J. went over to him. 'Hi, is Paul about?' The waiter nodded, picked up a telephone and pressed an internal line. 'You are?'

'His brother.' The waiter relayed the information and returned to his routine. A few moments later a door at the back opened.

'Hello, little brother, what brings you down here?'

'Cat,' he said smiling.

'J.J. don't go all strange and spiritual on me, I'm busy. If you are getting signals from feline friends it is time I got you laid. And I know just the place.' Paul walked forward and put his arm across J.J.'s shoulders. J.J. didn't look the slightest bit embarrassed, but Cat was.

'Unless of course by cat you mean pu—'

'I'm Cat,' she said quickly. 'Short for Catherine.'

Paul looked at her and raised an eyebrow slowly. 'Really?' Cat felt about two inches high. 'Well, Cat, short for Catherine, what can I do for you?' The guys at the bar dragged their attention from Sky sports and looked at Cat. Paul was happy to play to his punters. So much for the heartbroken, humbled man J.J. had described. 'Looking for a good time?' He clicked his fingers at the waiter. 'You've certainly come to the right place. How about a drink?' Cat shook her head. 'Come on, it'll loosen your tongue.' *Don't say it.* 'Or has the cat got it.' The men chuckled.

'Very original,' said Cat.

'Thanks.' He winked.

'I didn't mean it.'

'Hey, we've got a live one here, boys.' He took a step closer. J.J. was still caught under his arm. 'So what do you want with me, Cat? Heard about the amazing service that Madison's has to offer? Want a sample?'

'No thanks,' she said. 'I know what a cocktail saus-age looks like.' The other men sniggered quietly. Paul smiled, but it was tight-lipped. 'The only reason I am here is to ask you a few questions about Jane Wellby.' Then his expression changed. The smile disappeared completely.

'I'll see you in my office,' he said sharply, releasing J.J. from his brotherly grip and walking quickly back to the door he had come through. Cat looked at J.J. nervously, he signalled for her to follow. Paul had left the door slightly ajar. She walked through it into an office. Cat noticed the large sofa immediately and wondered whether Madison's services were sampled there. Paul was standing behind his desk. Cat closed the door behind her. He looked up at her slowly.

'You remember her?' she asked.

'Remember her?' He laughed. 'I'll never be able to forget her,' he said as his head dropped back down.

Cat looked at her feet. She hadn't been expecting that. 'I'm sorry, I heard you had a . . .' She paused. He didn't know. Shit. *He didn't know either.*

'A what? I doubt *you* would understand.'

'You obviously cared very deeply for her, I'm sorry.'

Paul started shaking his head. 'What are you so sorry about, has she sent you here to laugh at me? Her handiwork? She has no power over me any more so you can get out of my office.'

Cat bit her lip. 'Paul, Jane is dead.'

He was round the desk in seconds. 'What?'

'I'm really sorry, I thought you'd know. I feel terrible having to tell you the bad news.'

'Bad news?'

'I mean terrible, terrible news,' she said sounding as remorseful as she could. He was holding on to the desk, his eyes fixed on hers, a curious expression on his face. Cat thought he might burst into tears. 'I'm sorry you had to find out like this.'

'She's really dead?'

'I'm so sorry.'

'Why? Did you do it?'

'No!'

'Pity,' he said, standing up straight, 'I was going to offer you free drinks for the rest of your life.'

'What?'

'So who killed her then?'

'How do you know someone killed her?'

'Bitch like that was going to get her come-uppance some time. I just wish I'd had the fucking guts to do it. Still, no reason why we can't celebrate. Drink?'

Chapter Seventeen

Marcus pulled out a chair for Sandie. He'd asked for a table in the smoking section of the dining room. Less conspicuous. He didn't want anyone thinking they were out celebrating. Sandie sat down heavily. 'Jesus, I am exhausted. I need a drink.' Marcus beckoned the waiter over immediately.

'Two large vodkas and tonic,' he said.

'You not drinking?' she said smiling.

'Very funny.' He looked up at the waiter. 'We'll order the food later.'

'Thanks for coming with me, I feel like everyone is watching me when I go anywhere near home. Fucking spies, watching my every move, waiting to pounce. Just holding my tongue is driving me mad.'

'We're lucky they even gave us bail, Sandie.'

'With your eyes, darling, and my money, they couldn't refuse.'

Marcus knew better than to argue with her.

'That fucking bitch,' said Sandie, shaking her head.

'Hey, come on,' said Marcus, not wanting a scene.

'Well, she was a fucking bitch. You know I was actually relieved when I saw that she was dead. I thought thank God, it's over. Freedom,' she said, waving her hands in the air. The waiter approached with the drinks. Sandie smiled warmly at him. 'Thank you so much,' she said. The boy smiled back. Sandie waited for him to leave before continuing. 'And now the trouble-making little cow is still fucking at it. You know I heard them, Fiona and Robert, discussing Jane's death in the middle of the night. They had me nailed before they had even found that fucking diary. Where's our copy, the police are deliberately stalling.'

'Concentrate on ordering. You're losing weight,' he said changing the subject. He didn't want Sandie seeing the diary.

'I could go on chat shows with this new wonder diet, weight loss guaranteed, only murder required. Easy.'

'Shh,' he said watching the waiter return with the menus.

The boy went straight to Sandie. 'What's the best thing The Fox has to offer?' said Sandie coyly. Marcus kicked her under the table. She smiled at him.

'Um, well, the um, steak and Guinness pie is excellent.'

'Is there anything a little less –' she paused, looking him up and down, 'meaty?'

'Dover sole,' he said beginning to sweat.

'Perfect.'

'Make that two,' said Marcus. 'And another round of these,' he said picking up his glass.

'Oh, and the wine list if you wouldn't mind,' said Sandie.

'You are incorrigible,' he said in a whisper as the boy left.

'Hey, I'm a condemned woman, I'll get my kicks where and when I can.'

'We'll sort this, Sandie, promise.'

Sandie looked away. She stared out of the window. 'I can't believe she wrote a fucking diary,' she said as she downed the rest of the vodka and tonic.

CAT WATCHED PAUL POUR another vodka and Diet Coke down his throat. It was the colour of pale ale. She could smell the fumes as he walked past her. He was visiting the gents for the fourth time. His feelings for Jane Wellby completely confused her, one minute he was toasting her demise, the next a look of unbearable regret came over his face and he sat as still as stone, staring into space. Then he'd start whistling the tune of 'The Wicked Witch Is Dead' and laugh. It was beginning to freak her out, but she didn't want to leave until she'd made some sense of their relationship. Which made her think of Dan. On impulse she picked up the phone on Paul's desk and dialled his number.

'Hi. It's me.'

'Cat.' He sounded surprised. 'Where are you?'

Why did that sound so accusing? 'Essex. I was wondering, could we meet up later?'

'At Amelia's?'

'You want to meet at Gran's?'

'No. Are you with her now?'

'Why is it so important where I am?' she said. 'What is the difference? Do you want to meet up or not?'

'Why are you being so cagey? I don't mind.'

'Dan, please, I don't want to fight any more. I hate it.'

'So do I. Look, I'm sorry, I don't know what's got into me, I'm sure this is all my fault.'

'Probably,' said Cat, smiling, butterflies springing up in her tummy.

'Why don't we meet up later, spend some time, just you and me?'

The door to the office opened. Cat looked up guiltily. Paul was holding a bottle. 'I think this calls for champagne,' he said loudly, 'then we can get down to the really hot stuff.'

'Who's that?'

'Um—'

'I thought you said you were at Amelia's.'

'I'm not. I'm in a bar in Chelmsford. Thought you'd be pleased.'

'Not just any old bar,' said Paul, 'the best fucking bar in Essex, with sexy, well-endowed staff.' Paul started laughing.

Cat heard the phone click on the other end. She stared at it for a moment then replaced it. 'Sorry,' she said, 'had to phone home.'

'Was it something I said?' He passed her a glass, still laughing.

'Where's J.J.?'

'I've sent him home in a cab.'

Before Cat had a chance to voice her concern. 'You understand,' said Paul, 'he's my kid brother, I don't want him to know anything about that sordid part of my life. And we've got some celebrating to do.'

BRAMLEY WAS ACTUALLY ENJOYING himself. With a woman too. She laughed at his jokes, let him talk about his job, the difficulties that came with it, she seemed very sympathetic indeed. Her obvious delight at being out with his good self was so endearing that he'd decided to do something he hadn't done for years. Spend some money. Bramley was not fond of spending money for spending money's sake. In fact he loathed it. But Lynne Reed, with her rosy cheeks and heaving bosom, had brought about in him a desire to spend some money on something other than his green fees. This was the one good restaurant outside town, a country pub which served steak and Guinness pie, wild boar sausages with Cumberland sauce and bubble and squeak. Bramley had done a few favours for the owner, by getting them planning permission for the expansion of the conservatory that they now sat in. He liked the extra fuss he got there.

Quite right for a man of his standing. He thought it might impress Ms Reed, she certainly looked like she was enjoying herself.

LYNNE REED WAS ENJOYING herself so much she thought she'd died and gone to heaven. The astrologer had been right all along. They'd said a man of great integrity was about to enter her life. She had, as the astrologer suggested, been looking out so as not to miss him. And all thanks to Jane Wellby. As she lifted her glass of Baileys to her lips, she toasted the dead girl.

'What are you smiling about?' asked Bramley.

'Oh, nothing, just thinking how nice it is not to be in the office. I feel like I'm playing truant.'

'Well, I'm sure you deserve it. It must be hard, working all day then going home to cook for your . . .' He paused. Lynne had rings on every finger. It was a defence mechanism.

'. . . Mother?' she finished for him.

'Indeed. Your mother. Is she . . .' His hand circled, trying to find the word.

'Incapacitated?' offered Lynne.

Bramley nodded.

'Yes, I'm afraid. She hasn't got long to go.'

'I'm terribly sorry.' He was lying. He hated old people.

'Don't be. It will be a blessing. She can't do anything for herself any more. Very undignified. Sorry, there I go again banging on about my silly problems when you have so much to think about. It must be terribly stressful being a policeman. I hope you have someone very gentle to look after you when you get home. For instance your—'

'Mother. Actually she passed away last year. As you said, a blessing really.'

'Do you ever get lonely?' Lynne asked. For a moment Bramley seemed startled. 'I'm sorry,' she said, 'that was terribly impertinent.'

Then Bramley surprised himself by smiling. 'No it wasn't. To answer your question, yes, actually, I do get lonely, though, funny thing is, I don't think I ever notice it.'

'Oh,' she said, deflated.

'Until now, that is.' Lynne's face lit up. It was the Christmas tree in Trafalgar Square and the Oxford Street lights all rolled into one.

THE DRINKS SANDIE POURED down her throat barely touched the sides. Marcus realized he should take her home before anyone saw them. The pub was off the beaten track, and quiet, but he was not a man who liked to take chances. He ordered the bill. Sandie protested.

'Oh, come on, just a little more fun for the murderess,' she said, slurring her words.

'Sandie, please, finish your water.'

She picked up her wine glass and drained it. 'Oh dear, wrong one.' He shook his head disapprovingly at her.

'Oh, for Christ's sake, give me a goddamm break. If I had known you were going to be a party pooper as well I wouldn't have asked you along for the ride.'

'Sandie, please?' He looked around nervously. The waiter approached. 'The bill please,' said Marcus.

'Oh, come on, don't get the cheque yet, just one more.' She stretched her arms high in the air and arched her back. The tight cotton dress stretched over her breasts. The boy stared. 'Please?'

'Bill?' said Marcus impatiently. The boy backed off.

'Do you think he'd fuck an old lady like me,' she said looking after him. Marcus's eyes widened. He cleared his throat nervously. 'Oh, don't be such a stiffy, pity that stepdaughter of mine never brought any nice ones like that back. God, she was a sour old thing, a nice boy might have cheered up the place, young juicy blood—'

'Sandie!'

'What!' she said mimicking his alarm.

'Mrs Wellby,' said the familiar sing-sing voice behind her.

'Shit,' she said loudly before turning round. 'Detective Chief Inspector Bramley, how auspicious, we were just talking about you.'

Marcus stood up. 'My client has been under an enormous amount of pressure, talking now is not a good idea.'

'Drowning your sorrows, Mrs Wellby?' said Bramley.

'Something like that, Detective Chief Inspector,' she said as her eyelids flickered up and down.

'Very understandable,' he said, 'to lose someone is a terrible thing.' Sandie nodded. She was too drunk to get to grips with what he was saying. 'To lose your freedom is something entirely different.' The expression on Sandie's face changed. The colour drained from her face. She stood up shakily.

'There is no way on God's earth that you are going to pin this on me.'

Bramley pulled away from the alcoholic fumes. 'Mrs Wellby, I don't have to. You are doing a fine job yourself.'

She pointed a finger at him. 'This ain't over.'

'Sandie,' interrupted Marcus, 'we're going.'

'I suggest you take your lawyer's advice and leave before you say something incriminating.'

'Douglas!' called Lynne Reed, uncomfortable at having been left alone for so long. Bramley swung round. 'I'll be there in a minute,' he said anxiously, 'stay there.'

'Where are you?' called out the voice.

'What are you getting so nervous about,' said Sandie, watching him. He shot her a look of loathing and marched out to head off Lynne Reed. Sandie followed. Lynne stood at the entrance peering in. She had a lump of trifle lodged in the corner of her mouth.

'Well, well, well,' said Sandie.

'Mrs Wellby,' said Lynne startled.

'Ain't this a nice little conspiracy, what have you been saying, *Ms* Reed?'

'I, I . . .'

'Surely there is an easier way of getting laid than falsifying evidence against me, shit, *I* could have paid someone.'

'Sandie, that's enough,' said Marcus, taking her arm.

'Get off me.'

'Sandie. Enough.' He pulled her towards the exit, she nearly fell twice.

'You'll regret this,' she said turning back to them. Marcus pulled her again. This time she lost her balance completely and fell.

'How very unladylike,' said Lynne, stepping over Sandie. The young waiter ran over, and with Marcus on the other side took an arm and helped her across the car park to the car. Marcus shoved a wad of cash into the boy's hand.

'Keep the change,' he said, 'and keep quiet.' The boy nodded. After watching the car leave he walked back to the pub counting the money. They'd left him a fifty quid tip. This was turning out to be quite a profitable day. He half-turned back to the car park, saw the journalist and gave him the thumbs-up sign.

CAT LEFT HER GLASS untouched on Paul's desk as he continued to drink.

'I can't tell you how relieved I am to hear about Jane, I suppose you think that is a terrible thing to say, but you didn't know her.'

'I'd like to know more about her though.'

'Why? Call me old-fashioned but you don't look the type of girl to get involved with a slag like that.'

'I'm more involved with the family,' said Cat. 'There are a few things about her death that don't add up.'

'Don't tell me, they can't understand why she would hang herself from the back of her bedroom door with a dildo up her arse?' Cat grimaced. Paul didn't seem to notice. 'Or was it a bad E. I wouldn't be surprised if someone slipped her one on purpose.'

'Are we talking about the same Jane Wellby? She was rather religious at college and had a group of very square friends.'

'Yeah, well, it's always the quiet ones.' Paul stood up and walked around to the front of the desk. 'You really don't know what she was like, do you?'

'I don't think anyone did. You see her stepmother has been accused of killing her. Apparently the woman had been abusing Jane for years.'

'I don't think so,' said Paul laughing bitterly. 'She'd take too much pleasure out of that. She liked pain.'

'Well apparently this was more mental than physical,' she said cautiously.

'Yeah well, she was pretty good at fucking with your head as well.' He shook his own head to demonstrate. 'They must have been quite a pair,' he said looking down.

'Paul,' said Cat tentatively, 'can you tell me what she did to you?' He started shaking his head slowly. 'I really need to know, you see, something I said has put Mrs Wellby in the frame for Jane's death, she is being nailed by the police, everyone else thinks Jane was an innocent naïve little thing. Please?'

'Why should I?'

'Because otherwise no one will know what she was like.'

'Sorry, mate. I don't want anyone knowing that I was duped by the twisted cow.'

'Then Mrs Wellby will go to prison and it'll be your fault as much as mine. Looks like Jane wins again.'

'You reckon? I'd've killed her if she was my step-daughter, you have no idea . . .'

'Then *tell* me,' Cat pleaded.

Paul took a long drink. He sighed. 'I used to supplement my earning power quite nicely through rich girls like Jane Wellby. And before you give me the fucking how could you do that to women lecture, you lot have been doing it for years. Dinner, drinks, money for taxis, you name it. What did I have to show for it? Fuck all. A shag.' He sneered derisively. 'So I decided to turn the tables on the stuck-up tarts. Trick is to go for the insecure ones. Working behind a bar for years gives you a pretty good insight into people. You can spot them a mile off. The desperate ones. Got it wrong with Jane though, oh yes, missed that one.'

'What do you mean supplement?'

'I was the sexy barman with the sob story, got the patter down to a fine art. I'd appeal to their over-privileged consciences, they'd start handing out gifts and cash before I got to the bit about the living rough in my teens. All bullshit of course. I was their project, you see. Their new toy. I can't tell you how many barbecues I've been dragged along to and paraded around like a poodle at Crufts. Nine times out of ten Daddy would try and see me off. I'd do my bit, tell him that I loved his daughter, beg her to come with me, ten times out of ten, they did. After that it was easy. And the beauty was, I still had the pick of the bunch wherever I worked. Sweet as . . .' He looked at Cat. 'Not so long ago I could have done it to you.'

'Sorry, but I haven't got a rich daddy.'

'Oh, I wouldn't do you for money. I'd flatter your intelligence. Ask you why more women weren't like you. Your spirit, your sense of humour, your whole being, I wouldn't be able to get you out of my head, I'd tell you I'd never met anyone like you. I'd flatter you into submission. You'd come back to my bar. You wouldn't be able to help yourself.' Cat looked at him. He was good-looking, there was no denying it. He was the sort of male you would want to pay you attention, even if it was only to turn him down. Which you probably wouldn't.

'But not now?' she said.

Paul shook his head. 'I'm afraid you would be very disappointed.' His voice was beginning to crack.

'What did she do to you, Paul?'

After a while he spoke. 'It started with little things at

first. I was impressed actually, usually it's me who teaches them. But Jane was different. She liked to be different.'

'What, clothes, hair, what?'

Paul laughed. 'Sex. I'm talking about sex. Lots of it, and not very nice. Get it?' Cat stared blankly. 'No, course you don't. Never been tied up? Bet you haven't. You'd call the police if your bloke slapped you around. That is the sort of sex I'm talking about. She was playing with me all along. Here's a leather jacket, let's go to bed and I'll let you fuck me up the arse, new parts for the bike, tie me up. Nothing unusual to begin with.'

Nothing unusual? Cat watched him push himself away from the desk and walk over to the drinks cabinet. He found another glass, another bottle. 'Then it changed,' he said turning back.

Cat sat down. 'Why?'

'She knew it was time for me to move on, you know, she had no intention of letting me get away with it.'

'Getting away with what?'

'Haven't you been listening? I controlled them. I dictated everything they did, said, wore. I spent their money. Everything. Jane didn't like not being in control, don't you see, that was what made her tick. So I had to be punished. And that is what she did. Not a simple, cut up your clothes, throw your CD system out of the window revenge, oh no, she was much more inventive. Cunt ruined my fucking life.'

Cat ignored the comment. 'What did she do?'

'She'd got my confidence, I let her tie me up.' He hit

his head. 'How could I have missed it, the madness, it's in the eyes. If you look hard enough. I let her tie me up. She goes to the bathroom and comes back with a fucking knife. A knife!' Paul walked over to where Cat sat. He put each arm on either side of her and leant down. Cat shifted further back in the chair. Vodka fumes. Exhaust fumes.

'No sweet-talking me out of this one was there, oh no. She starts quoting the religious shit, she said that people like me should be banned from the kingdom of God, like what the fuck do I know about that crap? I told her I wasn't interested in no pearly gates, when I die, I rot. End of story. Big deal. I begged her to let me go. She never had any intention of letting me go, but she got a big kick out of watching me squirm. She had the power. She was in control of my fucking destiny.'

'I don't understand.'

'Yeah, well, neither did I until I read the Bible. The wrath of God. You ask me, he got the devil to do his work. Some might say I had it coming, but no one deserves this.' Paul stood up suddenly, walked over to the door and locked it. Cat looked around quickly for another way out. There wasn't one. 'You want to know what Jane was really like?' Cat nodded nervously. She watched in horror as Paul slowly undid his trousers.

'Look Paul, I um, there's been a misunderstanding here.' She tried to get up. He pushed her back down.

'Shut up!' Paul yanked his trousers and boxer shorts down to his knees and stood up. Cat was about to scream when she saw for the first time what Jane Wellby was really like. All around his groin were small scars, twenty or thirty of them. Taut, white, puckered flesh against the rest of his tanned skin. But the scars were nothing compared to the mangled object that lay in the place where his penis should have been.

'Like you said, cocktail sausage,' he said looking at Cat. As he pulled his trousers up he started to cry. 'Deuteronomy, chapter twenty-three, verse one,' said Paul. 'No man whose testicles have been crushed or whose organ has been severed shall become a member of the assembly of the Lord.'

Cat shook her head. 'Oh, Paul, you can't take that literally . . .'

'I don't want to go to hell, Cat, she'll be there.'

Chapter Eighteen

It was a dingy pub hidden in the back streets of the Great Eastern Road that provided a slow route out to the East and Hackney High Street. Wholesale territory. Robert sat in his car and watched the black-painted door of the pub nervously. He fingered the crisp fifty-pound note in his pocket and hoped that it would be enough. It was now or never. If he didn't get back to Fiona's soon she might start to get suspicious. It was a simple question. Would the landlord of this particular insalubrious establishment tell anyone who may come asking that he was in the pub during the hours of twelve to two on the Friday Jane died. It wasn't the police Robert was so worried about. The landlord didn't like the police, he would have no qualms lying to them, it was Marcus England and his high-performing purchasing power. The landlord would sell to the highest bidder. He didn't owe Robert any favours. Robert took out his wallet and withdrew another fifty-pound note. Surely that was enough to ensure total co-operation.

Robert locked the car and walked to the door, this was it.

'Mr Wellby,' said the landlord as Robert entered. 'Where have you been? I get nervous when I lose one of my regulars.'

Robert put his briefcase down and shook the man's hand. 'Family business.'

'Very important, families. Hope everything is sorted out now.'

'Not really.'

'I'm sorry to hear that,' said the landlord, wiping his hands on a red-checked drying cloth.

'Well that rather depends on you.'

'Oh really?'

'The Friday before last. I was here, at lunchtime.'

The landlord nodded. 'Go on.'

'And then I left to go to a meeting.'

'You did?'

'But not until about two thirty. And while you're trying to remember, perhaps I could trouble you for a glass of my usual.'

'Certainly, Mr Wellby.' He took a glass off the shelf above him and put it under the nozzle and pulled down on the arm. 'Friday before last. Well you were certainly here when we opened up' – he passed the beer to Robert – 'as usual.'

'Thank you,' said Robert, accepting the glass and reaching into his pocket to pay. He handed over the money. The landlord looked at the notes in his hand. 'The money I owe for my tab,' he said nervously.

'Your tab?'

Robert nodded. 'My tab.'

He looked at Robert for a while. Robert brought the glass up to his lips and let the warm, bitter liquid slide into his mouth, he watched the landlord over the top of the glass, silently praying. Eventually he pocketed the money. 'The slate is clean,' he said. Robert opened his mouth and took several gulps of beer and breath. 'Now about that Friday. I remember that day clearly, because you helped me throw out a couple of scally-wags trying to sell stolen Adidas sportswear, for which I am truly grateful. I bought you a round of smoked salmon sandwiches, the best in the area, to say thank you.'

'They were delicious,' said Robert, finishing his beer quickly. 'Thank you.'

'All part of the service.' Robert tipped his head and left the pub. It had cost him one hundred pounds for half an Adnams and an alibi. He returned to his car. It was only a matter of time before they caught up with him. Before Sandie caught up with him. He couldn't protect the family name any longer. Robert watched an over-weight middle-aged man enter the pub. The man walked with dejection in every step, he too was headed for the bottom of a bottle. Robert looked away. What had he done? Dear Lord, what had he done?

CAT REACHED HER CAR in a daze. Nothing Paul said was consistent with anything else she'd heard. Most of the time she had to remind herself she was discussing the same person. If Paul was to be believed Jane was twisted, but was it a phase or was she twisted enough to get herself killed? Cat studied her notebook. The computer teacher thought she might have been depressed and/or on drugs; Camilla Simpson thought she was a trouble-maker, possibly a bully, but certainly very bright; Paul thought she was the devil incarnate and yet her three college friends virtually canonized her. And despite the conflicting nature of this information, Jane's parents thought she was a perfectly normal happy child even though she was allegedly being repetitively abused at home. It just didn't make sense. It wasn't like she was an innocent six-year-old who couldn't defend herself. She obviously could, Paul was proof of that. Unless, thought Cat, he was lying. It was possible that the scars were the result of a sex game gone wrong. She shook her head. Those markings were as deliberate as cross-stitching. Something else, she was missing something else, then she saw the word. Calorie Carers. She had scribbled it in her notebook. Jane went to Calorie Carers? Why would a girl confident enough to play sex games and pick up barmen go to a place like that? She decided to pay them a visit. Cat called Anna and left a message on his answering machine, saying she would be home before six. Thirty minutes later, wearing an old raincoat, she pushed open the door of Calorie Carers and went in. It was pink. The colour of excess flesh. Cat instinctively pulled her tummy button towards her spine and held it there.

'Hello, can I help you?'

Cat looked at the tall, well–toned woman behind the counter on her left. She was smiling warmly at her. Cat didn't like being mistaken for a punter.

'Yes, I was wondering if I could speak to someone about Jane Wellby?' said Cat putting on an officious, *I'm not here to diet*, voice.

'Jane?'

'Yes, she used to—'

'I know who she is. I thought you'd already been in. Lynne said you wouldn't have to speak to me.' Cat frowned. 'Guess you are not the Keystone cops I had you down for.' Cat chewed her lip. 'Sorry, didn't mean to be rude, to be fair you don't even look like the police, so I should stop pigeonholing. Please, come through to my office.'

More confused identities. She should put the woman right, impersonating a police officer was a criminal offence, but then again, information was hard to come by . . . Cat followed the woman, despite herself, past expensively printed signs: 'Twelve Weeks To A New You. Enrol Now And Become A Member For Only £9.95. Lose Weight Without Weighing and Still Eat Your Favourite Food ! ! !' Cat pointed to the sign 'Chicken Tikka Masala Balti and Cheesecake, surely that can't be possible.'

'Isn't marketing a wonderful thing,' said the woman,

showing her into an office and offering her a seat. Cat did not remove her coat when she sat down. Instead she just took her notebook out of her bag. Get information and get out.

'Your name?'

'Carla Hammond.'

'Could you describe Jane Wellby to me?'

'Well she wasn't overweight, that's for sure, dark, curly hair—'

Cat remembered. 'I was thinking more of her personality,' she said interrupting. 'How did she come across to you?'

Carla Hammond frowned as she put together a mental picture of the girl. 'Well it was obvious she was a disturbed child.'

'Disturbed? As in suffering from abuse?'

'Lord no. Disturbed as in disturbed.'

'Go on,' said Cat, encouraged.

'Look, I know this is not what you want to hear, and I know that you have arrested Mrs Wellby, I'm sure you have good reason, but as far as I am concerned, if anyone was giving anyone else the run around it was Jane.'

So it seems. 'What makes you think that?'

Carla stretched before answering. 'Jane went straight for the weak ones and played them like a fiddle. Like Lynne for instance. Lynne could not see it.'

'Lynne?'

'Lynne Reed, my colleague. You've already spoken to her.'

'Oh yes, of course, sorry. What couldn't she see?'

'That she was being manipulated. That girl had less of an eating disorder than most of the women in this country. And I am not talking about my clients. First opportunity she had she stripped off naked. Butt naked. In all my years of this business I have never seen that happen. Women who have been told by partners, parents or anyone in authority, that they are fat, ugly, whatever, believe exactly what they are told. I have to coax most of my clients out of their jackets let alone anything else.' She eyed Cat's coat as if to make a point.

'Why would there be friction between Jane's stepmother and Mr Wellby over coming here?'

Carla shrugged. 'The man probably didn't like to think his daughter had a problem with food.'

Cat looked at her notes. 'But according to you, she didn't have a problem with food.'

'Well no, but she got Mrs Wellby to pay for a course. That means she had to convince Mrs Wellby she had a problem. She would've told her husband, and he would have gone mad.'

'What if it was the other way round? Sandie Wellby convinced Jane she had a problem and that she needed to lose weight. Same reason why she wanted Jane to go to the hairdresser's — to improve her looks. You see Jane wrote a diary. It says her stepmother systematically bullied and belittled her over seven years,' said Cat, reading the notes she had made at the police station before she was busted for impersonating a dead girl. Dead girl. Police-woman. What next?

Carla had been staring into space, suddenly she shook her head. 'I just don't buy it,' she said after a while. 'She did mention some things to us but I was so sure she was making it up that I left the room. She was crying wolf, I'm positive. So Lynne dealt with it after that, I couldn't stomach her. Lynne fell for it all right, hook, line and sinker. But not me. And she knew it too, Jane, she knew she didn't have me on her side. I caught her looking at me with an expression that sent shivers down my spine. I tell you that girl was disturbed. No, not disturbed, warped. She could warp a person's perception of her. She couldn't do it to me, so she concentrated her energy on Lynne.'

'Her energies being?'

'Making us think she had been tortured in some way.'

'What could she have possibly gained by making people think her stepmother had abused her? Why bother?' It still didn't make sense to Cat.

'Attention?' Carla shrugged. 'You would be surprised what kids do for some attention.'

'But she was an only child, all reports are that she had plenty.'

'Look, I don't know, maybe she was just mental, maybe it runs in the family, maybe she had an affair with a member of the family and was punishing them by making everyone believe she had emotional problems.'

Cat wrote it all down furiously. Carla Hammond was

better at this than her. Cat realized she was going to have to think warped if she was going to understand what had been going on at Cedar Hall. 'One more question. Did she appear a possible suicide case?'

Carla shook her head. 'No way. Not that one. Far too busy enjoying herself with her little games.'

Back to square one. 'So you do think someone else killed her?' said Cat disappointed.

'I'm beginning to feel like the investigator in this.'

'Sorry, it is just my way of thinking things through,' answered Cat, aware that she was slipping out of her role too easily.

'Who else stands to gain by her death? Or alternatively, who wanted her out of the way? Have you checked the writing of the diary? Are you sure it is hers?'

'I certainly hope so.'

'That is where I would start. If *I* were the police.' Was that a loaded tone, or was Cat imagining it? 'For instance, did you find the diary immediately, who found it, could it have been placed after the body had been found? Could it be a fake?'

Lord only knows. 'Thank you for talking to me, and thanks for the advice. I'll go straight back to the station and see about that handwriting. I doubt anyone checked,' said Cat thinking about Bramley.

'Maybe someone has been relying on that.'

Cat laughed. 'Ever thought of becoming a detective?'

'Oh, I am, in my spare time.'

'Really?'

'Oh yes, I'm Inspector Morse on Wednesdays, I'm Poirot or Holmes most evenings, I devour crime writing and I always, but always, guess the end. You see a writer has more of an imagination than a real killer. Think of the story as a book, reach your conclusion, and then simplify it. If you want to guess the ending of a book, do the opposite. Look at all the possibilities and then con-volute them. The more unlikely the scenario, the more probable you've guessed the ending.' Cat looked at Carla with confusion. 'It's a hobby of mine.'

'Maybe you should join the force.'

'And have to deal with all that macho crap? No thanks.'

'Fair enough.'

Carla smiled and opened the door for Cat. 'I take it back what I said earlier. You don't seem like a police officer at all.'

Cat smiled.

'In fact,' continued Carla, 'I would go as far as to say you were a reporter, or a private investigator, imperson-ating a police officer.' Cat felt the colour drain out of her face. 'But that would be ridiculous unless, of course, you have the imagination of a writer. In which case, anything is possible.' Cat thought she might throw up on Carla's feet. The entrance of the studio swung open with a tinkle of bells. Cat and Carla looked in the direction of the door. What Cat needed more than anything was an obese woman to barge through the door, break down, collapse on the carpet and weep. Thus allowing her to slip away

unnoticed in the commotion. That is what she needed.
But of course, that is not what she got.

BRAMLEY RETURNED TO THE station. He had intended
to drop Lynne Reed on the way, but he had received an
urgent message to speak to forensics. Calorie Carers was
out of his way and he wanted to nail the American bitch
in record time. He fancied the Chief Superintendent's
chair. He ordered Mike to take her back. At which point,
she had started sulking and made a fuss about how scared
she was of Sandie Wellby and that she wasn't sure she
could stand up in court after all. So he had agreed to see
her that evening. She'd been grinning when she left. The
price of justice, he thought as he rang through to
forensics.

‘We've got a complication,’ said the voice down the
phone. ‘I'm very embarrassed that we missed it before.’

‘Missed what?’ said Bramley impatiently.

‘The guy was looking for finger and glove prints.’

‘I should hope so.’

‘They are hard to detect,’ said the man nervously.

‘What are?’

‘Latex gloves.’

‘What?’

‘It looks like someone wearing latex gloves also
handled the hose.’ Bramley did not respond. ‘Kind of
opens up the murder scene. Sorry.’

‘How the hell could you miss a piece of evidence like
that?’

'It was a trainee dusting it, I'll have the report delivered to you for your case papers immediately.'

'Don't bother,' said Bramley, 'I'll come and get it myself. I don't want to entrust anything else to you lot.'

SHE SHOULD HAVE LEFT earlier, thought Cat, as she watched Lynne Reed swaying in the doorway silhouetted against the bright sunshine outside. Ms Reed walked forward a few steps then turned back to the doorway.

'Thank you so much for dropping me back. It was very kind of you.'

'That's all right, ma'am,' said DS Chambers.

'I don't deserve all this fuss, I'm just happy to help the course of justice.' She paused as she stroked her forehead in a theatrical way. 'It really means something, the lift, knowing it is appreciated.'

'We couldn't have let you drive.'

'Please, come in, let me offer you a drink, to say thank you.'

'Say no,' said a voice behind him. Mike turned around allowing Cat to see the crutch and the woman holding on to it.

'Clement?' said Mike. 'What are you doing here?' He looked back into the room momentarily. Lynne had moved further into the room.

'I could ask you the same question?' said Clement in a tense whisper. Mike shrugged. She narrowed her eyes at him. They were trying to investigate a murder and Bramley was wasting manpower having his lunch date driven home. It had obviously been a good one. The woman was swaying and the taxpayers were paying.

'Ms Reed,' said Clement walking past Mike, 'I was wondering if I could go over a few of the questions again?'

Lynne looked horrified. 'Actually I have a bit of a migraine coming on,' she said clutching her head. 'And I've told everything I know to Bramley. Over lunch.'

Cat, terrified of being caught, swallowed the bile that had risen into her throat and half turned away. Bramley and Lynne had lunch?

'Your colleague then,' Clement consulted her note-pad, 'Carla Hammond?' As she searched the room she spotted the lady in the raincoat standing on the opposite side of the room. Carla looked at Cat, Cat looked to the wall.

'Cat?' Cat turned reluctantly towards Clement.

'Yes?' she said quietly. Clement limped further into the room.

'What are you doing here, Cat?' Clement sounded furious. Cat was terrified.

'I um,' she swallowed hard, 'needed some information about, um . . .' Where the fuck was that hole in the ground?

'There is no need to be embarrassed, Cat,' said Carla, the question mark over her name screaming the intended nuance at her.

Cat looked at Carla. 'There isn't?' she said.

Carla shook her head. 'No. Not at all. Most women

want to lose a bit of weight before they turn thirty. After all if you believe the urban myth that weight stays constant after a woman turns thirty, then you are starting at the right time.' Cat opened her mouth then closed it again. Clement took a few steps towards them. The disbelief was apparent to all.

'You,' she said, 'losing weight. I don't believe it.'

'Now, Cat,' continued Carla, 'I want you to take those notes I gave you, have a good think about your dedication to the subject, and if you need any more help, you have my number. We can start a programme as soon as you want.' Cat opened her mouth again. 'Don't say anything now, off you go.' Cat didn't move. 'Go on.' Finally Cat broke free of her inertia and moved towards the door. Halfway across the floor she started smiling.

'Thank you. Thank you for all you help.' She walked past Clement. 'WPC Clement, I'm sorry about your knee. Hope it gets better soon.' She felt all eyes on her as she left. On the street she started running. She had made it. She was free.

'Cat Torrant!' shouted the voice. 'I want a word with you.' Cat didn't have to turn around. She knew who the voice belonged to. 'Bugger,' she whispered then turned around and smiled. 'WPC Clement, what can I do for you?'

Chapter Nineteen

Clement eyed Cat suspiciously.

'Honest,' said Cat, sounding far from it, 'I just want to lose a few pounds.'

'I had you down for a lot of things, Cat Torrant, but not a self-obsessed dieter.'

'I'm not, I'm just . . .' Her voice trailed off.

'A liar.'

Cat's eyes widened. 'How dare you—'

'I strongly suggest you stay off the moral high ground. Bramley may think your involvement in this case is purely accidental, but I'm beginning to think differently. The wide-eyed innocent look doesn't work so well on other women.' Cat was in shock. 'Does it?' She stared blankly at the stocky policewoman. 'So are you going to tell me what you are up to or am I going to have to take you to the station myself.' Still nothing. 'Cat got your tongue?' Cat's eyes narrowed venomously. She really did hate it when people said that to her.

'What I am doing here is none of your business, consultations at Calorie Carers are confidential.'

'Nothing is confidential when murder is involved. If you are not going to help me, then I can't help you.' Clement turned around. 'Mike,' she shouted, 'bring the car over here will you. Miss Torrant is coming with us.'

'Where to?' he said confused.

'The station.' Mike nodded, a signal of comprehension, and opened the car door.

'What for?' The panic was creeping back into Cat's voice. Clement turned back and studied Cat's face. 'You can't take me to the police station without a reason.'

'Oh,' said Clement breezily, 'I have a reason.'

Mike turned the car around and pulled up next to the two women. 'Hop in then.' Clement gave him a tired look. 'Sorry, no pun intended.' Mike was laughing, Clement was frowning and Cat was beginning to sweat.

'What reason then?' Cat pleaded. No one answered. 'I'm not going,' she said shaking her head. 'No way.' Cat turned and began walking to her own car.

'For impersonating a police officer,' said Clement. Cat's step faltered. 'Most probably,' continued Clement to Cat's retreating figure, 'me.' Cat stopped. 'Since you don't know any other policewomen, I'd say that was a safe bet. That is a criminal offence, Miss Torrant. So, as I said, you will be accompanying me to the police station.'

Cat stood rooted to the spot. She stared down at the grey pavement, her foot was placed directly over a crack that traversed the length of the stone slab. A fault line. Along which eruptions occur. She should have been more careful. Slowly she turned, Clement stood, resting wearily against one of her crutches. She looked worn out.

'Okay, okay.' Cat didn't know what else to say. 'But it was unintentional and I didn't say I was you, Carla Hammond just presumed I was you.'

'And you didn't put her right.'

Cat shook her head. 'I know it looks bad, this whole thing just got out of control. I only wanted to . . .' Her voice trailed off. *I only wanted to get a story*.

'You are in a lot of trouble, young lady.' Cat rolled her head back and closed her eyes. Dan was going to love this. 'I think we should go to the station and have a chat. Then I'll decide what to do with you.'

'Can I drive myself?'

Clement nodded. 'But I'll come with you.'

ROBERT LOOKED AT THE alien set of keys that Fiona had given him. He tried unsuccessfully to open Fiona's front door. Three bloody locks. At Cedar Hall the door was always open. Someone was always there, the daily, the gardener, Sandie. By a process of elimination he fitted the right key into the corresponding lock and pushed the door, he fumbled for the light switch and swore loudly when he couldn't find it. It was dark in the house, someone had drawn all the curtains, it took him a while for his eyes to get accustomed to the sudden change of light. He felt his way down the long thin corridor and into the kitchen on the left. A red cigarette end glowed

in the darkness. Robert's heart jumped into his throat.
They were coming for him.

'Who are you?' he shouted in a panic.

'Stop being so bloody melodramatic, Robert. It's me,
Fiona. Who did you expect, it is my house.'

'Why are you sitting here with all the lights out?' he
said, finally finding one and switching it on.

Fiona squinted. 'I prefer it. Everything I look at
reminds me of what we've done.'

Robert frowned. 'We? We haven't done anything.'

'Oh please, stop being so sanctimonious.'

Robert reeled from the insult. Simon had said the
same thing. Don't be so sanctimonious. Well they didn't
understand the pressure he was under. It was *his* daughter
and *his* wife. He'd like to see someone else handle it
better.

'That's better,' said Fiona, 'quiet is much better.'

'Have you been drinking?' he asked, amazed at
Fiona's uncharacteristic aggression.

She laughed. 'Not like some people I know.'

'What the hell is that—'

'I said,' Fiona was raising her voice, 'cut the sanctimonious crap.'

'Okay, okay. Jesus, what has got into you?' said
Robert heading straight for the drinks tray.

'What, apart from killing our daughter?'

'Stop it!' he shouted. 'Stop it. Don't ever say things
like that.' He ran over to her and took her by the

shoulders. 'Hallifax is right, we should get you something, some medication.'

She turned to him slowly. 'Like Sandie did. Drug me up so I don't do anything rash, is that it? Wouldn't want me upsetting the apple cart now, would you?'

'What has got into you? Fiona, please?'

Fiona took a long drag on her cigarette before pulling another from the pack and lighting one from the other. She threw the butt into the ashtray and watched it burn. Robert picked it up with over-exaggerated disgust and stubbed it out.

'You shouldn't smoke, Fi, it's bad for you,' he said, like they had been discussing the weather. She looked at him. 'I thought you'd given up.'

'No, Robert, I gave up because you made me. Actually it has always been a favourite pastime of mine. It was one of the joys of being single again. I could smoke without you constantly bickering in my ear telling me to give up. You got Jane doing it as soon as she could talk!'

Robert looked hurt. 'I didn't want you to get—'

'Yes, yes.' She sighed. 'I know.'

'It upset Jane.'

'No, it upset you, you told Jane to be upset. God she could be a pain.'

'Fiona, what are you saying, don't ever talk like that!'

Fiona put her hand to her chest. 'Of course I wouldn't do it in public. I've kept my tongue long enough. Don't you fret. I just wanted to see if I could talk like that in front of you. Honestly. But we can't talk about it can we, Robert, don't you see, we never could.'

'Talk about what?'

Fiona stood up and screamed. *'Jane!'* Robert stepped away from her. She stopped screaming and looked at him. 'What are you doing here anyway?'

Robert frowned. 'You gave me keys.'

'That was stupid of me. You should go back to Cedar Hall.'

'I can't, Sandie is there.'

'So? What are you, chicken? Think she'll get you too? The bogey man.' She waggled her fingers around.

'Don't be ridiculous.'

'What are you scared of, hmm, that she'll find out the truth?' Robert slapped her in the face. Fiona stared at him for a few moments then started to laugh. 'Thank you for that, Robert,' she said through the laughter, 'I'd almost forgotten how good at it you were.' Robert stared at her with horror then grabbed the nearest bottle off the tray and left the kitchen. He opened the front door and was startled by the brightness outside. A couple of kids ran off. He imagined himself: dishevelled hair, squinting excessively and clutching a bottle like his life depended on it. He looked at it. Gin. He hated gin, he thought, unscrewing the cap.

INTERVIEW ROOM ONE. SHE'D been here before. Clement passed Cat a cup of tea.

'I didn't think prisoners got privileges like tea,' said Cat sliding the saucer over the plastic surface of the table.

'This isn't the Tower of London, and so far you are not a prisoner. But you will be if you don't start telling me exactly what your interest in the Wellby family is. I would like to warn you that perverting the course of justice is also a criminal offence.'

Cat stared at the concentric rings in her teacup.

'You are in luck though, Bramley is not at the station, so far what takes place in this room is just between you and me.' Cat looked nervously at the tape-recorder on the wall. 'It isn't on,' said Clement reassuringly. Cat nodded.

'You won't like it,' said Cat.

'Try me.'

Cat took a deep breath. *Here goes.* 'I'm in my final term at the London School of Printing. I'm trying to do an investigative radio piece.'

'A journalist?' said Clement, not sounding convinced or impressed.

'Broadcast journalist,' she said, 'hopefully.'

Clement made a note on her pad. 'So was this investigation taking place before or after Jane's death?'

'After. I got into trouble with BBC Chelmsford because I didn't get a report in on time. Why? Because I hit that dog, then got stuck at Cedar Hall with you lot.'

'Don't blame us.'

'I'm not, I just wanted to do something impressive to make up for it.'

'Your grandmother resides not far from the house, you must pass it every time you drive there from London.'

'Yes, but . . .'

'Pretty impressive view isn't it? You say that you had a look around the house before you found Jane. You spent precisely one hour looking around. I would say that registers a high level of curiosity. You must've been curious before. Maybe you'd been to the house before. Had a snoop around. Found out something about Jane Wellby she didn't want anyone else to know.'

'No.'

'Maybe you were threatening her with that infor-mation.' Cat shook her head. 'Maybe you got into a fight, hit her over the head and accidentally killed her.'

'No way, no.' Cat's throat had tightened, she could barely speak.

'You put her in the car, hit the dog with a spade or something, which explains the lack of dog hairs on your bumper, put it in your car and drive to the pub, ask directions and return to Cedar Hall. You wait an hour because you don't know how long it takes for carbon monoxide poisoning to work, during which time you write her suicide note, then you run into the house and call the police. The presence of Sandie Wellby at the top of the stairs alarms you, you didn't realize she was there, you panic and apologize. We record it. You go back into the garage with Mrs Wellby where she touches the hose, as she says she did, you realize this is your way out and let it drop accidentally into a later conversation with Bramley that Mrs Wellby never touched the hose. Are you still with me?' Cat stared at her unblinking. 'Then the diary is found, you knew nothing about that, double whammy, so when your suicide note is read out in the police station, you say it is yours and you wrote it for the dog. You have the luck of the devil because as if by magic the dog appears. You have contact with old people, it isn't beyond reasonable doubt that you masterminded that as well.' Clement sat back in her chair. Cat didn't know what to say. She felt guilty just sitting there. Every step the policewoman had described Cat had taken, she could even see herself hitting Jane over the head.

'What a horrendous scenario,' she said.

'Isn't it,' agreed Clement.

'I didn't do it,' said Cat. 'I had never been to Cedar Hall before, I did feel guilty but only because it was my evidence that helped get Mrs Wellby arrested. I felt terrible about that, and then I met Jane's old teacher and immediately things didn't seem to fit. Of course, I knew nothing about the diary, but I know a lot more now. I'll tell you everything I know, and all you have to do is talk to the people whom I got this information off and they will tell you that I never met them before Jane's death. Okay?'

'Unless you were all in it together.'

Cat looked around the small, coffee-coloured room and shivered. 'First I'll tell you, and then you can decide whether you think I am lying.'

'You are a good liar Cat, you've proved that already.'

This was getting worse and worse. 'Please, just look at my notes, listen to the mini-disc, the date and time is recorded.' She thought about Anna at Camilla Simpson's, J.J. at the college, the men in the bar at Madison's, surely the police wouldn't think they were all in on it.

'Mini-disc?'

'It's a digital tape, we record interviews on it.'

Clement looked at Cat for a while, then stood up. 'Let me see if DCI Bramley is back.'

'Oh please, not him, can't I just tell you?'

'I'm afraid I can't do that. Please wait here.'

Cat watched the door close. 'Shit.' She began spreading her papers over the table, assembling them in chronological order.

Clement went down the hallway to Bramley's office. She knocked on the door. His secretary was on the phone. She looked up nervously, saw Clement and relaxed again. 'Oh hi, I thought you-know-who was back.'

'Where is he?' asked Clement.

'Optician's,' said the young girl.

Clement looked confused. 'Since when did he need an optician?'

'I don't know, he said he was going to the opticians and did not want disturbing even if the station house was burning down.'

'Weird,' said Clement. 'Do you mind if I leave a message on his desk?'

'Not at all . . . and anyway, then he said to her . . .'

Before she had time to write her own message a yellow post–it note caught Clement's attention. It was a message to call the forensic lab in Colchester, urgently. The secretary was still gossiping into the phone when she left the office. '. . . and *she* said to him . . .'

'You didn't see me,' said Clement. The secretary looked at her quizzically. 'And I didn't hear you,' Clement continued. The girl nodded. Fair enough. 'Good.' Clement walked as quickly as her knee would let her back down to interview room one. What had forensics found out that was so urgent, and why had Bramley decided to choose today to go to the opticians when he had everybody else on full throttle and he'd already wasted time at lunch? He wasn't the best boss by any stretch of the imagination, but he liked to oversee everything on a big case. He was a glory boy. His superiors called it thorough, she called it enlightened self-interest. Cat was bent over the table studying pieces of paper when she returned to interview room one.

'Are you sure the handwriting in the diary is Jane's?' said Cat as the door opened.

'Excuse me?'

'In the diary,' said Cat looking up.

'Well her mother found it, she should be able to recognize her own daughter's handwriting.'

'Where was it found?'

'Jane's room, why?'

'Could have been put there by anyone, Jane's mother even.'

'Possible,' said Clement, her mind on Bramley.

'Well, it's just a thought.'

'Why don't you let us do the police work. All I want to do is clear your name from our list of suspects.'

'So you do have more than one suspect?' asked Cat.

Clement didn't respond. Actually the answer was no, Bramley had concentrated exclusively on Sandie Wellby, but she wasn't going to tell Cat Torrant that.

'Personally,' said Cat, 'to understand this case I think you have to get to know the central character.'

'I presume by your acting analogy you mean Sandie Wellby.'

'No. The cause of all this. Jane. What was she like? Why did she die?'

'Her stepmother killed her is the popular belief,' said Clement sounding alarmingly like Bramley.

'Doesn't make sense, she was twenty-three, she didn't have to stay at Cedar Hall. She could've seen her dad in London, he goes in every day and Mrs Wellby doesn't live far from the city. I know your boss thinks Jane was as pure as the driven snow but I've been told that she took E, that she liked to be a recipient and perpetrator of violent sex, and that she found God. Doesn't sound like the same person, does it?'

'Are you trying to tell me she was schizophrenic?'

'I don't know, but it's worth investigating, isn't it?' Cat looked hopefully at Clement.

'We'll do the investigating if you don't mind. Amateur journalists can leave it well alone.'

Cat slumped back into her chair. After a while she began picking up the pieces of paper and putting them into a pile. 'Suicide is the third biggest killer of sixteen- to 24-year-olds,' said Cat.

'Thank you, I know the statistics.'

'Well maybe someone else was relying on that.' The excitement crept back into her voice despite her efforts to remain nonchalant. 'They were hoping you wouldn't dig too deep.'

'Like Mrs Wellby?'

'I know your boss wants it to be Sandie, but there is so much you don't know about Jane. Just listen to what I have, it could've been anyone.'

'Why?'

'Don't you want to get the right person?'

Clement sat down slowly, she was supposed to be resting her knee not running about after a wannabe Roger Cook. 'Are you always this tenacious when it comes to uncovering the truth, Cat Torrant?'

Cat thought about Anna. 'No,' she said truthfully.

'Are the Wellbys that newsworthy, I mean, why be selective, or is it the only crime you've ever had the misfortune to be part of?'

Cat finished putting her papers away in her bag. Clement didn't seem too pressed for an answer, but the question was burning a hole in Cat's brain.

'WPC Clement,' the policewoman looked up, 'if I gave you a copy of all of these would you do me a favour?'

'Cat, I can take those papers and I don't owe you anything.'

'Please?' said Cat softly, afraid to continue, but afraid to stop.

Clement straightened in her seat. 'Go on.'

'A friend of mine was raped. He didn't want to report it but I've got some evidence. If I gave it to you, would you do something with it?'

'Why didn't he report it?'

Cat gave her a knowing look.

'Who was raped?' Clement saw the look on Cat's face. 'It's okay, I won't tell anyone.'

'My housemate, he was with me when Bramley first dragged me in here.'

Clement recalled the day. 'Anna Prokton?' Cat nodded. 'Of course,' said Clement. 'Tall, blue eyes, hugging like your life depended on it.'

'Sorry?'

'You were seen. Anyway, what do you want me to do?'

'I thought I knew who'd done it to him, but Anna said the boy he'd gone off with didn't do it, I think he was just bait. Anna feels too ashamed and angry with himself to come forward.'

'Where did it happen?'

'Soho, I think, Central London anyway. Have there been any other attacks reported?'

'I don't know, but I do know the chief down there,

and he's an excellent man. He'll know. Have you got the evidence here?'

'It's in the car.'

'Go and get it, Cat, I'll wait here.'

Cat returned to the car park through the side door and walked over to her car. The sports bag containing the offending articles was squashed into a cardboard box in the boot. Just as she retrieved it another car pulled into the police station and stopped in front of the steps. Bramley got out and slammed the door. Cat ducked. She was scared of Bramley. Cat looked at the bag in her hand. What the hell was she doing? Anna's rape was nothing to do with the Essex police. What could Clement really do about it? Handing over the bag might appease her own conscience but it wouldn't help Anna. Cat threw the bag back in the boot, ran round to the driver's seat and climbed in. She saw Clement in her rear-view mirror just as she turned out of the police station.

CLEMENT STARED ANGRILY AFTER the car. Duped.

'What are you doing, Clement?' said Bramley looking behind him. The car had disappeared from view.

'Just getting a breath of fresh air,' she said rubbing her knee.

'You ought to go home, Clement, rest up a bit.'

Like you care? 'Thanks, but I'm fine. Sir, are we sure that it's Jane's writing in the diary? It could've been planted.'

It disappeared as soon as it had appeared, but Clement saw the flash of anger in his eyes. 'Clement, I'm ordering you to go home. We don't want you injuring yourself any further.' Bramley walked past her.

Something was up. 'Thanks, sir,' she said brightly. 'Don't mind if I do. By the way, how was the opticians?'

Bramley turned slightly. 'Fine,' he said, drawing out the word.

'Do you go to the one on the High Street? They're great in there,' she said enthusiastically. 'I've got an appointment myself tomorrow.'

'Really?' Bramley did not sound interested in her welfare any more.

'Who did you see?' continued Clement brightly.

'Actually I had to go to a specialist in Colchester. I'd rather not talk about it.'

'No, of course, I understand,' said Clement. 'I apologize.'

'I thought I told you to go home.'

'I'm gone,' she said, holding the smile until Bramley had entered the building. 'Colchester,' she whispered to herself. A coincidence? 'Coincidences don't exist in this business.'

'Talking to yourself again?'

Clement turned round. 'Mike, you've been flirting with the witnesses again.'

Mike looked embarrassed. 'I wondered if you'd heard about that.'

'I'm dying in the car park and you're busy getting a date. Thanks.'

Mike smiled. 'Got one too.'

'Take your puzzler book, you'll run out of conversation after two minutes.'

'Who's talking about conversation,' said Mike, pleased with himself.

Clement raised her eyes to the heavens. 'Men.'

'Well if the boss can screw the witnesses, why can't I?'

'Bramley and Lynne Reed?' Mike nodded. 'Don't be disgusting.' Clement began to walk slowly down the steps. Then turned. 'Really?'

'Wouldn't be the first time.'

Clement thought about this for a moment. 'Mike, what do you think about the Wellby case?'

'I'm not paid to think, Clement,' said Mike, reaching for the door.

'I take it back,' said Clement, 'you and Suzie will be very happy.'

Clement was left alone in the car park. Dismissed and depressed. She'd never liked Bramley for personal reasons. Now she didn't trust him professionally. Cat Torrant, the amateur journalist, had found out more information on the Wellby family than a team of detectives had managed to uncover in two weeks. Clement looked at the entrance that the Fiesta had disappeared through, then back at the double doors of the police station. She knew who she wanted to follow but jumping ship was not advised without a proper life jacket. She walked slowly back up the steps.

Chapter Twenty

Cat called Dan's number as she drove down the road. She already regretted running off like that, Clement would never believe her now. But she couldn't go back; everything she did to achieve relegation to the role of spectator sucked her further into the heart of Jane's death. If she'd given all her information to Clement, it might've been used against her. She did have stuff on Jane, significant stuff, they might try and use that in their bribery theory. Maybe Dan was right, she should drop this now before it got completely out of control. Eventually Dan's phone was answered. But not by him.

'Is Dan there?' she said startled by her reaction to the girl's voice. Her heart was pounding.

'Hang on . . . Dan! Phone!' Cat could hear the music in the background. Dan didn't hurry to the phone. 'Who was that?' she asked immediately, though she had been swearing to herself for the previous few minutes that she wouldn't. 'A mate from university.'

'Anyone I know?' said Cat.

'No, she isn't a post-grad.'

A young girl. A blonde. With big tits. 'Oh.'

'What do you want, Cat?'

'That's not very nice. I really need your help, Dan.'

'Don't tell me, lover boy got a bit rough.'

'What?' Cat pulled the car over. 'What are you talking about?'

'Look, Cat, why can't you just say it, why drag it along.'

'Are you pissed?'

'Just having fun, Cat, some people do that from time to time.'

Cat felt sick. 'What is that supposed to mean, I have fun,' she said, rising to the bait.

'Oh yeah, running around pretending to be a dead girl, sorry, I forgot.'

'What the hell has got into you recently?'

'Cat, if you can't work that out, I don't really know what the point in carrying on is.'

Cat couldn't believe she was hearing this. 'What are you saying, Dan, I mean, I know things have been a bit tricky recently but—' She paused. She could hear the girl giggling in the background. It pissed her off. 'What is really going on, Dan?' she said bluntly.

'I've got to go. Bye.'

'Dan?' The phone went dead. She looked at it. Press end? Obviously. They had never fought like this before. Cat felt very strange. A mixture of sadness and nothing. She would never be unfaithful to him, he must know that. They had a great relationship. Always laughing, never ran out of things to say, enjoyed doing the same things. She considered herself very fortunate in the boy-friend stakes, some of the horror stories she'd heard from girlfriends were appalling. Boys who were discovered sleeping with their girlfriends' sisters, or mothers, or brothers. Cat put her foot on the accelerator. One more reason to be thankful she didn't have any of those. There wasn't much chance of Dan trying to seduce Amelia. They just needed some time, thought Cat, then again, what was he doing with some bimbo at five in the afternoon, pissed? Didn't take him long before searching for a pair of sympathetic breasts. Why give up on the Wellby case, which is what he obviously wanted her to do, if he was going to bail out so easily. Was she important or not? Cat drove slowly through Harlow, getting angrier and angrier at each red traffic light. By the time she reached the motorway she was resolved. She wouldn't phone him, he had to apologize to her, and if he didn't, then she'd know the answer. Not important enough. Not by a long shot.

THE BOY HAD LEFT his post outside the members only club and was making his way to an unlicensed drinking room where he knew the money collected could get him a well-earned drink before bedtime. It had been a good night, the punters had been generous, maybe he would allow himself more than one nightcap before he put his head down in the doorway of the gentlemen's tailor shop on the Strand. He took a back alleyway through the red-light district and walked behind the peep shows and 'exotic' bars. There were a number of fruitful skips there, if you could bear the stench. He rummaged through the first two, nothing but the odd item all coated in the same stiffening by-product of the sex industry. He moved to the third, unhopeful but hungry. He could tell by the lipstick-coated tissues that this was rubbish from the girl's changing room. He dug deeper. He pocketed the half-eaten sandwich. The antiperspirant would come in useful. The squashed Tampax would not. Then he felt the material, it was thick, lined. Decent clobber. He could get a good bit of money for a coat like that. He yanked at the material, but it wouldn't budge. So he leant further into the skip to determine what was pinning it down. He had found drunk men in these skips before. But never a dead one.

IT WAS HARD LOVING someone who didn't need you. She went to Amelia for everything. If it was because she was scared he'd run off and leave her too then she was forcing him to do the very thing she feared. He wanted to get in. She wasn't letting him. He had hoped that he'd force her out into the open, make her say something about how she felt, put up a fight, something, anything. He should've known better. Dan got no reply from Cat's doorbell, so he tried Anna's.

'Oh,' said Anna when he saw who it was.

'Gee, thanks for the welcome,' said Dan. 'Can I come in?'

Anna stepped back. The flat was a mess. 'Don't say anything,' said Anna. 'I'm not in the mood.'

'I can clear up for you.'

'Is this your macho way of apologizing to me for your behaviour last week?'

Dan sighed. 'Emotions were high, Anna, we all said things we shouldn't have.'

'Just a simple sorry will do,' said Anna. Dan looked at him for a while. Then Dan sighed and slumped down on the sofa. 'I'm really in the dog house,' he said putting his head in his hands. The beer he had drunk earlier was giving him a headache. Anna sat down on a chair opposite. He was wearing an old Cambridge tracksuit, and studied his former room-mate. Why do men always think they are hard-done-by, thought Anna, hoping Dan wasn't going to go all self-pitying on him. He'd prefer to do one round with the Dyson than that.

'Have you seen Cat?' asked Dan.

'She left a message saying she would be here by six. I've been asleep, what time is it?'

'Ten,' said Dan.

'Really? What are you doing here so late?'

'Cat and I had another fight.'

'So I take it you're not coming to Paris.'

'Paris?'

'Amelia is taking us.'

'Cat didn't mention it.'

'Not surprisingly, the way you've been acting. Cat has been a star looking after me, she is also working really hard on this story, you should be proud of her, not giving her a hard time about it.'

'I should have known . . .' said Dan.

'Should have known what?'

'You two, all thick as thieves over this.'

'What?'

'Well, you would take her side, you've been spending all your time with her.'

'We've hardly been having fun, you know. She spends most days washing my sheets and putting them back on the bed so that I don't have to be reminded by the blood. I wake her up most nights with bad dreams and she stays awake with me until I fall asleep again. She has fended off my agent, she has lied on my behalf, she has in fact been a true friend. I don't know what the hell has got into you. For someone as intelligent as you are, you're being remarkably stupid.'

Dan studied his feet. He always wanted to say so much and always found it so difficult. Cat and Anna could always talk to each other, right from the very beginning, maybe he was a little jealous of that.

'I know you find the emotional bit a little tricky,' said Anna, reading his mind, 'you've been like that since we first met. I used to think it was because you were a repressed homosexual, now I realize it is the straight man's affliction. Emotional paralysis.'

'Bullshit.'

'Really, Dan, you are up there with the worst. That is why you and Cat worked so well together. She is so self-contained. Everything is very black and white with her. It is her way of defending herself,' said Anna less aggressively.

'What do you mean?'

'Amelia couldn't do everything, could she? Cat was the strange kid with no parents. I bet she was teased at school. I've been thinking about it a lot. Cat puts her faith in very few people. She hasn't learnt to share herself with a mother, father, brother, sister, cousin, whoever. So when she does, she'll give it her everything, but she expects the same in return. She isn't getting that from you. Once you've let her down, I very much doubt she would have you back.'

'She said that?'

'Aren't you listening to me? She didn't say that, nor would she. She is incredibly loyal to you. But she's changing, I don't think she even knows it herself. She has worked so hard this year on her course, slogged her guts out for the exams, every piece is researched and edited to perfection. She really wants a secure, rewarding career out of this. I think she wants a good base for later life. Amelia isn't going to be around for ever as you so charmingly pointed out.'

'She told you.'

'Dan I was only upstairs. Don't interrupt me again. I think her mother's behaviour scares her, like it might be genetic. That is why she is so self-contained and also why she doesn't want to be. Why else do you think she is so fascinated by this family. Surely you worked that out.'

Dan sat down next to Anna. 'Cat always said she didn't have problem parents because she didn't have parents.'

'And you believed her?'

'Seems pretty clear to me.'

'I think she's threatened by the very idea of a family, but what does she *really* want? A family. Amelia is right to worry about this Wellby thing. Cat is confused.'

'I didn't want her to do it either,' said Dan in his defence.

'Different reason. Doesn't count.'

He should've known Anna would be selective.

'Personally,' continued Anna regardless, 'I think it is a good idea. She has to realize sometime that what you want to feel and what you really feel isn't always compatible. I should know.' Anna turned away from Dan. 'I would've been a great dad.' Anna stifled a yawn.

'I'm sorry, this is the last thing you need. Why don't we put you to bed.'

'I'm not a child,' said Anna, snapping his arm away from Dan.

'Let me help you.'

He looked at Dan. 'You're not very good in the nursing role are you?'

With a self-contained girlfriend and an extrovert for a

best mate what did they think? 'Out of practice,' said Dan.

Anna smiled at that and took Dan's hand. 'The best thing you can do is go before Cat gets back. She is changing, Dan, but I don't think she realizes it. What you've got to decide is whether you want that change, I mean really want it. You've had an easy ride so far. You're young, there's been no pressure from her. But what happens when Cat realizes she wants a big family full of screaming kids, a husband who'll always be there, the whole works? You look pale, Dan,' said Anna ushering him to the door, 'I'll put myself to bed.'

DCI JONES STUDIED THE pathologist's conclusions. Caucasian male. Brown hair. Brown eyes. Age: 30–40. Big build – six foot in height. Weight: Fifteen and a half stone. Cause of death: Heart failure. Injuries: Jones read the jargon and interpreted. Kicked to shit. Sexual Interference: None. Number of assailants: As yet unknown. Distinguishing features: None. Items found with body: None.

'Poor bugger,' said Jones to himself. He'd been called in at five in the morning after the emergency services had received a call alerting the police to the presence of a corpse in a skip behind a bar imaginatively called GIRLS GIRLS GIRLS. It was a 24-hour joint. The owner had been questioned. The security video had been studied and the girls shown a picture. No one resembling the deceased had entered or left the place. As it turned out the questioning had been a waste of time. The man had been dead for two days. The skip was only emptied every three. Jones would be wasting more time asking any of the other establishments, they were too slick to dump a body on their own doorstep. Bodies from Soho turned up on the wasteland under the M40 flyover, half-submerged in a watery ditch alongside the Westminster city car pound and with all forms of identity on the body. It helped the police do their job and lessened the likelihood that they would have to come knocking on doors. The knocking shops didn't like it. It was a funny place to put a body, Soho, difficult because it was busy twenty-four hours a day. It implied that the death hadn't been planned. A mugging gone wrong? In which case what was he doing in Soho? Maybe a sex game gone wrong? Jones hated these sorts of cases. You'd break some woman's heart with the news of her husband's death then break it all over again when you told them why.

ROBERT HAD ENDED UP in a dirty, illegal drinking club where he had forced warm cans of Tennants Xtra down his throat in a vain attempt to black out the feelings of guilt and anger and depression that were consuming him. He felt that everything he said was incriminating, and everything he held back was mortifying. He knew he would have to stop drinking, he hadn't binged like this for a long, long time, but he couldn't see any other way out of it. Jane was dead. And whatever way he looked at it, her death was his fault. If only he'd told the truth in the first place. Drink didn't help but he enjoyed the self-destructive kick it gave him. He liked the feeling of being out of control. He could jump under a train, fall out of a moving vehicle, shoot himself in the head in this sort of mood. Leave them to discover the truth. Robert walked back to Fiona's house. It took him two hours, he had no money for a taxi and the idea of getting on a tube scared him. He knew commuters. He didn't want to be seen. It was nine a.m. when he finally put the key in the door. He could feel the tentacles of his hangover unfurl in the back of his head. The curtains were still drawn, the house felt empty. Thank God. He found a one-and-a-half-litre bottle of Safeway's own brand blended whisky. It was cheap but it would get the job done. Stave off the hangover. No matter what.

Chapter Twenty-One

Clement heard someone coming down the stairs. She braced herself. The door opened.

'Oh God,' said Cat.

'Oh God indeed,' said Clement. 'I'd like a word with you. Again.'

Cat nodded grimly and held the door open wider. Clement, having ditched the crutch for a walking stick, limped in. The door to Anna's flat opened.

'Dan?'

Cat turned to him quizzically. Why was he expecting Dan this morning?

'Oh sorry,' said Anna, 'I was . . .' He noticed the woman's uniform. 'No police,' he said, his voice quavering. 'Cat? No police.'

'It's all right, it's about Jane Wellby.' Anna looked nervously at them both. He'd obviously had another bad night. 'We'll be in Paris soon,' said Cat soothingly. 'We all need a holiday. You get packing, okay?'

'Okay,' said Anna quietly, closing the door.

Cat showed Clement upstairs, it was a slow journey. 'You shouldn't be walking around,' said Cat, watching her take one step at a time.

'I wouldn't have to be if you hadn't run off.'

'I'm so sorry I left like that,' she said when they were inside her own flat. 'I saw Bramley and got scared, you know . . .'

'You are not helping yourself doing things like that, Cat.'

Clement sat down heavily.

'Are you feeling all right?' asked Cat, looking at Clement. She nodded. 'Would you like something to drink, some water, tea?' Clement didn't respond. 'Is your knee hurting a lot?'

'It's not great. Bramley has given me time off. I thought I'd look into your report. Just to double-check.'

Cat hesitated.

'I won't show them to anyone else.'

Still she hesitated.

'I thought you wanted this solved.'

'I do, I'll get them.'

'I noticed your friend, downstairs,' she said tentatively.

'I shouldn't've told you about that.'

'Maybe not, but you have and your friend doesn't look so good. They'll do it again you know.'

'That's what I said,' said Cat.

'The truth is your evidence isn't valid anyway. Forty-eight hours after the crime, forensics are inadmissible, it just might give the police a direction to look in. I used to work in London, I know the man in charge, he's a great policeman.'

Cat studied her warily. 'Why now? Yesterday I was a murderer.'

'Don't be so dramatic. I was just testing you.'

'Guess I passed.'

'Cat, apart from an unpaid TV license, you are as clean as Bramley's nine-iron.'

Cat looked guilty.

'Plus, you wear your emotions on your face.'

'Yeah, I've been told that.'

'So what I'm proposing is that you and I help each other out. I look into the rape, and we swap info on the Wellby case.'

Cat went to the fridge and pulled out a carton of orange juice. She poured two glasses. 'Are you going to Paris because of Jane Wellby?' asked Clement.

'Yes.'

'Will you let me know what you find?'

'Will you?'

Clement nodded. Cat passed her the name and telephone number of the hotel.

'Hôtel des Tulipes, sounds romantic.' Cat looked away. Clement didn't notice. 'I'll leave you to pack.' She stood up. 'Can I have that evidence?'

Cat chewed her lip. 'You won't hassle Anna will you?'

'You tell me what happened then.'

Cat gave her a brief description of the boy at Madame JoJo's. She didn't know any more.

'Take my card, my number is there if you want to talk about it. I promise you, you're doing the right thing.'

'I hope so,' she said, hearing Dan's disapproving voice in her head. They walked slowly out to the street. Cat ran ahead to the car and fetched the sports bag from the boot. She had just passed it to Clement when Anna walked out of the house. Cat jumped back nervously, distancing herself from her crime. A taxi rumbled down the street, Clement hailed it.

'West End Central, please,' she said quietly through the driver's open window.

She grabbed Cat's arm and heaved herself into the taxi.

'Don't say anything to Anna, nothing may come of this,' she whispered in Cat's ear. Clement closed the door and opened the window. 'Thanks for the Wellby stuff, you've been a great help.'

Reluctantly, Cat turned back to Anna. He was watching her. Inspecting her.

'Are you packed?'

Without answering he walked back into the flat. Cat followed him.

'Why did you think Dan was coming over?' she said, trying to lead the conversation as far away from the police as possible.

'No reason.'

Anna wasn't even looking at her. *He knows*. What

was she going to say to him? Anna walked over to a pile of black plastic bin liners.

'You've been having a clear-out?' she asked.

Anna looked forlornly at the sacks of history at his feet and nodded.

'What do you think?' said Cat, picking one up. 'Salvation Army?'

'Is there one?'

I hope so, thought Cat, putting her arms around him. 'You bet,' she said, 'I'm the Major General.'

CLEMENT SAT IN THE back of the cab and willed the traffic to evaporate. Up ahead the road was being resurfaced, Clement closed the window to protect her from the vile fumes of heating tarmac. But the cab's interior was still caked in a thick fetid smell. It didn't take very long for her to work out the source. Clement opened the bag, put her hand in and pulled out a corner of plastic sheet. 'What the . . .!'

'What you got there?' asked the driver.

Clement looked at him.

'Not a body I hope, it stinks.'

'Could I borrow your driving gloves?' she said, opening the window between them.

He made a face in the rear-view mirror.

'It is police business.'

He relinquished the precious articles, it wasn't his cab, officially he worked nights. Sun-lighting, his wife called it.

Clement put her hand further into the bag and pulled out a pink, furry G-string.

'I'm a married man, luv,' said the driver, turning in his seat. A horn blared. Clement was thrown to one side as the cab swerved.

'I'd like to get there soon and in one piece, if you don't mind.'

'Sorry.' He eased out of the traffic jam and pulled across the oncoming traffic. He drove quickly, weaving in and out of bus lanes and running two red lights. Clement made no comment. He pulled up outside the police station in record time and told her he wouldn't take her money. Called it his good deed. He wouldn't take his gloves back either.

THE RENDEZVOUS WAS TWO o'clock at the check-in barrier. Cat had offered to collect Amelia but she had mysteriously refused, saying she had arranged her own transport. Cat hoped she hadn't decided to freewheel to the station again. Cat searched the bustling crowd under the chrome and glass of the Eurostar terminal.

'She'll be here,' said Anna.

Cat turned back to him. 'I wasn't looking for Gran,' said Cat sadly. She never thought he'd give it all up this easily. How had their relationship declined so rapidly? Forty-five degrees and sliding out of sight. Cat sighed loudly.

'Did you think he'd come?'

Cat shrugged.

'This is all my fault,' said Anna.

'Rubbish.' Cat put a reassuring arm around his shoulders. Anna hadn't confessed to the tête-à-tête he and Dan had had.

'This isn't about what he said about you any more, Anna. You can't blame yourself. If Dan wanted to make it up to me, he'd have been around. He hasn't. I think I've got the message.'

'You don't understand—'

Cat wasn't listening. She watched as a taxi pulled up and a young man got out and ran towards them. But it wasn't her young man. He ran on.

'Have you got the tickets?' asked Cat.

'Actually no,' said Anna.

'No! Oh God, we have to go back.' Cat looked at the clock nervously. 'We don't have time, what are we going to do?'

'Don't blame me, it's your grandmother, she is up to something. She told me not to buy any. Blessing in disguise, I couldn't face Prick-a-dilly Circus.'

Cat laughed and kissed him on the cheek. 'What a sad old pair we are, look at us, off on holiday to Paris and we're acting more like it's the gallows that await us.'

'As opposed to gallettes, gallons of gorgeous wine and garçons.'

Cat laughed. 'You never know.'

'Indeed,' said Anna.

'This means a lot to Gran, so . . .'

'Can we put on a brave face,' said Anna ruefully. 'I

know. Of course we can. As long as you watch my back, I'll watch yours.'

'Deal.' Cat leant back against Anna. He was losing weight at an alarming rate. She made a mental note to fatten him up in Paris.

'Darlings,' called out a familiar voice.

'Cutting it a bit fine, aren't we?' said Cat standing straight.

'Rubbish, we've got oodles of time.'

The man wheeling Amelia pushed her over to where they stood.

'Thank you so much,' said Cat. He bowed his head briefly. Cat expected him to leave. But he didn't. Maybe he was part of the Eurostar service. Or a crazy limo service Amelia had treated herself to. He was dressed in an extraordinary uniform of pink. 'Yes, of course,' she said, confused, and rummaged around in her bag for her wallet. A tip. He's waiting for a tip. She opened it. Three pound coins. Was that enough? Well it would have to be. She scooped out the coins and leant over her grandmother with her hand extended.

'Thank you so much,' she said again pressing the coins into his hand.

The man roared with laughter. Amelia started too. Cat looked agitatedly at Anna. He shrugged.

'Darling,' said Amelia, barely able to speak, 'this is Mr Blaine. Camilla Simpson's father.'

'Oh God,' said Cat. Then gently smacked Amelia

on the leg. 'Why didn't you tell me. God, I'm so embarrassed.'

'How do you do,' said Mr Blaine, 'please don't feel embarrassed, I've always wanted to be paid for my services.'

'Three quid is a little over-optimistic,' said Anna, looking him up and down. Amelia shot him a furious look. Anna didn't have time to respond.

'You must be Anna,' said Mr Blaine, still laughing. 'Good thing I've been warned about you.' Cat and Anna looked at each other frowning. Who was this man in pink? For the first time since the attack Anna wished he were wearing heels, fishnet stockings and a huge blonde wig. He would have enjoyed taking Mr Blaine on.

'We'd better get a move on,' said Amelia.

Cat walked round to push Amelia, but Mr Blaine intercepted. 'Allow me,' he said. Cat looked down at Amelia. She was grinning like a Cheshire cat. Amelia winked at her granddaughter before pointing forward.

'On, on MacDuff,' she exclaimed loudly as he wheeled her off.

Cat and Anna were left standing like a couple of stuffed marrows. What on earth had been going on? 'I leave her for one minute and look what happens,' said Cat eventually.

'Shakespeare.' Anna smiled. 'Well at least one of us has been having some fun.'

'What do you mean?'

'Oh, come on, look at her, I've never seen hot pants like it.'

'Please, a little decorum.'

'Someone has been undergoing an intense course of injections—'

Cat swung round to face Anna. 'That is my grand-mother you are talking about . . .' She shook her head. 'If you don't mind.'

'He certainly looks fit—'

Cat put her hand up to Anna's mouth. 'Let's not go there.'

'Come on, you two slow coaches, the train won't wait for ever!' cried Amelia from the barrier.

'I hope you have the tickets,' said Cat approaching her grandmother.

'Mr Blaine does,' said Amelia happily.

'Does he indeed?' said Cat, taking a sly look at the teacher's father. He looked like something that had stepped out of *Hello, Dolly!* Pink trousers, cream blazer, pale pink crisp cotton shirt and bright pink socks. Cat bent her head slightly. Gucci loafers? She straightened.

'You live at Heaven's Gate?' she said incredulously. He just smiled and handed her a glossy envelope.

'Camilla Simpson's father you said?'

He smiled again. She shook her head as Mr Blaine pushed Amelia through the barrier. Something was amiss. Camilla was a, well, a sensible woman. Not likely to be a descendant of this apparition. Maybe he was a con man?

A dirty rotten scoundrel after Amelia's millions. He would be sorely disappointed. Any money had long ago been invested in Cat's education and the return wasn't exactly piling up. The insurance money from the two burnt houses was fast running out and now even her mother's account had been emptied. She pulled her ticket out of its envelope to pass through the electronic barrier. It was only then she noticed it was a first-class ticket. Anna noticed at exactly the same time.

'Well, well, well, Amelia has come up trumps again.'

'She couldn't afford these,' said Cat.

'I think she's been working overtime.'

'Please, don't start on that again.'

'You don't think *she* bought these do you?' Anna raised her eyes to the ceiling. 'How terribly naïve you are, pussy cat.' Cat stuck out her tongue. At least Anna was enjoying this. 'I wonder what he wants,' said Cat idly as they went up the escalator to the platform.

'I would have thought that was perfectly obvious.' When Anna got an idea into his head there was no stopping him. 'This is going to be one interesting trip. The emotionally wounded middle youths and the love-sick octogenarians,' said Anna.

'She's only seventy-six,' said Cat, 'and you're the only middle youth around here.'

'Pedant.'

'You taught me everything I know, Miz Prokton.'

'Ouch.'

As they arrived Mr Blaine was pushing Amelia out of the special lift. 'Do you think it would suit me?' asked Anna walking towards the first-class carriage.

'What?' said Cat, briefly looking behind her one last time.

'Pink.'

Cat stopped walking and stared at Anna. He turned back to her and half-smiled. He was beginning to mend. She nodded. Afraid that if she spoke, she'd cry. Anna took her hand and led her to the train.

'First class,' said Anna. 'My dear, there is no other way to travel.'

FIONA HAD GONE TO the studio to escape Robert's drunkenness. She hadn't told him where she was going, and she wasn't going to phone him to tell him she wasn't coming back. The more time he spent in her house the more acutely she remembered what living with him was like. They were like two negative ions, the more they were pushed together, the more the sparks flew. Jane, their sealant, actually drove them apart. They were being forced to reunite in grief over Jane's death and it was happening all over again. What worked with them was distance and mutual contentment. She had her life. She had someone to spend time with when and if she wanted. Robert had Sandie and the money he had always craved and a wife who really loved him. Jane, so Fiona had thought, had the best of both worlds. Two happy homes instead of one unhappy one. Fiona couldn't really believe that unbeknownst to her Sandie had been torturing her daughter. At first she thought it was only her fault that Jane was dead. *She* should have noticed. Then it dawned on her that the reason she hadn't noticed was that there was nothing to notice. Sure Jane occasionally slagged off her stepmother, but what kid didn't slag off their parents at one time or another. Why didn't Jane oppose going to stay at Cedar Hall? Why didn't she complain about life there? It didn't make sense. Fiona had so many questions, so many things to work out. She couldn't talk to Robert, it didn't work. Their inability to communicate was demonstrated nicely when he'd hit her. She wasn't surprised he did, she was surprised she'd forgotten that he did. Ten years was a long time. Long enough for her mind to trick her into remembering the marriage fondly. How stupid of her. Good marriages don't end in divorce. Affection and kindness don't result in talking through lawyers. Her marriage wasn't good. It was a nightmare. She didn't spend time with Robert, she just thought she did. Sure he came over to see Jane in the beginning, but she had forgotten how she would make herself scarce. She had forgotten that it was with Sandie that plans about picking up Jane had been made. Robert never did it. Even at parent nights Robert and Fiona were careful not to spend time alone. They went together, put up a united front for Jane but they could only play to an audience. The lights came up, the act went down. Sure, she knew what he did day to day but only because Jane talked of little else. That was why she *felt* she knew him. But Robert and she weren't friends. They were strangers. Or should have been. The most time she'd spent with him was the day Jane died. They probably hadn't shared anything like that since her birth. Poor Jane. She was born of two people who should have known better. Jane was dead; she didn't have to pretend any more.

THE MAN IN PINK was charm personified. At first Cat felt a need to be suspicious of him, it was her job to look after Amelia, but as the train cut through the South of England to the coast, she had been happy to hand over the reins. She was feeling overwhelmingly tired. She had been brave on Anna's behalf for over a week and now, when there wasn't much courage left in the tank, she had to be brave for herself. She rested her head back on the plush velveteen seat and watched as the tunnel descended into the bowels of the earth. It was a strange feeling entering it. The first-class carriage, already quiet, quietened further still. Mobiles didn't receive under the mud and slime of the sea floor. Conversation seemed to dry up as well. The hush was almost reverential. Give the tunnel the respect it deserves and it may not crack open while you're inside. Cat crossed her fingers under the table as she imagined tectonically created fissures running parallel to the high-speed train. With every bump and jolt, the fissures became fractures, until the whole thing burst open and sea water came flooding in. The train would crash, people would run in panic, opening doors, smashing windows, letting water in everywhere, Cat would drown holding Amelia above her head, Dan would collapse in tears at the funeral and have to be taken out . . . Cat sat up.

'Darling, aren't you well? You look terribly pale all of a sudden.'

She shook her head. 'I'm fine Gran, just fine.'

'Not another hangover,' said Amelia. 'You lot are terrible. I suppose you were seeing Dan off.'

Cat frowned. She didn't think it was really a cause for celebration. 'Excuse me?'

'The job, driving some fast car in the desert.' She turned to Mr Blaine. 'It is extraordinary how much these people pay. Dan alone gets a fortune for having his hands on the wheel in the photo. How can they justify spending such obscene amounts of money on car ads?'

'A young Stirling Moss?'

'No, a hand model, and a Ph.D. student.' Amelia looked pointedly at Cat. 'A remarkable young man. Pity he can't be here.'

'Please don't—'

'Amelia,' interrupted Anna, 'when did you talk to Dan?'

'Yesterday. I phoned to tell him what train we were getting and he said he was sorry but he wasn't going to be able to make it. It is a good thing we didn't book in advance. We would have wasted all that money.'

'We?' said Cat.

Amelia giggled and changed the subject. 'So what are we going to do in Paris?'

'What time did you speak to him?' Cat persisted.

'Darling, don't interrupt.'

'What?' Cat couldn't believe she had heard Amelia right.

'Where are we staying?' asked Anna trying to break the tension.

'Hôtel des Tulipes,' said Cat, quickly, before turning back to Amelia.

'Actually, no. The Hôtel Mansard,' said Mr Blaine, 'a fantastic hotel spitting distance of Place Vendôme. And to answer your question, Amelia, we are going to do a great deal.'

'But I booked it,' complained Cat.

'And I unbooked it,' said Amelia.

'Near the Ritz,' exclaimed Anna, still trying to break the tension. 'All those lovely shops. Armani, Gucci . . .'

And who the hell is paying? Cat tried to get Amelia's attention, but Amelia refused to catch her eye. Dan had gone abroad without even putting up a fight. He'd dropped her like a stone. Cat sat and simmered in silence as the threesome listed galleries and places they wanted to see. The Eiffel Tower, of course, the Louvre, couldn't miss it. Cat did not join in. Eventually Mr Blaine excused himself and went to 'freshen up'. Cat pounced on her grandmother.

'Why is Mr Blaine paying for us to go on holiday when he has never met us before and you have never mentioned him?' *And why are you in cahoots with Dan? He left me.*

'Well there's gratitude for you.'

'Gran!'

'I think he is perfectly charming,' said Anna.

'Charming enough to be fleeced.'

'You are so like your mother sometimes.'

Cat shuddered. Her breathing quickened. 'My mother spent her whole life living off men, please do *not* say I am like her.'

'I meant the acid tongue,' said Amelia calmly. 'When it comes to morals, you are indeed quite the opposite.'

'Why are you being like this, Gran?'

Amelia didn't seem to see the distress she was causing Cat. Anna stepped in to help. 'It does seem a little odd, Amelia, you must agree. First-class tickets, a posh hotel . . . I can see why Cat is concerned.'

'I thought we all needed a little R&R.'

'You've been watching too much *M*A*S*H*,' said Anna.

'Not at someone else's expense, Gran?' pleaded Cat, ignoring Anna.

'He's a lonely old man, with a bit of a crush and a lot of cash,' said Amelia smiling broadly.

Cat was horrified. 'You know there is a word for what you are doing,' she said in a tense whisper.

'Catherine Torrant, I did not bring you up to talk like that. I thought you knew better than to cast aspersions before you knew the facts.'

Cat stared at Amelia. The wheelchair even got her sometimes. Fragile Amelia was not. She shot from the hip, even if it was immobile.

Mr Blaine came walking up the aisle. He stood over their table. He was a tall man with white hair and pale, drooping eyes. 'I thought this might happen,' he said. 'But I couldn't hold on any longer, one of the many disadvantages of age.'

'You should get a plastic bag, much less bother,' said Amelia, still looking at her granddaughter.

'I told your grandmother to fill you in, but she said you wouldn't have a problem with me. She was wrong wasn't she?'

'Mr Blaine,' said Cat uncomfortably and furious with Amelia for putting her in this position.

'It's quite all right, I'd think it strange if an old duffer resplendent in pink, my favourite colour by the way, whisked me and my family away.'

'This isn't about you,' said Cat. 'Really.'

'Oh, but it is. I offered to pay for your holiday because I have a huge amount of money and only a terrible family who are waiting for me to die. I'm trying to spend it all.'

Anna sniggered. Cat was flabbergasted. 'I thought Camilla was very nice actually.'

'You're wrong, she's more than that. She's wonderful. Though she is, sadly, not my real daughter. In other words she is not my blood daughter, people seem to put a lot of unnecessary onus on that, do they not.' Cat looked confused. 'She is my stepdaughter. Her mother, my second wife, died in a car crash. My ex-wife and our mutual offspring are the vultures, they only ever visited me when they wanted money. The pre-bleeding chitchat was more painful than you could possibly imagine. So I moved to Heaven's Gate to be under the protection of Nurse Cleveland, who I'm pleased to report they are all terrified of.'

'Unsurprisingly,' said Anna.

Mr Blaine smiled. 'And to meet people. To have some fun. I've been rattling around in my big old house for long enough. Camilla is very busy and I was beginning to put too much pressure on her to visit all the time. God, I was bored.' He paused, remembering the endless days, making one small errand stretch for hours, the daily stroll to the local shop to buy milk which he ended up throwing away. He didn't want to die but he found himself waiting for death. Now he didn't mind how long he had left as long as he lived it. 'Also,' he said with a smile, 'as I'm sure your grandmother has told you, I have contracted a small infatuation for her.'

'Small!' said Amelia shooing him away. 'Get back to me when it's life-threatening.'

'Everything with you is life-threatening, I'm surprised Nurse Cleveland hasn't suffocated you with a pillow yet,' said Cat.

'Or worse,' said Anna.

'Quite,' said Mr Blaine. 'So you see, Amelia isn't doing anything wrong by agreeing to let me pay, though I agree she ought to have told you, and you would be doing me a great honour if you would let me indulge you for a few days in gay Paris. We'll have a wonderful time.'

Cat was too taken aback to answer.

'Come on, Cat, let me have a little bit of fun. It's a premium at my age.'

She realized everyone was looking at her, but still she couldn't answer. Her mind was stuck like a record on one thought. Mr Blaine looked at Amelia regretfully and sighed. Cat went on staring at him regardless.

'I'm sorry, I didn't realize you'd find this so hard. Of course, I'm intruding in your family trip, I'll . . .' he paused.

Cat suddenly put her hand on his. 'She calls you Dad,' said Cat. 'My old Dad.'

'Camilla?' said Mr Blaine somewhat perplexed. 'Well, she would.'

'But you're not,' said Cat.

'Cat!' exclaimed Amelia.

'Oh, I am,' he said, not in the slightest bit perturbed. 'Absolutely, I am. Bonds don't always have to be blood related you know, Cat. Not all step parents are wicked. I wish more people knew that.'

Chapter Twenty-Two

A key sounded in the lock. The door opened. Feet brushed on the mat. Robert peeled his chin off his chest and looked up in the vague direction of the noise. He blinked, waiting for the darkness to clear, but it didn't. He looked out of the window. Where had the day gone? He couldn't remember how long he'd been there. In fact, he couldn't remember anything about the day at all. His daughter was dead, he could remember that. Robert pushed himself unsteadily to his feet and walked out of the room adjoining the kitchen. He didn't want Fiona thinking he couldn't take the pressure, Jesus, he'd been taking the pressure all his . . . Someone was standing in the dark at the other end of the hallway.

'Jane,' he croaked, inaudibly. Speaking sent him into a coughing spasm.

'I'm sorry, I didn't know Fiona had company.' That was not Fiona's voice. Nor was it female.

'What?' said Robert through the coughs.

'Sorry, that sounded a bit rude. Are you all right?'

The man slid his hand down the wall and found the light switch that had escaped Robert time and time again. The hall lit up. The man took off his coat and threw it on the banister. There was a level of informality in his movements and tone that alarmed Robert. 'I take it she isn't at home?' He looked at Robert. Glued to the tiles, frowning at him. Suddenly the man's hand jerked upwards, he ran his hand through his hair.

'God, how stupid of me. You must be Robert.' The man walked forward. 'I'm so sorry. Such awful news. I still can't believe it. I've only just found out. I've been abroad you see. She isn't here is she? Fiona?' Robert shook his head. Who the hell was this person? 'No. Sorry. Already established that. A drink. You look like you need it.' He walked past Robert straight to the cupboard above the sideboard and retrieved two tumblers. He knew his way around all right. He went next to the cupboard in the adjoining room. Whisky. He held the new bottle up to Robert, who had taken two steps back and now stood on the threshold of the kitchen. Fiona hadn't told him about that cupboard. Robert could see his empty Safeway's bottle sticking up from between the cushions on the small sofa. He walked over to it quickly while the stranger had his back to him and threw one of Fiona's hand-made cushions over it.

'This is your medicine, isn't it?' he said turning. Robert nodded again. 'Thought so. Ice and soda.'

'Just ice,' he croaked as the stranger poured double

measures into each glass and threw in some ice from a metal tin in the freezer. He passed it to Robert.

'I know how hard this must be.'

'You do?' Robert sounded very suspicious.

'My wife. Emily. She died of a brain tumour. One minute she was complaining about a headache and by the time I'd made her some tea, she was,' it still hurt, 'well. It was a shock. So I know how hard this must be. I can't believe Fiona didn't get hold of me, I would have come back immediately.' He glanced at the answering machine. Twenty-three messages. He pointed. 'You haven't been listening to the—'

'Excuse me,' said Robert, forcing himself to speak. 'But would you mind telling me exactly who you are, what you are doing here, and why you have keys to this house?' The man looked shocked. He laughed once. It was a nervous laugh. 'It's just,' continued Robert, 'you seem to know so very much about my family, I thought it might be considerate to introduce yourself. You see I have no bloody idea who you are.' The man frowned. 'Really. No idea at all. Not an inkling. You could be a mass murderer for all I know. Jane's murderer even, why not? You had keys to the house. I guess you were sleeping with her. Though, if you don't mind me saying you're a bit old for her. What was she, a rebound after your wife died? A bit of young comfort. You must be forty for God's sake. Think that is normal do you? Christ, what sort of household has Fiona been running? And where the hell is she anyway? She knew about this I suppose. I always thought her free-thinking ways would lead to disaster. Chuck her did you? Had enough? Poor kid, she was a child, for Christ's sake.'

The man stood up. 'That's enough, Robert.'

'How dare you speak to me in my own . . .' His voice trailed off.

'Fiona's house. We are in Fiona's house. I have a key because Fiona and I are having a relationship. I know all about your family because Fiona has become part of my family. I know Jane because I have spent a great deal of time with Jane. A great deal of time, yet you seem to know nothing about me. In that respect I am as surprised as you are.' He sat down and took a sip of the dark liquid. 'Fiona and I met up on a skiing holiday six years ago. We became friends and started seeing each other about three years ago.'

'What? I don't believe it.'

'My name is Attlewood. Ring any bells?' Robert shook his head. 'Last Easter Jane and Fiona came to stay with me on my boat on the Solent. Remember that?'

'Jane told me about the holiday. But she never mentioned you.'

'Christmas. You had Jane, Fiona and I went to India.'

'Fiona went to India with a girlfriend.'

Attlewood stood up, walked to the bookshelf above the drinks cabinet and retrieved an album. He flicked through it for a few moments. 'Here we are. Fiona and me at the Red Palace in Agra. This Easter. Together. Alone.'

'You are Jo.'

He nodded.

'Jo Attlewood?'

'Short for Joseph.'

'The trip through France two years ago?'

'Exactly.'

'Scotland. Walking. Last June.'

'Right again.'

'Italy. Skiing in January. Jane told me everything Fi did.'

'Obviously not everything,' said Jo.

Robert sat down at the kitchen table. He ran his hand through his hair. 'I can't believe it. Jane told me you were a woman.'

Jo laughed. Forgetting himself momentarily. 'Cheers Jane.' Robert looked at him. 'Sorry.'

'Or maybe I just assumed you were a woman. Jane said Jo, I saw Jo short for Joanna. She never told me that you weren't a woman.' Robert looked at Jo. 'I never imagined there was another man in Fi's life.'

'There isn't another man, Robert.' Robert looked confused. 'There's only me.'

THE FIRST FEW DAYS in Paris went so quickly Cat didn't have time to think about anything other than *pain au chocolat, demi-pression de bière* and promenading. The first night Mr Blaine had treated them all to dinner halfway up the Eiffel Tower. It had set the mood. Cat was grateful it was a good one. It was only when they sat talking and drinking late every evening that Cat realized how much she needed a break. She'd been working flat out and she was knackered. In a week she was back at college for her final term. She wasn't going to let Dan ruin her chance of a laugh. She stubbornly put him out of her mind and set about throwing herself at Paris. Amelia was on such cracking form that Cat soon found herself developing a small crush on Mr Blaine herself. He was so worldly and knew so much about everything. He said it was one of the pay-offs of being a widower. Time to explore history. Anna liked him because of the bright colours he wore. He felt a surge of joy when he looked at his dreary black jeans and felt fraudulent. He wasn't ready for drag, but he was beginning to feel an aversion to drab. He didn't tell Cat, he wanted to see whether the snippets of Anna Prokton were stronger than the cold hard terror that had gripped him since the attack.

THEIR HOTEL WAS WONDERFUL. Cat had felt a twinge of misery when Mr Blaine first wheeled Amelia across the ultra-chic marble-design floor of the lobby. But she didn't have to have Dan next to her to absorb the romanticism of Paris. Mr Blaine was on first-name terms with the constellation of concerned staff in orbit around the reception desk. It obviously wasn't his first time. Cat took him aside on the second day and thanked him, the staff were treating Amelia like the queen. He had said, careful, they chop their queens' heads off.

Amelia and Mr Blaine had separate bedrooms and Anna wondered if it would stay like that for the duration of the holiday. Cat said she didn't want to talk about it. Cat and Anna on the other hand shared a room. Neither of them wanted too much time alone. The room had high ceilings and two double windows opening on to small balconies overlooking the narrow street below. Apart from the Irish pub over the road, it was *vraiment* French. One of the first places they visited was the Louvre, a stone's throw from the hotel. Having descended into the infamous glass pyramid, Anna and Cat made a few wrong turnings and found themselves standing in a dungeon-like room with thick curved walls and a disquieting aroma. Mr Blaine told them later they'd found the recently excavated walls of the bastion that once guarded Paris before Louis XIV came along and built the magnificent Tuileries Garden and palace that the Louvre is now part of. But at the time, it had felt like they'd stumbled into a prison. No one else was down there and the temperature had dropped.

'Looks like dungeons,' said Cat, her voice disappearing into the thick damp curving stone wall.

'I dread to think what went on down here if it was,' said Anna. Thinking about incarceration.

'Unimaginable things,' said Cat. Anna didn't agree. Cat saw the look on his face and took him by the arm. 'It's giving me the creeps, let's go and find ourselves a nice, calming da Vinci to study.'

'You're on,' said Anna. He closed his eyes. *Think pink.*

A FEW DAYS LATER, as promised by Mr Blaine, they went to the Conciergerie where the aristocracy spent their last days awaiting the guillotine. Again the atmosphere changed as they descended into the huge medieval Salle des Gardes and saw the tiny dank cells where the prisoners were kept. The stale air lodged itself up the nose and prickled the skin. Marie Antoinette's cell was marked out for the tourists. Anna stood on the ledge where she would have been taken out and had her hair and dress collar cut off before being thrown in the back of the tumbrel and taken to the guillotine.

'Madame Tussaud became famous by making death masks of the beheaded,' said Mr Blaine.

'Really?' said Cat fascinated.

'Their way of keeping a record. They're exhibited at the Musée Grevan – we could go tomorrow.'

'Full of death masks, no thanks,' said Anna.

'No, it's got all sorts of waxworks.'

'Sounds great,' said Cat.

'Very macabre,' said Amelia.

'Paris has a history of the macabre just like any other city. Don't be taken in by the intricate façade, *malfeasance* runs deep.'

Cat studied Mr Blaine's face in the shadows and thought about Jane Wellby for the first time since arriving hin Paris. She hadn't even rung the college that Jane attended.

'Wherever past evils have chipped away at national pride, they've made up in tourist revenue,' he said smiling as he guided Amelia down the wheelchair ramp.

'Think of all those people,' said Anna, walking along the corridor of narrow cells, 'waiting to die.'

'Reminds me of Heaven's Gate, only with French food,' said Amelia.

Anna didn't respond to the joke. He was listening to the wails of prisoners, he could see their soft, expensively kept hair falling to the rat–infested floor, he could feel the hatred of the guards, consumed with jealously and rage because their prisoners had lived lives they'd never be privy to. Only when defenceless and completely at their mercy would they feel victorious. When victims turned their superiors into victims. Not all men are equal, thought Anna. They never will be. There will always be discrepancies and there will always be atrocities. Anna stared into the cell. Marie Antoinette in her full regalia curtseyed, before the cell gate opened and three big guards pulled her down. Marie Antoinette stared at Anna as she was forced to the floor. The men took it in turns to clamber on top of her. Rape, thought Anna, of course. The easiest way to debase a human being. He waited for the chilling sensation of fear to invade him as he watched his daydream unfold.

'What are you staring at, Anna?' said Cat.

The cold didn't come. 'History repeating itself,' said Anna, nodding to himself. As long as there were people, terrible things would happen. Human beings were blessed and cursed with emotion. Yes, he'd gone willingly to a man's studio but what had taken place in that room was not all his fault. Another day he could have been caught in crossfire. Another day it could have been a bomb. Another day he could have wandered into a gang of homophobic white trash . . . Anna had as much control over his life as he didn't. If you were lucky, it was balanced in your favour, if you were unlucky, it wasn't. He wasn't to blame. There is no rhyme or reason why one life should be taken over another. God giveth and God taketh away. Bullshit. He may giveth, but it's the bastard car thief that knocks down your child who taketh away.

FIONA HAD BEEN HOLED up in the studio for a week. No phone. No TV. No newspapers. The peace calmed her. She spent most of the days thinking about Jane. Trying to work her out. The more she thought about her daughter, the less she knew. Jane was a stranger to her. A two-dimensional daughter. The burning question was had she noticed this absence of life in her daughter all along and chosen to ignore it or had she simply not noticed. Hovering over the relentless repetitive thoughts was the little girl who had bullied her daughter at the age of nine and she didn't even know why. She wanted to talk to Sandie. She was the only person Fiona could talk to. She was too ashamed to talk to Jo, and too irritated to talk to Robert. So she'd left the safety of the studio and driven to Cedar Hall. She panicked when she saw the swarm of press outside the gates. Some of them were walking over to her, what the hell were the press doing there? She recognized a few people from the village. They snarled at her. The angry mob. Fiona didn't like being intimidated by anyone, she honked on her horn loudly and revved the accelerator. People started clearing to the side. She put her head down and drove on. They were tapping on her window, taking photos, she couldn't go back now so she continued to honk the horn. Sam Clough appeared at the gates, recognized her and opened them. Fiona drove through. The pack stood on the threshold. They knew they couldn't continue. Marcus England had issued a private property claim. Anyone stepping foot beyond the gate would be arrested for trespassing. She stopped the car and waited for Sam Clough.

'What on earth are they doing?' said Fiona, her adrenaline making her voice quaver. She was shaking.

'Bloody animals,' said the gardener.

'Why are they here?'

'Haven't you seen the papers?' Fiona shook her head. Sam Clough's expression changed from exasperation at the press to sadness. 'Best you talk to Mrs Wellby. I'm afraid things have got very bad.'

'What's happened?' said Fiona, alarmed.

'Your daughter has been causing mischief from beyond the grave.'

Fiona blinked at him. *She isn't in a grave, stupid, she's on a slab.* He turned away from her and disappeared behind the cedar trees. Fiona quickly wound the window up and sped along the drive covering the onlookers in a cloud of gravel dust. Fiona ignored the doorbell marked 'push' and forced the heavy wooden front door open instead.

'Sandie!' she called out. Her voice echoed around the room. She remembered the scream. Her scream. The diary. The plane ticket. What the hell was she doing here? She checked herself. Nothing was clear. She must try and keep an open mind. 'Sandie!' Still no answer. The kitchen was empty, but the kettle had only just boiled, so she must be somewhere. Fiona recrossed the hall and went into Robert's study. Sandie was sitting behind the big mahogany desk. She looked terrible.

'Sandie?' Her eyes were red, her cheeks were blotchy, she looked exhausted. 'Are you all right?' Fiona walked round to where she sat, staring out of the window to the cedar trees that gave the house its name. When Fiona touched her shoulder Sandie slumped forward. For a few moments she cried like a child. Then she sat up and, with a sudden movement, swiped everything off Robert's desk and stood up. Fiona nearly fell over.

'I'm so fucking angry! Everything I have worked for,' she shouted, 'everything! Ruined!'

'Calm down, Sandie, please?'

'I hope you haven't come here to gloat. You're not the one being hounded, I can't even go to the shops, I can't even leave my . . . It is all sympathy for you, and hatred for me. Well I did nothing but try with your fucking daughter, and it wasn't easy, I tell you, but murder her I did not, tell that to Robert, my dear husband, when you next see him.'

Stunned, Fiona stared at the woman unravelling before her.

'My business is haemorrhaging money as people cancel huge orders, even Simon has turned on me. Whatever I've done doesn't deserve this I tell you, not this. Jesus, she wasn't even my child, you should take responsibility goddammit, not me. I was just her stepmother.'

'Sandie, you threatened to cut her.'

'*Cut* her?'

'Genital mutilation.'

'For fuck's sake . . .' Sandie picked up the phone and dialled the internal line. 'Marcus, you little shit, why didn't you tell me . . . I don't give a damn . . . Have you got it? . . . Jesus, Marcus, what were you thinking, bring it to me now!' She slammed the phone down. 'This is bullshit. And you know it. Come on, Fiona, you are an intelligent woman, what the fuck is going on here?'

Fiona didn't know how to respond.

'Is it about money? Fuck it, I'll write a fucking cheque, just call off the dogs.'

'I came here to talk, I didn't know the papers had got hold of the story and I don't want your money.'

'Talk?! Jesus, I've been so naïve. I was set up you know. You ought to know that before you read the paper.'

'What did it say, the article?'

'They. Articles!'

'What?'

'Where have you been, Fiona? Off on a trip with lover boy?'

Fiona frowned. 'Jo?'

'Oh no, course not, he called here looking for you. I said, don't be stupid, she wouldn't dare come here.'

Fiona ignored the challenge. 'He's back?'

The patronizing tone in Sandie's voice was ferocious. 'I've had other things to worry about than the where-abouts of your lover.'

Fiona winced. She was too British for open discussions about her love life. 'When did he call?'

Sandie turned. 'What are you doing here?'

'I want answers!' Fiona was raising her voice. So much for the peaceful approach.

'Okay, here's an answer, your daughter was a vain, twisted, psychotic bitch.' Fiona's eyes widened. 'See, knew you wouldn't like it.' Sandie turned back to the window. She slumped forward again. 'Why did you have to give the diary to the police, Fi?' she said sadly, 'now we'll never know what happened. You think they are doing a comprehensive investigation, bullshit they are.

Bramley, who obviously has friends in high places, has only gone and rushed the court date through. Clever, don't you think, for such an asshole, leak info to the press, get the locals screaming for blood, a few holier-than-thou schoolfriends quoting what a bitch I am, and hey presto, court date gets set.'

Fiona turned away from Sandie and walked over to the ceiling-high bookshelf. The questions she'd wanted to ask sprang randomly into her head.

'Why did you tell the police Jane had been acting strangely for months?'

'Because she had. She didn't sleep at night. She drank during the day. She never had friends over. Do you think that's normal?'

'She wasn't like that at home.'

Sandie scraped her hair back and tied an elastic band round it. 'So I gather.' She turned back to Fiona who stood pressed against the bookcase. 'Look at me, Fiona. I'm a wreck. I didn't kill your daughter. I can't defend myself alone. I need you to help me. Robert is . . .' Sandie shook her head from side to side. 'I'll never forgive him.'

'He lost his daughter, Sandie,' she said in a pleading tone.

'He didn't have to lose his wife as well.'

'The diary.'

'It's a fake. Do you know Jane's writing that well? You must have had less than five minutes looking at it before you called the police. Not for one second did you think that you were being tricked. Whatever's in it, I didn't do it. If Robert loved me, if he'd ever loved me, he'd have known that. That's what frightens me the most. You know me too, Fiona, and think I could do those things: cut her. Imagine what the jury will think? Off with her fucking head, that's what they'll think. Do I sound pissed, well I am fucking pissed. You, my husband, Simon.' Sandie clicked her fingers. 'Gone. I haven't got a chance.'

'Maybe it was an accident, she fell, you panicked—'

Sandie stood up. 'Get out of my house, Fiona. Go back to Robert, I hope you'll be very happy. Tell him, he won't get a dime outta me, you tell him that. It is about time somebody other than me was hurting.'

Sandie walked over to Fiona, forcing her backwards to the door.

'I don't want Robert.'

'Too late.' Sandie looked murderous.

'I think he should come back here.'

Sandie laughed. 'Gee thanks. A drunk who thinks I killed his daughter. I'd prefer a divorce. I'm sure you'll both be very happy.'

'I told you,' said Fiona, backing out of the room. 'I don't want Robert.'

Sandie gave her a final shove. 'You can do whatever you like with him, just please don't have any more children, there is quite enough evil in this world without you two playing happy families,' said Sandie and closed the door. Fiona felt like she'd been kicked in the stomach.

She walked backwards away from the study, hoping to wake up and be arriving clear-headed, not departing more confused than ever. Her mind reeled with the things Sandie had said. Jo, she wanted Jo. There was a newspaper on the hall table. Fiona walked over to it and picked it up. It was two days old. On page three was a photograph of Sandie being helped into a car by her lawyer. The caption read: 'A TRULY WICKED STEP-MOTHER. Sandie Wellby went on a drinking binge with a man only days after her stepdaughter was found dead in her husband's car. She was overheard in the dining room of The Fox near the village of Thuckley, saying even a murderess needed a little fun . . .' Fiona grabbed it and ran to the car.

Chapter Twenty-Three

Anna and Cat lay on their beds after another exhausting plate of *steak frites*. Cat rubbed her belly and groaned. The *tarte tartin* had probably been a mistake.

'Now that's attractive.'

'I've eaten far too much.'

'No shit, Shylock.'

'Sherlock, you fool,' said Cat laughing.

'Just testing you're still with us. I've asked you the time thrice and you haven't answered.'

Cat propped herself up on her elbow. 'Really,' she said taken aback.

Anna nodded.

'Actually I've been thinking about Jane Wellby, it was something that Mr Blaine said—'

'Isn't he a dish.'

'Hands off, he's taken.' Cat shook a warning finger at Anna.

'He's also not gay, small point, but worth mentioning.'

'Yes, but you're as bad as the Jesuits when it comes to converting.'

'Don't you mean the—'

'Piss off. Do you want to talk about Jane Wellby or not?' asked Cat, tentatively doing up the buttons on her jeans.

'I'd rather talk about Dan.'

'Dan? Why?' Cat disappeared into their en-suite bathroom and stared at herself in the mirror. Anna wasn't put off.

'Well, you've hardly mentioned him since you got here, so I guess it isn't consuming your every waking hour?' Anna sat up on his bed.

'No.'

'Really?'

'I'm fine as long as I don't think about it.'

'Hmm,' said Anna. 'I think you have too many male hormones.'

Cat reappeared. 'In which case we should make the perfect couple. Let's set up home and adopt.'

'Ha. Ha. I mean it, it's usually boys who can switch off emotion, not girls. Do you want to know what I think?'

'No,' said Cat, knowing to resist was futile.

'I think you're too self-sufficient for your own good. No brothers and sisters, you've grown up depending on only yourself by –'

'I'm not listening . . .'

'– working out a system of protecting yourself by

projecting an image of someone who can cope with having a useless mother and a crap father—'

'I never had a father to be protected from.' Cat hated it when people talked about him.

'See. Your exterior personality has been acting for so long, making out it can cope with your, well let's be honest, pretty weird set up. Your internal personality believes it too. You switch off when you don't want to think about things that are too emotional. Like Dan. The thing is, I think you *do* want to think about him, and I think he wants to think about you, he came over looking for you, I told him to back off, it's my fault he isn't here, I feel terrible . . .' Anna looked at Cat, waiting for her reaction. She was staring at him open-mouthed, but no sound came out. Instead she turned away, walked over to the window and pushed it open. Anna got off the bed scolding himself. He hadn't meant to dump quite so much on her at once. He walked out of the second set of windows on to the other small balcony. Cat was leaning too far over the railing.

'Cat,' said Anna gently, 'I'm really sorry, I didn't mean to . . .'

Cat turned slowly to face him. 'You're right, you know. Of course. You're a fucking genius.' She straightened up quickly and started pacing the room. Anna watched her, fearful that he had started something that neither of them could stop. Take the lid off psychological repression and fuck knows what happens.

Cat was throwing punches into her hand like an

American pitcher. 'It adds up,' she said. 'She protects herself from her parents' situation by pretending all is fine in the family home. She does it for so long and so well, she starts to believe it.'

Oh God, she's talking about herself in the second person. 'Why don't you sit down, Cat,' said Anna. 'Drink?'

'No. But . . . Not at home. She can't do it at home, can she? So at home she is the perfect daughter. It is all part of the plan. Be good. Bring Mummy and Daddy back together again. One big happy family.'

'Cat,' said Anna, terrified of what he'd started, 'your parents were never going to do that, we better talk about this, I can help you.'

'Me? What has this got to do with my parents. Shut up, Anna.'

'It's because of Dan. The body clock. I scared him off.'

Cat stopped pacing. 'Anna, what are you talking about?'

Anna frowned. 'What are *you* talking about?'

'Jane Wellby of course. It's what you said. When your conscious mind begins to control your subconscious mind.'

Anna looked lost.

'The conflicting recollections of Jane. She was one thing to one person, like her mum, then another to others, like her teachers and Carla Hammond. Aren't you with me?'

Anna shook his head.

'It started way back when she was a kid, right? At school Jane's persona was that of a happy child with two loving parents. Not true. Parents were divorced. Rumours of bullying are ignored, she gets away with it. Then it gets complicated. The personality splits again. Camilla said Fiona and Robert always came to the school together, it would've been easy for her to imagine they'd get back together eventually. But then Sandie arrives. The enemy. Come to break up Jane's virtual family. As she gets older the personalities keep splitting.'

'You're saying she was a schizophrenic.'

'No. Schizophrenics have no control over where or when the personalities split or emerge. Jane was always the same thing to the same people. She was always good at home. She was always in trouble with teachers. She was always vulnerable and holy to her college friends and she was always a twisted sex fiend with Paul Hound.' Cat took a deep breath. 'Now are you with me?'

'Hm, well, hm.'

Cat raised her eyes to the ceiling. 'Don't be taken in by the intricate façade, *malfeasance* runs deep. That's what Mr Blaine said. She kept it hidden. Her malfeasance. Wickedness, Anna. That is why she was killed.'

'By Sandie?'

Cat sighed deeply. 'I don't know, but I'm going to find out.' Cat immediately picked up the phone.

'Okay, Shylock.'

'Sherlock.'

'That's what I said, didn't I.'

DARREN CLOSED THE DOOR and leant against it. He was sweating profusely and his heartbeat was right up there with the angels. He didn't think the fucking police would find the body so quickly. And once more, for the record; he didn't think they'd find it at all. Okay, so it may not have been the most intelligent place to put it, but it was kind of difficult lugging a dead bloke around Soho on your own. With everything that had been going on, he hadn't been keeping up his gym subscription. Darren had dragged the fat bloke as far as he could down the back streets, hoping he looked like a good sort helping out a mate who'd had a few. It was the first skip he'd come to. When they did find it, the body had been striped naked. He hadn't left the poor bloke naked; some frigging tramp had stolen his clothes and left him exposed. They'd been sniffing around the whore houses making him only too aware of how fucking close the skip was. Darren stood and stared at the place where the dead bloke had lain and wondered what he could possibly have done to deserve this. Years ago he had stood on the Tyne bridge and thought about ending his own life, but despite the shit, he'd known then that life was a privilege. Now he'd robbed a man of that privilege, he'd dumped his body in a skip and gone back to work. Because the men who liked to watch other men and women raped of their decency and dignity wanted more. They didn't care about the dead bloke, they just wanted more. This time it had to be a girl. A young one. That meant hanging around parks and shit. There was a kindergarten in Soho, in a normal situation he'd hang around there choosing someone. It was a trick of the trade. Always get them to come by their own volition. That way not only did they feel tortured and fucked up for life, they'd never go to the police. Why? Because it was their fault. Because they went back there. They had guilty consciences which meant the evil would go on indefinitely. Conclusion: a guilty conscience was a weakness. It made you a victim while allowing the wickedness to go on and on and on. Darren had killed a man. He had blood on his hands. All his life he had tried not to become like them. His parents, the johns, the men in the home, his boss, but now he'd killed a man and whichever way he looked at it, that changed things. Did he have a guilty conscience? *Yes*. He did. His fingerprints were all over the corpse, the police would find him eventually. They'd pin it to him and it would stick. Institutionalization. No thanks. He'd been up that road before. He stood in the empty studio and decided the time had come to end all of this. He remembered standing high above the polluted river, looking down on the crap. Free. He wanted to feel it again. He wanted to be free from his shitty little life. This time he was going to jump; but not alone.

CAT HELD THE DOOR to the college open as a flood of English-speaking youngsters spilled out. None of them said thank you.

'The least they could do is tip,' said Anna, over the sea of sunglasses that donned the selection of blonde, highlighted heads.

'I don't take American Express,' replied Cat. None of the Euro-babes noticed. They had cafés to go to, thé to drink and white-tipped Marlboro Lights to smoke.

'I wish I was wearing my togs, show them a thing or two.'

'We can always come back,' said Cat, testing him.

Anna shook his head. 'I think I'll leave someone else to convert these lovelies.' Cat and Anna eyed up the 501-clad derrières of the young men.

'And I wonder why all my girlfriends are single.'

'Including yourself.'

'Bitch,' said Cat. 'Long live Andrew.'

'Just go and ask someone where this bloke is,' said Anna impatiently. Happy to dish it, less happy to take it. They walked through the entrance hall, groups of students leant casually against the wall.

'Woah,' exclaimed Anna as if he'd walked into an invisible wall. 'Just feel that attitude. These guys are pros.'

Cat laughed. 'I'm so glad I don't give a shit any more, trying to be cool all the time was so exhausting.'

Anna tutted. 'Cat, you were never cool. You've worn jeans and T-shirts all your life.'

'So?'

'So, it isn't cool it is boring.'

'Rubbish.'

'Okay, let me dress you this evening.'

'No.'

'There you go. Boring.'

Cat's eyes narrowed to slits. Anna was about to continue when a door across the corridor opened. A Jack Nicholson lookalike opened the door. Cat and Anna stared.

'You must be Cat Torrant?' The man smiled. Cat looked at his wedding finger. Gold band. *Bien sur.*

'Yes?' Cat nodded, still speechless. 'Come on in. I am Monsieur Tillier, I run the school.' He turned his back and moved around to his desk. Anna put out his tongue and mimicked panting. Cat nearly laughed. There were two seats ready for them. They sat. For once Cat wished she'd been wearing a skimpy, strappy thing, then she saw the family photo on the desk and banished the thought.

'Thanks for seeing us. As I said on the phone, I'll be recording this interview, if you're still all right with this?'

'For your college work?'

'Yes. London College of Printing.'

'Bien.'

Cat fiddled with her equipment, placed it equidistantly between herself and the teacher and wrapped the mike wire around her fist. She did a test for volume then nodded that they were ready. Monsieur Tillier began talking before she could ask a question. 'So, Jane Wellby.' He sighed. 'A very difficult young lady.'

'She seems to have been a very complicated person.'

Monsieur Tillier nodded. 'Possibly. Very sad that she is dead. I'm sorry her family didn't listen to what I said.'

'What did you say?'

'Well, she was expelled, you know.' Anna and Cat both shook their heads. 'Oh yes, *les drogues*.'

'Really? What sort?'

'I don't know the specifics, but she brought Ecstasy into the school.'

'Pushing?'

The French man leant back in his chair. 'I don't know, maybe it was for personal use, it was a lot though. She was definitely in with a bad set. Her attendance was low, she was very, how do you say, up and down.' He shook his wrist to demonstrate.

'Did you tell the police?'

'Of course.'

'Without giving her a chance to explain herself?' said Anna, shocked.

'I tried to talk to her. Her eyes were like black holes, her skin was like tissue paper and she is biting down on her lip so hard that she doesn't notice it is bleeding. What does she say? Drugs, Monsieur Tillier, I don't do drugs. I have a lot of young students here, some very naïve.'

'But to go to the police?'

He tutted. 'Non. They came to me. Showed me some photos of the illegal raves at the Catacombs. They thought colleges were being targeted.'

'So what happened?'

'We raided lockers of all the suspected drug takers at the college. Unfortunately they found drugs and fliers in Jane Wellby's locker. She never returned. Maybe someone saw, she had quite a little following, *toujours le même*, weak, unpopular kids. I telephoned her mother.' Monsieur laughed. 'Jane was very smart, she'd been phoning every week telling her mother she was very unhappy, homesick. So when she turned up on her doorstep, *voilà*, no problem. She said Jane looked terrible, that she would call the authorities. I told her the authorities already knew about her daughter, I never heard from her again.'

'You didn't follow it up?'

'Why should I, I had to clear up her mess here. She was no longer my problem.'

Anna raised his eyebrows. 'It seems that everyone turned their backs on Jane Wellby, she was in trouble.'

'Yes, yes, she was.' Monsieur Tillier tapped the side of his head. 'In here. Serious trouble.'

'It can't be the first time a kid has got mixed up in drugs, don't you think your approach was a little draconian?' said Anna, feeling sorry for the girl.

'It wasn't just the drugs. Though they probably made her worse.'

'What do you mean?'

'You turn the machine off?'

Cat nodded and pressed pause.

'Confidentiality should remain just that, don't you think?' said Anna petulantly.

Monsieur Tillier didn't seem at all put off by Anna's

antagonism. 'I understand why you are angry with me, you think I should have done more, as a teacher? Hm? You can't help people who don't want helping. Whose families don't see the need. I'll tell you this because it might help you see what Jane Wellby could be capable of. When the police went to her *appartement*, there were two people there. Naked.' Cat shrugged. She had heard of worse. 'A boy and a girl.'

'Well,' said Anna, 'you know what they say about variation?'

'They had been tied up.' Anna opened his mouth again. 'Against their will. Jane came back, packed a bag, took a knife into the room, they were terrified, then she put it on the floor, just out of their reach, and left. They would not press charges, they were scared of her. They've both gone back to their own countries, I wouldn't want this to, um,' he spread his hands wide, 'haunt them. You understand me?'

Cat nodded solemnly. 'She did it to people in England too.'

'Well, then you know.'

'She did?' Anna was confused.

Cat put her hand briefly on his arm. 'I didn't want to tell you,' she said quietly. Anna didn't speak.

'Here is the flier,' he said opening a drawer. 'I kept a few.'

'Thank you,' said Cat accepting it. 'We'll leave you in peace, thanks for everything.'

'I hope the report is enlightening. Maybe it will help others?'

'I don't know if it will get on air,' said Cat looking at the flier. A woman was in a cage suspended over the word LaBase.

'S&M,' said Anna. 'I believe it is quite popular in Paris.'

'I wouldn't know anything about that, I am a family man.' The teacher smiled.

Anna let out a sad laugh. 'If I had a pound for every time I'd heard that.'

Monsieur Tillier looked at Anna for a while. '*Comme c'est triste,*' he said. Cat and Anna nodded unconsciously. '*Bon chance,*' he said as they shook hands. Looking at the flier, Cat had a feeling they'd need it.

WPC CLEMENT ASKED FOR confirmation of injury leave and had been given it immediately. She'd telephoned the forensic laboratory in Colchester only to be told that all test results pertaining to the Wellby case had been passed on to the Harlow police. She couldn't get to see the case file at the station without bringing attention to herself so she decided to go to Colchester on a bogus errand. They wouldn't know she was on leave. She'd got as far as the reception area to find what she'd been looking for. On the afternoon in question, the time of Bramley's alleged eye appointment, there were three visitors to the lab. A Dr Guillard, visiting from Cambridge

University, a Mrs Sarah Norton, identification of her son's belongings, and Michael Evans. Clement had written down the address. No reason for his visit had been stated. She checked out the first two, both were genuine. The third address was not. It was a cleaning company and they'd never heard of Michael Evans. The name rankled her. She'd seen it somewhere before, but she couldn't place where. Clement had just returned home when her phone started ringing.

'Clement?'

'Jones.'

'You are not going to believe this, but we got a match between the sheet and the DOA,' said Jones.

'Great!' she said crossing her fingers. 'What match?'

'A fingerprint.'

'Got a name?'

'Yup, a kid called Darren White. He escaped the social service's net a few months back, the police have been looking for him in connection with an on-running investigation.'

'Bad boy?'

'Not quite. It's a long story. Our real trouble is that no one knows where he is. The sheet took a long time to decipher. Most of the prints were smeared with blood and sperm and strange substances like glue, paint stripper, food stuffs, I mean really strange. We only got one good print.'

'Charming,' said Clement, imagining what had been taking place on the sheet.

'There are a lot of plastic glove marks, latex type. Many more than fingerprints.'

'What does that mean?'

'Well Darren White obviously doesn't wear gloves, he's not security conscious, the other, or others, are. It means there is more than one guy.'

'Well that ties up to what my source told me. The victim was taken by a young man, probably Darren White, but not attacked by him.'

'Well, obviously I need to talk to both of them,' said Jones, getting straight to the point.

'Ah, well,' said Clement pausing for time, 'that may not be easy.'

'Clement, a group of men are systematically torturing for sexual enjoyment. They are getting a young man to catch their prey. Think of the substances on that sheet. Paint stripper. Glue. Dog shit and vomit. Come on, Clement.'

'They're in Paris,' said Clement, still stalling until the time was right.

'Do you know where?'

Clement put the phone under her chin for a fraction of a second and prayed silently. It was time to gamble.

'I need your help too,' said Clement.

'Go on.'

'The Wellby case.'

'The one that's been splashed over the papers for weeks.'

'Yes.'

'What about it?' said Jones treading carefully. Clement had forgotten what a cautious son of a bitch he could be. She tensed up. She wasn't going to be the only one scratching.

'It's being fixed.'

'What?'

She had hoped Jones would be less astounded. 'Bramley, sir, he's fixing the trial.'

'Detective Chief Inspector Douglas Bramley?'

'Yes, sir.'

'Are you sure? From what I've read it has been brought forward on account of the enormous evidence against the woman, and on account of her own callousness.'

'Surely you don't believe everything you read in the press—'

'But the witnesses are watertight. Three school friends wasn't it. A diary?'

'All leaked to the press, conveniently.'

'You know we use the press when we have to.'

'It hasn't served anything, except to bring about a witch hunt. Though hunt isn't the right word, everyone knows who she is and where she lives. I just need access to your computers and information. I've been put on medical leave.'

'Nothing suspicious about that. You've torn a ligament.'

'I could lose that address in Paris.'

Jones fell silent. Clement held her breath. 'You'll get me the interview,' he said eventually.

'Sir.'

'Okay, Clement, you've got yourself a deal, though I must say, I didn't think you were the type to deal.

'Needs must, sir, when the devil—'

'Yes, yes. Where do we start?'

Clement felt a sadness seep into her. He sounded disappointed in her. 'Michael Evans,' she said. 'He's linked with Bramley. I think he is using this Evans guy to tidy up evidence that doesn't fit.'

'Okay. What else?'

'That's enough to start with. But I've got plenty more on the man.'

'WPC Clement,' said Jones, sounding stern, 'I hope you're not dragging me into a grudge match.'

All boys together. 'I'm sorry you feel you had to ask me that, sir.'

'You're asking me to investigate a man of my own rank, Clement. I have to be sure you are genuine.'

'I am.'

She sat down in an old armchair and looked at the photos of her family on the mantelpiece. She was risking her reputation and her job for a family she knew nothing about. She'd had time to study families but they always amazed her. They could look so normal from the outside, until you discover one of them is a front man for arms dealing, or pornography, or drugs. Some families are totally shocked, can't believe it, even in the face of alarming evidence. Others knew exactly what their brother, father, sister or mother was up to. But family is family. Isn't it? And secrets are secrets. And Jane Wellby had her fair share of those. What would Mr Wellby do to protect his family name? Would he lie? Commit perjury? Murder? She had spent the previous days talking to everyone Cat had. The only person who hadn't talked was Paul Hound. He told her to piss off. If what Cat had written down was true, she didn't blame him. In fact, she'd sent him some literature and fact sheets about genital mutilation. His case was surprisingly common. Bramley was definitely being selective but bringing Jones in was very risky. She trusted him, yes, but hand-shakes were handshakes in the police force. The lodge wielded more power than the badge. Like blood, they thought it was thicker than the bonds of law. Clement hoped she hadn't made a mistake about Jane Wellby or Jones. She prayed she hadn't made a deal with the devil. Clement retrieved the number Cat had left her and dialled it. The long international tone sounded unfamiliar in her ear.

'Hôtel Tulipes?'

'Do you speak English?'

'Oui.'

'Cat Torrant, may I speak with her?'

'Um, I'm sorry she is not here.'

'Can I leave a message?'

'Mais non, I mean she cancelled her rooms. She is not here. Sorry.'

Clement put the phone down. She dialled Cat's flat. No answer. 'Shit,' she said loudly. 'Shit,' she said again. She was dealing with an empty hand.

Chapter Twenty-Four

While Amelia and Mr Blaine took a gentle tour of the first floor of the Musée Grevan, Cat and Anna descended into the room of horrors. It was Anna's idea. In the middle of the partially lit room was a cage hanging from the ceiling. Cat glanced up at it and for a split second saw Jane Wellby smiling at her.

'You okay?' said Anna.

'Uh-huh. Who is it?' She said banishing the image.

Anna read from the English translation. 'Cardinal Jean La Balue, imprisoned by Louis XI, known as the "Spider", who imprisoned the Secretary of State for disloyalty from 1469 to 1480. He couldn't lie, sit or stand in the 120cm high cage.'

Cat looked at the pale, tortured waxwork suspended above her. She put her hand in her pocket and brought out the flier Monsieur Tillier had given her. One of the bonuses of always wearing the same thing. She unfolded it carefully.

'And now they do it for fun,' said Cat comparing the two images. 'Anna,' she said seriously, 'I think we should go.'

'You spook too easily.'

'No, I mean I want to go *here*,' she said tapping the piece of paper.

'It might be a little over our heads,' he said looking up at the incarcerated cardinal.

'Now I know why you have a script writer.'

'Trannie.'

Cat began walking towards the exit sign.

'You sure you're not a trannie?' said Anna after her.

'Behave,' said Cat, without turning around.

'You're certainly bitchy enough to be a trannie.'

'Look who's feeling better,' said Cat, holding the door open for him.

He smiled at her and winked. 'Not to mention the facial hair. Cat took a swipe but missed, they spilled out into the sunlight laughing. As they waited for Amelia and Bertie a busker began playing on a violin. Anna stopped joking and walked towards the sorrowful, melodic music. Other people soon stopped walking and listened to the intoxicating aria. Then, in complete discordance to the music, Anna burst into laughter.

'The *Danse Macabre*,' he said. 'It had to be.'

'Are you all right?' asked Cat, concerned.

'Absolutely,' he said smiling. 'I'm absolutely all right.'

MARCUS ENGLAND LOOKED AT his client as she stared out of the window. She was more than a client to him, but he couldn't think of that. He just had to try and get her out of this mess. It wasn't going to be easy. He had one lead, one avenue that could cast enough doubt to force the jury to acquit her. The first stumbling block would be Sandie and whether she would go for it.

'The news ain't good,' said Sandie, turning back to face him.

'How do you know?' asked Marcus.

'Because of that dreadful look on your face. Don't tell me Jane managed to rig up a camcorder and they've got the whole thing on tape.'

'No,' said Marcus nervously. 'Please stop saying things like that, it's what has got us into all this trouble,' he said.

'Bullshit, Jane is what has got us into all this trouble. So what's the news?'

'It's Robert,' said Marcus, matter-of-factly. 'He's broke. Not only broke, somewhere near bankruptcy, I should think.'

'What? Rubbish. He is at work the whole time, when would he have spent all the money he earns? He certainly doesn't shop.'

'It isn't as simple as that,' said Marcus.

'It never is,' said Sandie. 'Gambling?' she asked. 'Maybe that is why he's been on edge these last few months.'

'I'm afraid it's worse than that. Sandie, he lost his job.'

'Of course. Bastards. He should sue. Whatever happened to innocent until proven guilty.'

'You don't understand, Sandie. He lost it six months ago. They sacked him six months ago.'

'Don't be ridiculous, he's been getting up and going to work . . .' Sandie's head dropped forward, her blonde hair falling in dirty clumps around her face. 'Of course,' she whispered to herself, 'I've been so stupid!' She shook her head. 'I knew something was up. I began to think he'd been having an affair. We were arguing, we never argued before. Jane, she loved it. You know, I think that was why she was here more. Ready to go to Daddy every time we had a fight. I admit, I started getting a little paranoid. Thought she was plotting to get rid of me. Luckily someone came along and got rid of her first.'

'If we may return to Robert, I told you, enough of that talk.'

Sandie sat down on the sofa opposite Marcus. 'Sorry. How are we going to use it, his bankruptcy?'

'Well . . .' Marcus paused. Sandie had always claimed to love her husband, regardless of what other things went on, sure she'd been spouting blue murder ever since he had deserted her, who wouldn't. This was different. What he'd discovered might put her on a fast track to the asylum.

'I know,' said Sandie, 'you could argue that because he'd left his job, things at home got tough, which is true, for me anyway. But you could say he began to ostracize his daughter too. Jane was already attention seeking, all that depressed adolescent crap, who knows what else was going on, imagine then that Daddy, her prize possession, stops paying her attention altogether. It sends her round the bend. The depression, because let's be honest, all those traits are linked to depression, pushes her over the edge. She kills herself in Daddy's car. It's symbolic, hence no note. Of course, that's it. You're brilliant. It is a brilliant defence.' She leapt up and ran to where Marcus sat. She kissed him on the cheek then sat down next to him. 'I knew you'd do it.'

'It's too circumstantial. Your word against Robert's and something tells me he won't be supporting you on the stand. What about the diary?'

Sandie looked agonized for a moment, then pulled herself together. 'I told you, she made it all up. Robert might come round, we could talk.' Her voice was full of vain hope.

'Sandie, listen to me, when I say he was in debt, I mean seriously in debt.'

'Even better. He was totally obsessed with his money problems.'

'To the sum of 750 thousand pounds.'

Sandie whistled then nodded. 'It's a lot, but I can sort it.'

'Maybe that is the trouble.'

'What on earth do you mean?'

'Sandie,' said Marcus ignoring her, 'he took out a family life-insurance policy with your money.'

'So? He looked after all the family matters.'

'In the event of any of your deaths, the surviving receive 750 thousand pounds.'

'I didn't think they paid out for suicides,' said Sandie.

'Exactly.'

Sandie stared at him. 'Come on, Marcus, you don't really think that Robert is behind this? Kill his own daughter and frame his wife? No.'

'Where was he at the time of Jane's death, Sandie?'

'At wo . . .' Sandie stared at him. 'Oh shit.'

NOTHING COULD HAVE PREPARED Cat for the sight of the catacombs. The dark, dank tunnels seemed to twist for miles, criss-crossing other smaller underground routes. The earthy walls were compressed by the weight of Paris above and perfumed by the sewers below. Anna and Cat had borrowed two old overcoats that the hotel owner's dogs slept on. Anna had explained there were two ways in. The S&M route or the tramp route. Just out of gimp suits, they'd decided to go the tramp route. The catacombs were littered with smacked-out vagrants, it was drug pushers' stomping ground. Anna had gone to town with his flair for the theatrical, transforming Cat into the lady of the swamp. The dog smell was making her sneeze. Anna said it was a nice bubonic touch. Neither of them had ever looked so ugly, yet down in the tunnel, they looked like royalty. Nothing could recreate the fetid, purulent look of the vagrant population Cat and Anna came across as they searched for the back entrance of

LaBase. Cat grabbed Anna's hand. They could hear the music, but the tunnels were deceptive. Every time they might be getting nearer, the pulsating beat of rave music would disappear.

'Maybe this isn't such a good idea, Anna. I can't believe a middle-class girl like Jane would wander so far off the path of righteousness. Even if she did like dicing up men's genitals. Anyway, she'd found God since then.'

'So would I if I spent too long down here. Nothing else more likely to make you into a believer than being lost in purgatory.'

A young woman ran at them from the shadows, Anna pulled Cat out of the way just as she vomited and collapsed quivering on the earthy floor.

'Jesus!' Cat's heart was pumping in her ears.

'Leave her,' said Anna.

'But—'

'Leave her!'

They ran down the tunnel, came to a junction, turned left and suddenly they were there. Hell. They peered over the edge of the truncated tunnel and looked down. Fifty foot below them a swarming mass of emaciated bodies writhed, arms up-stretched, staring at them. Cat stepped back and leant against the wall.

'We can't go down there,' she said. 'What are they doing?'

'I've never seen anything like it,' said Anna, amazed as he stared down.

'I can't believe she had anything to do with this, I mean, drugs fine, but this? It's fucking twisted.'

'Exactly.'

'Come on, Anna, let's go.'

'We've come this far, Cat, take off your coat and leave it here.' They were wearing black jeans and black T-shirts underneath. 'Stick to the side of the wall where it is darkest, there'll be a VIP bit somewhere, if Jane was heavily into this, they'll know her in there. Ready?'

Cat nodded. But she didn't feel it.

There was a narrow staircase carved into the side of the wall, along with hundreds of arched recesses each containing a lead box.

'Coffins,' said Anna.

'Shit,' said Cat and kept her eyes down. At the bottom Cat looked back up, they had entered three-quarters up the right-hand side wall of the cavernous room. Higher than their entrance hung the cages. Each one spotlighted. Each other holding captive a naked figure chained, arms spread, legs spread. Cat stared at them. She crossed her fingers. 'Wax works?' she shouted in Anna's ear. He shook his head. She looked up again. A woman's head rolled rhythmically from side to side. A man urinated on the crowd below. Cat stifled a scream. The noise of the music was deafening on ground level, semi-naked bodies clad in strips of rubber, strange body armour adorned with metal spikes and harnesses pushed against them as they made their way around the wall to a lit doorway. Cat saw a man drag a razor blade down another man and lick the blood. Her stomach heaved. She'd grabbed Anna's hand. It was freezing. He squeezed it back when she squeezed his. From nowhere a man in a black leather spiked G-string threw himself against Anna and started thrusting against him. Cat watched in horror as the sharp metal spikes tore into Anna's jeans. Anna was shouting but Cat could only see his mouth form the cry for help, the music took it for its own. Cat felt a surge of such anger that she lashed out at the man catching him right on the temple and sending him flying. He lay on the ground, but kicked back. He missed, Cat didn't. Someone else slapped her. She turned around. A woman with metal clamps attached to her nipples smiled at her. The man on the floor sprung on to all fours and grabbed at Cat's T-shirt. The woman joined in. They were slapping each other and tearing at her clothes. Cat tucked her head under, stretched her arms out and backed out of the T-shirt and ran to Anna. She glanced behind her to where the man and woman were tearing the cloth to pieces.

Cat put her arm through Anna's. 'Run!' she screamed in his ear. She felt hands claw at them, people appeared out of the shadows and pulled her hair, the only place to go was into the writhing mass of bodies. They were too drugged to notice Anna and Cat crawl between their legs to the other side. Cat saw another entrance and surged forward. She pushed Anna into the corridor and ran down it, they came to a wall and collapsed against it, sliding down on to the floor to catch their breath.

'Who the fuck are these people?'

'Doctors, lawyers, secretaries, ministers of state . . .' The absence of humour was painfully noticeable. But he hadn't curled up into a ball.

It was quieter in the dark recess of the tunnel and as far as Cat could tell they were alone. 'I'll get you out of here,' said Cat, she reached into her pocket and retrieved a small torch. She turned it on and pointed it down the corridor. No way out.

'Shit.'

She aimed the torch along the wall of the narrow passageway looking for another exit. There was nothing but pictures. They'd run into a cul-de-sac. A gallery of photographs. Cat stood up slowly and walked towards them. The music pulsated from outside. She walked slowly along the wall of erotic art and sadomasochistic images. She stopped and stared at one. The girl was in a cage. Cat knew it was a girl because her genitalia had been prominently spotlighted and displayed. Cat looked closer. Her labia had been stapled open, her clitoris had been clamped to a chain which was attached to the top of the cage. But it wasn't long enough. She had to balance on the balls of her feet, her knees bent, her body arched over, her hands clinging to the bars. Her head hung between her shoulder blades, the rings of her oesophagus showed up on the grainy film. Her hair hung down. Dark frizzy hair. Cat took the picture off the wall and turned it upside down. She stared at the face. The grotesque, smiling face. 'Sweet Jesus.' She exhaled. She wouldn't've believed it if she hadn't seen it with her own eyes.

'Anna,' she said, 'we've found her. We've found Jane.' Cat smashed the frame against the wall and grabbed the photo. 'We've got to get to the staircase,' she said to Anna. 'Come on, take my hand, don't look up, just keep moving. Okay?'

Anna nodded. At the threshold of the cavern they went down on their knees. The bottom of the stairs was fifty feet away. Everyone in the crowd was looking up, worshipping the tortured souls in the cages. They'd be safe as long as no one looked down. They weaved in between legs. The staircase was getting nearer. Once someone collapsed on Anna. Cat pushed him off, dug her knee into his balls and moved on quickly. Pain was pleasure, she didn't feel guilty. Finally they got to the narrow flight of stairs. The coats were where they'd left them. Cat put one on over her bra and taking Anna's hand she ran.

Chapter Twenty-Five

Robert had been sober for a week. He'd had to be; Jo had been watching him like a hawk. The cloud had passed. He was beginning to see things more clearly. Fiona had returned, she didn't say where she'd been and he didn't ask. He knew they wanted him out of the house. Fiona approached him while he was making coffee. He stiffened when she touched his shoulder. 'I'm glad that you've . . .' She paused. In the past bringing up his drinking would only start it off again.

'I'm moving out, I won't be a bother—'

'You're not a bother, it's, well . . .' *You are a bother actually. A huge bother.* 'Jo and I are thinking of getting out of London for a few days, it's about Jane actually. I'd like to tell you about it. I think that she was a very—'

'I need to go, Fiona. Let's talk about it when I get back.'

'Work, is it?'

Robert studied her face. *Was that a dig, you smug cow?* He smiled and nodded.

'I was just wondering,' she said, sceptically, 'you've been away a fair while now.'

'My daughter died, Fiona. I think they'll understand.'

So did mine. 'Yes, of course. We won't go until you get back. I would like to tell you what I've been thinking.'

'Don't wait on my account—'

'But, Robert,' Fiona sighed heavily, 'this is important. It's about Sandie and Jane.'

'I'm late,' he said and backed out of the room. Fiona watched him go. She turned back and watched the coffee Robert had begun to make drip through to the jug. His cup and spoon waited patiently nearby. The door slammed shut. *Late my arse.* A few seconds later she heard the footsteps on the stairs.

'He's gone then?' said Jo, walking over to the coffee machine and pouring the steaming liquid into the cup Robert had left.

'Oh yes,' said Fiona.

'Did you manage to talk to him about Lottie Hawk?'

Fiona shook her head. 'He couldn't get out of here fast enough. I don't know what it is, me I suppose. I wanted to say something, but I just ummed and ahhhed like a pathetic little woman. If I'm not shouting at him I'm walking on eggshells. Maybe it is better if I wait until I talk to this girl before I try and tell Robert that I think there was something very wrong with our daughter.'

Jo put his arm around Fiona. 'She'll be an adult by now.'

'Yes, I suppose so. All I can see is that little girl's face. Jo, she was terrified and I ignored it. Like I've ignored any trouble Jane was ever in.'

'Like Paris?'

Fiona looked up at him. 'You're angry with me aren't you? For not seeing it.'

He shook his head.

'Why didn't you tell me Jane was foul to you whenever I was out of the house.'

He kissed her forehead. 'I did try, Fiona.'

Fiona sighed, fighting her own blindness but still not wanting to see. She sat at the kitchen table and sifted through the condolence letters that lay open. 'It's these that really bother me. The poor girl who used to babysit was terrorized by Jane. She said the news about Jane being abused by Sandie explained all that, but, oh, I don't know, something just doesn't fit. I don't think Sandie was even around then.'

'I think you should go and see Lottie Hawk. I'll come with you, if I may.'

'Why?'

'Because the incident happened before the divorce. If Jane was showing early signs of some personality disorder then you can stop blaming yourself, the divorce and even Sandie.'

'What about Robert?' said Fiona as she was ushered out of the kitchen.

'What about him?'

'He was her father, Jo.' Fiona sounded apologetic.

'When will you two realize, the best things you two have ever achieved are what you've done separately. Do this without Robert, tell him about it later when you know more.'

CAT DROVE AMELIA AND Mr Blaine to Camilla Simpson's house. After the catacombs they were ready to go home. Everyone but Amelia, that is. She protested furiously against being made to return to Heaven's Gate. Cat wouldn't hear of Amelia staying without her, but she had to get the evidence of how far Jane had deviated back to England. Amelia was furious. Cat was upset. Anna tried to mediate and felt the tempers of both Torrant women. It was Mr Blaine, their knight in pastel armour, that came to the rescue. He declared he was going to open up his house again. If Amelia agreed, and with Cat's permission, he would be delighted if Amelia lived at Brook House until it was time to wheel through the pearly gates of heaven. Amelia's only complaint was that she would be waltzing through the gate, not wheeling, having got some corruptible angel to throw her chair on Nurse Cleveland's head from the heady heights of eternity. Cat gave her permission immediately. Mr Blaine called Camilla and she had agreed to begin the dusty duty of making the house habitable. She said she would settle them in on their return. Cat wanted to call Nurse Cleveland. But Amelia forbade her. She said after so many years of such kind care from the woman, only the personal touch would do. Cat feared for the woman. Camilla was waiting at the gate of her house with her children. When Mr Blaine got out of the car, they went ballistic. Cat covered her ears. Amelia just laughed.

'How adorable,' she said. Cat helped her into her chair and she wheeled herself towards Camilla. Amelia took her hand. 'It's so nice to see you again, your father talks of little else but you and your delightful children.'

'Apart from history of course,' said Camilla, giving Mr Blaine a kiss on the cheek at the same time.

'Oh yes, I noticed that,' agreed Amelia smiling.

'Hard not to.'

'Charming,' said Mr Blaine, under attack. 'Right,' he said, 'present time.' More eruptions.

'Now look what you've started.'

Cat meant to get straight on. She wanted to show Clement the picture they'd found and taken from LaBase but the family atmosphere was so enticing, she found herself agreeing to stay for lunch. Camilla seemed particularly insistent. It was only after eating Cat discovered why.

'Cat, I doubt you saw any of these,' said Camilla passing her a see-through file. 'I've been keeping all the clippings.'

Cat flicked through them. 'Stupid woman,' she said looking at the photo of Sandie sprawled on the floor.

'She gave an interview. It backfired.'

'Of course it backfired. Look at this, every account describes Jane as the ideal child. Well we know that's bollocks.' Cat looked at the teacher. 'Sorry.'

'So you did find out something then, about Jane?'

Cat nodded solemnly. 'She was a very twisted young lady.'

Camilla seemed saddened by the news. 'I was so hoping you wouldn't say that.'

'I don't understand.'

'I have something to give you.' She passed Cat a letter. 'I'm sure you'll know what to do with it.' Cat frowned. The letter was addressed to Camilla, the post-mark was two days ago. 'Read it.'

Mrs Simpson
Now you know, don't you. Fourteen years I've
waited for this news. I shouldn't need an introduction,
but I'll do it anyway. Mrs Hawk. Ms Hawk actually
since my husband left me after Lottie died. Oh yes,
Mrs Simpson, she died. Didn't you know? She was
fourteen. Why has this got anything to do with me,
you ask. Do you remember, the little dark-haired girl,
little Lottie Hawk. Pigtails, she loved pigtails. They do
at that age. Nine years old. A child. But her life was
being irreversibly ruined by one of your pupils. And
then the worst thing in the world happened. You
believed the spoilt little bitch over my daughter.
Lottie was there on an assisted place, we didn't have a
chance. She wouldn't go back after that. She was too
scared. So we sent her to the local school but it was
too late the damage was done. Lottie was terrified.
Easy pickings. She was bullied over and over again
until she was a terrified wreck who wouldn't leave her

room. She was diagnosed a manic-depressive aged twelve. At fifteen she jumped off our roof and killed herself. She left a note.

I don't hold you entirely responsible of course, but the cycle started with you, at your doorstep. You are not fit to be a teacher.

I have one comfort now. Jane Wellby is dead. And she will rot in hell. She will suffer like Lottie suffered. Like I suffer. Only her suffering will last for eternity. And mine will last only as long as I breathe. There is no peace for the wicked.
Ms Hawk

Camilla was in tears.

'You didn't have to show me this,' said Cat.

'Yes, I did. I'm afraid we all played our part. Ms Hawk is right, I took one look at Fiona and Robert Wellby and thought, well —' Camilla looked over at her children '— they seemed so together. When Jane broke down in tears in my office, it was brilliant, I believed every word she said. I questioned Lottie too, of course. Well, she just looked terrified. I thought she was terrified because she'd been caught. When I told Jane that Lottie wasn't coming back she smiled at me. It has never left me. That smile.'

Cat didn't know what to say. She folded the letter up and held it out to Camilla. Camilla declined. 'I'm sorry,' she said to Cat.

'Don't apologize to me.' Cat was confused.

'I should have told you, from the beginning.'

'You did mention something about it, remember.'

'Exactly,' she said. 'I *mentioned* it.'

Cat made her way over to the car, Amelia and Mr Blaine were waiting. Cat kissed him.

'Thank you so much for looking after Gran, you've got my mobile number?'

Mr Blaine nodded.

'And the doctor's?'

'Yes.'

'And my flat?'

'Cat, she'll be fine.' Mr Blaine pointed to the letter Cat still held in her hand. 'Don't you have some rather pressing things to attend to?'

Cat looked down. 'Oh, yes, yes I do.'

He put his hand on Camilla's shoulder. 'Remember, Miss Torrant, just because it isn't blood, doesn't mean it's bad.'

'I'll remember that.'

'Then my work here is done.' Mr Blaine smiled broadly.

'Hang on,' said Camilla, 'what about all the dust sheets we've still got to get off, the ramp for Amelia, Cat's room . . .'

'My room?'

'Of course,' said Mr Blaine, 'it will be the perfect place to recover from your dalliances with the devil.'

'What about Anna?' said Amelia.

'Gran!'

'Anna too. Everyone is welcome. Now off you go and leave your impertinent grandmother to us.'

'Thanks,' said Cat, suddenly hugging him. 'And thank you, Camilla, not for this,' she said holding up the letter, 'for everything.'

Amelia and Camilla, her stepfather and children waved as she drove off. By the end of the road she had to pull over. The tears erupted from nowhere. Well, maybe somewhere.

Chapter Twenty-Six

Cat dumped her bags in the hall and kicked the door shut behind her. She found a can of soup, heated it up and settled herself on the sofa. There were twenty messages on the answering machine. She ignored it for the first hour, but the luminous flashing green light sent pulses to her subconscious. She finally pressed play and heard the tape rewind. It didn't click for ages. Cat grabbed a pad and waited. There was Amelia the day they'd left for Paris telling her with a knowing smirk that plans had changed. Too right they'd changed. A few from friends, none from Dan. Then there were five from WPC Clement. Her messages got increasingly frantic, then stopped. The last few days were just friends, still none from Dan.

'Shit,' said Cat loudly. She'd never told her about the change of hotel. She dialled the number Clement had left on the machine.

'Hello?'

'Clement?'

'Cat, where the hell have you been?'

'Sorry, we moved hotel, I should have called.'

'Yes, you should.'

'I've found out some amazing stuff about Jane Wellby,' she said, trying to pacify the irate policewoman.

'That is not important. You have to ring this number, speak to DCI Jones.' Cat wrote down the number and listened as Clement told her about the body in the skip. 'More people may die. This is important.'

'But—'

'No buts, Cat. You can't be selective about justice. Call him.'

'But Anna is so much better, I can't put him through—'

'More is riding on this than you could possibly know. You have no choice. Anna has no choice. You have to call Jones. We'll speak tomorrow at eleven.'

'Shit,' said Cat, after replacing the phone. She couldn't ring the policeman until she'd at least told Anna about what she'd done.

CAT TAPPED LIGHTLY ON Anna's door. He was humming to himself. Show tunes. It was a good sign.

'Amelia settle in okay?'

Cat nodded.

'You a bit upset, you know, Amelia and Mr Blaine?'

'No.'

'You seem a little . . .' He paused. 'Did Dan call?'

'I'll call him, it's okay. Anna, please sit down. I need to talk to you about something.'

'Heavens, sounds serious,' said Anna. 'Drink first.' He walked through to the kitchen. 'Have you called your copper friend and got an update? Sandie hasn't gone to the gallows or anything has she?' Cat heard the cork pop. Pink champagne. Another good sign. And here she was about to obliterate them all. Anna passed her the glass.

'To us,' said Anna.

'To us,' repeated Cat quietly.

'Okay, fire away.'

Cat put her glass on the table without drinking from it. 'I'm afraid I've done something you are going to hate.'

'Darl, I could never hate you.'

'A man was killed the other day.'

'What you do in your spare time is up to you,' said Anna gaily.

'He'd been manacled, stripped naked, beaten up and dumped.'

'Oh.'

'Anna, the police think that victims are being hand-picked by some group of people who are . . .' Cat struggled for a word. She didn't know. But Anna did. He was staring at her.

'I gave the plastic sheet to the police, fingerprints and DNA on it match up with those found on the corpse. They need to talk to you, Anna.'

'You gave them that thing . . .?'

Cat bit down on her lip. She felt a stake plunge through her. Yes, she had. She'd given it to the police in order to help a person or persons unknown. She'd never know who she'd saved and they'd never know they'd been saved. For that she had betrayed her most valued friend. Anna stood up. He walked over to the bottom of the stairs and stood with his back to Cat. Cat held her face in her hands and prayed for forgiveness. Anna walked slowly up the first four steps, then stopped. He turned slowly and looked down at Cat. Cat couldn't speak. The cat had got her tongue. Finally.

'Cat?' said Anna. Cat nodded. 'I think I'd like to get dressed now.'

Cat coughed as the saliva gathering in her mouth slid down her windpipe.

'Will you help me?'

'Of course, Anna,' she said through the coughs, 'of course.'

CAT FOLLOWED ANNA PAST the bathroom and into his dressing room.

'We'll need a good exfoliation before we do anything. After the scrub, a cleanse and tone and possibly, if we are lucky, I'll dig out a moisturizing face mask.'

'Anna?'

'Shh, darling, I know what I'm doing.'

Cat and Anna sat side by side in front of the mirror slopping on cream, wiping it off. Every time Cat tried to speak, Anna quietened her.

'It's okay,' he'd say. After the buffing and polishing was over, Anna put make-up on both of them, then he began to undress. Cat stared as he removed the jeans he'd been wearing for days, the long-sleeved T-shirt and the Nike trainers. He clicked his fingers. 'You too.'

Cat pulled off her clothes obediently. She stood in her bra and pants in the middle of the room.

'You have a great figure, you little minx, it's time you did something about it.'

Cat sat down feeling self-conscious. She'd leave the parading to Anna. Or not.

'Anna?'

'Not now Kitty-Kat, I'm thinking.' He pointed a finger at her. 'It is time, Cat. Long past it, actually. I should have done this years ago.' He disappeared into the walk-in wardrobe that housed his best drag outfits. Cat waited five long minutes. Cat got up once when the reassuring sound of coat-hangers scraping and chinking against each other stopped. She put her head round the door.

'No peeking,' he shouted.

Finally Anna came out. He looked like a 1920s flapper, adorned with feathers, tassels and pearls. 'Men look much better in these dresses, no bosom you see.' He wore a slivery-blonde bobbed wig on his head with a string of pearls wrapped around the crown. 'You look absolutely fantastic,' Cat exclaimed walking around him. 'Truly amazing.' Anna started doing the Charleston. Cat joined in until she caught a glimpse of herself bouncing up and down in bra and pants. She collapsed on to the chaise longue laughing.

'Now for you,' said Anna.

'No, I don't—'

Anna held up her hand. 'Don't speak,' he said theatrically. 'You will do as I say. Now put this on.' Anna handed her a dress in a pale silvery satin. She looked at it with awe.

'Wow,' she said feeling the material.

'Put it on.'

Cat, stepped into the dress and pulled it up her.

'Havana, 1940s,' he said. 'Suits the curves and your dark swarthy looks.'

Cat laughed again. 'You make me sound like a pirate.'

He did up the thirty small material buttons at the back. 'Hardly.' He made her step into some shoes, fiddled with the plunging ruffled neckline, and pulled the material straight over her waist. It fitted perfectly, flaring out below her knees.

'Now look.'

Cat turned to the mirror and stared at someone she'd never met before. She twirled. The material swished. 'It is amazing,' she said.

'It isn't. You are.'

Cat looked at Anna. 'But . . .?'

'I'm ready now. Let's go and have that chat.' He fetched two more glasses of champagne, dimmed the lights in the dressing room, and reclined on to the chaise longue.

'I'll tell you, Cat. I am strong enough now to do that, but not the police. I'll tell you everything. You tell them. I know how your mind works. I know your power of recollection is amazing. You tell them.'

'I'm so sorry it has come to this. I know you didn't want this to happen.'

'Cat, do you really think I didn't know you'd give it to the police.' He laughed briefly. 'Secretly I was probably relying on your tenacious nature. You are a strange girl, Cat Torrant. That is for sure. Morally you are very exact. Emotionally also. Good and evil. Right and wrong. Black and white. That is how you see the world. You are very like men in that respect. You don't go for emotional grey porridge. I admire that in you, I also hope it will change. I can't go to the police, it is too emotional for me. I can tell you. I can't tell them. That is emotional porridge. Thick, lumpy, sticky, difficult to traverse. Do you understand?'

'Absolutely.'

Anna laughed again. 'My point exactly.'

'What?'

'Never mind. Let's get this over with. We had a lock-in at the club . . .'

'Girls,' says Anna, 'what do you think of this divine creature?'

The transvestites look him up and down. He is a good-looking boy. A bit thin. But they envy that. The barman pours more drinks. The boy hovers possessively around

Anna, who is relishing every moment. Adoration is hard to
come by in this self-obsessed world. Anna makes a
decision to go back with him. He doesn't do that very
much these days. Too risky. This boy is different. He is so
. . . eager to please.

'Course he was,' said Anna. 'His objective was to get
me back to that hell hole.'

'Drink up, Fannies, it's time for beauty sleep,' shouts the
barman.
'Don't say it.'
'Don't we know it.'
'Piss off, brute.'
The chorus of girls. Anna is pleased it is time to go. He is
full of fuel-injected bravado. Tequila. He is Marlene
Dietrich, he is Mae West, he is Lana Turner rolled into one.
He takes the boy's arm. 'Take me to your pleasure dome.'

Anna shudders and falls silent for a while. Cat says
nothing.

Anna and the boy turn right out of the club. They walk
along Brewer Street and turn left down Lexington Street.
Anna is staggering a little. He sees someone he knows on
the door of a drinking club he sometimes goes to after
slow, depressing nights. They wave. Anna tries to show off
his catch. The boy turns away and hurries him on. They
make two right turns in relatively quick succession. Anna

gets a bit disorientated. He thinks they are doubling back on themselves. He sees a shop he's just seen before. It sells videos. He thinks he must be drunk and is led on. The tequila high is peaking. There is a lot of rubbish on the ground. Brown paper bags. Squashed cherries. They arrive at a narrow cul-de-sac with three arched doorways. Anna is guided through the middle one. He notices a broken window above the door.

'You should get your caretaker to take a look at that,' says Anna. The boy does not respond. He looks around nervously. Anna tries to look around nervously, but is seeing double. Did he really drink that much? The smell inside is foul. 'Tramps,' says the boy. The stairs go on for ever. Up and up and up. Anna's shoes are hurting him. Finally they arrive, a door, another narrow flight of steps, *et voilà*. Pretty fucking nice pad considering the location. There is a rug on the floor. The walls are white. The furniture is chrome and glass. Anna sits on the black leather sofa. It's fake. Anna frowns. The boy passes him a drink. Anna doesn't really want it but feels compelled to enter the spirit of things. The boy toasts them and knocks back his. Anna follows suit. The boy has a strange beauty about him. His skin is almost translucent under the bright electric light. Anna tries to stroke his cheek. The boy pushes him away. Anna feels the very first tremors of fear. He dismisses it as the boy toasts again. He repeats the process three times. The drink tastes funny to Anna. Salty. Thick.

'What is this stuff?'

The boy laughs. 'Have another,' he says. Anna can barely
hold the glass, let alone drink it, the boys helps. He'd been
doing a lot of that.

'I tried to leave, Cat, he called me a faggot, I knew
then I was in trouble. God knows what was in the drink.
It tasted like spunk. It was definitely drugged. It suddenly
hit me, I tried to make it to the stairs, I just couldn't.
That's when I saw it, the beaded curtain. He guided me
towards it. They'd been waiting there all along. The
bastards.'

Anna collapses to his knees. He falls forward on all fours.
He tries to be sick. Nothing comes up. Whatever was in
the drink is now pounding through his heart. He clenches
his fists, they are the only muscles that seem to be
working properly. There are three of them. Dressed in
black. They wear hoods. Not S&M hoods. Although there
are manacles on the wall. These are like the medieval
hoods of the executioner. Anna thinks he is going to die.
He says it out loud. To make sure it's real. 'I'm going to
die.'
'No,' says the voice, 'but you're going to wish you were
dead.'
Anna tries to beg. They hit him over the head. The shock
vibrates through his body. His heart beats faster. They drag
him over the plastic sheet and remove his clothes. This is
done slowly. With precision. Everything, including his
watch, his jewellery, his pay packet is passed to the boy.

Anna looks at the boy as he is pulled naked off the floor. The boy shrugs and leaves. They place Anna over a table and tie his hands and legs to the legs. The humiliation begins. Hours of it. Anna periodically passes out. He comes to. He is tied up against the wall. They taunt him with torture weapons. Spiked objects. Razor blades. There is a mirror. He can't watch what they are doing to him. He hovers between hell and his imagination. He passes out again. He is back on all fours when he comes round. Parts of his body are beginning to hurt. Sting. Throb. They want him to beg. Then they want him to cry. They force drugs down his throat and he passes out again.

'That is when they raped me,' said Anna. 'The last time I fell unconscious. I never saw any of their faces and I didn't come round until I saw you standing over me. They spoke with American accents but not genuine ones. It was to disguise their voices. One was six foot, about, the others were smaller, about five foot eight. Educated, probably quite rich. I remember noticing a glint of gold watch. The socks, too, had an emblem – Armani I think. It wasn't about rape. It was about reducing me to nothing. It was about punishment. I don't know what or why. I believe the rape was secondary to them. They get off on the retribution thing, they knocked me out for good, I could've been the girl next door as far as they were concerned. And why drop me off? I've thought about that long and hard. My only conclusion is this. They wanted me to know that they knew where I lived.

What I did. Where I'd go. Who I'd talk to. No wonder none of the other poor bastards has gone to the police.'

'What happened with the boy?' asked Cat.

'I didn't see him again. Druggie. I recall working that out at some point, must have been before he took me into the room. He's doing it for hits. Nice-looking guy, you saw him, heavily disguised of course, certainly not gay, northern I think, the London accent dropped towards the end. They probably send him out hunting female targets too. Tell that to your policeman. This isn't a gay thing, Cat.'

Cat exhaled. 'You've been thinking about this a lot then,' she said, fiddling with the material of her dress.

'Until Paris, little else. You know, why me, all that shit. What did I do to deserve this? Paris was the cure. That's why I don't want to go to the police. Because I'm cured of that now and I don't trust the police not to lace their questions with guilt. I can't feel guilty about going to that flat any more – it's too crippling. Remember those dungeons, the guy in the cage, the guillotine. Think about it, all those injustices. In its grim way, it all helped.'

'How?'

'You remember that piece of music we heard in the street?'

'The *Danse Macabre*,' said Cat.

'Exactly. Well that was what I had been on. A dance around Paris of all the terrible things mankind has done over the years. Bad things will always happen. I was just unfortunate. It happened to me.'

It was a strange philosophy but if it worked, she didn't mind. 'Will you go back to Madame JoJo's?'

Anna stood up and did a little Charleston again and sighed. 'I am so much more than a drag act,' he said, 'but equally, it is so much a part of me. I shouldn't bury that part because some twisted, depraved men put me through hell. If I do, they win. And they don't deserve to win, Cat. That is why I am pleased you went to the police. Really I am.'

'When I heard the man was dead . . .' Cat's eyes wandered over the walls of the dressing room. Photos of Anna, all dressed up.

'Cat, you did the right thing, so please don't worry about it.'

'You are amazing you know, Anna.'

'We both are.' They clinked glasses.

'To the mutual appreciation society,' said Cat.

'To you, for looking like a girl for once.'

Cat smiled.

Chapter Twenty-Seven

For the first time Cat could remember, she didn't dream about Jane Wellby. She woke up in her own bed and saw the dress Anna had given her hanging up. Havana 1940s. Her jeans stared angrily at her from the armchair. She pushed the sheets back, sprang out of bed, scooped up the offending article and bunged it in the laundry basket. She found a dress in the back of her cupboard, put white plimsolls on and didn't put her hair up. She picked up the pile of post that had collected behind the front door and went through to make herself some coffee. Bills, bills, bank statement, a cheque for a news piece she'd put together weeks ago. It didn't cover half the bills. Big stiff brown envelope. The kettle clicked off. She looked at the steam. And saw only steam. She returned to the envelope with her coffee and opened it. Inside was a scribbled note on a piece of A4 paper.

Dear Cat,
So not the ex-directory girl I had you down for. I tried

to ring you but always got the answering machine. Hate them. They steal your voice and distort it.

'J.J.,' said Cat, searching the bottom for proof. She smiled, it could be no other.

I don't know what happened with my brother, but the police came, he got very angry, then very sad. Now he has taken a break from work and has gone to a special clinic. He told me what had happened. They are treating him. He's going to have an operation. It was the policewoman who sent him the brochure. He wants to say thank you and sorry but doesn't know who she is. I took some photos of you the day I first met you at the college. You didn't know I was taking them, the results even surprised me. They are beautiful despite your terrible lack of confidence in that department. Or were you bluffing? Anyway I developed them. It is my way of saying thank you to you. I enclose five 10 by 8 pictures and a gentle reminder that I'm available for weddings, funerals and bar mitzvahs. Come and see me soon.

Your friendly lens wizard.

JJ

Cat laughed and spilled the pictures out on to the kitchen table. Each of the black and white photos was of her. Slightly right of the middle, and slightly out of focus. The way the light skimmed across her face made her eyes look dark and mysterious and her hair float around her head. The expression on her face was of deep concentration, her wide mouth slightly open, her hand halfway behind her head, the movement incomplete. She turned the others over. They were in sequence. Her removing the ethnic hat she wore to the college, sweeping back her head, shaking out her hair. Cat stared at them. She picked up one of them and brought it closer to her face. She did the same with all of them. She couldn't believe what she was looking at.

'You little beauty,' she exclaimed, standing up. 'J.J.,' she said, kissing the letter, 'you are a genius. An absolute genius.'

The phone rang, she looked at the kitchen clock. Bang on.

'Clement,' she said picking up the phone.

'I take it you don't get many calls.'

'Bramley trapped me into saying Sandie didn't touch the hose.'

'Excuse me,' said Clement.

'The fingerprints on the hose, he knew they were Sandie's all along?'

Clement was intrigued. Cat had no way of knowing that. 'Mrs Wellby is indeed accusing of him stealing an object from Cedar Hall and obtaining them illegally. Her lawyer tried to get the case dropped on a legality. The judge didn't go for it. They play golf together, if you know what I mean.'

'A coffee mug?' asked Cat pacing up and down as far as the cord would allow.

'Yes, actually,' said Clement.

'Then you've got him, Clement. You can get him taken off the case, fired, whatever—' Cat was completely overexcited.

'What do you mean?'

'I've just been sent the most amazing photos.' Cat picked one up again and laughed.

'Cat?'

'They are of me actually—'

'How nice for you, now you know what you can do if all else fails.'

Cat ignored the facetious comment. 'In the background Bramley is throwing a mug out of his car window and driving over it. No doubt about it.'

'You're kidding.'

'I saw the mugs in Cedar Hall. All neatly lined up on the kitchen dresser. It's the same pattern, the same tulip shape. I really think I've worked her out.'

'Sandie?'

'No, Jane Wellby.'

Clement didn't reply immediately. 'Cat, the story broke, while you were away.'

'I know, but it isn't about that any more, really.'

'You want to meet then?'

'As soon as possible.'

'Great. Do you remember where Calorie Carers is?'

'How could I forget.'

'There is a café next door, meet me there. One hour okay?'

'Perfect,' said Cat. First she'd talk to Clement. Then she'd talk to Jones.

CAT RAN DOWN THE stairs to the ground floor. A jiffy bag lay on the mat. Cat picked it up. The package had been delivered by hand and was addressed to Anna Prokton. Inside was a video tape. Cat could feel it through the brown paper and the layer of bubble wrap. Instinctively she opened the front door and looked out. No one was in their street. She tapped the parcel against the palm of her hand unsure of the feeling of apprehension it evoked in her. She was wondering what to do with it when Anna appeared. He was wearing white linen trousers and a turquoise shirt.

'That's an improvement,' said Cat.

'Ditto,' said Anna. 'Give us a twirl.' Cat did so. 'Legs, you *do* have them. What's that?'

Cat looked down at her legs.

'The prezzie, silly.'

'Oh, tape, for you.'

Anna shrugged as he took it. 'Either it is a gyrating pansy desperate to get into my show or,' Anna beckoned Cat into his flat, 'a German promo video, we'll make you a star sort of thing, porno star of course.'

'Get them a lot?'

'Hundreds. I sell the worst.'

Cat pretended to look shocked. 'How are you today anyway?'

'Fabulous, I feel like a new person. I know exactly what I'm going to do with my life.'

'Great.'

'And where are you off to, dressed like that, all innocent and wide-eyed.'

'To meet the policewoman.' Cat looked at her watch.

'Oh.'

'You still all right with this?'

'Yes, really, I am. I want you to do this.'

'I need to give her the stuff we found in Paris too,' said Cat.

'Two birds with one stone.'

'Something like that.'

Anna smiled. 'Thanks, Cat, if I was a girl I'd like to be just like you.'

'Ditto,' said Cat.

Anna pulled the jiffy bag apart and pulled out the black VHS tape. He turned it over. There was a label.

'Watch Me,' said Anna.

Drink Me. Push. 'Who is it from?' The feeling of apprehension returned when she saw the label.

'Won't know until I watch it. Good trick, arousing my curiosity. Usually there is all sorts of glittering fanfare with them.' Anna pushed the tape into his machine, picked up the remote control and stood back. Cat and Anna waited for the image to appear. It wasn't clear at first what is was. A ruffled mess. Out of focus. Shaky. Then the imaged sharpened. Cat drew in her breath sharply. It was Anna. Drunk. But flirting with the camera.

He was dressed in the outfit from his last show. Anna looked at Cat.

'Turn it off, Anna.' She tried to grab the remote control, but he jerked it away from her hand. 'Turn it off. Turn it off.' Anna walked closer to the TV set, eyes unblinking, as he watched himself flirt, laugh, lean forward, stroke whoever it was who was holding the camera. Cat pushed past him to turn the TV off herself. Just as she was about to press the button Anna shouted at her.

'Don't touch that!'

'Anna, please, please—' She looked down. 'Don't do this to yourself.'

'I don't remember *him* filming. I don't remember that,' he cried, pointing at the television screen. 'Cat, I don't remember that—'

'Turn it off.' Cat ran for the mains.

Anna screamed at her to leave it. She switched it off anyway. The telly plopped electronically and went black.

'*Bitch!*'

Cat swung around. 'It is for your own good, Anna, please I'm only—'

'*Meddling little bitch!*'

Cat heard the words. They filled the room. But Anna's mouth wasn't moving.

'*You'll be punished for this!*'

Someone was hammering on their door. Cat and Anna stared out of the window. A man in a leather jacket was shouting through the letter box.

'*I know you're in there!*'

'The video,' said Anna quietly. 'They're going to stop me going to the police.'

Cat pulled Anna away from the window.

'No one is going to stop you. Listen to me, call this number. Ask for DCI Jones.'

'*Open this door!*'

Cat moved towards the corridor.

'What are you going to do?' asked Anna.

'Keep him here until the police get here.'

The banging on the door continued.

'No, Cat.'

'Anna, it's my fault he's here, I'm not going to let him hurt you. Just call the police,' she said in a frantic whisper before opening Anna's door, running down the hall and bursting through the front door.

'The police are on their way you bastard!' she shouted, pushing him to the ground.

'What the hell are you doing!?' the man shouted back, pushing Cat's forehead as far back as it would go. Cat was forced to look right at him. For a second everything stopped, sight, sound, sense, smell. But just as quickly it came roaring back to her.

'Simon Proudlove?!'

'Get off me, you crazy bitch. What is wrong with you?'

Cat was so stunned she let go. Simon stood up quickly, rubbing the back of his head where he had hit the pavement. Cat's neck was already tensing up after the pressure exerted on her forehead. She pushed herself on to her knees.

'God my head hurts,' said Simon, less aggressively.

'What the hell are you doing?'

Simon looked at her furiously. 'I want to know what you are up to, Catherine Torrant. Sandie wouldn't be in this mess if it weren't for you. They stand at the gates of Cedar Hall every day, shouting, chanting, threatening. Why couldn't you leave it alone? Everything would have been fine.'

'They have been hiding behind those imposing gates for long enough,' said Cat, remembering the lions.

'Envious little cow. You'll burn in hell for this.'

Cat stood up. 'I don't have to listen to this shit, what have you been doing to—'

Simon acted like he didn't even hear her. 'The dog. The fingerprints. You've lied all the way through this.'

'You are the one who lied, Mr Proudlove. I was there, remember.'

'Oh yes, I remember, faking fucking suicide notes, I just want to know why?'

'Don't we all.'

Simon sneered at her. 'You haven't got a clue what Sandie Wellby is like. You are persecuting the wrong person. She doesn't deserve your punishment.'

'But Jane did?'

'What do you mean?'

'I know what she was really like, Mr Proudlove.'

Simon looked like he'd been hit in the solar plexus. 'That has got your attention, hasn't it? Wouldn't have hit a nerve would I?'

'I don't know what you are talking about.' Simon spat the words.

'Sex, Mr Proudlove, a lot of it, and not very nice—'

'Great, not content with fucking up Sandie's life, you are going to throw wild accusations at me—'

She hadn't been talking about him, but it introduced the possibility. 'Were you sleeping with her? Is that why you are so defensive, wouldn't want dear old Sandie to know, or maybe it was both of them?'

Simon Proudlove looked at her with utter disgust. 'How dare you? She is the only woman I have ever truly loved.'

'Did Jane find out about your affair, was that it?'

Simon didn't reply. What Cat heard instead was a scream from inside.

'Anna!' She ran back into the house, Anna had fled the sitting room, she glanced at the TV set. He'd turned it back on. An image flickered. Black and White. Good and Evil. Right and Wrong. Anna was manacled face down against the wall. Blood was running down his spine. HIV + was written on the wall.

'Oh no, please God,' Cat looked up the stairs. The bathroom was on the first floor. '*Anna!*' she screamed. She ran up the stairs, tried the door, but it wasn't budging. 'Anna, open the door, open the door. Please.' She heard another crash. The tears welled up in her eyes as she started hitting the door with her fists, what the hell had she been thinking, leaving him alone. Would she ever learn? 'Please, Anna, let me in.' She kicked it. It wouldn't open. 'Anna, open the door, I'm sorry I left you, please, don't do anything stupid . . .' A hand landed on her shoulder. She shot round, ready to hit him, but Simon Proudlove caught both her hands and held them.

'Calm down.'

Cat was shaking, unable to speak, her eyes stuck open in terror.

'Calm down.'

Her friend was going to die and it would be all her fault. 'Help me,' she said quietly. 'Please?' Simon nodded. Moved her aside and threw his weight against the door. It burst open, Simon lunged forward and grabbed Anna's right arm just as he was about to dig a razor into the soft flesh halfway up his arm. The razor nicked him slightly as Simon pulled his hand away, a line of bright red blood immediately sprang up. Cat gasped at the sight of it. 'It is okay, we missed the artery,' said Simon cradling Anna as he slumped to the bathroom floor. Anna seemed oblivious to their presence, he just stared at the trickle of blood.

'Be careful,' said Cat quietly, staring at the blood.

'It's okay,' said Simon, 'I know what to do.'

Anna slowly turned to look at Simon. Cat watched the haunted expression on his face and knelt down beside them.

'Anna?' said Cat, softly.

'It's all right,' said Simon, 'leave him with me. Really, I know what to do.' He stroked Anna's head, Anna closed his eyes and huddled into the same ball he had been in the night he was attacked. Cat stood for a moment. Unsure of what to do.

'We should get him to the hospital,' she said, staring at them, feeling redundant. Useless. Simon didn't say anything, continuing to stroke Anna's head like Amelia used to do after she had had nightmares. Cat stared at the blood that Simon periodically dabbed away.

'I have to call someone, cancel an appointment, will you look after him for a second. Then we'll go to the hospital.'

'Go.' It was Anna.

'Anna?' Cat crouched down and took his hand.

'Go,' he said again.

'But I don't want to leave you.'

'I'm here,' said Simon, 'I'll look after him. I swear to you.'

'But—'

'Go!' said Anna.

'Where are you going?' asked Simon.

Cat looked at him. 'If you really want to know, I have a lot of evidence that should get Sandie off the hook. That's what I've been doing, at the cost of every-thing and everyone else—'

'Don't worry,' he said, 'Anna will be fine with me, trust me – I'll get him to a hospital. I've got a car. Please, go and help Sandie.'

Cat's head was full of a thousand thoughts. She didn't even know this man. She shouldn't leave Anna. She should go to Clement. She should call the police.

'Look,' said Simon watching her, 'I'll call the police, get them to have a look at the video. I'll take Anna to the hospital and get him tested. Now go. He's in safe hands.' Cat hesitated.

'You look after Sandie, I'll look after Anna. Deal?'

What choice did she have? 'Take this,' she said passing a piece of paper to Simon. 'Call it. Speak to a man called Jones. Get that video tape to him as soon as you can.' He nodded. 'Maybe I should call him now.' Cat looked back down the stairs to the telephone.

'Cat, I'll do it. I'll do it straightaway. I promise.'

'Don't let any of them near Anna though, Simon, promise me you'll protect him from them.'

'I promise,' said Simon.

Cat kissed Anna lightly on the forehead. 'Call me on my mobile,' she said.

Anna grabbed her wrist and stared at her. 'Two birds,' he said, then he let go and closed his eyes. Cat ran down the stairs, out of the house and into the street.

STUPID LITTLE COW, THOUGHT Darren, he wasn't going to do anything to her. She would have been quite safe with him. She'd seemed to fall for his little plot. Hanging around the gates of the Soho Parish School for a couple of days. The girl was always collected by a driver. All he had to do was get in early, dressed like a driver, crumpled suit, beard, he wouldn't go as far as a chauffeur's hat. She'd gone along with it, walked halfway up the street, got to the corner and said where is the car. Before he'd had time to respond, she'd belted. He couldn't run after her, there were too many people around. So now he had to go back to the drawing board. Either he'd find another little girl or he would have to go to plan B and that was very risky. Darren walked quickly back to the studio. The beggars and the tramps littered the way. He hated them all. They reminded him how dependent he had become on the bastard who was behind the sordid little set-up. Darren often wondered what these privileged men had suffered to turn them into monsters. Over-indulgence. Too much of everything. No one saying no. Well the time had come. All he needed was a girl. Like a fisherman needs a worm. Schools were just breaking up for the holidays. There'd be plenty around. If you knew where to look.

'I'M SORRY I'M LATE—' said Cat, out of breath.

'Sit down,' said Clement bossily.

Cat put her mobile on the table. She didn't want to miss Anna's call. 'Something very strange happened this morning—'

'The photos, let's have a look.'

'Photos?'

'Bramley?'

'Oh yes, here.' She pulled the envelope out of the bag and placed the photos in sequence on the table.

'That is amazing,' said the policewoman. 'You say you didn't know they were being taken?' Cat shook her head. 'The odds on that happening must be a billion to one. Or you have someone up there pulling strings,' said the policewoman pointing to the heavens.

Cat looked up at the ceiling. 'Just luck,' said Cat looking at the grease stains.

'That isn't luck,' said Clement, 'that's a miracle. But it won't get Sandie off.'

'But it will undermine his investigation. What else has he been hiding, destroying.'

'Probably quite a lot.'

'What do you mean?'

Clement paused before answering. She had no reason not to trust Cat. But it didn't come naturally to her. 'I was sure Bramley was up to something so I paid a visit to the forensic lab in Colchester, they're working on the Wellby case. They had a visitor named Michael Evans. That is the name of the first man Bramley put away.'

Cat frowned.

'At first I thought Evans was doing Bramley's dirty work, but the bloke is back in the nick, so I reckon it's Bramley's pseudonym, which means he's definitely covering up something they found at the lab.'

'So, what are you waiting for?'

'I can't just steam in there, I need more evidence, more time, I need to convince my superiors that they should open up the case to someone else. I can't do this alone.'

'These will help,' said Cat pointing to the photos. 'And so will this.' Cat brought out her pièce de résistance. Jane in a cage.

'God Almighty!' exclaimed Clement loudly, then quickly covered the picture and looked around to see if she'd offended anyone.

'She was into drugs, big time, S&M, serious stuff, I'm not talking about the odd nipple clamp, this is deep sexual deviance. She had well and truly been led off the path.'

'It's still not enough.'

'Who is this Jones guy. Can't he help?'

'He's at West End Central. He's looking into the Soho death.'

Cat frowned. 'Death?'

Clement didn't say anything.

'You mean murder, right?'

Clement blinked several times before answering. 'The man wasn't actually killed, he suffered a heart attack while being held.'

'A heart attack?'

'They still killed him.'

'But they didn't mean to, he could've had that attack any time. You said it was murder.'

'It is.'

'It isn't,' said Cat, her temper rising. 'It isn't the same at all. You purposely led me to believe more people would die without Anna's help.'

'Well, Cat,' said Clement harshly, 'you'd know all about that. Suzie, Carla, shall I go on?'

'That's not the same thing. You're doing this to further your career. You help Jones with his case, Jones helps you with yours. You're doing this to get Bramley.'

'You can think what you like, Cat. I promised Jones Anna would talk to him.'

'Well he won't now,' said Cat. And nor would she.

'He found out about Michael Evans for me, he went out on a limb.'

'That's bullshit, Clement, he should have done that anyway, Bramley is bent, you don't need a reason. Was there even a match between the plastic sheet and the dead body?'

'Of course there was, Anna is our only hope.'

Cat pointed her finger warningly at Clement's face. 'You leave him alone, you hear me. Anyone goes anywhere near him, I'll . . .' Cat's face creased. She was so angry. 'You're all the bloody same.' She stood up. She should never have left him. Anna just tried to cut his wrist and she left him with a stranger.

'You impersonated a dead girl to further your career. It's exactly the same thing, Cat.'

'Change the record, Clement.' Cat reached for her jacket.

'I'm sorry if Anna had a hard time, but that isn't my fault. It's the people who are doing this. And unless Anna helps, it *will* be someone else.'

'You tricked me.'

'You tricked yourself. This is a serious case of sexual assault, imprisonment, rape. You *knew* Anna would eventually have to tell his side of the story. You knew that.'

Cat shivered, despite the steamy warmth of the café. 'Come on, Cat, it'll be someone's father, boyfriend, brother. Don't you care?'

'It's just as likely to be someone's sister,' said Cat quietly.

'He'll talk then?'

Cat looked around the café. Normal people doing normal things. She didn't feel like she had done anything normal since hitting the dog. 'Anna said it isn't a gay thing. It's a punishment thing. They'll do it to anyone.'

'I am sorry, Cat . . .'

Clement was right. She had done the same. When information meant everything. Cat sat down slowly. She opened her bag again and pulled out the letter Camilla had given her the day before. She handed it over to Clement and then slumped down into the seat and stared out of the window. Jane had bullied Lottie Hawk to death. Not directly, but effectively. Those three men who attacked Anna had done the same to the man in the morgue. Scared him to death. Just for kicks. They all did it for kicks and Jane had been ten when she started. She would talk to Jones. She'd tell him everything Anna had told her. They would put an end to this sordid chapter but leave the world no better. She'd like to take Amelia and Anna, Mr Blaine, even Camilla and her kids and hole them away somewhere safe. She'd like to take Dan too, if he'd let her. Her family might look insubstantial from the outside, but at least they were solid on the inside. Mr Blaine was right. Blood wasn't as important as the bond. Sandie Wellby was a victim of that prejudice. Jane Wellby had been very clever. Very clever indeed. Cat stood up again.

'Where are you going?'

'To interview Ms Hawk, the address is on the top of the letter.'

'What about Jones?'

'I'll go and see him afterwards.'

'Cat,' said Clement, 'why don't you come and meet me at Cedar Hall, and we'll go together? It might make it easier.'

'Will you help me when I tell Anna I've gone behind his back and now the police want to interrogate him?'

Clement didn't answer. *No, didn't think so.*

DCI JONES READ THE two tags. Torrant and Upyerbum. He rang the top one first, he'd like it if Cat were present. There was no reply, so he rang the other. Still no reply. He didn't have time for this, Jones hammered on the front door and was filled with dread when it swung away from him.

'Maybe he popped out for some milk?' said one of the officers. Jones shot him a withering look. 'The bloke's been raped. Doubt he is in a trusting, I'll leave my front door open, sort of mood.' He pushed the door wider. 'Mr Prokton!' Jones stepped into the neat, tiled hallway. There was a narrow staircase leading to the upstairs flat and a door on his right. He signalled for two officers to check out upstairs. He walked soundlessly over to the painted wooden door of the downstairs flat. It was ajar. Jones's heart sank. He was too late. He'd waited for Cat Torrant to contact him. He shouldn't have. DCI Jones didn't like to use his gun very much. But in cases like this it was better to be safe than sorry. He wouldn't like to lose any of his team. He slid it out of its holder, clicked the safety catch off and walked slowly, gun first, into the room. Someone had been throwing things about. The sofa was upturned, pictures were hanging askew on the wall, a china pot was scattered in pieces across the floor. He stepped up on to the staircase. It creaked. He pointed the gun above him. Nothing. He crept on up, stealth and patience, it had kept him alive this long. On the landing was a bathroom. All the bottles had been smashed, the mirror lay in shards on the white-tiled floor mixed up with spilt shampoo, broken jars of cold cream and blood.

'Shit.' He continued upstairs. As he reached the bedroom, one of his lads shouted from downstairs.

'Gov!' He turned back. 'Gov! Think you better come and look at this.' Jones ran back downstairs. One of his men pointed to the TV screen. They stood in the up-turned sitting room and watched Anna Prokton, blindfold and naked, strapped to a wooden table. A pair of hands came into view.

'Latex gloves,' said Jones sadly. 'Get that to the lab immediately, John, you wait here, and you,' he said, pointing to another officer.

'Sir,' said another. 'Look at this.' The telephone had been knocked to the floor. Next to it was a crumpled, bloodied bit of paper. It had Jones's number on it. 'Looks like he tried to call you before he was taken.'

Chapter Twenty-Eight

Cat approached the plum-coloured door. The paint was peeling off it. She checked the address. It was the right house. There was a lightweight knocker above the letter box. She tapped it three times. It wobbled on its hinge. She heard a chain slide and the door opened a few inches.

'I'm sorry to bother you—'

'We are not interested, thank you. No need to waste your time.' The woman started to close the door.

'Mrs Hawk,' said Cat quickly.

The woman frowned. 'Who wants to know?'

Cat stuck her hand through the gap. 'I'm Cat Torrant, I'm a friend of Camilla Simpson.'

'Who?'

Cat frowned. 'Where is Mrs Hawk?'

'You're looking at her.'

'With all due respect I don't think that is true. Mrs Hawk wouldn't, couldn't forget Camilla Simpson.'

The woman looked at Cat suspiciously, then

exhaled loudly. 'Of course I know who she is. Lottie's teacher.'

'And Jane's. She got your letter. I thought you should know that she has been very helpful in finding out the truth. You were right, she did know what Jane was like, she's been racked with guilt ever since. She is very sorry. But she did try to tell Jane's parents, they weren't having any of it.'

'Jane was fine at home.'

'Exactly. Can I come in and talk to you?'

'No. Please go away.'

'Mrs Hawk,' said Cat ignoring her, 'Jane had many sides to her, a few of them deeply antisocial. When they surface Sandie Wellby is going to be blamed. It's obvious, the child was abused by her stepmother, therefore she bullied kids at school, but *you* know it started long before Sandie Wellby came along. You're the only one who can prove how far Jane would push a victim. Don't blame Camilla for Lottie's death, blame Jane.'

'Who are you, why do you know so much?'

'I found Jane's body—'

'You! I know all about you. Go away. Leave us alone.'

Cat frowned. 'I'm on your side, Mrs Hawk,' she shouted as the door closed. Cat banged the door and heard the peeling paint crackle under the impact of her fist. She stopped. 'I know Jane was a bully. That is not all, she punished people sexually, she took drugs, she was probably verging on the paranoid and suffered bouts of depression. But she managed to turn it off and on; her parents didn't have a clue about any of this. Sandie was probably the only one who saw it.' She leant her head against the door. 'Sandie Wellby didn't kill Jane, don't you see, Jane killed Jane.' The door didn't reopen. Cat retreated down the pathway. Nettles had grown up on either side. Stinging nettles. She looked up at the roof. The girl was falling towards her. Cat shrank back. A pigeon flew by. Cat exhaled loudly. This was really getting to her.

FIONA WELLBY WATCHED FROM the window of Mrs Hawk's house.

THE PACK STILL HOUNDED the perimeter of Cedar Hall. The press hadn't let up. All condemning evidence had been leaked by Bramley. And all inaccurate. Cat drove through them to the gates. Sam Clough opened them for her. She was expected. She drove past the lion statues and the gardener. Sandie's defence. Cat walked into the hallway and was met by the woman herself.

'Of all the people I thought might someday believe me, you were the least likely. WPC Clement arrived a few moments ago, she tells me you put the local CID to shame. Thank you.'

Cat shook her hand. 'It wasn't easy, the evidence is nicely stacked against you.'

'Isn't it. Though I didn't help myself either. I'm afraid my little drunken scene was rather undignified.' She looked thinner than when they had first met on the stairs. But she also looked more alert, brighter. Sandie showed her through to the living room, where WPC Clement was waiting.

'I'm dying to know what it is you've found out about Jane.'

'I'm not saying I know exactly what went on but I can prove that Jane has had problems since she was nine. How they went undetected for so long is either a reflection of appalling parenting or proof that her mental state was much more intricate and entrenched than anyone will ever know.' She was thinking aloud.

'She spent hours locked away in her bedroom. When Robert went away on business and she was here, it was terrible. She wouldn't sleep, eat, talk to me, God only knows what she was doing in there. Then Daddy would return and suddenly Spring itself would skip down the stairs, all sunshine and flowery. I tried to tell him, but when she denied it so vehemently, I started to feel like I was going mad.'

'Did you know your stepdaughter was into drugs and sex?' asked WPC Clement.

'No.'

'Not even an inkling?' asked Cat, surprised.

'You must understand, my stepdaughter was a very accomplished actress. Certainly put me to shame. I wondered about the drugs though, Fiona says she found pills on her, of course Jane said *I* gave them to her. Little yellow pills, which she said was Melatonin. I'm allergic

to Melatonin, it gives me a terrible migraine. And anyway, Melatonin is white. Fiona did nothing about it.'

'You didn't follow it up.'

'I didn't know anything about it, and if I had?' Sandie
poured coffee into tulip-shaped mugs. Cat and Clement
exchanged knowing glances.

'I couldn't do anything about it. It is hard being a step
parent, harder because I was American. Am American. In
the beginning I tried to love her, I loved Robert, why
shouldn't I love what is part of him. When I got close to
her it was Fiona and Robert who seemed to stake ownership, do the *our* daughter bit. The parent nights, the plays,
the sports days, I don't think they realized what they were
doing, they thought they were being supportive. I have
spent a long time with Fiona, she didn't want Jane caught
in the middle of the two of them, so effectively they lived
apart from each other without ever truly separating. But
actually they spent very little time with each other. I'm
not explaining this very well, am I? You should talk to
her, she is going through a terrible time, but she is an
intelligent woman, she'll come round.'

'I've never met her,' said Cat. 'I would like to talk to
her though.'

Clement raised an eyebrow. Cat just caught a glimpse
of it.

'I never did discover why you got involved in all of
this,' said Sandie. 'Apart, of course, from nearly killing
my dog, who is fine now by the way, living with those
two sweet men, I thought she'd get scared with all those

thugs out there braying for blood. They demonstrate against fox hunting, but they'd all come to a public hanging, I'm sure.'

Cat smiled. 'You seem remarkably cool, Mrs Wellby.'

'Call me Sandie. And thank you but actually I've been a mess. Your news has helped.'

Cat looked at the American woman and felt guilty. 'I wanted to do a radio report on you, the family, the wicked stepmother and all that. I guess I am suspicious about extended families, if you knew me better, you might be able to understand my narrow-minded ways. Though I must say you were acting a little strange when I first came into the house.'

'Do you know I can barely remember that day. I think I might have been ill actually, but because of what happened, I ignored it. I felt terrible. I'd had a headache earlier that was a killer.' Everyone looked at her. 'Sorry, bad choice of words.'

'I'd like to talk to you about that day if I may. Try and work out exactly what happened.'

'To do the piece?'

Cat shook her head. 'Only if it means putting it right. I've read the papers, you are the new Rosemary West. You have become the central pawn in the "bring back hanging" argument. What started off as a flip and rather stupid comment in a pub has turned into a full confessional. The waiter from The Fox must have retired to Tenerife by now.'

'Bastard.'

'It wasn't all his fault, Sandie,' said Marcus England entering the room.

'Yeah, yeah, kick her while she's down.' The man looked hurt. 'Sorry, hon.'

Clement and Cat looked at each other again. Clement's eyebrow rose a fraction. Again.

'I have evidence of Jane's instability, and you can have it all, but any lawyer will tell you it is circumstantial, it doesn't prove you didn't kill her. The diary is still a big problem.'

'You're not accused of the odd slap, Mrs Wellby,' said Clement.

'I know that now,' she said looking pointedly at Marcus. 'And none of it is true. That is the fantasy of a sick girl. She framed me.'

'In which case she got you into that indefensible position. No alibi, plenty of incentive. You have to remember every little detail of that day. She will have left clues. For instance, Suzie told me it was Jane who cancelled your hair appointment. She obviously didn't want any interruptions.'

Sandie looked at Marcus. He nodded. 'The morning of Jane's death, Robert went off to work, well went somewhere anyway . . .'

'Sandie,' said Marcus warningly.

'I'm sorry, how rude, I haven't introduced you. WPC Clement you know, Cat, this is my ever-cautious lawyer, Marcus England.' They shook hands. He was very good-looking.

'Why do you think your husband didn't go to work, Mrs Wellby?' asked Clement.

'He was fired. Six months ago. He's been pretending all that time. I thought it would help my defence but, well, anyway, I'm surprised you didn't know.'

'Bramley's investigation is very much concentrated in certain areas,' she replied tersely.

'How very diplomatic of you, WPC Clement,' said Sandie, almost laughing. 'You better know now I'm going to bust his balls when this is through, I'm going to make his life a misery and I won't rest until he is out of the police force. Apart from a mean armlock, you've always treated me kindly, I wouldn't want to see you go down with him.'

'I can look after myself thank you, Mrs Wellby.'

She smiled. 'I remember, I've still got the bruise.'

'Sandie really can't remember very much about the day, Miss Torrant—' said Marcus, interrupting the two women.

'Call me Cat. She has to try.'

'I don't know if going over it again will help,' he said.

Cat shook her head in disagreement. 'A friend of mine went through a very traumatic experience the other day. He didn't remember the details until he was prepared to put himself back there. It is difficult because your memory is clouded and rewritten by subsequent events. You've just got to go back to that morning, and relive it as if it were this very second. Take your time and don't start talking until you remember how you felt when you woke up.' Sandie nodded and sat back in the floral sofa. Soon after she closed her eyes.

Jane keeps running up and down the stairs all morning. Sandie can hear her from the study. It annoys her. She wonders for the umpteenth time when the girl will go home to her mother. She'd got used to the sulky presence in her house. This jubilant overexcited creature with an I-know-something-you-don't-know attitude was beginning to piss her off. She couldn't tell Robert, he'd been in a weird mood too. If she asked her to quieten down a bit, she'd tell her father some distorted version of the truth and it would be her word against Jane's. She'd lost that one too many times to try it. Jane knocks on Sandie's door.

'Do you want some coffee?' she says. 'I'm making.' The clock in the hall strikes twelve thirty. 'That can't be the time, where the hell did Suzie get to? I was expecting her at eleven.'

Jane shrugs. 'Guess she forgot.'

'Not like her—'

'Coffee then? I'll make us some sandwiches if you like.'

'Yes, that would be great.'

'Thinking back on it,' said Sandie, opening her eyes, 'that was not normal behaviour for Jane. In fact I don't think she'd made me a cup of coffee, or anything for that matter, in eight years.'

They drink the coffee. Jane didn't make the sandwiches
after all. Sandie doesn't mention it, she's not hungry
anyway. Lucy starts scrabbling at Sandie's feet, running to
the door, then scrabbling at Sandie's feet again. 'Haven't
you been out, little one? Jane, has Lucy been out?' She
shrugs. 'It's my fault, I can't believe the morning went so
quickly. Come on, Lucy, walkies.'

Sandie doesn't change into jeans, she just puts some
trainers on her stockinged feet. They are going straight to
the meadow. No roads. It's a short walk, but she's wasted
a lot of the day on paperwork. Soon Sandie begins to feel
the pain behind her eyelids. She recognizes it immediately.
The beginnings of a migraine. She calls Lucy, the sound
hurts, already the brightness of the midday light begins to
sear through her pupils and bounce off the back of her
skull. She covers her eyes and stumbles into a rabbit hole.
'Shit,' she says, and regrets it, the sound of her voice
vibrates through her. The pain is intensifying quickly. She
barely makes it over the stile.

'I can't remember helping Lucy over, she is too small
to jump up, it's a stone wall, she always needs a hand.
Poor little mite, she must have been terrified. I just left
her. She must have scrambled through the hedge to the
road. How awful, she doesn't really know about roads.'
Sandie looked distraught. 'I don't really remember getting
home, I just got there. Have you ever had a migraine?'

Cat shook her head.

'You wouldn't understand then.'

The clock strikes one forty-five, it feels like she is standing in the bell of Big Ben. She collapses on to the hall table and sees the note, takes in what it says, Jane video shop, thank God, no more thumping up and downstairs. Sandie grabs on to the banister and hauls herself upstairs. All she does is kick off her trainers she'd put on for the walk. She falls on to the bed, scrabbles about in the bedside-table drawer and finds her headache pills. She's only supposed to take two. She takes three. She expects to be lying there, not daring to move until the migraine wears off. The pills rarely hit it hard enough. But instead she feels herself get heavier. The pain doesn't subside, but her muscles relax anyway. Her head doesn't belong to the rest of her. She is on the verge of blacking out. Someone walks into the room, Sandie can't open her eyes, she passes out.

'I didn't go to sleep,' she says alarmed, 'I passed out. There was someone in my room.' Sandie shuddered. 'I didn't see who it was, I just knew it. Why didn't she just smother me, get me out of the picture that way, rather than a convoluted plan that she'd never benefit from.' No one said anything. Cat hadn't worked that bit out. 'The next thing I knew I was standing at the top of the stairs.'

'You were wearing stilettos. Do you remember putting those on.'

'No. I remember feeling like death, trying to take in you on the phone. I remember you saying Jane was dead,

I mean I know she and I had our differences, and she was a pain in the butt, but to feel nothing, you know, it was strange. Even walking into the garage with you felt other-worldly. I felt very guilty about that.'

'You didn't touch the hose did you, Sandie?'

Sandie looked at Marcus who had hovered through-out. 'No, I didn't.'

'Why did you say you did, Mrs Wellby?' said Clement coming forward.

'Everything was against me at that point, it was my only hope, my word against Cat's. If she was saying that and getting away with it, why couldn't I. I didn't touch the hose, but I couldn't tell you when I touched it last. Sam does the garden. My speciality is dried flowers and I don't wash cars. I don't know how my prints got on that hose, and that is the sad, pathetic truth.'

'What pills do you take, Sandie, for the migraines?'

'Imigran.'

'That is common knowledge is it?'

'Don't know about common, but I do keep two bottles of pills by my bed, Imigran and Valium. And before you give a lecture on Valium, I'm American, I was breast-fed on the stuff.'

'Always two bottles?'

'Yes, I don't like taking medication.'

Cat laughed, confused.

'I know, Valium, everyone has one weakness, at least mine wasn't taking drugs and chaining myself to walls—'

'Why did you say that?' asked Cat, standing up.

'Okay, smoking then . . .'

'Yes, but why that?'

'No reason, just an example.'

'Pretty strange example don't you think,' said Cat looking in Clement's direction.

'Mrs Wellby,' said Clement, 'you have staff, where were they on Friday?'

'It's their day off. Shopping for the weekend.' She turned back to Cat. 'I didn't mean to offend you—'

'It doesn't matter.' Cat sat down again. 'The pill bottles must have been swapped, or the contents anyway.'

Marcus and Sandie looked at each other. 'How do you know?'

'Listen to what she said, she grabbed the bottle, she was in a state of real pain—'

'It was definitely the right bottle, I wouldn't ever get the two mixed up.'

'But you may not have known what you were swallowing. You said they didn't work like usual, your muscles relaxed, Valium does that, three of them would've knocked you out pretty fast, Jane was probably coming in to check on you. Could we have both bottles?'

'Sure, I'll get them.'

Clement stood up. 'I'll come with you.'

Sandie smiled sadly. 'Not quite out of the firing line, am I?'

Clement smiled back. 'Unlike my boss, Mrs Wellby, I like to be thorough.'

After they left the room Cat turned to Marcus. 'How long have you known Sandie?' she asked him.

'All my life. We're cousins.'

'Really, what a good-looking family.' Cat swallowed, that wasn't supposed to come out like that.

'Thanks.'

'There is one thing puzzling me though,' said Cat, returning to safer ground, 'the timing of it all. Sandie returned at a quarter to two but I was here by two fifteen. If it was Jane who came into the room, and I'm sure it was, it must have been about two. It isn't enough time. Maybe she got the prints off Sandie when Sandie was out cold. Then she had to get the hosepipe into the exhaust pipe without touching it, that must have taken some time. It was a very still day, I would have heard something. And why did Jane want to have coffee with Sandie that morning when she'd never done it before?'

'Well she did say that the morning passed very quickly,' said Marcus. 'Perhaps Jane fixed the clock in the hall, it's the only one the loony woman tells the time by.'

'Really?'

'Yeah, she is mad about it, the American fascination with antiques, I guess. Sandie loves them. As soon as she started making money she started buying antiques.'

Clement returned with the two bottles in a plastic freezer bag.

'Could you get the clock in the hall dusted for prints,' said Cat walking up to her. 'Yes, sir, Inspector Torrant,' said Clement quietly into her ear. Cat looked around nervously to see if Sandie's cousin had heard. He was smiling at them. Cat felt her cheeks redden.

'Let's go and look at that clock,' said Cat grabbing Clement's arm. They walked out of the sitting room into the hall. 'It's quite a story, isn't it,' said Cat in a whisper. 'I mean I know Jane was strange—'

'That is one way of putting it,' said Clement.

'But would she really kill herself to get at Sandie? It's sort of extreme.'

'Unless the drugs had pushed her over the edge. Ever heard of Ecstasy-induced paranoia?'

'Sort of.'

'It's a huge problem in Essex. Perfectly normal kids started to lock themselves in their rooms, unable to cope with social situations, in extreme cases, it led to suicide. Every case led back to Ecstasy. Rave culture has had a stronghold in Essex for a good ten years. No signs of abating. I spent months going to raves, trying to warn these kids. But no one thinks it's ever going to happen to them. They don't consider the long-term effects, let alone the fact that one pill can kill you. Two to three pills every Friday and Saturday night for two to three months is all it takes to irreversibly damage the brain.'

'Paris?' said Cat.

Clement nodded at Cat. 'She was already pretty unbalanced. We'll never know for sure, but it could've been that. As the teacher said, she wasn't the same after Paris.'

'And what about her father?' Cat whispered. 'If he

wasn't at work, where was he? Maybe he did find out about her extra-curricular activities in Paris. He pretended to go to work to protect his reputation, how far would he go with his daughter?'

'I've already thought about that, I'll check him out. He certainly hasn't been defending his wife's innocence all along.'

'Exactly.' Cat looked behind her as she heard Sandie and Marcus.

'Right now,' said Clement turning round, 'I want to get these bottles to the lab in Colchester. If we want the results by tomorrow morning I'd better hurry.' Clement headed for the door purposefully. Cat watched her go to her car, get in and drive away. She found herself waving from the door then looked back at Sandie and Marcus, embarrassed. Clement wasn't her guest, this wasn't her house.

'I'll be off too,' said Cat, self-consciously.

'Why don't you stay here?' said Sandie answering the question. 'You don't want to have to drive all the way back to London, then come back out tomorrow.'

'Why not?' said Marcus. 'Sandie and I have been rattling around in this big old house for weeks.'

'Come on,' said Sandie, chiding him, 'what about all those parties we've been invited to, the constant flow of guests, it has been non-stop party, party, party.'

'Very funny.' He turned back to Cat. 'We are social lepers. I am too young to be incarcerated in my cousin's house, please stay, I cook a mean spaghetti meatball.'

Cat pulled a face.

'I can lend you a toothbrush and some clothes,' said Sandie. 'By the way, it is nice to see you out of jeans.'

Cat smiled uncomfortably.

'So will you stay?' said Marcus.

Cat's mobile rang in her hand. She jumped.

'Hello?'

'Cat. It's me.'

'Anna,' said Cat, turning away from the others. Hardly the ideal spot for an intimate conversation. 'Where are you?'

'Home.'

Cat glanced at the number.

'Why is the number different?'

'I'm calling from a phone box.'

'Why?'

'I can't explain right now.'

He sounded strange. 'I'm coming straight back.'

'No, Cat, I'm fine.'

'Please stay,' said Sandie, loudly behind her.

'Yes stay, Cat,' said Anna, having heard the woman's voice. 'I'm being looked after.'

'Is he still with you?'

'Yes.'

'Is that okay?'

'Yes.'

'Anna, you sound so—'

'I'm fine.'

'But?'

'Please. I don't need you to watch over me. Stay there. I've got to go now. Bye, Cat.'

Cat hit her phone, the batteries were running out. She stared at the small plastic object in her hand then turned if off. She felt as run down as it was.

'You look exhausted,' said Marcus.

'Thanks.'

'Beautiful but exhausted.'

'Come on, you two,' said Sandie. 'Let's have a drink.'

Cat nodded, allowing herself to be led into the kitchen.

DAN HAD DONE NOTHING but think. He'd lied about the job to Amelia and gone to stay with some friends in Wales. He'd been a miserable bastard for the whole week and finally arrived at the root of the problem. He loved her. He couldn't imagine life without her. But Cat wasn't the happy-ever-after type, she didn't need him like he needed her, and the truth was it pissed him off. Anna said she was changing, but what if his so-called feminine intuition was wrong. Cat called him a gender whore. Dan felt a strange flutter of anxiety in his stomach as he approached the front door, he hoped Anna was in the mood for a manly chat. Anna would know what he should do. He let himself in and was just about to knock on Anna's door when it flung open and two policemen charged at him, knocked him to the floor and handcuffed him.

'Name?'

'Daniel Starling.'

'Address?'

'Look I wasn't breaking in—'

'Address?' One of them rummaged around in his jeans pocket for his wallet.

'Oi,' shouted Dan. 'That is close enough, it is in my back pocket.'

'Address?' shouted the uniformed man.

'Who wants to know?'

'What are you doing here at this time of night, Daniel Starling?'

'My girlfr— My ex-girlfriend lives here. So does my old room-mate from Cambridge. Upstairs.' He pointed. The two officers looked at each other. It made Dan panic. 'What is it? Why are you here?'

'You queer?'

'What?' said Dan, turning around.

'Your girlfriend the piece who got raped?' Bile rose in Dan's throat. Cat had been raped? 'Guess it isn't really rape, not if you like it up the arse anyway.'

'What did you say?!'

'You heard me.'

Dan brought his handcuffed hands to his face and buried it in them. 'Oh no,' he mumbled. 'No.'

'You all right?' said the other plain-clothes policeman.

Dan shook his head. He could hear his own voice in his head. *Somehow it seems worse, guys raping guys*. He could see the look on Cat's face. The dark, disappointed eyes. Horrified eyes. He had given the policeman the same look. He hated the policeman in the same way. *That sort of thing fucks with a guy's head*. No wonder Cat hadn't called. He hadn't even apologized. *Just making an intellectual point*. About penetration? He disgusted himself. This policeman disgusted him. He disgusted Cat.

'You are a sad, bigoted idiot,' he said to himself.

'Right that's it,' said the policeman who'd made the offending comment. Dan closed his eyes, waiting for the foot, fist or truncheon to come whistling through the air.

'Don't even think about it,' said the plain-clothes policeman. 'Take a walk, calm down.' The two police-men stared at each other; the one in uniform finally backed down and went out to the street. The remaining policeman undid the handcuffs.

'Thanks,' said Dan.

'Call me John, I'm with the CID. I'm afraid my officer doesn't much care for . . .?' He waved his hands demonstratively.

'I figured. So what are you doing here?'

'Who did you say you were again?'

'Anna was my room-mate, Cat was my girlfriend. I was just dropping by to . . . Well you know.'

John nodded. 'He was attacked. Some weeks back.'

'I know, I was here when he was dropped back.'

'Dropped?'

'Yeah, Cat was awake. Hasn't she told you?'

'We haven't managed to get hold of her yet.'

Dan frowned. 'I'm sorry, I'm being thick, what do you mean?'

'The fingerprints of one of the boys who attacked your mate turned up all over a dead guy in a skip.'

'How did you know that?' asked Dan, confused.

'From the autopsy.'

'I mean how did you know about Anna?'

'The plastic sheet he was brought back in,' said John thinking Dan's memory needed jogging. It didn't.

'Yes, but how did you get hold of it, the plastic sheet?'

'Your ex-girlfriend—'

'I don't believe it,' said Dan angrily, walking away from the man. After everything Anna had said. They'd promised him no police.

'She did the right thing,' said the policeman tentatively. 'You all should have come forward earlier.'

'When a friend begs you . . .?' Dan ran his hands through his hair. 'It is difficult.'

'I realize that, but that is what these guys are relying on. A man died. He didn't get to come home and be nursed by his friends. He ended up naked in a rubbish dump in Soho. Your ex-girlfriend was doing the right thing. I only wish we could have got here earlier. You can't take the law into your own hands, it never works.'

Dan looked at him. 'I don't know what you mean.' The man raised a disbelieving eyebrow. 'Really, Anna just wanted to be left alone.'

'If that is the case, why did his attackers risk breaking in and doing this.' John pushed Anna's door open wider. 'If that isn't a calling card to back off, then the video was.'

Dan stared at the room. 'What video?'

'The video of Anna's attack.'

Dan turned to face him. His mouth was open in horror. He walked around the flat in a daze. Someone had turned it upside down. Anna always fancied himself taking part in bad TV dramas. The room looked like a set from Charlie's Angels. All they needed was Anna to walk in, dressed in a seventies-style catsuit and floppy hat, and say, 'They must have been looking for this,' as he pulled a microfilm out of his gaudy clip-on earring. At which point the girls would throw themselves around his neck and he would get his wish. To meet Charlie.

Dan finally found his voice again. 'So where is Anna now?'

'That's the trouble,' said John. 'No one knows.'

Dan looked around the room again, he started walking up the stairs. Dan saw the bathroom. 'Shit!'

'It looks worse now that forensics have been. Honest.'

Dan didn't believe him, he ran down the stairs and dialled Cat's number upstairs, when that went unanswered he tried her mobile.

'*The vodaphone you are calling may be switched off. Please try again later.*'

'Shit!'

Chapter Twenty-Nine

Dan rang anyone he could think of but no one had seen Cat or Anna. Even Amelia had disappeared. She'd suddenly left Heaven's Gate and hadn't come back. Nurse Cleveland was as useful as the ox she was. If Amelia was in trouble, it was her own bloody fault. And Anna's. And Cat's. Towards dawn John's replacement had turned up, they shook hands and admitted to hopelessness. Dan was furious with himself for staying away so long. He was trying to prove a point to Cat. Trying to show her that needing someone wasn't such a bad thing, all she had to do was call. It was pathetic childish crap. Hadn't he grown out of that? The truth was he'd been hurt by Cat's ability to cope without him. Her ability to get involved in something and see it through to the end. The ability to do the right thing even if it meant going against Anna. He didn't know she'd succeeded. But he knew she'd try. And what had he done? Fuck all. And now Anna had disappeared. So had Cat and so had Amelia. What he wouldn't give to see them all walk through the door now. Safe. Alive.

'Think, Dan,' he said to himself. 'There must be something I can do, God help me . . .' He went over the night of the attack. He'd practically thrown Anna into the bastards' waiting arms. Cat had been right then too. She was still having bad dreams at the time about the dead girl. She'd been up, watching the world wake up when she saw the car . . . Dan stood up. The car. He took the number John had given him and dialled the police station.

'Jones please?'

'Who is calling?'

'Dan Starling. I'm a friend of Cat Torrant and Anna Prokton.'

'Just putting you through . . .' It was coming back to him, the details, he rambled them off to the man who had answered.

'. . . I'm sorry to call so early, I didn't remember at first, the shock, Cat saw it, we used to go out, I've known Anna for—'

'Dan,' said Jones gently, 'what did Cat see?'

'Sorry.' Jones heard him inhale deeply. Calming himself. 'A black saloon car pulled away from outside the flat the morning Anna was attacked. Cat didn't think anything of it, thought it was a minicab or something. But a minicab driver wouldn't carry a naked unconscious man to his doorstep, wrap a plastic sheet around him and stuff a pair of pink fur pants in his hand, would he? Especially not one driving a decent car. I know it is just speculation, but I thought it might be of use?'

Jones wasn't really listening. He was standing up frantically turning pages of his report notes. Finally he found what he was looking for. He held the interview page up in front of his eyes.

'Do you remember what make of car?'

'Afraid not. Cat never said.'

'Any number plate, markings?'

'Just that it was in good nick. A smart car, she said. Executive cab, something like that.'

Jones sat down heavily and pressed the phone to his head. 'It might not be anything—'

'What might not be anything?'

Jones could hear the panic in Dan's voice, but he couldn't give him false hope. Anna Prokton was more than likely in trouble.

'Dan, would you say that Miss Laing from next door is a trustworthy witness?'

'Gaby? Yeah, lovely lady.'

'She told one of my officers that following screaming coming from the street yesterday, she saw Anna get into a black Rover before being driven off by another man. "A smart man".'

'Coincidence,' said Dan. 'He would never have got into a car with the guy who attacked him.'

'She said she thought she saw him "slump" forward in the car. "As though he were drunk",' read Jones.

'Oh, no, no. That can't be right. Where was Cat?'

'Don't know, I was expecting a call myself. But we know one thing now, she isn't with Anna.'

Dan was silent for a moment. 'Do you think it's the same car?'

'It's possible.'

'He'll be alright, won't he?'

Jones didn't know what to say. The odds that he was alive had been pretty high. Up until then. Clement was right; coincidences didn't exist in their business. A black car meant death in his book.

'I don't know, son. But right now things are not looking good.'

Jones replaced the phone, having taken Dan's number and agreed to call him as soon as he heard any news about Anna. Clutching his coffee, he walked out to Trudi's desk.

'I want an APB put out. I want all black Rovers pulled up in the greater London area. We are looking for a male, well-dressed.' Jones paused. It was hopeless. 'Tell them to get registrations, names and addresses . . .' His voice trailed off. It was like looking for a person allergic to oysters in a city that didn't serve them. You wouldn't know him until he accidentally blew up in someone else's face in someone else's city.

NO ONE HAD SLEPT well at Cedar Hall. Too much was going on. Cat had given Sandie a brief description of what had happened with Simon Proudlove without giving anything away about Anna. She respected his privacy.

Even though she was going to tell the police everything as soon as she had the chance. Cat put the dress back on and went in search of some coffee. Halfway down the stairs she could smell it. Marcus was in the kitchen, wearing nothing but a towel wrapped around his waist.

'Oh, sorry,' said Cat startled.

'Been swimming,' he said. 'You should, it's great.'

'Is that coffee?' said Cat pointlessly given the strong smell in the room.

'Uh-huh, want some?'

'Yes please, Clement called yet?'

'Cat, it's eight thirty in the morning, I doubt the lab is open.' He passed her a cup. His hand rested on hers for a fraction of a second. Cat didn't look up. Unsure whether she was reading the situation clearly. Was he flirting with her? At this time in the morning? Cat sat at the kitchen table and pretended to flick through the newspaper. There was no mention of the Wellby case. Perhaps Sandie's fifteen minutes were over. Perhaps she'd start doing the morning TV slots after all this was over. Cat sighed. What was she doing here? Did she really know what was going on? It wasn't impossible that Sandie swapped her own pills around, faked the headache, pretended to be Jane on the phone to Suzie . . . No, how could she know that a busybody like herself would come snooping around and follow the trail to Paris. That was too risky wasn't it? But then there was the diary . . .? Was it true, or was it another of Jane's twisted fantasies?

'Do you always pull that face when you're thinking?'

Cat looked about the room nervously, thinking up a
response. He'd been watching her?

'I was just wondering,' said Cat slowly, 'what are you
going to do, if the pills were swapped around, and the
clock tampered with, are you going to wait until it goes
to trial?'

'Not if I can help it, Sandie's business is losing money
fast, reputation is everything. I'll go to the CPS with the
evidence, hopefully get the case dropped. Or at least
thrown open. You know Robert is broke as well, Sandie
doesn't want anyone to know, though God only knows
why she protects the stupid fool after the way he has
treated her, his first marriage was a disaster, why she
thought she could do better—' Marcus looked up suddenly to the doorway. 'God, I'm sorry, I didn't mean
to . . .'

Cat turned round expecting to see Sandie. She was
astounded to see the person standing in the doorframe
was Ms Hawk.

'Wait a second,' she said, her mind galloping at full
speed. She was in on it too? Was this some kind of *Death
on the Orient Express* thing? No, no, Cat stood up. Marcus
moved past Lottie Hawk's mother saying he would fetch
Sandie. Cat stared at her, unable to speak. The woman
didn't move from the doorway, she just looked back at
Cat with an unfathomable expression on her face. Something was wrong. How did Marcus know who she was?
He hadn't asked her name. Her mind raced back over
her visit to the woman's house. She didn't know who

Camilla Simpson was at first. She defended Jane's behaviour at home. How did she know that? Leave us alone, who is us? Ms Hawk lives alone. Cat looked at the woman in the doorway as if for the first time. The accent hadn't matched the crumbling house, the peeling paint. How could she have been so stupid, of course . . .

Cat stood up. Sandie appeared behind the woman.

'Fiona,' they said simultaneously.

'What are you doing here?' said Sandie.

'Why didn't you tell me who you were?' said Cat.

'Because I was afraid,' said Fiona walking into the kitchen followed by Sandie. 'And I'm here because of you, because of what you said.'

'I thought I was talking to Lottie's mum, I would never have said any of those things if I'd known—'

Fiona held up her hand. 'I'm glad you did. I've been protected long enough, don't you think?'

'If I'd known,' said Cat again.

Fiona turned to Sandie, taking her hands in hers. 'I owe you an apology,' she said, 'we all do.'

'I don't understand,' said Sandie. 'Who is Lottie? Why the sudden turnaround?'

'I'll explain everything. I went looking for some answers myself. Things just kept cropping up that didn't tie in. She was foul to Jo you know, she told her father that Jo was a *girl*friend of mine. I found her passport, it was out of date, yet she'd booked a holiday to Portugal. She was never intending to go, Sandie, this was all planned. Her results came through, she got the lowest mark possible, she wasn't revising all that time, she was planning this.'

'What? Getting me locked up?'

'No, getting Robert and I back together again. Isn't it obvious?' Sandie frowned. That was ridiculous, nothing on earth could bring those two back together. Fiona continued. 'How could Robert love you if you killed his daughter? But he does, he has all through this, that's why he started drinking again, because he hates himself for loving you still. He barely touched a drop of the stuff while you were married, but he drank all the way through ours. He hated himself then, he hates himself now.'

Sandie sat down in a chair and put her head in her hands. 'You overestimate him. He's drinking because he got the sack and he's too ashamed to tell me, his own wife. He's a stupid, selfish, arrogant man. He's been hell to live with for six months because of it, how dare he put me through that. This.'

'You'll work it out.'

'I won't. All this is his fault. If he'd stuck by me. If he'd disciplined his daughter once in a while. If he'd taken my side, once, just once.'

'It isn't all his fault, Sandie, it's mine. Jane had a completely distorted view of our marriage, we let her; buried in the church she said in her diary, there was no church. And she killed herself ten years to the day that we told her we were splitting up. But none of that is anything compared to these.' Fiona threw a bunch of letters on the kitchen table. Sandie looked up as they skidded past her. There were thirty or so letters addressed to Lottie Hawk. Cat stared at the writing on them.

'Who are they all from?' she asked, fingering through them.

'Jane,' said Fiona.

'All of them?' Cat looked at Fiona for confirmation. 'But the writing isn't the same.'

'Exactly.' Fiona sighed and sat down next to Sandie.

'I don't understand,' said Sandie.

Cat was still rummaging through them, putting them in order of dates. The most recent was two month ago. 'Jane didn't know Lottie was dead.'

'Jane went on persecuting Lottie for years and years, reading them broke my heart.'

'Are you sure they are all written by Jane?' Cat couldn't get over the variation in the style of writing.

'I paid a visit to Camilla Simpson this morning, as you said, Jane and Lottie's teacher. We went through Jane's files together, by the way Cat, your grandmother is a peach.' Cat smiled thankfully. 'Jane's handwriting has varied enormously all through her school and college life.'

'So?' said Sandie.

It suddenly dawned on Cat. 'The diary,' she said.

Fiona nodded sadly. 'The writing is consistent throughout. That is what she was doing when she was supposed to be revising. She was rewriting the past eight years. Maybe it started as a sick fantasy and because of all the drugs became real, all consuming, or maybe I was just blind and refused to see what is now plainly obvious. We were terrible parents, our marriage was terrible, you, Sandie, are the best thing that has happened to all of us. I am so, so sorry . . .' Fiona cried as Sandie leant towards her and hugged her.

'This wasn't your fault,' said Cat quietly. 'I never met my father, and my mother ran off after I was born – I don't go around bullying the rest of the world because my parents are fuck-ups. You take responsibility for your own life. Jane was sick, it isn't your fault.'

'She's right,' said Sandie. 'None of us knew how bad she was, maybe none of us wanted to know. But ultimately Jane did this, no one else.'

'So determined was she to incriminate Sandie, she hit herself to cause a bruise to add suspicion,' said Cat.

'I can't believe it,' said Fiona. 'It would have been too painful. She hated pain.'

Cat looked at Sandie. It was time Fiona was told what her daughter had become. Cat stood up to leave them alone, and as she did she saw the Jaguar pull into the empty garage opposite. She walked into the hall and leant on the round polished table. Dried flowers. She'd made a full circle.

CLEMENT RETURNED TO THE lab first thing in the morning. The reports were almost ready, she was told, if she wouldn't mind waiting. She was shown into an office to wait while the report was typed up. She could see the filing room that stored the old case papers through one of the glass doors. A woman sat with her back to Clement, audio typing. Clement looked from the woman to the door of the filing room. If she was careful she could make it. Clement got up, checked to see that no one was coming along the corridor, then carefully and silently opened the office door. The woman carried on typing away furiously. She edged around the back of the room, keeping well out of the woman's eye line while keeping a careful watch on her foot. Every time the woman's foot came off the pedal, Clement stood dead still. When the typing started again, Clement moved towards the door. When the woman bent over to scratch her calf, Clement dived into the filing room. She went straight for E. E for Evans. Clement pulled Michael Evans' file. She heard someone come into the room. Her heartbeat soared as she looked around nervously for a hiding place. She slid the drawer closed and moved further into the room. Clement smiled. She'd found it. All the forensic evidence Bramley had done on the sly. Or hidden? Or accidentally lost. She recognized some of the case names. She had him. Finally she had him. Clement flicked through them until she found what she had been looking for. Porcelain coffee cup. One set of fingerprints. Traces of lipstick and saliva. Remains of coffee with traces of the drug commercially known as Melatonin. She crept round and replaced the files. Clement peered round the door. The gods were on her side. The woman must have taken a break. Clement couldn't see her anywhere. She made a dash for the door, as she opened it, the outer door opened. The secretary stared at her frowning.

'I was just looking for you,' she said.

'I was just looking for you,' replied Clement. 'I had to find a loo, you weren't here when I got back. I really need those reports in a hurry.' The secretary clutched the manila file to her chest.

'I'll just make a copy for the Wellby file,' said the woman.

Clement hadn't told her what case she was working on. 'How did you know they were for the Wellby case?'

She rolled her eyes at Clement's stupidity. 'These are prescription drugs, the woman's name is all over them.'

'Of course.' Clement sighed with relief. She was getting paranoid.

'I'll make a copy then shall I, for the backup file.'

'Yeah fine, thanks.'

Clement watched as the secretary returned to her desk, opened the manila file and fed it through a strange machine that looked like a mixture between a PC and a fax. Digital boxes appeared on the screen, the woman touched one. More boxes appeared.

'Wow, what is that?'

'Great, isn't it? This is my baby. No one else knows how to work it. I love it. We still keep the hard copies of course, but this has made archiving a joy.' The typed page disappeared into the machine slowly. 'It's scanning it now. If I want it back, I go into the file, press print and Bob's your uncle. No more broken nails and damaged back from heaving huge boxes around. They're all in here.' She tapped the machine.

'Is that the Wellby file?'

'I wouldn't be doing my job very well if it wasn't.'

'Could you pull out an attachment for me?'

'Attachment to what?'

'The record of the fingerprints found on the hose?'

'Sure.'

Clement looked around nervously.

Within moments the original report on the pill bottles came back out with a copy of the attachment. The secretary handed them to Clement. Clement speed read them both. Residue powder of Valium was found mixed in with the Imigran and vice versa. Conclusion. The contents of the bottles had at one time been swapped. Glove marks were also on the bottle. Latex. As for the attachment, Clement nearly kissed the woman.

'Is that all you need?' asked the secretary.

'And more,' said Clement, backing out of the office. 'Thanks.'

ROBERT PARKED THE JAGUAR alongside the space left by the impounded BMW. He stared at the gaping hole. It was nothing compared to life without Sandie. Life without Jane. His mistakes with his daughter couldn't be rectified. The mistakes with his wife . . .

'Robert?' Fiona tapped on the glass. 'What are you doing here?' She looked back at the house nervously.

Robert got out of the car.

'I killed Jane.'

'What?'

'You heard me—'

'I don't understand—'

'Robert?' Sandie was standing at the kitchen door. He ran to her. Fiona shouted after him. He ignored her.

'Forgive me?' said Robert. 'Please?'

Sandie stopped him. 'Robert you can't just turn up like this.' Sandie started crying against her will. 'Thinking everything is going to be—'

'Robert!'

'Fiona, please,' said Sandie. 'This is between me and him.'

'I want to know what you meant. Robert? For God's s—'

Robert turned to Fiona. 'I killed Jane.' He looked back at Sandie. 'I'm sorry I put you through this.'

Sandie took a step back. 'Jane killed herself.'

'Yes, but I should have been here to stop it. I told her I was coming home and that we'd play tennis.'

'She knew you worked too hard for that,' said Fiona. Robert and Sandie looked at each other.

'Where were you?' said Sandie slowly.

Robert lowered his head.

'Drinking?'

He nodded.

'Oh, Robert—'

'What's happened, what's going on?' said Fiona, interrupting.

'I was fired. I haven't been going into work for months, the pub was the only place I could go. I could've been home that Friday.'

'Robert, Jane didn't want you to stop her, she wanted you to find her. You'd never get the image out of your mind and you and I would be finished. Diary or no diary. Jane manufactured the whole thing.'

'She's right,' said Fiona.

'But I told her I'd be back early.'

'Darling, she was dead by one. You'd find her in the car and me asleep in bed, my fingerprints on the hose, no note, the diary. If Cat Torrant hadn't turned up it would've been an open and shut case. We'd never have found out about Jane and all our lives would've been ruined.'

'I still can't believe she wanted to die.'

'She probably didn't see it as dying. Who knows what state of mind she was in.'

'I'm sorry, Sandie, I should've known the diary was . . .' He searched for an appropriate word.

'A sick fantasy,' said Fiona.

Robert walked over to the mounting block and sat down. 'What happened to my little girl?'

Fiona and Sandie looked at each other. Fiona signalled for Sandie to go to him. She hesitated.

CLEMENT RAN OUT OF the lab to the car park. She immediately dialled the number of West End Central police station.

'Trudi, it's WPC Clement here, can I have a word with—' The phone clicked in her ear and Jones came on the line.

'Where the hell have you been?'

'What?'

'Where is Anna?'

'Who?' asked Clement disorientated.

'Anna Prokton, where is he?'

Clement swore silently. 'I meant to call, he isn't coming to talk to you, Cat is, you see he's—'

'Disappeared! Where is Cat?'

'What do you mean disappeared?'

'A young girl was accosted by a man outside the Soho Parish School. Good-looking, smart suit, said he was a driver sent to collect her. The girl had the good sense to run. She called the police. The lad had gone. It's connected, I know it is. The bastards are going for a girl next.'

'Cat said they would.'

'Now she tells me.'

'I'm sorry—'

'I couldn't wait, I went to their flat at three yesterday afternoon. The door was virtually off the hinge, the flat is upside down and there is blood everywhere. I find my number on a bloody piece of paper and a video of the torture chamber this girl was next on the list for! Where the hell have you been!?'

All of Clement's joy evaporated. 'Colchester,' she said quietly.

'Bramley,' said Jones exasperated.

'Yes,' said Clement.

'I told you I would investigate it, but there is a life in danger, for God's sakes get your priorities right. Where is Cat?'

'Cedar Hall.'

'Jesus, what are you two up to? What's the number?'

'I'll call,' she said. 'Please?'

'Tell her Anna was seen leaving in a big black car, a Rover, she'll understand, and Clement, ask her if the name Darren White means anything to her. Call me straight back!' The line went dead. Clement stared at it. She started dialling the number of Cedar Hall.

THE PHONE ON THE HALL table rang. Cat stared at it. All three Wellbys were outside. She picked it up. Completing the story. Cat looked up the staircase where she had first seen Sandie Wellby, in heels, walking down the stairs. A lifetime ago.

'Cedar Hall?'

'Cat, thank God.'

'What!? You've got the results?'

'It isn't about that, Cat, it's about Anna.'

'What about him?' said Cat warily.

'Where is he?'

'At home, why?'

'Cat, the flat has been trashed, the police have been there since three yesterday afternoon.'

'What! Impossible. He rang me, you'd just left . . .'

Her voice trailed off. The phone box. His insistence that she didn't have to come home.

'Simon Proudlove . . .?' she whispered, a cold fear sweeping over her.

'Cat, they left together in a big black car.' Clement waited for the information to sink in.

'Where to?'

'You're not listening. A black saloon. The car you saw that morning, could it have been a Rover?'

'Oh my God—'

'Cat, does the name Darren White mean anything to you?'

'What?'

'Darren White?'

'No!' she shouted angrily.

'Stay there, don't go anywhere, I'm on my way . . .' But Cat wasn't listening. She was running back through the hall, back through the kitchen, out to the courtyard.

'Sim . . . on . . . Pro . . . udl . . . ove,' said Cat, her voice disjointed and hoarse.

Sandie released Robert from an embrace and rushed over to her. 'What's happened? Fiona!' she shouted, 'get a glass of water! What is it, Cat? What has happened?'

'Bl . . . ackRover . . .' Cat was breathing too fast.

'Yes,' said Sandie, encouragingly, 'Simon's car.'

Cat stopped breathing completely. Then she pushed Sandie away from her and ran back to the hall, she knocked the table, the dried flowers and phone crashed to the floor, she yanked open the heavy wooden door, climbed into her car. The gates were closed. Cat screeched to a halt, got out of the car, the crowd started to jeer, Cat screamed at them, no words just a loud, delirious, enraged scream. The crowd stood back. Cat opened the gates, returned to her car and sped away.

SANDIE PICKED UP THE phone from the floor.

'Hello?'

'Mrs Wellby?'

'What the hell—'

'Where does Simon Proudlove live, Mrs Wellby?'

'What is going on?'

'Just answer the question!' shouted Clement. Sandie gave her the address. Then, putting down the phone, rang Simon's home number. His cleaning lady picked it up.

'Is Simon there?'

'No, Mrs Wellby, he hasn't been here for a few nights. Not to worry, he does that occasionally.'

Sandie put the phone down.

Robert and Fiona appeared. 'What is going on?'

Sandie shrugged. 'I have absolutely no idea.'

Chapter Thirty

Cat stood with her back to the door of Madame JoJo's. Her mouth was moving constantly though no words came out. She closed her eyes for a few seconds. The panic was blocking her mind. She couldn't remember a word Anna had said. Cat shook her head. *Concentrate!* She waited, eyes closed, for the words to come back to her.

'We turned right out of Madame JoJo's and walked along Brewer Street.'

Cat stepped away from the entrance and moved along the pavement. Anna had been drunk, but he knew Soho well, she could only pray that his recollection had been accurate. Lexington Street came into view. Cat turned down it. The drinking club was there on her left, as it should have been. It was just a plain, bolted door, but she knew what was behind it. Soho was busy. Early evening. People everywhere. They were making it harder for her to concentrate. Two right turnings. Anna wasn't specific. She went down the first. A dead end. She swore and returned to Lexington Street. The second had no other right turn for ages, Cat made a decision to try for the third. All the time she wasted, all the wrong turnings, Anna might be dying. Somehow Simon had found out Anna was prepared to talk and that Cat was going to the police, why else would he send the video to scare him? Why else would they take him? Simon Proudlove. Cat felt sick, she'd left Anna with him. It must have been his plan all along. Did Sandie know? Was that why she'd asked her to stay at Cedar Hall? The phone call from Anna was so suspiciously well-timed. The third right had another right turn soon after it, Anna had been more lucid than he'd thought, pink pants did double back on himself. The road bent round back to Lexington Street, she saw the video shop she'd seen before. Cat began to feel a surge of hope. She'd find Anna if it killed her. And it might. Cat banished the thought. Ahead of her was the market. A line of fruit stalls on one side and cheap imitation clothes on the other. Squashed cherries and brown paper bags. She walked through the stalls zig-zagging back and forth until she found the cul-de-sac. Three arched doorways, the middle with a broken win-dow. Cat stood and stared at it. She'd found it. Anna's voice faded from her mind.

THE SMALL, DIRTY STREET was deserted, despite the bustle of the market and the building of the evening buzz behind her. Cat looked around, then up. Gentrification had ignored this little spot. Cat approached the door. There were no buzzers or names or anything.

'Shit,' she said, banging the door.

A door below her bumped closed, she looked down to the basement, the door swung on its hinges. She had to climb over the padlocked gate, why the fuck wasn't she wearing jeans. She jumped and ran down the steps. The room was damp and dark, the warm evening air didn't reach that far down and the stench was violent. Cat covered her nose and walked in. She could hear people moving about in the shadows. Tramps, the boy had said to Anna. This was where they congregated.

'Who the fuck are you?' someone shouted.

'I don't want any trouble, I just need to get upstairs,' said Cat trying to keep the tremor out of her voice.

A woman and her kid came into a puddle of light from the grimy window. She pointed to a doorway.

'Thanks,' said Cat.

'You won't tell them we're here will you?'

Cat didn't answer, she ran up the stairs to the ground level.

'The stairs went on for ever, my feet were killing me,' said
Anna.

'Excuse me?' said a voice. Cat swung around. 'May I help you?'

Her heart was beating so loud it was almost all she could hear. 'No, thank you.'

'Young lady, I don't like to interfere but this isn't the sort of place you should be in.' He spoke in a Birmingham accent.

Cat tried to walk on up the stairs. 'Thank you, I'm fine.' He ran up after her. Cat swung round startled when he touched her arm.

'Whoa,' said the man, grabbing on to the rusty metal railing. 'Have you got any money in that bag?'

Cat looked at the bag and frowned. Great, now she was going to be mugged. 'Yeah,' she said, 'have it.'

The man laughed. 'I don't want it, I just inspect this foul place, it's a halfway house, you know, for druggies. Halfway to hell more like. I just wouldn't want you to be, well anyway, I'm sure you know what you're doing.'

Cat looked at the man. He had a beard and glasses and badly kept hair. His cheap grey suit hung off his body. He began to walk away. 'I was looking for someone,' she called out after him.

'Well I hope you don't find them here,' he called over his shoulder waving his clipboard at her.

'I think someone is being held here, against their will. Do you have keys?'

The man turned. 'You've certainly come to the right place, everyone in here is against their will, but it is the only way they get the government to pay for their drugs. Methadone, that sort of thing—'

'A flat on the top floor,' she said getting the feeling he'd stood on that particular soapbox before.

He looked up and beyond her. 'That one is rented, it isn't part of the programme. Pays for it probably. Can't imagine the rent is too high though.'

'That's it, I need to get up there.'

The man looked nervously around him. 'I can't do that, sorry.'

'Please.' Cat ran down the stairs towards him. 'Please? My friend is in big trouble.' The man looked at her for a while, then sighed and raised his eyebrows. 'Oh, all right then.'

'Thank you,' Cat said already running back up the stairs, 'thank you.'

At the top was the door as Anna had described it. The man took out a bunch of keys and fiddled through them, counting silently. Cat didn't think it odd that he had the key, she just wanted to get in. Find Anna. The door was opened for her. She stepped quietly up the narrow flight of stairs and peered around the banisters into the flat. The rug. The glass and chrome furniture. The fake leather sofa. She espied them all. She turned back to the man and put her finger to her lips then went up the last few steps and listened. She couldn't hear any noise. She went further into the room until she saw it. The beaded curtain. This was it. Absolutely. Cat picked up a knife from the kitchen sideboard and crept over to the curtain, she counted to three silently in her head, then burst through the curtain. She swung left and right, her eyes darting from corner to corner, her mind registering the objects of torture, she turned round and started again. Left, manacles, right, heating tongs, below, plastic sheet, above, more manacles. The room was empty. No Anna.

'We've got to phone the police,' said Cat, coming back through the curtain and making her way to the phone in the corner. 'This is definitely the place.' Suddenly Cat stopped dead in her tracks. She was only halfway across the room. For a second or two she didn't say anything, then she lowered her head and let her hair slip either side of her face. 'Shit,' she said in an angry whisper. 'Shit.'

'Drop the knife,' said the voice from the other side of her hair.

Cat let the knife fall to the floor.

'Good girl.'

Eventually Cat turned to face what she had only seen for a fleeting second from the corner of her eye. He was smiling at her. He would do. He had the gun.

'I was looking for something younger,' he said, still smiling. 'But you'll do.' Cat watched as the man pulled off the beard and removed his glasses.

'You bastard,' she said in a dread whisper.

'Remember me then?' he said in a cheerful Geordie accent.

Cat closed her eyes and nodded.

CLEMENT'S KNEE WAS HURTING. All the running and driving was irritating it. She stopped the car outside the front door of Cedar Hall and ran in. Fiona, Sandie and Robert were waiting.

'What on earth is going on?' said Sandie. 'Cat ran out of here like a panther, she looked terrible, and why was she asking about Simon Proudlove?'

'Mrs Wellby, if we could sit down,' said Clement leaning against the righted hall table. She noticed the bowl of dried flowers had gone.

'Cat's in trouble, isn't she?'

'That depends on Simon Proudlove. He went round to Cat's flat yesterday in a rage, would you be able to tell me why?'

Sandie nodded slowly. 'We had a terrible fight. We were trying to make up for our last fight, it just seemed that everything I said made it worse. I was angry, I couldn't help it.'

Clement nodded, she'd been on the receiving end of Sandie's fury herself.

'It felt as if the world was closing in on me, I was lashing out, he kept asking me if I remembered anything, anything at all, well I didn't, not then, he was pushing me, I just blanked.'

'Why was he so interested in whether you remembered anything, Mrs Wellby?'

'To help me of course,' she said impatiently.

'Are you sure about that? You see I've just been on

the phone to my old boss in London, they are looking for a well-dressed man, who drives a black car and is responsible for a series of kidnappings, tortures and possibly a killing. He is a fetishist, he likes to see people punished. The same man attacked Cat's flatmate. The same man dropped a video recording of the attack at the flat yesterday morning. And now the flat has been trashed and Cat's flatmate has disappeared. The tape has already been sent to the lab, they found glove marks on it. Latex glove marks. The same type of glove marks found on the pill bottles—'

'You have the results?' said Sandie. 'Had the pills been swapped?'

'Yes, by someone wearing latex gloves. Probably the same latex gloves that were used to put the hosepipe in.'

'But I thought there were only—'

Clement held up her hand. 'The same type of gloves used in the attacks in London, on the dead body, on the evidence Cat had regarding her flatmate's attack. So,' said Clement, rising to a crescendo, 'when I ask you whether you are sure Simon Proudlove wanted to know whether you remembered anything in order to help you, I mean are you *really* sure?'

Sandie blinked at her, her mouth slightly open. 'What are you saying?'

'Cat left Anna with Simon and now he has disappeared. In a black Rover. When Anna was dumped after the attack, it was in a smart black car. When I first met

Mr Proudlove he was driving a Mercedes estate.' Clement rubbed her knee subconsciously.

'The Mercedes is the company car. The Rover is his.'

'The day Mrs Wellby found the diary—'

'Fiona, please,' said Fiona, her hands clenched tightly in her lap.

'Mr Proudlove turned up, he'd been walking in Cumbria?'

'Hmm—'

'You seemed a little surprised by that at the time.'

'Did I?'

Clement nodded. 'Mrs Wellby, I know he's your business partner, but Cat Torrant is the reason why you won't be going to jail. I doubt you'll even go to trial after the evidence she has found. Cat talked to Anna, she was going to the police with details of his attack, and now she's gone alone to look for Anna. So please answer my questions. Did Simon often go off on strange weekends, trips, days off?'

'Well, um, yes sometimes. I can't believe he'd have anything to do—'

'Does he have an apartment in London?'

'Um,' Sandie ran her fingers through her hair, 'I think he stays with friends.'

'What friends?'

Sandie was beginning to sound panicked. 'I don't know.'

'He's your partner and you don't know who his friends are?'

'He can be secretive—'

'Secretive,' repeated Clement.

'He doesn't talk about personal things much.'

'He doesn't talk about personal things much,' repeated Clement again.

'Why are you repeating everything?' said Sandie desperately.

'So you can hear how you sound. Secretive about his personal life, Mrs Wellby, you said it. How well do you really know him?'

'Very well.'

'Mrs Wellby, your stepdaughter had some pretty ferocious sexual practices and you didn't know about those.'

'What?' said Robert, standing up. 'What do you mean?'

Clement ignored him. 'It could be that Simon did too. Manacles. Latex gloves. Think about it, Mrs Wellby, maybe Simon was responsible for Jane's behaviour, or maybe their paths crossed, maybe she was going to tell everyone, maybe Simon panicked, maybe Simon killed her and knowing about Jane's fake diary decided to implicate you.'

'Will someone tell me what you are talking about?' shouted Robert.

Clement still ignored him. 'So once more, Mrs Wellby, why do you think Simon was asking you whether you remembered anything? Could it be because the person who walked into the room was not Jane, but Simon.'

'No.'

'Why did he go round to Cat's house shouting that it was all her fault? Her fault that he was going to be found out?'

'No.'

'Does Simon have another house?'

'No. Wait, um, shit, I don't believe any of this—'

'Where is the house, Mrs Wellby?'

'He doesn't have another house.'

'Are you sure, Mrs Wellby?'

'He used to, in Norfolk, I'm sure he sold it.'

'Where?'

'I don't know.'

Clement stared at Sandie then stood up. She walked over to the telephone and without asking permission dialled a number. 'You are looking for an address of a Norfolk residence, he may have another house,' said Clement down the phone.

'That can't be right,' said Jones from his office.

'Why not?'

'They've found Cat's car, Clement.'

'Oh no—'

'No one in it, it was on a single yellow line on Glasshouse Street in Soho. They are bringing it to the pound now, I've got forensics there ready.'

'Shit,' said Clement.

'I've also got someone outside Simon's house, I'll send them in, maybe they can find this place in Norfolk. But I don't think they are there.'

Clement replaced the phone.

'I'd like to know what you meant by fetishes?' said Robert, standing in front of her. Clement looked beyond Fiona to Sandie.

Sandie took the hint. She stood up and took Robert's arm.

'Sandie?' said Robert, his voice cracking. 'What is this all about?'

Clement picked up the phone again and dialled Harlow Police station.

'Mike, it's Clement here—'

'How's the knee?'

'Get to Cedar Hall as quickly as possible.'

'But—'

'Just do it, Mike, and don't tell Bramley.'

'WHERE IS ANNA?' SAID Cat.

'Belt up, bitch!' shouted Darren. He had wrapped tape around her legs and her wrists. She hadn't made a noise since dropping the knife, she knew if she did, he would tape up her mouth and then her chances of survival would dissolve into nothing. She'd been sitting there, good as gold, for three hours. The first few minutes were the worst. She thought she was dead for sure. Amelia would be so angry with her. She wondered whether Dan would care. And Anna? He might be dead already. But the boy hadn't killed her, he hadn't attempted to touch her, he hadn't phoned anyone to tell them he had new prey, he hadn't done anything except tie her up. It gave her hope. But not much. She'd been watching him. He was preparing for something, moving furniture, putting her in a place that could be seen from the stairs. He had even tied back the beaded curtain as though he was expecting someone. Cat decided she probably didn't have much time before that someone showed up.

'Darren?' she said tentatively. He pounced up from where he'd been sitting and hit her across the face. Cat heaved herself upright again. 'I need to know about Simon? Where is he?' Darren brought his hand back again. Cat stared at him. 'I just need to know,' she pleaded. 'Please?'

'Know what? I haven't a frigging clue what you're on about.' He lowered his arm.

'Simon—'

'Oh yes,' he said, 'Simon. Simple Simon's going to the fair.'

Cat frowned. 'Very funny,' she said, 'like nursery rhymes do you? Your mother sing them to you often? I'm sure she'd be very proud of you now.'

Darren stared at her. 'Don't bring that whore into this, I'm nothing like her, nothing.' He walked away angrily and opened a drawer in the kitchen.

Please tell me where Anna Prokton is. The guy you took from Madame JoJo's?'

'Fucking faggot. Got what he deserved. Men like that abuse small boys, they should all be stopped. He'll think about it next time he fancies buggering some poor defenceless kid.'

'Actually Anna was abused as a kid, sexually and physically. He didn't deserve it then, he didn't deserve it the other night, and he doesn't deserve it now,' she said softly.

'So what, he likes it up the arse, fucking faggot. What has he got to complain about.'

'That gives you no right. He never hurt you, he's never hurt anyone. Ever.'

'Not my frigging fault, man, so fuck off.'

'Yes it is. You brought him here. Let him go or you're just like them. The men in the hoods.'

Darren stepped away from the open drawer and swung his arms out in a wide circle laughing. He walked up to the manacles on the wall and pretended to undo them.

'All right, coz you asked me so nicely.' He took his imaginary prisoner's imaginary hand. 'I declare you a free faggot, God be with you.' He turned round and bowed at Cat. 'Anything else I can do for you, ma'am?'

'You are Darren aren't you? Darren White.'

The smile disappeared. 'Enough of your frigging lip, got it!' He stormed up to where she sat with her back against the wall. 'You should be begging me to let you go, not nagging me like an old whore.'

'Like all the others you kidnapped and brought back here.'

'They came because they wanted to come. Your friend, he couldn't fucking wait to get into my pants, the slag deserved it.'

'He didn't want to be tied up, raped, humiliated—'

'He's still alive, isn't he!'

'Is he? What about the guy in the skip?'

'What?!'

'Darren, the police have your name. Anna said all you did was bring him here, none of this is your fault, they'll understand, just tell me where he is.'

'Bullshit. Who the fuck are you?'

'My name is Cat. I'm twenty-eight. Single. I wanted to be a broadcast journalist, but now I'm not so sure.'

'Don't like the real world, eh, girlie? Sorry to be the one to break it to you, but life is a shit hole, it always has been.'

'Where is Anna?' said Cat again, sure she could talk him into telling her. He didn't answer. 'Why should you take the blame for what Simon Proudlove is making you do, don't let him victimize you too.'

'Who the hell is Simon Proudlove?' Darren laughed. 'You think you can blabber your way out of here throwing false names. You think I even know their names? I've had men, women, beg me, offer me money, cars, jewellery and you think you can talk me into letting you go. No one is going to victimize me. Not any more.

And you, pretty little Cat, are going to help me. So bad luck, you are not getting out of here until I hit the water.'

Cat looked at him. 'What do you mean?'

'Shut the fuck up.'

'I found you, they'll find you.'

'You reckon? No one's given a damn about me before, they're not likely to start now, are they. They don't know where I am and you, you stupid cow, came alone. So don't threaten me. You're tied up,' he walked over to the open kitchen drawer, 'and I'm the one with the gun. So shut the fuck up!'

Cat didn't say another word. She watched him continue to move the furniture around the room like he was preparing a set. Then he sat down and started to write something on a lined pad of paper. Cat could see it was frustrating him. She could also see it annoyed him. He kept standing up and going to the small fridge. There was a bottle of cheap vodka in it. He'd take a slug and go back to the pad. He was also watching the clock. Cat couldn't see it from where she was, but she knew it was late because it was finally getting dark. Cat hoped they'd found her car, even though she knew it wouldn't lead them to her. If only Anna had been here, at least then she'd know he was alive. Darren had covered three pages before he folded them up and put them in an envelope. It made her think of Jane's letters to Lottie Hawk and she stared at the manacles. Jane had everything. Looked like

Darren White hadn't had much. But looks could be deceiving. She knew that now. Privileged or otherwise, no one had a right to torture another person.

DARREN WALKED OVER TO her and dragged her on to her feet. 'Play time,' he said smiling at her. She tried to struggle but with her hands and feet bound it was pointless. He grabbed her under the arms and pulled her over the wooden floorboards to the wall with the manacles. She started struggling more, writhing around in his arms.

'No!' she shouted, 'Please God, I'll do anything . . .'

Darren smiled. 'If I had a pound for every time I'd heard that, I would be a very rich man. A very rich man.'

'Help,' shouted Cat at the top of her voice. 'Help!' She tried aiming her voice at the narrow window that stretched the length of the adjacent wall.

'Oh dear,' he said, 'I thought you were more intelligent than that.'

'Please, Darren, please don't do this.' Cat breathed heavily, trying to keep herself from crying, she didn't think she could keep it up for very long. He clamped one of her tied wrists into the manacle, untied her then put her other arm in the other one. He did the same to her legs. She didn't even get a chance to kick him. He was too careful. He knew what he was doing. He'd been doing it for some time.

'My granny is in a wheelchair, she needs me.' Cat bit

her lip, but she couldn't stop the tears. Darren stepped back to admire his handiwork.

'Perfect,' he said. He went over to the kitchen drawer.

'Help,' shouted Cat, 'someone help me! Please God!'

'No good asking him for help,' said Darren returning with the roll of tape. He tore off a piece and walked up to Cat.

'Darren, whatever happened to you, this isn't going to make—' She couldn't finish the sentence. Darren pressed a finger to her mouth.

'Yes it is,' he said.

'But—'

'Trust me.' Then he pressed the tape hard across her lips. Cat couldn't move her jaw. She couldn't move at all. She was a sitting duck. Darren walked over to the kitchen drawer again and took out the gun. He snapped open the chamber and one by one removed the bullets. He looked up at Cat, she did not take her eyes off him. Holding her gaze, he clicked the gun shut, slipped the gun into his trousers and walked up to Cat. Darren stared at Cat for five long minutes. Cat had tried to plead with her eyes, but it was useless. He had a glazed expression on his face. Then he brought up one of his hands and traced his finger along the edge of her dress. Cat closed her eyes and prayed. He undid the top button of her dress, then the second, then the third. Cat started to cry. When Darren wiped the tears off her cheek she opened her eyes again and watched him remove the envelope from his pocket and slide it beneath her dress and under her bra strap. Then he did the buttons back up. He continued to stare at her, then stroked a strand of hair away from her eyes. Cat was about to press her cheek into his hand when he suddenly moved away. He strode over to the telephone and began dialling.

'Got one,' he said. 'Oh yes,' he was smiling strangely, 'she is very pretty.'

Chapter Thirty-One

Sandie shattered any remaining illusions Robert had regarding his daughter. He and Fiona had cried. She had looked on sympathetically planning her escape. Finally she told the policeman she was going for a walk. He didn't stop her or follow her. Hours she'd wasted being watched over by the idiot and then he hadn't even batted an eyelid. The policewoman should learn that if you want something done properly, do it yourself. She found the extra set of keys in a drawer and opened the back door. A hand landed on her shoulder, she spun round, then sighed when she saw Sam Clough.

'Sam, would you do me a favour?'

'Anything.'

'I need to get out of here but without that darned policeman cottoning on. Will you start the mower, it'll disguise the noise of the engine?'

He nodded and quickly walked off. When she heard the mower, she reversed out of the garage, past Sam Clough's cottage and down the track that led to the main road. With any luck she'd get to the motorway before they noticed she'd gone. She took the back route to the motorway, keeping a watchful eye on her rear-view mirror. Not until she turned on to the M11 and headed north did she begin to relax.

A POLICE CAR SAT on the flyover and noting the Jaguar pull out to the fast lane and radioed through to head-quarters.

CLEMENT RECEIVED THE MESSAGE in Jones's office. It was the best news they'd heard for hours. Dark blue Jaguar number plate WWW 33 was heading north on the M11. Clement had begun to worry she'd got Sandie wrong, but the car was travelling at a steady 100 miles an hour, she was in a hurry to get somewhere. The police car on its tail had been given strict instructions to ignore the violation and keep a safe distance. Mike had done her proud.

'I knew she knew something, what a cow, after everything Cat has done for her. Are you sure there is no record of a Proudlove residence on the coast?'

Jones shook his head. 'Maybe she is the wicked stepmother after all.'

Clement pulled a face. God she hoped not. Not only would Bramley have her badge but Cat would feel responsible for everything for ever after. If she survived, that was. Clement stared out of Jones's window. It would be dark soon.

'She didn't say anything to you?' said Jones, clutching, clutching, clutching.

Clement looked at him exasperated. 'Don't you think I would've told you by now.' Then she apologized. This wasn't his fault. It was hers. She should have known Cat would do something like run off. Dan was at the station too. He had got increasingly frustrated waiting at the flat, looking at the mess, so he'd turned up offering his help. Jones had tried to send him home. But he wasn't budging.

'So what do you know about Darren White exactly?' asked Clement.

'He's had a terrible life. That's all I know.'

'Go on,' said Clement.

'His mother is a prostitute, oldest girl on Tyneside I think, his father is in prison for GBH. Practised on his son a few times. Not surprisingly, he hasn't spoken to the boy in years. Darren was taken away from them when it was reported that his mother had been using him, you know, for her clients. I've told you everything else I know. That boy has been let down by everyone he's ever come into contact with. He's had nothing all his life. He needs serious help.'

'He's got Cat, he raped Anna, I really pity the guy,' said Dan.

'Sir,' John put his head around the door. 'I think I've got something.' Dan, Clement and Jones stood up immediately.

'Stay here, Dan,' said Jones and followed John back down the corridor to the tech room.

'I thought I'd look over that tape again,' said John semi-looking back over his shoulder, 'when I noticed this.' He pushed open the blue swing door into the small, hot room piled high with TV and video equipment. The image of Anna chained to the wall flickered on the screen. Jones looked at it and felt revulsion shiver through him. He must have seen it ten times by now, and it still made him ill. 'Watch this,' said John. The picture zoomed in on the window high up on the wall. It was about eight inches high and six foot across, hinged at the top. It was propped open about four inches.

'Look at the window.' Clement and Jones leant forward to get a better look. John pointed out the repeated markings across the glass. It was a faint pinkish colour. 'It was the colour that made me think that it was a reflection from outside.'

Clement and Jones looked quizzically at John.

'A neon sign, outside. Must be. Look.' John pulled out a blank piece of paper. He transposed the pattern on to the paper and showed it to Jones. It looked like a capital C. A right angle. A two-sided isosceles triangle. A short capital I. And a sickle. Jones shook his head. 'Okay. Assuming it is a reflection, we have to turn it round. So the actual sign looks like a backwards C,' he said drawing it, 'a short L, a two-sided triangle with the left side going straight up and the top side coming down at an angle, the stumpy capital I and finally a sickle turned back to front.'

'John?' Jones threw up his hands.

'Okay, here is where the true genius comes in. The pattern is repeated three times. Each time separated by a gap. It must stand for something, repeated three times. The window is narrow. It can't be the top half of the word, I've tried. No letter matches these shapes, but imagine it is the lower half of a word and what do you get?'

Jones looked at it hard. 'The bottom half of an S, an L.' He studied the third. 'K?'

John shook his head.

'An R,' said Clement, catching on.

Jones looked again. 'Okay, then an I. And heaven knows what the inverted sickle is.'

'G,' exclaimed John triumphantly. 'With a fancy stem.' The smile slowly dissolved. 'Trouble is,' he said, running his hands through his hair. 'I have no idea what S. L. R. I. G. stands for.'

Jones's jaw dropped open. 'Girls,' he said quietly. Then shouted 'GIRLS, GIRLS, GIRLS!' He shook John. 'You've done it!'

Trudi pushed the door open. 'Sorry to interrupt the shouting,' she said, 'but an anonymous 999 call has just been reported. Someone heard cries for help from a top-floor apartment on Ingestre Place.'

Jones let go of John. He barged passed Trudi, sending her flying, and ran back down the corridor. 'What street?' he shouted from his office.

Trudi, followed by Clement and John, spilled into

Jones's office where he was poring over a map of Soho. His patch. Trudi repeated the name of the road. 'Look,' he said excitedly. 'Call reported of cries for help here, and GIRLS GIRLS GIRLS is here.' He pointed to the street perpendicular to it. 'Get all the cars we have! Now!'

Dan pushed into the room. 'What's happened?' he asked, looking around wildly.

'We've found them,' said Jones.

DARREN WAITED IN THE middle of the room as though he were waiting for the bus. Cat watched his profile as he watched the door. He had moved the gun. It was in his pocket. The unloaded gun. Cat had tried to shout at him through the tape but only a strangled moan escaped through the thick plastic. Suddenly she'd worked it out. She knew what he was going to do. After the first telephone call she thought it was over. Everything that happened to Anna would happen to her. But they wouldn't let her go at the end. She knew where they were, who Darren was, she could identify them. She was going to die. She wished she were dead. But then he'd made the second telephone call. And that had really confused her. Then suddenly, like a vision, she had worked it out. She knew what he was going to do. He had summoned the men with the first call and the police with the second. Darren wanted out, he wanted an end. Darren didn't turn around and look at her once in the forty minutes that they waited from the time of the last phone call to the moment the studio door opened. Then he did. Just once. For a split second. It broke her heart.

THE MEN WALKED UP the stairs so Cat knew it wasn't the police. She craned her head round to see. Pinstripes. The bastards. The fucking, twisted, privileged, bastards. If Cat could have, she would have killed them all.

'Why the fuck is that open!' shouted the first and tallest man pointing at the curtain.

'Jesus, Darren, she can see us.'

The third stepped through from the human side of the curtain. 'She isn't young. What is going on?'

The other two joined him.

'She can see us!' Cat looked at the three men one after the other. She looked again. Her shoulders dropped and she let her head fall forward. No Simon. No Simon Proudlove.

'I'm leaving,' said one of them.

'Sorry,' said Darren, 'but that's not possible.' Cat looked up as Darren pulled out the gun and aimed it at the men.

One held up his arms. 'Now, Darren—'

'Shut the fuck up!'

The men crumpled against the back wall. He kept the gun pointed at them until the police burst in. And then he aimed it at Cat. And finally she knew. Darren's plan. Well she wasn't going to let another one die.

SHE WAS SCREAMING THROUGH the tape. 'Don't shoot, don't shoot, please don't shoot.' But nothing other than the same strangled cry got through. No one even heard that. Everyone else was shouting.

'Drop the gun!'

'Get on the floor!'

The men dropped. The gun didn't.

Darren had no intention of letting go of the gun. Cat knew that. It was his ticket out of there. The men were shouting, Darren was shouting, waving the gun around, the police were shouting. The noise was deafening. Darren pointed the gun back at Cat and held it there.

'Police!'

'Put your weapon down!'

'I'll shoot!'

'Drop the gun!'

'Wankers!'

'Stay down!'

'Don't shoot!'

'Drop it!'

'Help!'

'Drop the gun, Darren!'

'Fuck off!'

'Stop it!'

'Drop the gun, Darren!'

'Jesus Christ!'

Cat watched as Darren squeezed the trigger. Then she saw Clement. Clement looked at her, saw the look in Cat's eyes and screamed 'No!' just as the first bullet went off.

'Don't shoot!' shouted Clement as Darren fell to the floor. Jones had hit him in the leg. The police edged forward. Still everyone was shouting. The men were begging. Darren was screaming. Cat continued to stare at Clement. Clement was telling people not to shoot. She was running in front of the police guns, patting the air, trying to calm the situation. It seemed like it was working, Darren stopped shouting, the police stopped shouting, one of the men started pleading innocence. Clement slowed down, the police lowered their guns, a man started whimpering. The noise subsided. But Cat knew it wasn't over. Just as Clement turned back to Jones, Darren lifted the unloaded gun once more and aimed it at Cat. Only she heard the trigger click as a bullet ripped straight through his chest. Darren's unloaded gun fell from his fingers, Clement rushed forward, kicking it further out of reach and pulled the tape off Cat's mouth.

'It wasn't loaded!' she screamed. 'Undo me! It wasn't loaded!' Cat fell out of the manacles and ran to where Darren was lying. Dying. She knelt down by him. 'You stupid idiot.' She picked up his head. She looked up at Jones standing above her. 'It wasn't loaded,' she said again.

Clement looked at Jones's face. 'Get the paramedics!' she shouted at the police dithering by the door.

Cat looked down at Darren White, for a split second he opened his eyes, she smiled at him.

'Water, water everywhere,' he said quietly.

'You are going to be fine,' she said, but his eyes stayed open and Cat knew he wouldn't be. After a few moments, Jones felt for a pulse. He shook his head. Suddenly there was no noise at all. Cat just continued to stare at Darren. Clement's radio fizzed and broke the quiet. She backed out of the room hurriedly. After a few minutes, she returned to Cat who still held on to Darren's dead body, staring down at him.

'Cat,' she whispered. Cat didn't look up. 'They've found Anna. He is okay. He was with Simon at his house in Norfolk, he is fine, absolutely fine.' Cat didn't respond. Clement tried again. 'The police are with him, Simon's been taking care of him after Anna had a fit in the flat, he just had a fit, Cat, smashed everything.' Clement put her hand on Cat's arm. 'You can't do anything for Darren now, he's dead, Cat. It's over.'

Darren lay in Cat's arms. A boy. A young boy. Pretty. Pretty fucking dead. Horribly dead. And he was staring straight at Cat with fixed, rigid eyes. Jones knelt down beside her. Cat looked across at him. She knew who he was. He took her hand. 'I'm sorry,' he said shaking his head, 'I thought he was . . .' His skin had paled to a milky white. 'I didn't want it to end like that.'

'He killed himself,' she said. 'It isn't your fault.'

'But—'

'He killed himself and he left a suicide note.' Cat pulled the envelope out from inside her dress. Jones looked at it for a moment then stood up and walked over to the three men, now handcuffed, standing against the wall.

'Name?' said Jones to the tallest.

The man sniffed and straightened himself up, brushed down his pinstriped suit jacket and lifted his head.

'Name?' said Jones again, impatiently.

'I want my lawyer,' he said in perfect Queen's English.

'Get them to the station,' said Jones with loathing. 'And summon the doctor, I want them all tested.'

Cat turned and stared at the men, her eyes stinging with tears. She had no idea whether it was a fraction of a second or a full scarring hour before she started running. All she knew was that she was running.

Epilogue

Cat replaced the phone in her bed–room and did a little victory dance. She caught a sight of herself in the mirror and started to laugh. She'd been so intent on the call, she'd forgotten she had no clothes on. Cat stood in front of the mirror and studied her naked form. Her parents would never know anything about the still–life sculpture that smiled back at her. But it didn't matter any more. It was better that way. She knew only too well how dangerous illusions were. Parents were people who brought up children. Producing them was the easy bit. Any selfish idiot can do that; it was the lifetime of finishing touches that was the hard bit. Darren White and Jane Wellby were proof of that. Jane was unbalanced, had been since childhood, she almost certainly had psychiatric problems, the tragedy was that neither of her parents had noticed them. All Darren needed was a break. Two more young suicides to bump up the statistics. Cat looked at her reflection. Her physical form looked strange to her. She had never taken much notice of it before. She didn't want to see her mother's feminine form or father's olive skin. Now she was looking with different eyes. She was part of a family, she had a beginning, middle and end. She liked that. Cat opened the closet and found a pale green dress with flowers on it and dressed quickly.

CAT RAN DOWN THE stairs two at a time, her cotton dress billowing around her thighs. She jumped the last three steps and landed on the wooden floor of the hall. She ran across the expansive hallway, knocked on a door and, without waiting for an answer, opened it. The man at the desk turned and smiled, put his pen down and opened his arms. Cat ran into them, hugged Bertie Blaine and kissed him on the cheek.

'I take it that phone call was good news?' he asked knowingly.

Cat nodded.

'You got the job?'

'Better than that, Anna's blood test came up clean and so did the others'. Jones says victims are coming forward every day, all prepared to testify. They'll be put away for good.'

'Thanks to you,' said Bertie.

Cat shook her head.

'So still no news about the job?'

Cat's smile broadened. 'Actually, I start at BBC Cambridge in two weeks. They loved the Wellby piece, they're putting me straight on to the news desk. And I get paid.'

Bertie clapped his hands. 'Fantastic. But we'll be sorry to lose you.'

'You're not. I'll be back and forth like a yo-yo.'

'Good, this house is too big without you.'

'Rubbish, there's barely room for all of us.'

Bertie smiled and readjusted his glasses. Just how he liked it.

'Where's Gran?'

'She vanished into the garden hours ago. I think she said she was pruning, though God knows what, we haven't got any plants yet.

'Do you mind if Anna and Simon come for the weekend?'

'To celebrate?'

Cat smiled knowingly. 'Something like that.'

'One room or two?' said Bertie.

'Bertie!'

'Gran,' said Cat turning at the sound of the familiar voice. 'Don't you knock?'

'Très droll, darling, leave the humour and that gorgeous man to me. You've got one of your own, haven't you?'

'I don't know what you're talking about,' said Cat. Amelia's eyes narrowed. Imperceptible except to those that knew her.

'Amelia—' said Bertie.

'Gran—' said Cat.

Amelia hushed them both. 'You didn't really think we believed you when you said you were going to yoga?

Why all the cloak and dagger stuff? You could have brought him here.'

All eyes on the guilty party. 'I just wanted to make sure we were doing the right thing, without Mother Hen clucking around me and warming milk.'

'That's quite enough cheek from you,' said Amelia. 'Look, I've brought the paper in, thought you'd be interested in this.'

Cat took the paper and read the front-page caption. 'Bramley's out, taken early retirement.'

'Yes, poor bugger, but look who's got a promotion.'

Cat glanced down the page. 'Fantastic.' She folded the paper. 'We'll have to buy the new Detective Constable a drink.'

'Why don't you ask her over for Saturday lunch as well. Go and phone her now,' said Amelia. 'I'd like to talk to Bertie alone, please.'

'You haven't left the electric blanket on again,' scolded Cat. Amelia pointed to the door. 'I'm going.' She kissed her grandmother on the way out.

'By the way,' said Amelia. 'Camilla and the kids are coming on the weekend too.'

Cat nodded. 'I knew that, I'm taking the kids swimming.' Cat closed the door behind her and ran back across the hallway. Then she stopped. Amelia listened to her receding footfalls, then turned back to Bertie.

'Dan turned up at the crack of dawn this morning,' she said in a hushed voice.

Cat crept silently back to the study door.

'He's asked my permission.'

'For what?'

'Oh, Bertie, you know perfectly well for what.'

'Did you give it?'

'Do you think I should? What about Cat?'

'I'm sure she's in on it, she's been leaping about all morning like an impala.'

Amelia raised an eyebrow at him. 'Do you really think so?'

'Anna, Simon, Camilla, the kids are all coming for the weekend. I should say the whole family is in on it.'

Amelia smiled. 'Well then, I'll say yes.'

'Where is he?'

'In the garden shed.'

'Oh, Amelia, I'll go and get him.' Bertie gave her a gentle kiss on the lips and left the room. A few minutes later Amelia wheeled out after him. Cat stepped in front of her.

Amelia put her hand over her heart. 'Cat! You'll give me a heart attack doing things like that.'

Cat winked at her, ran back to the staircase and taking them two at a time quickly disappeared upstairs. Amelia couldn't see the smile on her granddaughter's face. But she could feel it.